Books by Elizabeth Thornton

The Worldly Widow*

Fallen Angel*

To Love an Earl*

A Virtuous Lady*

Bluestocking Bride*

Highland Fire*

Cherished*

Velvet is the Night*

Tender the Storm*

Shady Lady

Almost a Princess

The Perfect Princess

Princess Charming

Strangers at Dawn

Whisper His Name

You Only Love Twice

The Bride's Bodyguard

Dangerous to Hold

Dangerous to Kiss

Dangerous to Love

*Published by Zebra Books

ELIZABETH THORNTON

THE WORLDLY WIDOW

ZEBRA BOOKS
KENSINGTON PUBLISHING CORP.
http://www.kensingtonbooks.com

ZEBRA BOOKS are published by

Kensington Publishing Corp.
850 Third Avenue
New York, NY 10022

All Kensington titles, imprints and distributed lines are available at special quantity discounts for bulk purchases for sales promotion, premiums, fund-raising, educational or institutional use.

Special book excerpts or customized printings can also be created to fit specific needs. For details, write or phone the office of the Kensington Special Sales Manager: Kensington Publishing Corp., 850 Third Avenue, New York, NY 10022. Attn. Special Sales Department. Phone: 1-800-221-2647.

Zebra and the Z logo Reg. U.S. Pat. & TM Off.

First Printing: January 1990
10 9 8 7 6 5 4 3 2

Printed in the United States of America

For my sons and the wonderful girls
they have brought into the family—

Stephen and Valerie, and baby Kaitlin
Peter and Susan
Tom and Anita

and for my friend, Georgia
who simply adores policies.

Chapter One

The sound of laughter came to her through the open window of her chamber in the Hotel Breteuil. It was, Annabelle decided, thoroughly improper in nature—the sport of a man with a maid. For a fraction of a second, her hand stilled. She gave herself a mental shake and continued with her toilette, skillfully smoothing a film of rouge along her lips, making no attempt to disguise their rather full and sensuous curves. The laughter came again as she was carefully applying the blacking to her lashes. Her hand shook, and a blob of the sooty substance landed on her cheek.

Muttering softly under her breath, Annabelle reached for the washcloth and carefully removed the offending smudge. She leaned forward in her chair and dispassionately surveyed her reflection in the looking glass. For a lady who had just celebrated her thirtieth birthday, she thought that she had little to complain about. Her chin was smooth, her skin fine-pored, her blue eyes large and fringed by a thick sweep of gold lashes suitably darkened a shade or two, and her lips and cheeks artfully and becomingly rouged. And if her patrician nose was a smidgen long, there was nothing to be done about it, and Annabelle never repined for the impossible. She touched her finger to the small dark mole on her left cheek, slightly to one side of her generous mouth. A lady with a decidedly rakish air, she thought, to which her luxuriant dark hair, the color of rich sable, was the perfect complement. Satisfied with what her reflection told her, she moved to the tall armoire against the wall.

Her fingers skimmed deftly over the outfits her maid had packed for the journey to Paris, fine kerseymere and velvet pelisses, and gowns in the sheerest silks and satins in shades of peacock blue, pomona green, and her favorite, full-bodied claret. In Mrs. Annabelle Jocelyn's wardrobe, there were no pallid mulsins in insipid pastel shades. She had an eye for color and fashion and had the temperament to carry off the bold look she preferred. She also had the advanced years, she admitted to herself with a faint sigh of regret.

Annabelle looked to the door as her maid entered. Among the other servants, Nancy, of an age with her mistress, was known as "The Queen," and deservedly so. At that moment she was at her most regal.

Annabelle diplomatically affected not to notice her maid's disapproving cast of countenance. She was well aware of Nancy's sentiments on the inadvisability of a lady of quality traveling to Paris at such a time and with only a distant kinsman as escort, and taking up residence in a public hotel with only maids as chaperones.

In the normal course of events, Annabelle would have been accompanied by her companion, Mrs. Beatrice Pendleton. But Annabelle had decided that Bertie should remain in London with young Richard, Annabelle's five-year-old son and the apple of her eye. Richard would have been just as happy to visit with his aunt and uncle to permit Bertie to make the journey. But Annabelle had rejected that suggeston. Richard had already spent the better part of the summer with his cousins in the country. And Annabelle reasoned that a boy needed a certain discipline and order in his life, especially a boy who had lost his father when he was a mere babe. Annabelle was sorry to forgo the pleasure of Bertie's company, but she was a conscientious mother and put her son's welfare first at all times.

Annabelle became aware of her maid's silence. "The blue silk today, Nancy, and the claret to go over it," she said cheerfully. "I thought Paris would be warmer in September, but as you see, it's no better than London."

Nancy accepted the blue silk, but made no move to retire.

Annabelle's blue eyes gazed speculatively at Nancy's thinned lips. That she was about to embark on an errand without an escort was a bone of contention between mistress and maid. Paris was a city of occupation, the Battle of Waterloo having been fought and won by the allies only three months before. Annabelle did not let that weigh with her. The capital was teeming with visitors, and the French whom she had met seemed civil enough, if not positively friendly.

Moreover, Annabelle had come to Paris for a purpose, and when Annabelle mapped out a course for herself, she was not to be diverted. Few people knew of her real design, and of those whom she had taken into her confidence, not one would approve her next step. There was no danger involved in the enterprise. Annabelle simply preferred to work alone, without interference. And though a certain modicum of prudence was essential, maids, chaperones, and escorts would prove an unmitigated nuisance.

Before the maid could voice what was on her mind, Annabelle's cultured accents, polite, pleasantly modulated, and slightly distancing, interposed, "The silk could do with a press. Then you can set about packing for the journey home tomorrow. Oh, and leave out the green. I'll wear that with the claret. D'you suppose our landlord can be persuaded to pack us a picnic lunch? Don't forget, Lord Temple is fond of beefsteak. He'll be calling for us at first light. Perhaps you would be good enough to remind Jerome. Thank you, Nancy, that will be all."

It was the voice Annabelle habitually employed to manage any difficult servant and, more especially, any difficult colleague at Bailey's Press, the publishing house of which she was half owner and managing editor. It never failed in its objective.

Nancy murmured an acknowledgment and obediently draped the silk across one arm. A quick look at her employer warned her that to remonstrate, however mildly, would be utterly futile. She made a dignified exit, promising that the gown would be ready within half an hour.

Annabelle returned to the dressing table and had just unpinned her long mane of dark hair when it came again—low masculine laughter followed by a trill of feminine giggles. To her surprise, she found that she was slightly irritated. She stood gazing reflectively at the vision in the looking glass, abstractedly combing her fingers through her shoulder-length hair. A flash of self-knowledge jolted her. The couple in the hotel gardens who were so obviously indulging in a little dalliance had brought to mind that she had attained her thirtieth birthday. For the first time in years, she was touched with a vague fear for the future and an equal regret for the path she had long ago chosen for herself.

"Fustian, my girl!" she told her reflection. "You're letting Paris get to you. You're here on business—not to engage in amorous adventures. Kindly remember that!"

There it was again, that low, seductive, masculine laughter, and so thoroughly tantalizing.

"Oooh!" said Annabelle, annoyed as much with herself as she was by the couple who were cutting her peace to shreds.

Clutching the edges of her delicate lace peignoir, she moved quickly to the window, intending to shut out the disturbing sounds. She was forced to lean over the sill to grasp the handle of the open casement, which had been thrown wide. She tugged on the handle. Nothing happened. She chanced to look down.

The owner of the disturbing masculine voice had caught sight of Annabelle's movement. He was staring directly at her. She recognized him immediately. In the four days since she had taken up residence in the hotel, she had been aware of his eyes following her as she came and went with Lord Temple. Annabelle was used to men's eyes resting on her—eyes filled with admiration. This man's eyes never registered any such emotion. If anything, he seemed to regard her with thinly veiled contempt. He made her so uncomfortable that she could not bear to be in his proximity. She never lingered in the hotel foyer or dined in the public dining room. Mostly, she kept to her rooms or made the odd excursion with her faithful escort, the Viscount Temple.

She allowed herself the luxury of assessing him slowly and carefully, knowing that she would never have been so bold if she had been within arm's reach. There was something about this man that made her nervous. She was not nervous now. Her confidence seemed to have increased in direct proportion to the distance that separated them. Her eyes were as insolent as his as she took inventory.

His jacket was looped over one shoulder and held negligently with two fingers. He wore no neckcloth and his white shirt was open at the throat, displaying a thick shag of dark hair. His skin was deeply tanned, the distinguishing mark of every military man Annabelle had had occasion to meet. If she'd met him on a lonely stretch of road, however, she would have taken him for a bandit, she thought, and suppressed a shiver. She had an impression of strength and predatory grace, but her gaze did not linger on the breadth of his shoulders nor on his supple, pantherlike form. His eyes, bold and brazen, dominated his harshly handsome face. She carefully avoided the compelling stare. One arm was clasped around a young woman whom Annabelle immediately recognized as the chambermaid who had turned down the beds the night before. The girl lifted her head to follow the unwavering stare of her companion, who seemed to have forgotten her very existence. Though the gentleman looked to be in his mid-thirties, it did not escape Annabelle's notice that the object of his attentions was a girl of little more than twenty or so. Unconsciously, Annabelle's lip curled. The girl had red hair. Annabelle was not partial to red hair.

The stranger caught that contemptuous look and grinned, showing a flash of white teeth.

Annabelle gave him one of her cool, intimidating looks which never failed to make the unfortunate recipient of such a chilling feminine appraisal feel that he had been caught with his breeches down. The gentleman in question laughed outright and, setting his companion to one side, made an elegant leg to the lady at the window.

Annabelle did not recognize the affront to her dignity with so much as the flicker of an eyelash. Thankfully, the window came unstuck and she shut it with a snap, blocking out sight and sound of the gentleman who, in some sort, she felt had just thrown down the gauntlet.

She turned back into the room and almost tripped over the peignoir which had slipped unnoticed from her shoulders in her struggle to close the window. Hurrying to the looking glass,

11

she gaped at her reflection. With her mane of unbound hair spilling over her shoulders and the transparent wisp of silk barely concealing her soft feminine contours, she might easily be mistaken for a wanton! It was not a look Annabelle cared to cultivate. She strove for a bold allure that showed the face of a woman of the world. This utterly feminine and flagrantly sensual appearance was one she would not tolerate.

Thirty minutes later, dressed for the outdoors, Annabelle was reassured by a quick glance in the looking glass. Her bold, cutaway, high-waisted claret pelisse showing a slash of peacock blue silk, was everything she wished for. Her hair was severely swept back from her face and twisted in several fat ropes to lie provocatively at her nape and shoulders. She gave her reflection an approving nod as she donned her best bonnet with its flashy show of peacock feathers. The lady, supremely confident, projected that slightly rakish air which invited every male to admire but dared him to do so except from a respectable distance. Her beauty, indisputable, was faintly intimidating. In the years since she had become a widow, it suited her purposes to promote that image.

From the Rue de Rivoli, opposite the Tuileries, where the hotel was situated, was only a short walk to Annabelle's destination, but she ordered her coachman to take the long way round to the Palais Royal. This was her last day in Paris and she settled herself back against the squabs to view the sights from the safety of an enclosed carriage.

In the Bois de Boulogne were the bivouacs of some English and Prussian regiments. In the Champs Elysées, the Scots seemed to have taken up residence. Uniforms of every color and description were very much in evidence, and Annabelle witnessed more than one altercation on the streets between soldiers of different nationalities. She'd heard that dueling was so common an occurrence that nobody batted an eyelash when the clash of steel or the shot of a pistol was heard coming from the Bois de Boulogne or some deserted street or other. As they passed the Arc de Triomphe, which was under construction, several groups of soldiers eyed the carriage speculatively, and Annabelle's unease grew apace. The capital, though reputed to be largely under Wellington's discipline, gave every evidence

12

of a license which she thought perilously close to anarchy. She was very glad that Nancy was not in the carriage to say "I told you so."

It was with no little relief that she felt the chaise roll to a stop in front of the Palais Royal. Directly opposite was the old Palais du Louvre, which had been turned into a museum. Annabelle had heard of the controversy which raged in diplomatic circles: the allies were insisting that the treasures Napoleon had lodged there—the spoils of war—should be returned to their countries of origin. The crafty curators denied such things even existed. Rumor had it that they had hidden them away in the labyrinth of passages in the foundation of the building. The Duke of Wellington, however, was proving relentless in his pursuit of the booty. It did not seem likely that he would lose this battle with the French any more than he had lost any other.

The coach door swung open, and with the aid of Jerome, her groom, and her coachman, Annabelle alighted. One comprehensive look at the throng of pedestrians and her unease returned in full force. The pavement outside the Palais Royal, the former palace of Richelieu and now a commercial district, was as crowded as Bond Street on any afternoon of the week. But though there were many fine ladies in the crush of people, they were of the painted female frailty and were flirting outrageously with the officers of the allied armies who lounged about.

Annabelle drew herself up to her full five-foot-six-inches and with a curt word to Jerome strode purposefully to an *allée* which gave entrance to the magnificent enclosed courtyard gardens. Within minutes, in one of the arcades, she had found the door beside a jeweler's shop which bore the address in her hand. She passed through without incident and bade her stoic coachman wait until she should return. One floor up and Annabelle came to the conclusion that she had made a grave error in judgment. For all its exalted title and past history, the Palais Royal was not what she had expected. To her left could be heard the unmistakable sounds of a gambling house. "*Faites vos jeux, messieurs,*" Annabelle heard, and waited to hear not one word more. She went forward, mounting the next flight of stairs in a kind of frozen chagrin. When she entered the scarlet doors at the top of the stairs, her steps slowed and finally faltered altogether. The decadent splendor, the drawn shades, the lingering perfumes, and the hushed murmurs of the "ladies" as they were roused from their slumbers for the beginning of a new day—and this at four o'clock of the afternoon—confirmed her worst suspicions. Damn if she had not stepped inside a bawdy house!

For a moment, she was severely tempted to turn on her heel and make a strategic retreat. Cooler logic prevailed, and Annabelle was nothing if not cool. The damage had already been done. And there were cogent reasons for her to remain. She could conclude her business inside of ten minutes at a pinch. It would be stupid to have come so far and then run off like some hysterical schoolroom miss. Good grief! She was a woman of the world! The risk of meeting any gentleman of her acquaintance was bound to be slight. She moved in only the highest reaches of London society. This was Paris. And she had made up her mind to meet with Miss Dupres in her own setting. So be it. Still, her fingers trembled alarmingly.

A very proper and demure maid accepted her card and showed her into a small waiting room. Only then did Annabelle begin to relax. Within a few minutes, the door opened to admit a strikingly pretty girl who looked to be in her mid-twenties. Her hair was dark auburn, a hue that was perfectly acceptable to Annabelle's sense of aesthetics. Her eyes were large and dark and clearly registered all the shock she was feeling at seeing a lady of quality in such a setting.

"How do you do?" said Annabelle, rising to her feet and extending her hand in a friendly gesture. "I am Mrs. Jocelyn. You must be Monique Dupres. I have come to make you an offer for the manuscript you so kindly wrote to us about. I must say that the opening pages of your memoirs were highly . . . diverting."

The girl came slowly into the room and eyed Annabelle in astonishment. "You are from . . ."

"Yes. I'm here as a representative of Bailey's Press." Annabelle was used to taking charge of conversations and did so automatically. "May we sit down?"

Miss Dupres obediently seated herself.

"I've no wish to inconvenience you during working hours . . ." said Annabelle, and came to a sudden halt when the infelicity of her remark occurred to her.

"No, no," disclaimed Miss Dupres, tying the belt of her almost transparent robe more securely around her waist, "I don't start work till ten, unless by special appointment."

It was years since Annabelle Jocelyn, née Summers, had blushed. She felt a small rise in temperature under her skin. By sheer strength of will, she forced the unwanted heat across her cheekbones to cool to a more acceptable degree.

"Excellent," she said, and would have slumped with relief, except that Annabelle never allowed herself to give way to slumping or to any other outward show which might betray that a crack had developed in her habitual ironclad composure. She gave a small self-deprecating smile. "I beg your pardon for descending on you uninvited. I know the arrangement was that we should meet on neutral ground. But I was curious, you see."

Truth to tell, it was more than curiosity which had brought Annabelle in person across the English Channel and to this particular establishment. She had no wish to buy a pig in a poke. If Monique Dupres was not who and what she represented herself to be, there would be, could be, no question of publishing her memoirs. Annabelle's object was solely to verify the girl's identity. Both ladies knew it.

"The reason I wished to meet with you on neutral ground," murmured Miss Dupres meaningfully, "must be very evident to you now."

Annabelle's smile was a trifle thin. "I apologize for misjudging you. If I had known what I was getting myself into, you may be sure, I would never have stepped over your threshold. If I've caused you any embarrassment, I'm sorry for it."

"Ça ne fait rien," responded the girl with a knowing twinkle in her eyes. "Think nothing of it. If you don't mind, why should I? And I assure you, when you leave, I shall forget that you were ever here."

"Thank you," said Annabelle, and meant it from the bottom

of her heart. "My one consolation is that I'm not like to encounter any gentleman to whom I might be introduced in a London drawing room."

Though Annabelle had not thought of saying anything humorous, her words produced a spate of laughter in the other girl.

She waited till the laughter had subsided and gently prodded, "Did I say something funny?"

"Oh *assurément,*" said the brunette airily. "In this establishment, we get only the *crème de la crème* of masculine society, whether English, French, Prussian, or Russian. You'll find them all here," and she rattled off a string of titles which any hostess on either side of the English Channel would have given her eyeteeth to have enter her portals.

Annabelle's dismay lasted only a moment. For one thing, she had no intention of encountering any gentlemen in that establishment. She was sure she would put a bag over her head before she would let her face be seen. For another, Miss Dupres's list of gentlemen included only military sorts, and Annabelle avoided them like the plague. She had once been married to one. The experience had left her with a thorough distaste for anything remotely connected with Wellington and his armies. Her opinion of men in general was not very high. Of soldiers, it was positively unprintable.

She listened politely as Miss Dupres began on a flood of anecdotes that would, thought Annabelle, provide enough material for a second volume of her memoirs. She stored the information away for future reference. By degrees, she politely and unobtrusively steered the conversation to Vienna and Brussels in the year during which Miss Dupres had been the mistress of one of Wellington's high-ranking officers before he met his untimely end at Waterloo. Within minutes, Annabelle came to the conclusion that Miss Dupres's memoirs, in diary form, were no fabrication. She considered herself a shrewd judge of character and had decided that there was the ring of truth in Miss Dupres's words. Having achieved her sole object in coming to Paris, Annabelle asked if she might see the rest of the manuscript. It was duly brought to her. She dipped into it at random.

16

From time to time, Annabelle's eyes lifted to gaze thoughtfully at the other girl. There was nothing spiteful or malicious in the racy and often witty stories in her diaries. On the contrary, there was a certain charm and vivaciousness in the girl's personality which was evident in her writing. Still, Miss Dupres's intimate knowledge of the bedroom antics of Wellington and many of his staff, not to mention diplomats and visiting dignitaries, was enough to rock both houses of Parliament.

Such sordid goings-on held no interest for Annabelle. But she was sensible of the fact that what she held in her hands, when published, would sell like hotcakes. Such a book would consolidate Bailey's Press as one of the leading publishing houses in London. It also represented future security for the employees who relied on Annabelle's business acumen as well as the means to provide for her dependents. That it would be an embarrassment to those who found themselves portrayed in its pages did not weigh with Annabelle. The gentlemen had sown their wild oats. Let them weather the scandal as best they might.

She made an offer, a very handsome one, but then, Annabelle told herself, this particular volume was like to sell as many as twenty thousand copies, and at a selling price of a guinea a volume, Bailey's Press stood to make a very handsome profit. The offer was accepted with alacrity. A bank draft exchanged hands. Thereupon, a hatbox was produced to store the four hundred pages or so of Annabelle's latest acquisition. She was feeling very proud of herself as she rose to take her leave of the other girl.

"You're a very talented writer, you know," she said sincerely. "You could quite easily make a living in that field if you had a mind to."

"Oh no, there's not nearly enough money in it," was the candid rejoinder. "I'm at the top of my profession now. In a year or less, I shall have the capital to open my own establishment if I continue as I am now."

Annabelle, who had only moments before handed the girl a draft for the sum of two thousand pounds, was thunderstruck. It had been on the tip of her tongue to offer the poor thing

17

temporary sanctuary in her own home in London until such time as she found a respectable position and might pursue a more settled way of life. She'd thought the girl an unhappy victim of circumstance. Evidently, the life of a demi-rep was more lucrative than she had credited and held an allure which outweighed its disadvantages. She became conscious that she was staring with her mouth agape.

She pulled herself together and held out her hand. With her habitual poise, she brought the interview to an end. "I'll say good-bye, then, and take this opportunity to wish you every success in your chosen profession."

The unthinking remark was no sooner out of her mouth than Annabelle regretted it. She'd used those practiced words, or words very like them, at the conclusion of many a business transaction. It did not seem proper, however, for the daughter of a vicar to voice such a sentiment and in such circumstances. As she slipped into her pelisse and donned her bonnet, she tried to view the whole matter philosophically.

Thankfully, her poor father knew little of his daughter's enterprises. His living was in Yorkshire; London held no interest for him. As far as he was aware, his only child lived the life of a respectable widow under the auspices of her late husband's relatives. It never occurred to him to question the why, or wherefore, of the generous bank drafts Annabelle sent to him regularly when she'd been left with only a very small competence. Annabelle was perfectly sensible of the fact that Jonathan Summers would not under any circumstances condone his daughter's mode of living if he ever learned of it.

That she was part owner and director of Bailey's Press was not generally known. To the world, she was a lady of fashion with nothing in her head but the next rout, ridotto, ball, or masquerade. She enjoyed the social whirl. She was the first to admit it. But she took far more pleasure in the challenges that the business world presented. She'd turned Bailey's Press around till it held its present position of eminence in the publishing world. It tickled her fancy to observe, on almost every sofa table in the most prestigious drawing rooms in Mayfair, a novel or diary or biography which Bailey's had published. That she had to conceal the extent of her involvement with Bailey's from the high sticklers of the ton or face public censure seemed totally nonsensical, in her opinion. It was, however, the way of her world. A lady might include any number of commercial interests in her holdings as long as she turned over the management of those same holdings to some enterprising male. But to be the driving force behind a thriving business could easily spell social ruin. It was an unwritten code that only a fool would think to trespass with impunity. Annabelle was no fool. She endeavored to keep the two milieus in which she was at home entirely separate. And she had succeeded.

Without warning, from the opened doorway a masculine voice interposed, "Monique, my little pigeon, I've brought you that trinket you so much admired."

Miss Dupres's face lit up with pleasure. "Dal!" she cried out, and crossing the room at a run, threw herself into the arms of the intruder.

Annabelle's heart lurched. She recognized the man as the dark and brazen stranger from the hotel. With great presence of mind, she edged away from the couple and turned her back on them, staring fixedly into the drawn shades at the windows.

"Diamonds," breathed Monique, and Annabelle surreptitiously glanced over her shoulder to see the gentleman fasten a thin rope of those gems around the lady's wrist.

"Now you can thank me properly," he said with a lecherous smirk, and suiting action to words, he brought his head down in an open-mouthed kiss that had Annabelle's toes curl inside her little high-heeled boots. What effect such an embrace might be having on the other girl Annabelle could scarcely imagine. She wished only that the floor beneath her might sink and she with it.

The minutes passed. The kiss continued with unabated passion. That she should continue as a spectator in such a scene of depravity was unthinkable. Marshaling every ounce of her composure, Annabelle put her head down and made a beeline for the exit. She had almost gained the threshold when strong masculine fingers closed round her arm and brought her up short.

"Not so fast, my lovely," that hateful voice said. "Who have we here?" And before Annabelle knew what he was about, the gentleman had removed her bonnet and sent it sailing across the room.

As it came to rest atop the bust of some female Greek deity or other, Annabelle observed its bright plumage bend and buckle. Her own feathers were no less ruffled. She knew that her mouth was opening and closing as if she were a fish on a hook, but to find words of sufficient condemnation with which to scorch the libertine's ears was temporarily beyond her power.

Her chin was grasped firmly and her head turned up toward the light. "So we meet at last," he said. There was laughter in his voice.

Annabelle went as rigid as a statue as cool gray eyes made a thorough inspection of her person, coming to rest finally on the hatbox in her hand.

"My God," he said, "you're one of the new girls! I can't believe my luck! You can start right this minute, *chérie*, and I'm buying all of your time, I don't care what it costs."

The dark head descended and Annabelle's pulse accelerated in alarm. "Make yourself scarce, Monique," were the last words he threw over his shoulder before taking possession of Annabelle's reluctant lips.

A sound of muffled laughter came from the other girl just a moment before she made her exit. Annabelle heard the soft click of the door and felt the betrayal all through her shocked body. While she had thought to offer that . . . that *Phyrne* the hospitality of her home out of a sense of obligation, she, Monique Dupres, had acted the part of procuress! Annabelle had known for a very long time that there was little justice to be had in the world. She took no satisfaction in having her conviction proved correct yet again.

"Pl . . . please," said Annabelle brokenly, but the gentleman's experienced lips were already soothing away her objections.

Stunned into immobility, Annabelle remained passive beneath the pressure of that exploratory embrace. After a moment, the stranger raised his head and observed her expression. "Open your lips," he commanded. Annabelle mutely shook her head.

As a deterrent, it was totally ineffective. She was hauled roughly against him, her head captured by unrelenting fingers as his mouth claimed hers with an aggressive passion which left her trembling. There was an element of flagrant masculine dominance in that kiss which Annabelle yielded to almost by instinct. When she realized how easily she was succumbing, she marshaled her defenses. In her right hand she still clutched the ribbons of Monique's hatbox. She carefully let it drop from her fingers and brought both hands up to tug at his hair. He released her mouth, and Annabelle took instant advantage to wedge both hands against his chest. They were both breathing heavily, but for different reasons.

"Cad!" she sputtered. "Get your hands off my waist." It was a voice that would have shocked Annabelle's employees. For Mrs. Jocelyn to lose her temper, even in the most trying of circumstances, was unheard of.

A dark brow arched sardonically. "Whatever you desire, sweetheart," he drawled, and immediately sank his fingers into the soft flesh of her bottom. The lower half of her body was dragged inexorably against hard, muscular thighs. As he ground himself into her, Annabelle's shocked cry of outrage was swallowed by another long, drugging kiss.

She was weakening. She could feel it all through her body. Her taut muscles were becoming pliant as she strained against his hard length. She'd been attracted to him from the moment she'd set eyes on him. If she had ever been in ignorance of that fact, her body made her aware of it now. He was stirring senses which had lain dormant for years, evoking an ache deep within her which Annabelle had prayed never again to experience. No man since Edgar had had this effect on her. The realization brought her to her senses as nothing else could.

The man was an unprincipled rake! In the space of a few hours she'd caught him red-handed, quite literally, with two different redheads both of whom were years younger than herself. Good God, it was evident that the man could not help himself! Nothing in skirts was safe from him! Well, she had a wealth of experience in dealing with men of his kidney. If ever she had need of that experience, now was the time to draw on it.

She went limp in his arms. The bruising pressure of his grip relaxed. In that instant she tore herself from him and caught him full across the face with the open palm of her hand.

His head jerked back from the force of her blow. Annabelle stood stock-still, knowing herself to be in the worst peril of her life.

"So," he said in a voice strangely devoid of anger, "you're not one of the new girls. Pity." And he offered a conciliatory grin.

Her voice shaking with suppressed emotion, Annabelle said, "Kindly step aside, sir, or I shall . . . I shall . . ."

Amusement lurked in the depths of the slate gray eyes he turned upon her. "Yes?" he murmured. "What exactly shall you do if I don't step aside?"

Annabelle had the good sense to remain silent, but she was far from conceding defeat. She had come up against an adversary who was worthy of her steel. It behooved her to deal with him cautiously, very cautiously. Her blue eyes gazed at him blankly, but behind that blind stare was a mind frantically casting around for a way of disarming her formidable opponent.

He observed each fleeting expression as it flitted across her face, waiting expectantly for her to make the next move. A casual observer could have told Annabelle that the gentleman was enjoying himself immensely. She was, at that moment, too preoccupied to notice.

"My husband," she murmured, "my husband will kill me if he knows I'm here."

"A wise man," was the dry rejoinder.

For an instant, anger blazed in her eyes. She suppressed it with a control he could not help but admire. She touched the tip of her tongue to her dry lips. "My husband . . ." she began again.

He cut her off without compunction. "Mrs. Jocelyn, your husband did not accompany you to Paris. I know that you arrived with another gentleman—your lover, I suspect."

Speechless, she stared at him for a long interval. Her worst fears were realized. Her shoulders straightened. "How do you come to know my name?" she asked him coldly.

"I made it my business to discover your identity," he told her.

"But why?"

He shrugged. "You're a beautiful woman. I don't think much of your lover. Without conceit, I think I may say that I am the better man. As it happens, at the moment, I am in the market for a mistress."

Annabelle did not know whether she should laugh or cry or have a temper tantrum. He was like no other man she had ever met before. She looked into the steel of those steady gray eyes from which every trace of amusement had been erased, and a frisson of alarm danced along her spine. The man was deadly serious.

For a moment she considered telling him the truth, that she had been a widow for a number of years and that the gentleman whom he presumed to be her lover was merely a distant relative who had very kindly given her escort to Paris. But the wisdom of throwing herself on the mercy of such a man seemed highly questionable. Better by far, she thought, that he suppose she had a protector at hand who would look out for her interests.

Striving to give the appearance of being in command of the situation, she gave a low laugh and moved about the room, retrieving both bonnet and hatbox. Over her shoulder, she essayed, "Did you follow me here?"

He had not moved from his position by the door, and though he permitted her the freedom of moving about the room, there was never any question in her mind that until he should decide to let her go, she was virtually a prisoner.

There was a slight hesitation before he answered, "Would you be flattered if I told you that I had?"

She slanted him a look that spoke volumes. He caught that look and laughed.

"Let's discuss it as we dine," he said.

"Thank you, no," said Annabelle through her teeth, and did not take the trouble to elaborate.

Once again her chin was seized in those unrelenting masculine fingers and her face turned up for his inspection. She glared up at him, anger shooting from her eyes like blue lightning.

"You're not very wise, are you?" he remarked. In a long, lazy perusal, his gaze traveled the mutinous set of her features. "It's my surmise that you're used to ruling the roost. You'll discover that unlike your husband and former lovers, I don't permit a woman to ride roughshod over me."

His voice dropped to little more than a whisper. "I don't wish to threaten you, but you leave me no choice. What would your lover say, I wonder, if he knew that we had an assignation here this afternoon? We might even fight a duel over you. Would that please you?"

"You wouldn't," she breathed.

"Wouldn't I? What makes you say so?"

Annabelle was speechless. A threat to her own person was one thing, but she had not dreamed that by her careless words she might be putting poor Lord Temple in jeopardy. Her thoughts took flight, and she trembled at the picture they conjured.

"That's better," he said. "I knew you would see sense. Aren't you going to wear your bonnet?"

His words and manner were so dispassionate, so negligent, that Annabelle was not quite sure how to take him. Without thinking, she slapped her very elegant *chapeau* with its broken feathers upon her head and tied the ribbons under her chin.

She was still trying to devise a way out of her predicament when his hand cupped her elbow and he propelled her from the room.

She heard his grunt of satisfaction and the sudden change in his breathing

Chapter Two

David Falconer, the Earl of Dalmar, visibly relaxed against the plush cushions of his straight-backed chair. As he surveyed his dining companion through the thick shield of his lashes, he raised the rim of his champagne glass to his lips, effectively concealing the small half-smile which threatened to degenerate into a self-satisfied grin. He judged it prudent, for the moment, to allow his companion time to adjust to her situation. One more evidence of masculine complacency and the lady might very easily take to her heels.

He'd been rough with her. He knew it. And more masterful than he'd ever suspected was in his nature. It wasn't that he'd lost his temper—far from it. He kept his more volatile emotions on a tight leash, and with good cause. But he'd known from the moment he'd set eyes on her as she'd swept into the hotel foyer that to betray any form of weakness with such a woman would be fatal. He'd recognized the challenge in that intimidating, touch-me-not stare which had warned any man worth his salt to keep his distance. And everything that was masculine in his nature had responded to the challenge.

He'd given up the chase before it had begun, however, when he had learned that the lady was married and that her escort was not her husband. He'd drawn his own conclusions. That the lady was conducting an affair with her milksop of a lover had filled him with a furious disgust. Even so, he'd continued to take his meals at the Hotel Breteuil, which was only a short distance from the Palais Royal, where he had his rooms. The arrangement suited him, and to change his habits merely because of a female was not to be countenanced.

He'd watched her comings and goings with a jaded eye; and he'd observed the man he had contemptuously nicknamed "The Milksop" dangle after her like a marionette. It was very evident that it was the lady who was working the strings. The poor devil, a minor lordling whom he vaguely recognized from school days, evidently wasn't even permitted to take rooms in the same hotel. It was his surmise that Mrs. Annabelle Jocelyn was afraid of reprisals should her husband ever discover what she was up to. Which left him wondering what manner of man would allow his wife the freedom to come and go as she pleased. Another milksop, he'd decided, and had been gripped by some primitive, masculine instinct which urged him to take and conquer the woman and make her his.

The notion amused him. He'd felt other primitive emotions before, but those had come upon him in the blood lust of battle. He'd never felt like this about a woman. When the drive to possess her had persisted, his amusement had converted to a slow, simmering anger. He'd grown restless. In an effort to banish the lady's image from his mind, he'd embarked on a night of frantic debauchery. It had availed him nothing. And then had come their silent exchange, when she'd caught sight of him from the hotel window.

He'd been stunned by the transformation in her appearance. Elated by the knowledge he'd read in her demeanor that he was a man to be reckoned with. And as she'd shut the window upon him that instinct to claim her, unbridled, full blown, had shaken him to the core. It was like an obsession. He'd come to a decision then—that if Mrs. Annabelle Jocelyn was fair game, he was entering the lists and he'd be damned if he would deny himself the pleasure of availing himself of the sensual fire she had so unconsciously betrayed. A moment's reflection had sobered him. The lady had a husband of some sort. It was inconceivable that a man with such a woman in his possession would forego all his claims to her. And he would not share her with any man.

And then fate had taken a hand. He'd walked into the Maison D'Or, and he'd found her with Monique. Not for a minute had

26

he mistaken her for one of that establishment's sisterhood, though some perverse impulse had urged him to act out that little charade. He'd surmised that in her ignorance, Mrs. Jocelyn had inadvertently entered the wrong part of the building. Now he was not so sure.

"How was the beefsteak?" he asked politely.

"Tolerable," Annabelle replied. In actual fact, it had been delicious, but she would not gratify his vanity by saying so. She was still smarting from the high-handed way the stranger had taken charge of her since he'd found her in that upstairs bordello. Her hired chaise and coachman had been summarily dismissed, and he'd hauled her off to the Trois Frères Provencaux on the other side of the Palais Royal.

Her eyes lifted to take in the other diners and her confidence increased. She was in a public place. It gave every appearance of being respectable. And though their table was in a private alcove and shielded to some extent from curious eyes, she had only to call out and every head in the restaurant would turn their way. She chanced a quick look at her companion, and her confidence ebbed a little.

He had formed a very false impression of who and what she was. Her own slightly rakish appearance was against her, for a start. And that he had found her at the Palais Royal and without an escort was bad enough, but to have discovered her in that awful establishment with Monique Dupres did not bear thinking about. The thought that she should confess the whole to him she dismissed out-of-hand. Though he'd shown her every civility as they'd dined, she could not trust him. The man might easily ruin her if he knew all that there was to know about her. No, decided Annabelle, better by far that he should think her a lady of tarnished virtue. It was evident to her that he meant to offer her carte blanche. Fine. She would hear him out and then politely decline his offer. That would be that. And by morning, she and Lord Temple would be long gone from Paris. She need never again set eyes on the man. The thought cheered her.

With her most disarming smile, she began conversationally, "You have the advantage of me, sir. I don't know your name."

"Dalmar," he replied at once.

27

Thankfully she had never heard of him and hoped she never would again.

He topped up her wineglass and adjured her to drink. She toyed with the stem of her glass, but made no move to obey him.

"What are you exactly?" he asked at length. "An actress, an opera dancer, a wife, or merely a professional kept woman?"

Her cool and cultured accents at odds with the fiery sparks that were shooting from her eyes, she said, "I am under no obligation to explain myself to you, Mr. Dalmar."

Ignoring the ice in her words, he remarked, "Please call me David." He could not say why he did not wish her to know that "Dalmar" was his title unless it was because, in some sort, he wanted to claim her first as man to her woman.

When she did not respond to his invitation, he went on, "Everything about you suggests a woman of means. Your husband would have to be very liberal, however, to agree to permit you to live in this style, and with so little restraint. Somehow, I can't quite see it. But I'm open to correction."

Annabelle did not deign to dignify his conjecture with a reply, and after a moment he mused confidingly, "If you're an actress, you must be at the top of your profession to afford the Hotel Breteuil and your own retinue of servants. Yet I've never heard of you. Ergo, that leaves the other alternative."

Her hand shook slightly as she brought her wineglass to her lips. She took a long sip and carefully set the glass on the table. Her eyebrows rose speculatively. "What are *you* exactly?" she asked, turning his words back upon him. "A soldier, a brigand, or merely a well-breeched philanderer?" She was not forgetting the diamond bracelet he had so casually bestowed on the French girl before dismissing her.

Humor kindled in his eyes, but he answered seriously enough, "A little bit of all three. How astute of you to deduce it. But no, I'm not a professional soldier, if that's what is troubling you. Don't worry, I can afford you."

"I'm sure you could, if I were for sale. But you see, Mr. Dalmar, I'm not." She spoke slowly and deliberately so that there could be no misunderstanding between them.

He slanted her a curious look but thankfully seemed to

accept her calm assertion. She almost jumped when he snapped his fingers, but it was only to attract the notice of one of the waiters. In faultless French, he demanded another bottle of wine and a selection of fresh fruit.

When the waiter had done his bidding, he asked casually, "What's in the hatbox?"

Striving to appear equally casual, Annabelle responded, "Why? What should there be in a hatbox?"

"I only wondered when you refused to let your coachman take it with him when he returned to the hotel."

She smiled enigmatically but said nothing, hoping that he would not press the matter. From the moment she had read the first pages of Monique Dupres's diaries, she had known that an unscrupulous person could quite easily use the information as a tool for blackmail. There was no doubt in her mind that the man sitting on the other side of the table was as unscrupulous as anyone she had ever met in her life. That she intended to publish the diaries without a ripple of conscience or regret did not strike her in the same light at all.

From the glass pedestal dish on the center of the table, he selected a peach and began to peel it with a small knife. "What were you doing upstairs in that den of vice?"

She had an answer ready but she could not resist a little baiting of her own. "I might ask you the same question."

He offered her a small section of the peach, which she courteously accepted. It occupied her hands and carefully averted eyes as she came under his intent scrutiny.

"I hardly think we were there for the same purpose," he said gently.

"No, I don't suppose we were," she returned and ruthlessly suppressed her quivering lips.

In a crisper tone, he demanded, "Were you there to meet your lover?"

At this her eyes widened fractionally. "No. Might I have?"

"It's possible. There are rooms for rent . . ." His eyes narrowed as she coughed into her table napkin.

When she had recovered, she murmured, "Thank you for telling me. I'll be sure to keep that in mind when I'm next in Paris."

He decided that he'd allowed her more than enough time to regain her equilibrium. If he wasn't careful, the minx would turn the tables on him. Trying to suppress his admiration, he said silkily, "If you don't tell me what I wish to know, we have only to retrace our steps and confront Monique Dupres together."

The laughter faded from her eyes. He was sorry to see it go, but more than anything, he wanted her to take him seriously.

"If you must know," she said, throwing him a reproachful look, "it was all a mistake. D'you suppose I would have entered those premises if I'd known that I was stepping inside a . . . a brothel?"

"Then where were you going?"

"That's none of your business."

He thought he understood. Like himself, her lover probably had rooms in another part of the Palais Royal. In all likelihood, her coachman had delivered her to the wrong part of the vast building.

"Does your husband know that you have a lover?"

Annabelle choked on her champagne. When she had regained her breath, she glared into his unsmiling eyes and said chillingly, "I make it a rule never to talk about my husband to strangers."

"It's as I thought," he said, and calmly bit into the peach in his hand.

"What is?" she asked cautiously.

He dabbed his lips with his table napkin. "I make no doubt that your poor husband is as henpecked as your erstwhile lover." He flashed her a knowing grin. "I suspect it's in your nature to try to master anyone who is weaker than you. Let me give you a piece of advice," he softly admonished. "You'll come to grief if you try that tack with me."

"I wouldn't dream of it," she readily assured him. That he had painted her as a managing female who emasculated the men in her life, even if they were a figment of his imagination, she found highly annoying. When her husband had been alive, she had been the most conformable wife in England. Much good it had done her.

"Do you live under the same roof?"

"What?" She could not seem to keep up with his thoughts.

He gave her a lazy, indulgent smile. "Mrs. Jocelyn, you're not paying attention. Your lover is old history now. Do you share your husband's roof?"

His eyes held hers in their mesmerizing depths. She saw intelligence there and a simmering passion which he held rigidly in check. She tried to imagine that passion unleashed against herself. The fine hairs on the back of her neck rose at the harrowing spectacle. As an enemy or as a lover, such a man would demand complete surrender, and whether or not he would be generous in victory was a matter of conjecture. For an unguarded moment, she allowed herself a small flight of fancy. To be under the protection of such a man, whether as his wife or as his mistress, would have its own compensations. He would hold and protect what was his should the whole world be against him. The fortunate woman of his choice would have a strong arm to lean on.

She would also have a very domineering and masterful man who would not tolerate any show of resistance to his will. To a woman who was used to a modicum of freedom, he posed a threat she'd be a fool to underrate. She did not deny that there was an attraction between them. But she knew, in that instant, that to give herself to him even once would be the most foolhardy and dangerous thing she could ever do. To a brief love affair, she might have been susceptible. She was not sure. Perhaps if he had courted her, gentled her of her fears, treated her with deference . . . but she was appalled at this stark show of masculine determination. Without volition, she shivered.

"Well?" he demanded.

She tried to recall what he had last said. Of course. Her husband. She felt as if she were groping her way blindfolded through a treacherous quagmire. One false move, and she would sink to her neck.

Drawing a deep, steadying breath, she said, "You have no right to ask that question."

"Will he fight for you?"

Careful not to issue a challenge in her words, but very evenly and distinctly she said, "Edgar won't fight for me because it won't be necessary."

"Is he or is he not a true husband to you?"

"What?" For an awful moment she thought he suspected the truth.

His eyes blazed as he reached across the table and sank his fingers into her shoulders. "Answer my question. Does he exercise his conjugal rights?"

Resentment flared in her. "I've told you, I don't discuss my husband with anyone."

"Annabelle!"

The threat in that one furious word brought her to a sense of her jeopardy. "No!" she said, her voice oddly breathless. "Edgar has not been a husband to me in years."

He studied her expression as if weighing the truth of her statement. Inexplicably his lip curled. "I can almost feel sorry for the poor blighter," he said, dropping his hands from her shoulders.

Annabelle fell back into her chair. Rubbing her shoulders where she could still feel the imprint of his fingers, she said resentfully, "What's the matter with you? I told you what you wanted to know. Don't blame me if you don't care for the answers."

There was a touch of self-mockery in his smile when he said, "Oh, I liked your answer well enough. But I pity your husband. He was a fool to let another man chase him from your bed. But then, it wasn't just one man, was it?"

"I beg your pardon?"

"The fact that he has not been a husband to you in years suggests a succession of lovers."

She read the condemnation in his expression. Very softly she said, "Spare me the censure. I'm not forgetting the girl in the hotel gardens or Monique Dupres. You're not exactly a patterncard of rectitude yourself, are you?"

"No," he agreed amicably, "but then, I'm not married."

"Congratulations," she ground out. "You're to be envied."

"So," he said, "the state of matrimony was a disappointment to you and you embarked on a string of affairs. It's a familiar tale, I suppose, though rather sordid. Which brings us to 'The Milksop.' I'd be obliged if you'd give me his name and direction. You needn't look at me like that." A slow smile

32

touched his lips. "Hopefully, it won't come to a duel."

Annabelle had a vivid impression of the Bois de Boulogne at dawn and two marksmen with pistols in hand turning on command to fire at each other. Her throat became parched; her hands became clammy. It had been one thing when her back was to the wall to pretend that she had a claim to the protection of some powerful gentleman. Now, she was beginning to see she had made a serious blunder. Fear loosened her tongue.

"I have no lover," she told him earnestly. "I'm sorry if I gave you that impression. The man you mistook for my lover is merely a kinsman who very kindly gave me escort to Paris. There's absolutely no occasion for you to threaten him in any way."

"A kinsman?" he asked incredulously.

"Yes. On my husband's side. I'm telling you the truth. I swear it! I hoped you would leave me alone if you thought he was my protector. Then, when you threatened him, what else could I do but come here with you?"

"You have no lover?"

"No," averred Annabelle vehemently.

He eyed her thoughtfully over the rim of his wineglass. She could not sustain that searching look and reached for the tray of sweets which a waiter had set on the table a moment before.

She nibbled delicately. "Marzipan," she said for something to say to break the unnerving silence which had grown between them. "One of my favorites."

Straightening in his chair, he said, "Why is it I have the impression that you're not being completely frank with me?"

That she was chewing on a marzipan gave her an excellent excuse to marshal her thoughts before rushing into speech. Finally she said, "I don't know why I have told you as much as I have."

"Oh we both know the answer to that," he said provocatively.

"Oh?"

As she reached for another marzipan, he grasped her wrist. Her eyes lifted to meet his. Very softly, he said, "You've finally met a man you cannot master. I'm willing to overlook your checkered past, but you'll find me very different from your husband if you don't play straight with me."

She meant to wrench herself from his grasp, but before she had that satisfaction, he released her. Once again, she found herself rubbing her flesh where his fingers had bruised her.

"If 'The Milksop' isn't your lover, it's not for the want of trying. I've saved the poor sap an ignominious fate. He should thank me for it."

"What's that supposed to mean?" For a man who professed that he wanted to bed her, she found his whole demeanor positively insulting.

"It means, my sweet," he drawled, "that the man is a weakling. The man who thinks to master you should be cast in the heroic mold—you know, someone who has been mentioned in dispatches and so on."

"Such as yourself?" she jeered.

"Precisely!" He made no attempt to conceal his laughter at her expense.

She was stung into goading him. " 'The Milksop,' as you are pleased to call him, is more of a man than you give him credit for. That he has some war injury which makes it difficult for him to jump on and off horses and pursue the so-called manly sports does not weigh with me."

"I assure you, it does not weigh with me either."

"Then what are you talking about?"

"I'm talking about the way he fawns over you like some domesticated lapdog, coming to heel when you snap your fingers. If you were to give the command, I'm sure the poor creature would lie down and play dead."

"He's a gentleman, for heaven's sake. He respects me. I respect him. More, I like him. He's been a good friend to me. How dare you call him a weakling and a milksop simply because he doesn't try to terrify a poor, defenseless woman? He knows the true meaning of the word *manliness!*"

"Some poor, defenseless woman?" he repeated, and his dark brows lifted eloquently. "And who might that be? You? Spare me the rhetoric. And as for the meaning of the word *manliness*, you're the one who's in need of a lesson. It shall be my very great pleasure to teach you what that word means precisely."

She waited in simmering silence until the waiter had removed the remains of their meal, then she began on a recital in which she was well versed, only this time, her words were etched with venom. "Mr. Dalmar, I am deeply grateful of the honor you have done me. It is with heartfelt regret, however, that I feel constrained to decline your offer. To be frank, we would not suit."

He smiled tolerantly and said, "In case you hadn't noticed, Mrs. Jocelyn, I'm not offering. I'm telling you how it will be."

"Why?" The word was almost a wail. "What gives you the right to force yourself on me?"

For the first time, his face gentled into an emotion that was very close to tenderness. His hand reached out and touched her left cheek in a butterfly caress. "You know why," he told her softly. "Don't try to gammon yourself. Electricity has been sizzling between us since the moment we met in that hotel lobby. But you're afraid of any man who comes up to your weight. If I don't make the push to capture you, some other man will." Amusement crept into his voice. "I suspect that this is going to be a battle royal—oh, not that that's how I want it. But you're going to fight me every inch of the way. You know, it doesn't have to be like this. You could surrender gracefully at the outset and save us both a great deal of trouble."

Every word that she heard was inflammatory. Every feminine instinct urged her to put some distance between them. But she ruled her temper and her natural inclination with a will of iron. In that softened, almost tender expression, Annabelle recognized weakness. And Annabelle was not above exploiting weakness in an adversary—not when that adversary had so ruthlessly brought her to a standstill. Bailey's Press was her natural arena, not the boudoir, as the gentleman had so insultingly conjectured. Some lessons she had learned the hard way. Some skills she had mastered just to survive in the competitive world of commerce. Prevarication, she had discovered, was a very useful tool.

"Time," she murmured. "I need more time. I scarcely know you. How can you expect me to put myself . . ." she almost choked on the next words, ". . . under your protection when I

35

don't know what manner of man you are? A little time to get to know you—surely that's not too much to ask?" She was careful not to overdo it. She held his gaze steadily and frankly, knowing instinctively that to resort to overt feminine lures with this man would achieve the opposite of her purpose.

For a long interval, cool gray eyes assessed her expression. His eyes warmed slightly, and he said, "There was never any question of my forcing myself upon you. I'll give you time. Just remember, I don't have a limitless supply of patience where you are concerned."

A slow, secretive smile suffused her face. The man had handed her the victory, though he had no notion of having done so. Time was her friend. In twenty-four hours she would be well beyond Dalmar's reach. Like bubbles in a bottle of champagne, her success mounted to her head. She felt suddenly lighthearted and quite in charity with her formidable adversary.

She became conscious that he was holding her chair for her. "The galleries?" she repeated.

"Just upstairs. Most of the shops are there. And I feel I owe you a new bonnet."

"Please. That's not necessary. I already have more bonnets than I know what to do with."

"That would explain why you acquired another earlier today," he intoned meaningfully, and his eyes touched briefly on the strings of the hatbox which Annabelle clutched tightly in her hand.

She shot him a quick look, but his attention had shifted to the *maître* as he settled for their dinner.

Her arm was taken in a firm hold as he led her through the *allée* which gave onto the gardens. In the upstairs galleries, shopkeepers were already lighting their lanterns as dusk settled over the city. The gardens and galleries were crowded with pedestrians. Most of the "ladies," thought Annabelle, for want of a better word, were obviously Parisians. She had previously remarked that the hems of their gowns were several inches shorter than her own. She made a mental note that when she returned to London, she would have Nancy shorten all her gowns by an inch or two, for nothing was more certain than that the fashions prevailing in Paris would in time cross the English Channel.

Ten minutes browsing in the plethora of distinguished *magasins* and *boutiques* in the galleries of the Palais Royal worked a remarkable change in Annabelle. It was a change that Dalmar noted with some surprise and no little fascination. Shopping was obviously one of the lady's pleasures, if not vices. She became entranced, and when Annabelle became entranced, she also became entrancing.

Gone was that mask of distancing aloofness. He might have dreamed the wariness in those eyes which had lightened to the unclouded clarity of midsummer sky. Her lips, so deceivingly soft and tremulous for a woman of her forceful disposition, were slightly parted, as if she were having trouble breathing. She flashed him a smile, and the mole on her left cheek suddenly seemed to be begging for his kisses.

"Annabelle," he said, his voice low and unnaturally unsteady.

But she was already floating away from him. She might have been Aladdin in his cave, wandering as if under some compulsion from one treasure trove to the next. Dalmar followed in her wake, thoughtfully absorbing the lady's profound involvement in a pastime she evidently enjoyed with a passion.

Within fifteen minutes, she had forgotten to be reserved with him. "David," she breathed, "what do you think of this?" Did she know that she had given him his Christian name? He thought not. He examined the ornamental dagger she held out for his inspection.

"Interesting," he replied cautiously. What did he know about weapons that were mere playthings?

"Look how the mother-of-pearl has been so intricately worked into it."

He looked. "Very clever," he agreed, not very knowledgeably. "For whom do you intend it?"

"For Richard," she replied absently, taking it out of his hand and turning it over.

"And who is Richard, if I may be so bold?"

Her eyes flew to his face. She noted the thinned lips. She

shook her head. "He's only a boy, for heaven's sake!" Another evasion, Annabelle thought with a prick of conscience, then grew impatient with herself. The less Mr. Dalmar knew about her, the less likelihood of his ever finding her again. She was not devious by nature. It was the man himself who forced her to such lengths.

"They're the worst sort," he responded gravely.

She chortled. "At five years old? No, what I was wondering, David, is—do you think a five-year-old boy is too young for something like this? I mean, I don't wish him to do himself an injury or anything of that sort."

He took the dagger from her and examined it carefully. "He can't do much damage with this little toy. Besides, a boy should learn early how to handle weapons. D'you know what I think?"

"What?"

"I think this is a letter opener. If it's a real dagger you want . . ."

"No! This will do fine."

"The boy may not think so!"

She gave him a brilliant smile. "His mother will," she said, and began to rummage in her reticule.

His hand closed over hers. "I'll pay for it," he said.

Wariness rekindled in the eyes that had a moment before been as transparent as crystal. "You promised me some time," she reminded him.

He relented immediately, knowing that he would do almost anything to preserve the easiness which had developed between them. Her brow cleared, and with that he forced himself to be content.

Without a moment's hesitation, she handed over the fifty francs the shopkeeper demanded. Once outside on the gallery, Dalmar upbraided her.

"Annabelle," he said laughingly, "we're in France, not England. Haven't you ever heard of haggling? The shopkeepers here inflate the prices of their goods outrageously. If I'd known you were such an innocent, I'd never have let you step through the door. Next time, my girl, I'll show you how it's done."

She had to be forcibly restrained from returning to the shop

38

and boxing the shopkeeper's ears.

"*Caveat emptor,*" said Dalmar with a taunt in his voice, and he dragged her away from what might very easily have turned out to be the scene of a crime.

She was soon distracted from her murderous frame of mind. The objects which caught her interest were oddly revealing. She had an eye for the old and unusual.

"David," she said again, on that strangely breathy note, and held out a pair of tortoiseshell-and-silver combs.

He wondered how his name would sound on her lips when he entered her with his body. There was a tremor in his hands as they closed over hers. He wondered if she noticed.

"They're Spanish," he said. This time he was knowledgeable. He'd spent five years on the Peninsula.

Some expression he could not name passed over her face.

"They're beautiful," he said.

She replaced the combs on the counter with something that might have been regret. "They're not Italian?"

"No. Definitely Spanish."

The combs lost interest for her. His eyes trailed her small, straight-backed figure as she moved at random through the aisles, oblivious of the more aggressive and voluble shoppers, who were mostly native Parisians. There were facets to Annabelle Jocelyn, he decided, that he would never have guessed at. In that moment, he sensed a vulnerability in her that she would never admit to. An unfamiliar emotion, something soft and nebulous, caught him unawares. He savored it, tested it, and tried to give it a name. *Careful, Dalmar,* he warned himself. *This woman will never respect a show of weakness in the man who means to claim her.*

He was examining a necklace of diamonds when she called his name again. Obedient to her summons, he returned the necklace to the jeweler, instructing him to wait on his decision.

The gold locket in her hands was old and ornate. On the front were engraved the initials A.D. He studied it closely. "French," he said without hesitation. "Mid-eighteenth century."

She fingered it with near-reverence, and all he could think of were those soft hands and how he craved the touch of them on his body.

"This time, *I've* found something," he told her, and drew her to the counter where the diamond necklace lay on its velvet cushion. In some obscure way he could not even explain to himself, he wanted to make up for the scene where Annabelle had witnessed him giving the French girl the bracelet.

She slanted him a look of amused tolerance. "Diamonds," she said, and he detected the teasing derision in her tone. "Oh David! They're so common," and she linked her arm through his and laughingly dragged him back to her latest find.

"I wonder who it belonged to and what the initials stand for?" she mused thoughtfully, her fingers lazily tracing the pattern of the letters.

Without thinking, he said, "Annabelle and David?" He was instantly sorry he had spoken.

Her eyes registered her shock, then slid away from his.

His fingers closed around the locket. "I'll get this," he said, in a tone that brooked no argument. She started to protest. He cut her off without a qualm. "I owe you for the bonnet."

"Only for the feathers," she argued, running to keep up with his long strides as he made his way purposefully to the counter.

"Where *did* you get those peacock feathers?" he demanded, angling a smile at her. He succeeded in distracting her.

"I got them for a song at Bartholomew Fair," she explained, preening a little.

Without blinking an eyelash, he paid over the sum the shopkeeper had named.

She was too dumbfounded to speak as he turned her by the shoulders and secured the locket at her neck.

Once out of the shop, she rounded on him. "You didn't haggle over the price!" She could not have been more scandalized if he'd walked away without paying for his purchase.

He had expected an argument about whether or not she would accept the locket from him. "What a delight you are," he murmured, and turned her to face him.

His lips, as soft as swan's down, brushed the small dark mole which had tempted him beyond endurance. Surprise held her

40

captive. He moved closer.

A shout went up from the courtyard below. There was the sound of shattering glass and booted feet running on flagstone.

A shot rang out, then pandemonium erupted in every quarter of the Palais Royal.

"*Les Prussiens! Les Prussiens!*" The cry was taken up and rang out through the gardens.

"The Prussians? What does that mean?" asked Annabelle, instinctively edging closer to the shelter of Dalmar's body.

He groaned. "Trouble," he said. "Come on. Let's get the hell out of here."

Chapter Three

The cry of warning acted on the bystanders as if someone had screamed the word *fire!* In the resulting hysteria, shoppers spewed onto the gallery, searching frantically for a way of escape. In their wake, canny merchants were dousing lanterns. The sound of bolts being shot home only added to the panic.

Down below, scores of soldiers in Prussian blue were streaming into the gardens. Their furious onslaught did not go unchecked. From every part of the Palais Royal, the officers of the Bourbonist *garde du corps* unsheathed their short swords and rushed to meet them. With mingled cries of *"Jenna"* and *"Vive la France,"* men went at each other as if the signal to join battle had been given.

There was no question of descending to the lower level, thought Annabelle. Already the Prussians, who vastly outnumbered the *garde du corps,* were cutting off the exits.

"Au toit, au toit!" someone cried out, and the press of people surged to the stairs, which would take them to the roof and away from the scene of slaughter.

"Steady," said Dalmar in Annabelle's ear as she tried to push past him. His left arm captured her shoulders protectively. In his right hand gleamed the wicked-looking short sword which most gentlemen in Paris seemed to affect. Annabelle had presumed it was mostly for decoration.

Every instinct urged her to flee with the herd. Her eyes searched Dalmar's face, and by degrees her panicked heartbeat slowed. His air of confidence seemed unshakable.

43

He smiled down at her. "May I offer you my protection, Mrs. Jocelyn?" he murmured in her ear.

She felt her knees buckle and leaned into him for support. "Oh David," she answered shakily, "this is no time to joke."

She caught the quick flash of his teeth before he answered her seriously. "We're going through the gardens. Don't argue. Just keep close and do as I tell you."

In that moment, if he had told her to follow him through a river of fire, she would have obeyed him. "All right. But how?" she asked, her eyes traveling to the staircases, which were dangerously choked with people.

She was released. She heard the shatter of glass before she realized what he was up to. Behind her the window of the shop they had been browsing in minutes before was completely demolished. He used the hilt of his sword to smash the few remaining shards of glass which protruded. She grasped his hand tightly as he helped her over the sill.

"The back stairs," he told her before striding away to the back of the shop. Annabelle, not daring to linger, hurried to keep up with him.

Their descent was torturous. They made so many twists and turns that Annabelle lost her sense of direction. It was evident that the man she followed knew exactly where he was going. And then she heard it—the clash of steel on steel and the hoarse cries of the combatants. Her steps faltered.

"Why don't we stay here?" she asked the back of his dark head, but before he could answer, she heard the rush of booted feet on the stairs behind her. Retreat was impossible.

"Stay close!" he shouted, and burst through the archway into the courtyard.

The scene which met Annabelle's eyes would remain with her forever. Nothing in her experience had ever prepared her for such carnage. Nor could she comprehend how men who professed to be civilized could be so filled with hatred of each other. She could almost smell the blood lust in the air.

Though her limbs remained frozen, her mind quickly registered several facts. The confrontation had spread to the upstairs. She wondered if Dalmar had surmised that it would. A troup of gendarmes had arrived to augment the

French officers, evening the odds somewhat. Nor were the British left idle. With something like relish, they turned on Prussian and French alike.

Her arm was seized roughly. "I said stay close!" Dalmar barked at her.

His harsh command galvanized her into action. Shutting her ears to the groans and cries of the wounded, she quickened her steps after him.

Two things happened simultaneously. From the darkest part of the gardens where the lights had been doused, a woman's scream pierced the air, and Annabelle was grabbed from behind. Her own shocked cry went unheard.

She was brutally manhandled, but whether the hands which closed over her breasts were French or Prussian was impossible to determine. Nor did she care. There could be no mistaking the design of the man who dragged her into the cover of bushes. She was spun to face him.

"*Für Berlin,*" he snarled, and his hand grabbed at her collar and tore her garments from throat to waist.

"David," Annabelle warbled. Then on a shriller, more compelling note as those strong, callused hands kneaded her breasts, "Da - v - id!" *Oh God,* she thought, *oh God, please . . .*

He loomed out of the darkness like a furious avenging angel. She was thrust aside as the Prussian swung around to meet him.

"Get your back to the wall," Dalmar shouted at her before lunging. Annabelle scooted to the side of the building and pressed herself against it.

Everything happened at once. Another form materialized from the shadows and attacked Dalmar from the rear. She cried out a warning. With the grace and speed of a cat, he circled, his sword arm slashing and parrying unerringly as he warded off the double attack.

From halfway up the stairs, an English voice hailed him. "Dalmar? It is you, you devil! I thought as much! Leave us poor blighters some of the action!" and one of the officers of the Horse Guards lightly vaulted over the railing and took up a position beside him.

"Mercer? Just like old times, isn't it?" said Dalmar without once breaking stride or deflecting the furious slash of his sword arm.

Shoulder to shoulder, they met the frenzied assault of the Prussians head on. Even from her obscure vantage point, Annabelle knew from the furious and frantic pace that no quarter would be asked or given. Never in her life had Annabelle been so close to such unbridled violence. For a horrified moment, she thought she was about to swoon away.

She saw one of the Prussians go down. As Dalmar deliberately wiped his bloodstained blade against the leg of his pantaloons, he calmly asked of the man called Mercer, "Need any help?"

"Don't you dare!" laughed the other man, and in one savage assault, he ran his adversary through without compunction.

Annabelle was shivering with terror. Only a sudden blooming of anger saved her from having a fit of the vapors. Damn if these men weren't enjoying themselves!

"Do me a favor, cover my back," said Dalmar casually, and with a quick, searching glance at Annabelle's stunned expression, he gathered her closely to him. "I'm conveying the lady to safety."

"I'll be right behind you," promised the other.

They crossed the courtyard unmolested. The incongruous note of the cascading waters of one of the fountains could be heard intermittently even above the noise of the pitched battle.

As they reached one of the doors, Mercer called out, "You're on your own. Here comes another!" and he turned away to meet the furious attack of a black-coated civilian.

The words *vive l'empereur!* trembled on the air as Annabelle was pulled roughly through the door.

"A Bonapartist," grunted Dalmar. "That's all we need."

She felt him stiffen and heard the hiss of his breath before she saw the figure blocking their path.

"We're English. Let us pass," said Dalmar.

In that moment, Annabelle's relief at having fled the combat zone died within her. It was an officer of the *garde du corps* who confronted them. In his hand he held a sword stained with blood. At his feet lay the body of a Prussian officer, his blade still grasped in one hand. In Annabelle's mind, the scene was

46

made more grotesque by the shadows cast by the few lanterns which hung on the walls.

"Dalmar," breathed the Frenchman on a note of mingled disbelief and triumph. "Last time we dueled with pistols. At that time I was compelled to concede that you were the better man. This time the choice of weapons is mine."

Annabelle's hand was grasped, and a key was pressed into her palm. In an urgent undertone Dalmar said, "At the top of the stairs, you'll come to a door. This is the key to that door. Use it." In a more normal tone, he addressed the Frenchman. "I'm still the better man, Livry, whatever the choice of weapons."

"Shall we put it to the test?" drawled the Frenchman, and as if to underscore his point, made several sweeping slashes with his sword high above his head. The sound was like the crack of a whip and just as terrifying. Annabelle flinched and he laughed softly, his eyes insolently sweeping over her disheveled figure. *"En garde,* Dalmar, and to the victor go the spoils!" His meaning was unmistakable.

Annabelle had never felt more helpless in her life. Though she was perfectly sensible of the Frenchman's threat, her most pressing fear was for the safety of the man she regarded as her champion. The skill of the French with the short sword was legendary. Dueling was one of their favorite pastimes. And this particular Frenchman exuded a confidence that made her blood turn to water. She wondered if the man beside her had brains enough to be frightened.

As the two adversaries warily circled each other with flashing blades, she tried a last-ditch, forlorn attempt to avert disaster. "Excuse me," she said, addressing both gentlemen, "if either one of you so much as scratches the other, I shall report you both to the authorities."

A gleam of mingled surprise and amusement momentarily registered in the Frenchman's eyes. Again that soft laugh fell from his lips. "Dalmar," he taunted, "where do you find them? This one, I look forward to taming."

"The woman is mine," said Dalmar, studiously casual. "If you want her, you'll have to kill me first."

"With pleasure!" Livry ferociously lunged and lunged

again, driving Dalmar back till he was pinned against the wall.

The hilts of their two swords locked. In a burst of strength, Dalmar wrenched the Frenchman round till their positions were reversed.

"Now!" he shouted over his shoulder to Annabelle. "Quick! The stairs!"

Clutching her hatbox in one hand and the key to Dalmar's rooms in the other, Annabelle scampered past the duelists. As her foot touched the first step, the combatants broke apart. She hesitated.

"Get going!" Dalmar snarled at her, and immediately made a slashing arc with his blade, forcing Livry to stumble back. Dalmar was on him in an instant.

Annabelle quickly mounted the stairs, but on the first landing she halted. Though she was shaking like a leaf and wanted nothing more than to find a safe hole where she could find refuge, everything in her rebelled at leaving Dalmar to his fate. Torn between a fear for his life and a fear of disobeying his commands, she faltered.

She glanced over the stairwell, and though she was not in a position to see the contenders, her eyes were drawn to the grotesque spectacle of their shadows on the wall—gray wraiths which seemed to be engaged in a deadly pas de deux. Only the ring of steel on steel, their harsh breathing, and their soft footfalls gave any indication of the awful reality. Mesmerized, Annabelle sank to her heels, her eyes riveted to the moving pictures on the wall.

She heard the soft cry before one of the shadows fell back, then sank to his knees. Annabelle was on her feet. *Which one?* her mind screamed.

Horrified, she watched as the other man closed in for the kill. In that moment she knew that Dalmar, stranger to her though he was, would never kill a wounded adversary. The man who was poised to administer the *coup de grâce* had to be the Frenchman.

She did not think of consequences. With an anguished cry, she hurtled down the stairs. Upon her sudden appearance, Livry's startled eyes were diverted from his target. It was all that Dalmar needed. With superhuman strength, he parried

48

the Frenchman's blade and thrust.

A look of pained surprise flickered in the Frenchman's eyes. He staggered, holding his chest. His back hit the wall, and he sank to his heels. The sword fell from his inert fingers.

Annabelle rushed to Dalmar.

"Stubborn woman," he growled at her. "Can't you ever do what you're told?"

At that moment, he could have cursed her up and down Britain from Land's End to John o' Groats and Annabelle would have thanked him for it. That he was not mortally wounded was more than she had hoped for. That he had the temper to take her to task in such uncompromising tones filled her with an overwhelming relief. Tears started to her eyes. She hiccuped.

Dalmar, correctly assessing the fragile thread which held her together, roughly interposed, "For God's sake, give me your arm. If anyone else comes through that door, we're done for. Now move!"

The harsh imperative acted on Annabelle exactly as Dalmar intended it to. She kneeled before him and said in a voice that was almost normal, "You're bleeding like a pig. I'll bind your arm with your neckcloth," and suiting action to words, she quickly untied his linen cravat and stemmed the flow of blood which seeped from the wound near his shoulder. With his good arm around her, she supported him till they had gained the stairs.

"What the devil is in that hatbox?" asked Dalmar, diverting her attention as they brushed by the prone figure of the Prussian.

Without thinking, Annabelle answered, "Papers."

Their progress up two flights of stairs was slow enough to fill Annabelle with renewed alarm, for sounds of what gave every evidence of becoming a slaughter seemed to echo through the dark corridors of the building. It was only as Dalmar locked the door to his rooms behind them and shot home the bolt that she allowed herself to sag against him.

"Ransome!" he roared.

The summons was answered immediately by a giant of a man who cursed softly under his breath as he took in at a glance the

49

torn and tattered dishabille of the woman who supported the injured man whose features were etched in lines of pain.

"What the devil?" he exclaimed, coming forward.

"Prussians and the hot-headed *garde du corps*," said Dalmar by way of explanation, and transferred his weight from Annabelle's slender shoulders to the more capable arms of the gentleman who waited on him.

With legs that were perilously close to buckling beneath her, Annabelle followed them down a long, dark corridor and into what was evidently a gentleman's bedchamber. As Dalmar was led to the great tester bed, she sank gratefully into an old-fashioned overstuffed armchair. The word *impropriety* never once entered her head. She had no notion that her breasts were practically bared to the waist, and was scarcely aware of the giant as he solicitously covered her with a blanket. For the last hour, she had been living on her nerves. Now that the threat to life and limb was removed, she was fast sinking into a state of shock.

A large glass of brandy materialized from nowhere. A voice, soft and kind, said some words to her. Obedient to the command, Annabelle choked down the fiery liquid.

The glass was miraculously replenished. Again Annabelle obediently drained it to the dregs. A shudder passed over her, and she became conscious that the soft-spoken giant was addressing her.

"The colonel asks if you would mind waiting in the dressing room. I've taken the liberty of setting things out for you."

From the depths of the bed came Dalmar's laconic drawl. "Annabelle, go and tidy yourself. For God's sake, woman, you're half naked, and the rags that are covering you look as if they've been baptized in blood." On a more gentle note, he added, "There's a good girl. I'll send for you when we're done here."

She rallied somewhat and allowed herself to be led to an adjoining door. For a moment, she could not recollect the purpose for her being in the small room. The sight of the washstand with its basin and pitcher and the commode

50

conveniently located behind a screen brought her out of her lethargy.

Absently, she accepted the garments that the man called Ransome draped over her arm.

"You'll be more comfortable in these in the interim," he said, and shut the door softly behind her.

The garments he had given her were a man's shirt and dressing gown. She laid them over the back of a chair and took stock of herself in a long cheval mirror. With her blood-spattered and torn gown and pelisse and wildly disheveled hair, she might have been taken for one of the witches in "Macbeth." Her bonnet was gone. She had no recollection of losing it. Miraculously, the gold locket which Dalmar had given her still nestled between her breasts. Though there wasn't a scratch on her, blood was everywhere. As memory flooded her mind, she quickly stripped out of her clothes and resolved to consign them to the fire at the earliest opportunity. The blood on them could not possibly have come only from Dalmar's wound. *Dead men's blood,* she thought, and was shaken by a shudder of revulsion.

When she was called back into the bedchamber, she found Dalmar propped up against pillows. Both right shoulder and forearm were bandaged. His face was drawn, his eyes closed. Against the starkly white sheets, his naked chest and shoulders glistened like copper.

Her eyes flew to Ransome, asking a question.

"He'll survive," he said. "He's lost some blood, but it's nothing to worry about. I've dosed him with laudanum to ease the pain. He'll sleep like a baby for the next hour or so."

"And a physician?"

"That's the least of our worries. Look, I must leave you here. I have to go out, and I can't leave him unattended." As he spoke, he removed a brace of pistols from a cabinet. "You'll be safe enough as long as you keep the door locked and bolted after me. I've left the bottle of laudanum on the mantelpiece. If he gets restless, you can give him a couple of drops."

"Where are you going?"

"To get reinforcements. Colonel's orders."

51

He took her by the elbow and walked her to the front door. "I don't suppose you know how to use one of these?" he said, extending one of the wicked-looking pistols.

Annabelle drew back. "No. I've never had occasion to."

He nodded. "Then it's best not to leave it with you. When I go through that door, I want you to lock it and bolt it behind me, and don't open it for anyone until I return."

As soon as the door closed behind him, Annabelle turned the key and shot home the bolt. She returned to the bedchamber and moved about nervously, her eyes coming to rest frequently on the still figure on the bed. From below, the sounds of rampage and carnage gave no evidence of lessening. After a time, she curled up in an armchair and brooded in silence.

She must have dozed. Her head suddenly jerked, and she was startled into wakefulness. Every muscle in her body ached with weariness and tension.

The man in the bed was stirring restlessly. She rose and went to check on him. There was no sign of fever, she decided, as she touched her fingers to his forehead. He opened his eyes and stared up at her.

"How do you feel?" she asked softly.

She had to strain to hear him.

"Water . . . please."

She held his head as she carefully offered the glass to his lips. His eyes never left hers.

After a few swallows, he turned his head away, but before she could draw back, his left hand came up to capture her wrist. "Stay . . . please," he whispered hoarsely.

"I won't leave you," she said, and offered him a reassuring smile.

His eyes fluttered closed. "Promise?"

She hesitated, sensing in the simple question more than she understood. His fingers tightened on her wrist. "I promise," she said.

By degrees, his fingers relaxed. "To the victor go the spoils," he murmured, and smiled to himself.

Annabelle's quelling frown came too late. He had already succumbed to sleep. For a long interval, she sat unmoving on the edge of the bed, drinking in every detail of the face and form of the man who had somehow contrived to slip under her guard. In repose, his hard-chiseled features were softened, lending him a less formidable, almost boyish aspect. The man was wounded. Drugged. Helpless. It was hard to imagine that in the last several hours she had considered that he posed any kind of threat to her person.

Daringly, she pursed her lips and fanned his cheek with a puff of breath. His nose twitched. He was, she thought, like a sedated lion from which claws and fangs had been surreptitiously drawn. At the unholy thought, her lips turned up at the corners. Very gently, with her index finger, she prodded him on his good shoulder. Nothing. The lion was at her mercy. A wave of feminine power surged through Annabelle.

With increasing confidence, she touched her fingers to his dark head. His hair was just as she had imagined—crisp, thick, healthy. Very tentatively, she tested the hard, corded muscles of his left arm. Under her exploration they rippled, and she pulled back her hand in alarm. A full minute elapsed before her breathing returned to normal.

With the pads of her fingers, lightly, cautiously, she stroked the dark mat of hair which covered his naked torso. Soft and silky, she decided, and as sleek as an otter's pelt. The sleeping man betrayed not a flicker of consciousness as her fingers skimmed over him.

In the secure knowledge that the object of her interest was drugged into oblivion, she became bolder. She began to play with him, feathering light kisses along every part of his exposed anatomy. She felt deliciously decadent—and utterly beyond his power. His masculine scent, a combination of sweat, soap, and something indeterminate, assailed her nostrils. She buried her nose against his chest and inhaled. Though his scent was not unpleasant, it was unequivocally disturbing. She drew back, letting the thought revolve in her mind.

Becoming more relaxed by the minute, she slipped under the quilted coverlet and stretched out, full length, beside him. Steadfastly she gazed into his sleep-softened features. She blinked once; she blinked twice. A slow, drugging lethargy began to steal over her. She decided to give in to it, but only for a moment. Her head floated down to the soft, inviting pillow.

"Annabelle."

She heard her name as if from a great distance. Her slumberous thoughts absorbed the word, testing the dark, syrupy flavor of the voice which called to her.

"Annabelle," said the voice again, and she felt it pouring over her like warm treacle—wet, thick, and infinitely sweet.

She tasted it on her tongue and opened her lips to take in more of it. It pooled, overflowed, and coursed down from throat to ankle, submerging her in its potent warmth, clinging to her like a lover's embrace. *Danger!* she thought, and felt herself, like an unsuspecting bee drawn to the jam pot, caught and held by the sweetness which had attracted her. She began to struggle.

Dalmar groaned as her fist caught him a glancing blow on the shoulder. He captured her wrists and held them over her head.

Annabelle's eyes flew open. For a terrified moment she stared up at the dark masculine shadow which loomed over her. Slowly, by degrees, she came to herself. Her tame lion had wakened, she thought drowsily, and smiled up at him.

Her lips were taken in a kiss that was anything but tame. When he drew back his head, Annabelle saw the flame in his eyes, and the sensual flare of his nostrils.

"David," she breathed on a note of alarm. She became conscious of several things at once. She was naked beneath the quilt, and the man who was sprawled so suggestively over the top half of her body, pinning her with his weight, was as naked as she.

She saw the stark and uncompromising hunger in his eyes and said his name more sternly, "David! Your arm! Your shoulder! Don't . . ."

He kissed her into silence, and though she squirmed beneath him, she was too solicitous of his injuries to struggle in earnest.

She dragged her head away and hoarsely managed to get out,

"I don't wish to hurt you. Please, David, don't make me fight you."

"Don't then," he muttered against her throat. "Give in to me. Please, Annabelle. We both know this moment was inevitable."

She felt the upward movement of his hand at her waist. It molded itself to her breast, and the air was suddenly stripped from her lungs. As the pads of his fingers grazed first one sensitive nipple, then the other, pulling gently on the swollen peaks, she cried out softly.

"Yes," he murmured. "Yes. Like this. Give in to me," and his mouth, hotly moist, followed the path of his fingers.

She felt the hard pull at her breast as he suckled deeply, and the tightening in her womb as it responded to his masculine demand. Her hands splayed out against his chest, gently restraining him.

"David, please," she cried out, scarcely aware of what she was saying. "You're sedated. You don't know what you're doing. You'll open the wound."

"Not if you make it easy for me," he coaxed. "Give yourself to me, love. Make it easy for me."

The hot, dark words stirred an ache in the center of her being. As his tongue laved the hollow between her breasts, the ache became a throb, and Annabelle felt her senses go spinning. Her head shifted restlessly on the pillow as she tried to absorb what was happening to her. In a forlorn attempt to evade the seduction of her senses, she inched herself toward the edge of the bed.

Her mild act of resistance provoked him to thrust her legs apart and settle the full press of one leg against the cradle of her thighs. Involuntarily she jerked away from the heavy masculine arousal which pressed so threateningly against her body.

"Where are my clothes?" she demanded on a strangled note.

"On the floor. You didn't object when I removed them."

She felt his hand at the back of her knee, lifting her leg slightly. "No, oh please, listen to me," she moaned, "I was dreaming. I don't want this."

His voice, low and thick, soothingly tried to calm her fears. "It's all right, sweetheart. I won't hurt you. I'll take care of you. You don't have to be afraid of me. Let me love you. It's what we both want. Don't fight me. Please."

"You don't understand," Annabelle cried out as his hand made a slow, proprietary sweep from breast to hip to thigh, setting off tremors of unbelievable longing all through her body. "I can't take the chance."

"Hush," he soothed. "I'll give you everything you want. You'll never have cause to regret that you came to me."

His masculine obtuseness was thoroughly upsetting.

"Babies," Annabelle wailed. "Can't you understand? You could give me a baby."

He went still, then suddenly pulled back, an expression of arrested surprise on his face. It was evident from the slow, smoldering fire which kindled in his eyes that her warning had not acted upon him as she had hoped it would.

"A child," he murmured, and his eyes, glittering with some new emotion, swept over her. "Don't worry about it," he soothed. "If you give me a whole brood of children, I'll welcome every one of them."

Shock held her speechless. He took instant advantage. His mouth slanted over hers again and again, opening her to the full force of his passion, his tongue penetrating her with a thoroughness which left her trembling.

He raised himself slightly, and his hand brushed over the nest of curls which concealed the center of her femininity. Deliberately, he forced her knees wider, opening her body to his touch. Ripples of sensual heat washed through Annabelle. For a moment she panicked. In that instant of total vulnerability, she knew that there would be no turning back once he had discovered how eagerly her body craved his caresses.

"David, wait," she choked out.

But even as she said the words, his probing fingers were becoming dewed with the hot feminine wetness which betrayed her arousal.

She heard his grunt of satisfaction and the sudden change in the tempo of his breathing. He stroked his fingers more deeply into her, and her own breath became suspended in her chest. She gasped, struggling to draw more air into her lungs.

"Oh David," she cried softly, and turned her face into his neck.

Her cry of surrender seemed to inflame him to the point of frenzy. Hot, dark words of passion spilled from his lips as he positioned himself above her. Suddenly, aggressively, he forged into her. Annabelle went rigid with the shock of his possession. It had been so long since she had known a man's passion that it was as if she were being made love to for the first time.

Sensing her physical distress, he went perfectly still, giving her time to adjust to the hard intrusion of his body. His lips coursed down, capturing her mouth in a lover's kiss, reassuring and infinitely patient. The moment of discomfort passed, and Annabelle melted against him. Slowly, powerfully, Dalmar set the rhythm for their lovemaking.

Lost in a riot of unfamiliar sensations, she grasped at the last shreds of her control. But her body was beyond her, answering his blatant masculine demand, yielding to the age-old feminine hunger which cried out for fulfillment. Passion and fear warred within her. Her hands clutched convulsively at his straining arms.

Her anguished confusion transmitted itself to Dalmar. He did not hesitate to use her passion against her. Suddenly his hands slipped under her hips, fusing her body to his, overwhelming her with the urgency of his ardor.

It was his hoarse lover's plea which sent her spinning out of control. "Give in to me! Hold me! Annabelle, please, love me!"

Emotion melded with passion, and she responded to him on every level of her being. Her capitulation was sudden and complete. She locked her arms around his neck and offered him her lips. He took what she was offering and asked for more. The hard, rhythmic drive of his body warned her that he wanted her with him, there, at the end, when he made the leap to ecstasy. Such a thing had never before been demanded of her.

"Let go," he told her hoarsely. "Let go and trust me."

And for the first time in her life, Annabelle surrendered the total control of her body to her lover. The pleasure became unbearable. Her body tightened. Far back in her throat, small animal cries erupted and became choked. The effect on Dalmar was explosive. As her own body went hurtling over the edge, she felt the wracking shudders of his as he poured himself into her.

The descent to reality was sweet and languorous, accompanied by his wet, open-mouthed kisses and half-coherent, drowsy exclamations of wonder.

"Annabelle, you can't know . . ."

"I know."

"I never expected . . ."

"Neither did I."

"You're mine. I'll never let you go."

"Hush, David. Go to sleep. We'll talk about it later."

Possessively, he anchored her with one leg thrown over her thighs. She nestled against him and waited till the soft rise and fall of his chest told her that he had drifted into sleep. Careful not to waken him, she slid from beneath the comfort of his warm body.

She shrugged into her borrowed dressing gown and stood gazing at him as if mesmerized. In the aftermath of spent passion, a thousand disturbing thoughts rushed in to confront her. She knew a sense of shock at having put herself, once again and against all reason, into a position of vulnerability with a man.

The unnerving thought that to allow this man to make love to her would be the most dangerous thing she could do in her life came back in full force. A spasm of alarm went rippling through her. She tried to suppress it, but her sense of panic grew.

She found her clothes where she had left them and dressed with quick, economical movements. The torn and blood-spattered garments were the least of her worries now. In the gentleman's press, she came upon a man's cloak. It trailed the ground when she draped it round her shoulders, but she

58

deemed it adequate for her purpose.

Before she left, she checked on him. He was moving fitfully in his sleep, but the bandage on his arm was secure and dry. Carefully, she measured the drops of laudanum into a half glass of water and held his head as she forced him to drink. His eyes opened once, and he said her name. She whispered something reassuring which seemed to settle him.

Though the finger of dawn had yet to penetrate to the candlelit interior, outside the window, on the avenue of limes, the birds and their nestlings were already heralding the new day. Inside, the vast corridors of the Palais Royal were blanketed in an unnatural silence. Annabelle slipped past two English sentries who guarded one of the exits to the Rue de Rivoli. They made no move to stop her.

She drew a deep, steadying breath and moved off at a brisk pace in the direction of the Hotel Breteuil. In another hour she would be on her way to Calais. In another week, Paris would be a memory; and with luck, in another month, Dalmar would seem like a figment of her imagination.

By noon, her hired chaise was entering the Forest of Chantilly. Back in Paris, inventory was being taken in the wake of one of the worse melees to have broken out since the occupation of the city. Scores of innocent and not-so-innocent bystanders were injured. Of the dead, fourteen were Prussian officers and ten were either known Bonapartists or of the *garde du corps*. In one corner of the gardens, beneath a thicket of mimosa, the body of a French woman was discovered. Her throat had been slit. She was later identified as a young prostitute, the drawing card of the Maison d'Or. Her name was Monique Dupres.

Chapter Four

Dalmar's glance, carefully neutral, touched briefly on the diverse uniformed gentlemen of His Majesty's Service, all four of whom were known to him, and who lounged at their ease in Sir Charles's elegant study in the British Embassy. Of their number, only Ransome appeared to have escaped injury in the recent fracas at the Palais Royal. Of the ambassador himself, Sir Charles Stuart, there was nary a sign.

"Mercer, Seymour, Bodley, Ransome," murmured Dalmar, addressing each gentleman in turn. Sheepish glances were exchanged. Dalmar strolled to one of the vacant gilt-edged chairs and carefully seated himself.

"How's the shoulder?" asked Major Seymour conversationally.

"Mending nicely, thank you. And your arm?"

"The same."

It was Captain Mercer who interrupted the spate of chitchat and civilities which this small exchange provoked. "What are you doing here, Dalmar? You're no longer under army discipline, as I hear."

From his coat pocket, Dalmar withdrew a small enamel snuffbox. He offered it round. "Is that why we're here?" he asked mildly. "To be disciplined?"

Mercer grinned. "Speaking for myself, it wouldn't surprise me. I was the officer in command that night. I've already been hauled over the coals once for not sending for reinforcements the moment trouble started."

61

"Thank God someone did," drawled Major Bodley, his fingers absently curling the ends of his handsome mustache. "We're lucky there wasn't a bloodbath. Well, we all know we've been sitting on a powder keg these last months. The French and the Prussians would like nothing better than to wipe each other off the face of the earth."

After a considering silence, Ransome remarked, "What I don't understand is how the devil the rumpus got started. I thought to catch forty winks before joining Lady Ashford's party for the theater. The next thing I knew, our friend here," he indicated Dalmar by a nod of his head, "was shouting bloody murder at the top of his lungs."

"D'you mean you missed the show?" asked Captain Mercer consolingly. Of the five gentlemen present, he was the youngest, and transparently eager to earn his spurs in any affair of honor which presented itself. He'd had the misfortune to take a trifling injury at Quatre Bras, two days before the main action at Waterloo, and had lamented his unfortunate fate ever since.

Ransome's lips were very grave as he answered, "It pains me to tell you, Captain, that I slept through the whole of it. Shall I ever live it down?"

Ignoring this idle exchange, Major Seymour took up the conversation. "As for how it got started, I think Bodley and I can answer that. We were there, you see, at the Café de Foy, when a score of those half pay French officers swaggered in. They were looking for a fight, of course, and they got it."

"What were you doing in the Café de Foy?" asked Ransome, mildly surprised. "It's a known Prussian rendezvous."

"They're not all barbarians," protested Seymour. "I'm on very good terms with a few of 'em. Well, I think you all know the gentlemen we were with that night—Hildesheim and Lenk. Dashed good fellows, officers and gentlemen, even if they are Prussians. Put 'em in a couple of redcoats and one might easily take 'em for our own chaps."

"Could there be a higher encomium?" murmured Dalmar ironically. Seymour sliced him a glance, but the Earl's innocent expression robbed his remark of any real offense. "Go on, old chap," encouraged Dalmar. "You were saying? How the fight got started, or something to that effect?"

"What? Oh yes. Well, the Prussians weren't looking for trouble on this occasion. As I said, we were enjoying a dashed good dinner when the place was invaded by those offensive half-pay officers. One insult led to another. A scuffle got started and spilled into the gardens. The rest you know."

Major Bodley took up where his friend had left off. "Thank God our chaps were on duty that night, or there's no telling how ugly things might have become."

"How was it brought under control?" asked Dalmar of Captain Mercer.

"Lord Hay himself arrived with reinforcements. It was touch and go there for a minute or two, I can tell you. By this time, you see, word of the fight had spread outside the walls of the Palais Royal, and men of all description were pouring in to aid their comrades. There were more than a hundred Prussians, and a whole troop of gendarmes had arrived. I shall never forget that last confrontation in the gardens—the French ranged on one side and the Prussians on the other, and each side on the point of charging. Lord Hay lost no time in placing our chaps, with muskets at the ready, between them and said that he would give the order to fire upon the first who moved."

"And no one moved, I take it?"

"Well, of course they didn't. These chaps may not have a very high opinion of our swordplay, but Waterloo has taught them to respect our infantry. They melted away like summer snow on the mountain."

All heads turned as the door opened to admit a fresh-faced, elderly gentleman of rather stout proportions. The occupants of the room recognized him as James Somerset, one of the ambassador's senior attachés.

"Please be seated," he said, one comprehensive glance taking in the five, who had risen at his entrance. He took his place behind the massive leather-topped desk and began to rifle through some papers. "Sir Charles sends his regrets. He's been detained at the Tuileries with our delegation." Addressing no one in particular, he went on, patently ruffled. "The Duke also is with His Majesty and at some pains to convince Marshal Blucher that there is more to this unfortunate affair at the Palais Royal than the exchange of a few insults between hotheaded officers of rival factions. I'm sorry to say that Marshal Blucher cannot be persuaded to temper the conduct of the troops under his command."

A considering silence ensued, each gentleman privately reflecting on the vindictive reprisals the Prussians had exacted against the French in retaliation for Napoleon's victory at Jenna and the subsequent savage subjugation of Berlin nine years before. Unlike the British army of occupation, Prussian troops were billeted in private homes, and the unfortunate inhabitants were obliged to provide for not only their unwelcome guests, but also their horses. But this was not the worst offense by any means. Scarcely a day went by but formal complaints were lodged with Wellington of some atrocity or other openly perpetrated against the defenseless populace by the dregs of the Prussian army. As every man in the room knew, the situation was highly volatile.

"The sins of the victors are now visited upon them by the former vanquished," murmured someone, framing exactly the thought which held each man silent.

Mr. Somerset laced his plump fingers together and placed his joined hands on the flat of the desk. Finally he said, "Forgive me for burdening you with my ill temper. These concerns are for the diplomats to decide. There is one matter relating to the unfortunate affair at the Palais Royal, however, which has fallen to my province. I refer to the murder of the French girl Monique Dupres, whose body was discovered in the gardens outside the Café de Foy. For reasons which I am not at liberty to disclose, it is this girl's death more than any other which interests us at present."

He could not have surprised them more if he had accused one of their number of the murder itself. Oblivious of any offense he may have given, the attaché said very deliberately, "Gentlemen, this is a matter of some delicacy. Once you leave this room, I am relying on your discretion."

It was Ransome, remote and controlled, who interposed, "And that is why we have been summoned to this . . . conclave? You think, perhaps, that one of us knows something about that unfortunate girl's demise?"

"Only in a manner of speaking," instantly responded the attaché. "None of you is under suspicion for the murder. You are, after all, English gentlemen first and foremost. No, my enquiry is altogether of a different order."

"But sir," protested Captain Mercer, "surely this is a matter for the French authorities?"

His voice etched wih patience, Mr. Somerset reiterated, "Didn't I just say that we are not primarily interested in the girl's death, but only as it touches on another matter?"

"Which is?" asked Seymour.

Mr. Somerset felt constrained to retrieve a large linen handkerchief from his coat pocket. He immediately set about mopping his pinkening cheeks and bald pate. When he spoke next, it was evident that his supply of patience was running thin. "As I have already explained, I am not at liberty to disclose the nature of our enquiry. Gentlemen, please, disabuse yourselves of the notion that any of you is under suspicion. If it were otherwise, do you suppose for one minute that you would be interviewed en masse?"

No one saw fit to contradict this inescapable logic, and on a calmer note the attaché continued, "Bear with me, please, as I simply try to reconstruct the events of that night. At the outset, let me say immediately that the French authorities are satisfied that Monique Dupres's murderer was a Prussian officer, a certain Captain Zeitler, who met his own demise at roughly the same time."

He chanced a quick look at his companions. Satisfied with what he saw, he went on, "To begin at the beginning. At four o'clock of the day in question, Mademoiselle Dupres had an interview with an English lady. What transpired during that interview, no one knows. Lord Dalmar, it is known that you arrived at the Maison D'Or during this interview and presented Mademoiselle Dupres with a diamond bracelet. Moments later you were observed escorting the English lady from the premises."

Dalmar said nothing.

Taking the Earl's silence for affirmation, the attaché continued, "An hour later, Mademoiselle Dupres also left the premises in company of the aforementioned Captain Zeitler, a Prussian officer of unsteady temper who was an habitué of the Maison D'Or. A short time later they were observed dining at the Café de Foy." He looked up from the paper he had been perusing. "Majors Seymour and Bodley were observed in conversation with the lady."

"Of course," answered Bodley without heat. "Why wouldn't we exchange a few commonplaces with Mademoiselle Dupres? She was well known to everyone who was a friend of Jerry Blandford."

"Ah yes." The attaché shuffled some papers and finally withdrew what he was looking for. "Major the Honorable Jeremy Blandford of the Guards, who lost his life at Waterloo. She became his mistress when he was a member of the British delegation at the Congress of Vienna, and afterward followed him to Brussels when he rejoined his regiment. Mademoiselle Dupres was his hostess on numerous occasions where the highest ranking officers of the British army, not to mention ladies of, shall we say, dubious reputation, were known to congregate and mingle."

"We went there to gamble," explained Dalmar with a twinkle in his eye.

"Quite," responded the attaché amiably. "But to get back to the Palais Royal. Soon after Majors Bodley and Seymour were seen in conversation with Mademoiselle Dupres, several half-pay French officers walked into the Café de Foy. Then all hell broke loose. No one is quite certain what happened next. What *is* known is that about thirty minutes later, a woman's scream rent the air. Captain Mercer, you were on duty, and were observed in the gardens at that time in the vicinity of the Café de Foy, going to the aid of an unknown Englishman."

"Was I?" murmured the Captain evasively.

"Who was the Englishman?" persisted Somerset.

"I recollect it was I," interposed Dalmar, studiously toying

66

with his gold signet ring. "What of it?"

"Only this," answered the attaché. "The Englishman was seen to be protecting a young woman. Was she Mademoiselle Dupres?"

"You have my word that it was not."

"Then she was the English woman whom you escorted from the Maison D'Or."

It was not a question, but a statement of fact, which Dalmar might affirm or contradict at his pleasure. He chose, instead, to ignore it. If the other gentlemen present found much to speculate on this exchange, no expression or movement or word of theirs gave any indication of it.

Somerset's close scrutiny was met by an equally steady stare from the Earl.

"Thank you," murmured the attaché, and turned his attention to Captain Mercer. "Captain, just one small item. You saw Captain Zeitler fall?"

"I did."

"Please, in your own words, tell us how it happened."

"There's not much to tell. After Lord Dalmar left the gardens, I found myself in the thick of it outside the Café de Foy. Zeitler was making short work of some Englishman or other. I wanted to help the poor fellow, but my hands were full. There was a shot. When the smoke cleared, Zeitler was on his knees. It was only later that we discoverd that Zeitler had been shot through the heart."

"Why do you refer to the Englishman as 'poor fellow'?"

Seymour seemed to consider the question. Finally, he answered, "He didn't seem to be handling himself very well."

"Do you think he put that bullet in Zeitler?"

Somerset's bald question startled a laugh out of the Captain. "It never once entered my mind," he exclaimed.

"Why not?" persisted the attaché.

Mercer's uneasy glance quickly traversed the stoic faces of his companions. "Because he was an English gentleman," he answered. "Zeitler's assailant was obviously a coward. One doesn't draw a pistol on an adversary when one is engaged in swordplay."

"Then what do you think happened?"

"It's impossible to say. Zeitler wasn't exactly a popular fellow, not even with his own kind. The man was a bully. Anyone might have used that melee as a cover for paying off old scores. If you ask me, the Englishman was just lucky. In another minute Zeitler would have finished him off. You don't really think the Englishman did it, do you?"

It was the attaché's turn to be evasive. Ignoring Mercer's question, he addressed himself to Majors Seymour and Bodley. "Getting back to the Café de Foy . . . who else was present that night?"

The two majors exchanged glances.

"No one of any significance that I can think of," said Major Seymour cautiously. "Mostly Prussians, and the odd Englishman."

"The odd Englishman? What does that mean?"

"Sightseers, I suppose, or history devotees. You know, 'Here I stand on the sacred spot where the French Revolution is reputed to have had its genesis.' There are some who are positively daft about such foolishness. Well, look at Waterloo. Visitors have been swarming over the battlefield like flies on a carcass. It's offensive, if you want my opinion. Where were these dandies when we needed them? I'll tell you where they were . . ."

"Thank you, Major Seymour," interposed Somerset with quiet determination. "I don't think there's a man here who doesn't agree with you. May I draw your mind back to the night in question?" His eyes touched on each man in turn. "Did anyone else happen to see either Monique Dupres or the unidentified Englishman outside the Café de Foy?"

When it was evident that no one had anything further to add, Somerset rose to his feet. "I rely on your confidentiality, gentlemen," he said. "For all intents and purposes, this meeting never took place. Ransome, Dalmar, I should like a word with you in private." And in very short order, the attaché escorted Messrs. Mercer, Bodley, and Seymour to the door. When he returned to his place behind the desk his alert eyes fell on Ransome.

That gentleman returned the look with raised eyebrows and remarked mildly, "I swear I was asleep in Lord Dalmar's rooms throughout most of the ruckus. Unfortunately, I was alone and can offer no alibi."

Somerset smiled at this mild rebuke. He observed, "At the risk of repeating myself ad nauseam, Colonel, may I say again that I am not investigating the slaying of Mademoiselle Dupres? The French authorities are satisfied that Captain Zeitler was the perpetrator of that savage act."

"Then how may I help you?" asked Ransome.

"An explanation, Colonel. That is all I require from you."

"I'm listening."

"What is your interest in Mrs. Annabelle Jocelyn?"

Colonel Ransome straightened in his chair, as if becoming aware for the first time of its inadequate confines. He stretched his legs without haste and by degrees settled his large frame into a more comfortable position. Lord Dalmar looked to be suffering from acute boredom. Finally Ransome remarked, "I have no interest in the lady."

"And yet on the very morning after the riot in the Palais Royal, you were at the Hotel Breteuil asking for her direction."

"How very well informed you are," drawled Ransome.

"Very," agreed the attaché. "Why, Colonel? Why the interest in Mrs. Annabelle Jocelyn?"

"I had undertaken the office on behalf of a friend, nothing more."

Somerset's eyes traveled to the bored figure of the Earl, then returned to the man he was questioning. "And your friend was unable to undertake this office for himself?"

"Something like that."

"May I have his name?"

Into the silence, Dalmar's bored voice drawled, "I am that friend, as you very well know, Somerset."

"Ah," said the attaché, and smiled benevolently upon his lordship. Colonel Ransome, having served his usefulness, was thereupon dismissed with as many civilities as had been offered to his fellow officers.

The door was hardly shut upon him when Dalmar exclaimed

violently, "What the devil do you think you're up to, James? You have no jurisdiction over officers in His Majesty's service. I'm surprised they didn't tell you to go jump in the lake."

The attaché laughed softly. "You know me better than that, my boy. This directive comes from the Duke himself. Your friends are under orders to cooperate."

"And for myself?"

"Ah well. Now that you've sold out, you're a free agent. I rely on the ties of friendship to secure your cooperation."

"The devil you do!"

"My dear boy, you're surely not forgetting who it was who plucked you from a watery grave when you were ten or thereabouts, yes, and saved your skin on more occasions that I care to remember?"

"You fraud!" said Dalmar, laughing. "You never rescued me from scrapes, but you administered a beating. In retrospect, I don't know why I always looked forward to holidays at Gilcomston."

"If I did beat you, you deserved it. You should thank me. Your uncle would have used you more severely. How have you been, my boy?"

Grins were exchanged, and hands clasped in a firm handshake.

"Capital," said Dalmar. "And yourself?"

"Oh, getting by. Here, this calls for a celebration. It's years since we last broke a bottle together. In the summer of six, wasn't it, shortly after your return from India? After Spain, you never came home on furlough. Why?"

Dalmar leaned back in his chair and crossed one foot over the other. A glass of brandy was thrust into his hand. "What was there to come home to?" he murmured.

Somerset's keen eyes swept over the relaxed figure of his companion. Very gently he said, "You refine too much on old history. No one blamed you for what happened to your father. The coroner exonerated you. Besides, that happened all of—what?—seventeen years ago? How old were you then? A lad of eighteen?"

"A man of seventeen," corrected Dalmar.

"It was an accident."

"Was it? Rumor said otherwise."

"Fustian! That fabrication that the duel with your father was over some woman or other? Nobody who knew you gave any credence to that particular piece of spite."

"Ah well, my father and I were never friends. It's not to be wondered that the gossip mongers made capital of that fact. When all is said and done, it was my hand that struck him down."

"Is that what your subsequent career was all about? To atone for your father's death?"

"Scarcely!"

The patent bitterness behind that one word held both men silent for a full minute.

Abruptly changing the subject, the older man asked, "How was Spain?"

"Hot as hell. But, as you see, I'm a survivor."

"You never married? I seem to remember, shortly after your mother's death, there was a betrothal . . ."

"Of very short duration. The lady's relations got wind of the old scandal. It's not every family that would welcome into its ranks a man who committed patricide."

"I suspect, my boy, you'll find that things are very different, now that you've come into your uncle's title and fortune," said Somerset cheerfully.

They sipped their brandies in companionable silence. After an interval, Somerset offered, "If it's any consolation, your uncle was inordinately proud of your military exploits in Spain. As of course was your mother, poor lady."

"Yes. I owe the old boy a debt of gratitude that can never be repaid. But as for you—you seem to have done well for yourself."

"Thank you. I've no complaints. As you know, I became secretary to Sir Charles on your uncle's death. When Sir Charles became ambassador to France, I came with him."

"You were always a modest fellow, James. A secretary is scarcely to be compared to an attaché."

"Who says it's not? Oh, 'attaché' has a ring to it, I'll give you that. But no secretary worth his salt sees himself in the role of a mere clerk. Tact and diplomacy are the stock-in-trade of both professions. Tell me, what are your plans, now that you've resigned your commission?"

Dalmar gave the older man an eloquent look. "My dear James, as we both know perfectly well, you are about to sketch my future for me. Though investigating a murder is scarcely in my line. If it's cloak-and-dagger stuff you are after, you would have done better to approach Ransome."

"Oh, you mean the mysterious Englishman who was at the scene of the crime? Forget it. It's merely a whim of my own. A loose end. I don't suppose we shall ever know who he was. Well, it's very evident, the fellow doesn't wish his identity to be discovered."

With the merest trace of exasperation, Dalmar exclaimed, "What, James? Is the Englishman a red herring you introduced to throw us off the scent?"

Somerset laughed. "No. You misjudge me. It's just that . . . well . . . I suppose I have a suspicious mind. His presence there that night may mean something, or it may mean nothing at all."

"Then why don't you stop beating about the bush and get to the point?"

Without further prevarication, Somerset selected a paper from his desk and proffered it to the Earl. "From Monique Dupres to one Bailey's Press in London. This appears to be a copy of a letter she sent. As you can see, the lady was trying to sell her memoirs. Note, item, Dukes: Argyle, Beaufort, Richmond, Wellington; Marquesses: Anglesey, Worcester; Earls: Dalmar, Jersey, Yarmouth; Viscounts: Castlereagh and so on down the line, and these are only the ones she used as bait."

Having quickly scanned the letter, Dalmar whistled. "Good God! These diaries must rival Burke's peerage."

"You've got it. But lacking something of the latter work's innocence."

"Where are the diaries now?"

"That, my dear boy, is a moot question."

Dalmar returned the letter to the other's hand. "Bailey's Press," he mused. "I can't say I'm familiar with the name."

"That's not surprising. At one time, as I understand, it was quite respectable. In the last number of years, it's degenerated into a spurious outfit which publishes a desultory bill of fare—you know, the occasional book of poetry, or philosophy to leaven an unrelenting diet of frivolity, or worse, obscenity. Well you must have read *The Confessions of a Footman*? It was all the rage when it first came out."

"Did Bailey's publish that? I thought it was hilarious."

"Well, of course it was," answered Somerset, in no wise discomposed by his lordship's humorous bent. "Just the same, you're not like to laugh when you find your own prestigious title blazoned for all the world to read between the purple bindings of a Bailey's special edition."

A crooked smile played upon Dalmar's lips. "Purple bindings? Sounds like a woman's caprice, if I know anything of females."

"Funny you should say that. Among Miss Dupres's possessions there was also a bank draft drawn on the account of an Englishwoman, Mrs. Annabelle Jocelyn."

"Ah," said the Earl noncommittally, and accepted the scrap of paper which Somerset tendered. The signature at the bottom seemed to jump out at him.

Somerset fixed the younger man with a look of keen interest. He smiled. "So," he said, "I've found the fly to bait my line."

Catching that look, compounded of devilry and rank smugness, Dalmar sheepishly admitted, "All right. I'm interested. Now shall we get down to brass tacks? I have a few questions of my own I wish to pursue. Evidently you think Mrs. Joceyn has the diaries. And you suspect that she will use them as a tool for blackmail or sell them to the highest bidder?"

Somerset inclined his head gravely and the Earl continued, "What I want to know is this. Do you think that there is some connection between Monique Dupres's death and the diaries?"

"It had occurred to me. Oh, I know that the French are satisfied that Zeitler slit her throat in a fit of jealousy. But he can't be questioned, can he? And *so* many coincidences and so close upon one another, in my opinion, are highly suspect. I wouldn't mind getting a look at those diaries, I can tell you. It's just possible that among all the titillating morsels there may be a real scandal concealed, something unexpected."

"A motive for murder?"

"It had occurred to me."

"If what you say is true, then Mrs. Jocelyn may be in some danger."

With a very steady look, Somerset replied, "Not if she's the murderess."

Equally grave, Dalmar answered, "She's not."

"Can you give her an alibi? It would gratify me if you could. We old men, you know, like to maintain a few illusions. And she is of the softer sex, and English to boot."

Dalmar recognized that Somerset's question, so casually thrown out, was not an idle one. There was a slight tensing of his jaw before he answered, "The lady spent the night with me."

"Does she have the diaries?"

Something flickered briefly in the steel of Dalmar's eyes. After a moment he said, "It would not surprise me if she had." His tone became crisper. "Is that what this is all about, James? You want me to destroy the diaries?"

"Not unless it's unavoidable. I should like to take a peek at them, remember? But at all costs, those memoirs must not be published."

"How so? If they are published, you'll get your peek at them. And as for the scandal they are likely to cause in Court circles, that is a mere commonplace nowadays, surely?"

Setting his empty glass aside, Somerset observed, "Frankly, I don't give a fig for Court circles. But these diaries could shake the government to its very foundations. It would be tragic to see so many fine men brought down."

Before Dalmar took his leave, Somerset cautioned him. "Mind your step, David. If there is a murderer loose, both you and Mrs. Jocelyn stand in some danger. Don't ever forget it. No need to alarm the lady, though. All things considered, I think it best to say nothing of Monique Dupres's unhappy fate. Yes, I think that is our best approach."

"Why?" asked Dalmar.

"Any number of reasons. You'll just have to trust my judgment, my boy." Before the Earl could protest, Somerset went on hastily, "If you start by telling her that there is a murderer on the loose, who knows what she might do? I am not a fool, David. Don't you think I put two and two together? She ran away from you once, didn't she? My advice to you is to gain the lady's confidence. And you won't do that by frightening her from the outset."

Hours later, at his rooms in the Palais Royal, as he absently watched his man pack his trunks and bags for the journey to England, Dalmar was still reflecting on the impulse which had provoked him to accept Somerset's office.

The infamy that might accrue to his own already tarnished name if the diaries were published, he discounted as a trifling irritation. Of all the gentlemen of distinction who were like to be embarrassed by the broadcast of their private lives, he deemed that he, a single man, had least to forfeit. There was no wife or family waiting for him in England; no sire or dame to whom such a scandal would occasion pain; no position of eminence in government circles to jeopardize. It had been on the tip of his tongue to say, "Publish and be damned." That Annabelle Jocelyn was in some sort involved in the ugly business, however, had stayed the refusal which sprang to his lips. He remembered the hatbox, and Annabelle's almost desperate attachment to it that evening, and the suspicion that she had possession of the diaries became a solid conviction. But who was she? And where was she? These questions continued to tease his mind.

She had slipped through his fingers while he had been immobilized, confined to his sickbed. And for those first few hours after he had awakened, he had chafed at his impotence, in a fever of impatience to discover what had become of the woman who had shared his bed and decamped in the wee hours of the morning without a word of explanation. Nor would he ever forget the fears he had entertained for her safety

75

till Ransome undertook to find out what had become of her.

When he learned that Mrs. Jocelyn had left the Hotel Breteuil that very morning in the hired calèche of an English gentleman, and that her servants and baggage had followed at a more leisurely pace, he'd felt as if the wind had been knocked out of him. Outwardly, when Ransome had given him the intelligence, he'd preserved a mask of impassivity, philosophically shrugging off the whole affair as of no moment.

Whether or not he'd fooled his friend he had no way of knowing. He thought not. But he could not hide from himself the resentment which gnawed at him.

He'd claimed her in the fullest sense of the word . . . that much he remembered. Evidently, like so many of her kind, the lady had regarded the act of love as a commonplace. That he himself habitually took his pleasures with no more thought than to satisfy an appetite, he discounted as of little significance. It was the way of men. But that a woman should use him in like manner when for the first time he'd felt himself respond at some deeper level was a bitter pill to swallow.

He'd resolved to put the jade from his mind. To his disgust, he'd found that Annabelle Jocelyn's image was not to be easily shaken. She haunted him at odd moments. He'd observe some lady with an elegant bonnet, and without conscious thought he'd find himself comparing her to Annabelle and that air of hers, a compound of bravado and sauciness, as she'd sported her ridiculous *chapeau* with its broken plumage when he'd escorted her through the galleries. Nor could he descend the stairs to his rooms or cross the gardens of the Palais Royal without reliving every minute of that escapade which had almost cost him his life. Like any callow youth, he had exulted in the danger, savoring the opportunity of demonstrating to the woman of his choice that the offer of his protection was no empty boast. Like a knight entering the lists for his lady, he'd wanted to prove his mettle. Later, though this part was hazier, he had claimed his reward. And though she had accepted him with such sweet surrender, in the morning, while he still slept, she had crept from his bed and had gone straight to the arms of "The Milksop." The wound to his dignity outweighed every other feeling of revulsion.

He wanted to punish her. He wanted to protect her. But more than anything, he wanted to stake his claim to her. He knew, then, that with or without the ambassador's commission, there had never been any question that he would run Mrs. Annabelle Jocelyn to earth. On that cheering thought, he doused the candle and went to bed.

Chapter Five

For a full fortnight, with unwavering perseverance, and until she was word perfect, Annabelle rehearsed in her mind exactly how she would handle the situation if she should have the unlikely misfortune to meet up again with Dalmar. She would be everything that was civil, Annabelle decided, but remote, perhaps even faintly regal, and should he be ungentlemanly enough to so much as hint at what had transpired between them in his rooms in the Palais Royal, she would widen her eyes just a fraction and plead ignorance. And if the gentleman should dare to go further and cast her conduct in her teeth, she would look him in the eye and call him a liar.

Dalmar's eyes held hers across the throng of people in the drawing room of her house in Greek Street, and Annabelle felt her knees turn to water. Since her return from Paris, she had refused every invitation, cutting herself off like some recluse, and all to avoid the calamity which had overtaken her like a bolt from the blue. He had caught up with her in her own drawing room, during one of her own parties. She could not quite take it in and stood rooted to the spot, her mind spinning in every direction.

Holding her in the steel of his gaze, Dalmar took one step into the room. There flashed before Annabelle's eyes a scene from a book she had recently published—the picture of a man-eating tiger stalking the poor little lamb which had been used as bait to lure the ferocious feline into the open. As far as she could remember, no one ever gave a fig for the fate of the lamb.

Dalmar took another step in her direction, and Annabelle let out a strangled yelp, one hand fluttering wildly at her throat as if to protect her jugular.

"Annabelle," said a feminine voice in her ear, "I think your protégé is on the verge of creating a scandal, and enjoying every minute of it, by the looks of him. Those unprintable words which he promised to eliminate from his vocabulary? They're tripping off his tongue as if someone had just opened the sluice gate to his mouth! Lady Holland looks to be in dire need of smelling salts, and she's no prude. Annabelle, are you listening? You've got to do something."

Annabelle's shocked eyes turned upon her friend and companion Beatrice Pendleton, a moderately handsome woman of fair complexion whose habitually serene expression had given way to a graver mode. "Bertie," said Annabelle, her voice unnaturally husky, "hold the fort! I'm needed in the kitchen," and she picked up her skirts and bolted.

Annabelle heard her friend's dismayed plea raised in protest at her back, but she did not so much as slow her stride to look over her shoulder. She came to a door and whisked herself behind it. By degrees she became aware that she'd shut herself in the broom closet at the top of the short flight of stairs which led to the kitchens. Though her breathing finally slowed to normal, her mind continued to keep pace with the thousand questions which rattled around in her head.

How had he found her? What was he doing here? How could she evade him? What had he learned of her? Should she ask him to leave? And if he refused, how could she make him? Oh, how had he found her, and what did he want?

It took every ounce of willpower to subdue her emotions and put her thoughts into some kind of order. It was just possible, she chided herself, that he'd come on a whim. After all, there were no gilt-edged engraved invitations to her literary soirées. Her parties, by Mayfair standards, were very informal affairs; her guests, with few exceptions, of a sort that were rarely met in ton circles. Friends of a literary bent vouched for their friends. It was understood that only those who held unorthodox views, were given to some eccentricity, or could claim an exotic background were assured a welcome. Perhaps Dalmar, at a loose end, had taken up a friend's suggestion and had come merely to satisfy his curiosity.

She examined her conjecture from all angles and almost immediately discarded it. He was here for a purpose which boded no good for Annabelle Jocelyn. She could feel it in her bones.

By the time she returned to her guests, she thought she had herself well in hand. Bracing herself for Dalmar's sure and certain onslaught, she paused just inside the arched entrance to the ground-floor drawing room. Her eyes quickly scanned the noisy, milling throng. She found him almost immediately. His back was to her, but she would have recognized him anywhere. She almost groaned aloud when she saw the man with whom he was deep in conversation. It was the Viscount Temple, the gentleman whom Dalmar derisively referred to as "The Milksop," and whom he had mistaken for her lover.

Annabelle expelled a shaky breath. From all appearances, the thought of a duel was the farthest thing from their minds. Dalmar was conversing as if he and the Viscount were on the best of terms, and his companion's lips formed a smile.

She wondered, then, if Lord Temple had taken a few drops of laudanum before the party. He seemed more relaxed than he'd been in an age. The rigid lines of pain and tension which frequently disfigured his finely chiseled features had softened, revealing a face that was more beautiful than handsome. Not for the first time the word *pretty* flashed into Annabelle's mind, and she suppressed it, feeling vaguely disloyal. If Temple lacked something of his companion's uncompromising masculinity, she counted it a virtue.

Temple looked up at that moment, and catching sight of her, beckoned with his index finger. Annabelle composed her features into a mask of well-bred civility and forced her legs to carry her to the small alcove where the gentlemen had secluded themselves. She steeled herself for the coming introduction.

"Annabelle," drawled Temple with that faintly proprietary air which she heartily disliked, "I'd like you to meet an old school friend whom I haven't seen in an age. I thought for a moment I'd walked into the wrong house when I saw him in your drawing room." His next words were patently derisory. "He's one of our brave soldiers who's given the best years of his life to king and country. A Tory and proud of it!"

Annabelle squirmed at the insult in Temple's words, and she flashed a look of apology at his companion. Though it was true that she held unshakable convictions about the inefficacy of war in general, and in particular on Tory policies in the last number of years, she made it a rule never to attack the man, but only his dogma. Temple's inflammatory remarks embarrassed her. If anyone else had said them, a quick rebuke would have sprung to her lips. But she understood the bitterness which had provoked her friend to rudeness. Those who fell in battle became instant heroes. The war-wounded became objects of pity. It was only natural that men such as Dalmar should incite their less fortunate comrades to envy.

The look she turned on Dalmar was eloquently expressive of all that she was feeling. Her smile was sincere. It wavered a little as she caught the surge of something not quite nice that came and went in the depths of Dalmar's eyes.

"Lord Dalmar," began Temple, "may I present . . ."

"Annabelle!" exclaimed Dalmar, capturing her small hand and holding it firmly. "I came just as soon as I could get away. Forgive me for the delay."

"You know each other?" asked Temple, his narrowing eyes flicking from Dalmar's roguishly taunting smile to Annabelle's frozen expression.

"Know each other?" echoed Annabelle, casting frantically around in her mind for a suitable answer. There was nothing to guide her, for in her exhaustive rehearsals of how she would manage the man who was now revealed not as plain Mr. Dalmar but as a tittled gentleman, she had never imagined that he would publicly claim an acquaintance with her.

"Know each other?" repeated Dalmar, and his accents deliberately colored the innocent words with a meaning that was far from innocent. "My dear Temple, when a gentleman takes up arms to defend a lady, I think you may safely say that they are more than a little acquainted. Yes, we know each other."

She gave what she hoped was a convincing laugh, and laying a restraining hand on the stiff-backed figure of Lord Temple, essayed, "I owe Lord Dalmar a debt of gratitude, Gerry. It was he who very kindly came to my assistance when I was attacked the night before we left Paris. You may remember I mentioned something of the sort to you." She had given Temple only the sketchiest account of what had happened, and only because her maid had inadvertently let slip that she had been missing all night. As far as Temple knew, it was the British army that had intervened to save Annabelle's skin.

Into the charged silence, Temple said, "Permit me to thank you for any trifling service you may have undertaken on Annabelle's behalf. You may be sure, Dalmar, that if the opportunity presents itself, the debt shall be repaid in kind."

Rather wildly, Annabelle interjected, "I don't believe either of you has had a chance to meet the guest of honor this evening. He's rather a rough diamond, but terribly clever. He's a sort of poet-cum-philosopher. His political commentary is biting, but amusing if one has a taste for irony. We'd better hurry if we want to catch him. He drinks like a fish and is almost always castaway before a party is half over."

For a moment it looked as if her ploy had succeeded. Lord Temple obligingly offered his arm, and Annabelle wasted no time in placing her fingers upon it.

They had taken only one step when Dalmar threw out, "Forget about the debt, Temple. Annabelle has already paid it in full."

Annabelle's hand tightened along Temple's arm, urging him forward. Beneath her fingers, he seemed to turn to stone. She could not move him. She felt a sense of dread wash through her as he gently turned her to face Lord Dalmar.

Temple's face was carefully blank as he said, "I beg your pardon. I don't think I understand."

"Ask Annabelle," said Dalmar, his gray eyes turning silver bright as they surveyed the Viscount.

With her face almost cracking under the strain of appearing

totally in command of herself, she looked from one to the other and said, "Lord Dalmar suffered some injury, and I helped nurse him. It was the least I could do under the circumstances." Her eyes dared Dalmar to reveal more.

He seemed to hesitate, but only a little. His eyes baiting, he said, "Annabelle's a wonderful . . . 'nurse.'"

Desperation unglued Annabelle's tongue from the roof of her mouth. "I'm delighted to see that you are fully recovered," she quickly interposed.

"Oh, I shall never fully recover from what transpired in Paris," said Dalmar, flashing Annabelle a complacent grin.

Lord Temple's eyes, hard with suspicion, darted from one to the other. Annabelle smiled weakly, and Dalmar affected an interest in the intricate plaster ceiling.

Suddenly the Viscount smiled. Relief swept through Annabelle as she heard him offer to fetch her a glass of champagne. She watched his progress until he was out of earshot, then she turned on Dalmar, her bosom heaving.

There was a slight break in her voice when she hissed at him, "How *dare* you embarrass me like that?"

With remarkable unconcern, Dalmar replied, "Temple deserves to know where he stands. Sometimes one has to be cruel to be kind."

"Kind?" repeated Annabelle, her voice wobbling alarmingly. "Was that kind to me? You might just as well have taken out an advertisement in the *Times* and blazoned our *affaire* for the whole world to read about." Her cheeks were vivid with color.

He jerked her round so that his broad shoulders shielded her from curious eyes. "Hush," he soothed. "You're exaggerating. Get hold of yourself, Annabelle. I told you in Paris that I would not tolerate that milksop hanging on your skirts. If you had listened to me then, it would not have been necessary to reveal as much as I did."

"You take too much for granted, my lord," she said scathingly. "I'll have you know, Lord Temple has asked me to marry him."

Eyes which a moment before had been as soft as velvet

hardened into flint. "Has he indeed? And what does your husband have to say about that, may I ask?"

"Husband? What husband?" asked Annabelle shrilly.

"Your *late* husband," said Dalmar.

"Oh," said Annabelle, and carefully lowered her lashes. "You've discovered that I'm a widow."

There was a silence, and Annabelle peered up at Dalmar. "I didn't really lie to you," she offered. "You jumped to conclusions. It seemed safer at the time to let your misconception stand."

"Safer?" he asked incredulously. "You let me think you were a woman of easy virtue. If I'd known you were a respectable widow . . ."

"Yes?" she encouraged, when he failed to complete the thought. "What then?"

He shrugged philosophically. "In the circumstances in which we found ourselves, it probably would not have made a jot of difference. Who can say?" His tone became brisker. "To get back to Temple . . . are you going to marry him?"

"No," she answered at once. "But why I should tell you so is more than I can understand."

"Oh, I know why," answered Dalmar. "Hold still," he said, and carefully removed a thread of something from the nape of her neck. "Cobwebs," he informed her. "Did you hide yourself in the cellars when you first saw me come in?"

Ignoring his levity, she demanded, "Why did I tell you that I've refused Lord Temple's offer of marriage?"

"Mmm? Oh, because you like him, of course, and you wouldn't want to see any harm come to him." Grinning, he elaborated, "I've never heard of anyone marrying a corpse."

She could not tell from his smile whether or not he was trying to bluff her, and she stared unblinkingly into his face.

Reading her correctly, Dalmar remarked, "You needn't worry. Couldn't you tell? 'The Milksop' will never fight for you, whatever the provocation."

"And so I would hope," answered Annabelle with feeling. "Haven't you heard? There's a law against ducling. And furthermore, Lord Temple is too much the gentleman to bring

85

scandal to my name by fighting a duel over me." The unpalatable thought that Lord Temple had decamped with unseemly celerity when provoked by Dalmar she ruthlessly quashed.

"Here comes Temple now with your champagne," said Dalmar. "We'll talk of this later. Go greet your guests, Annabelle. You're neglecting your duties."

He wandered away after that, deeming it expedient to keep his distance until the lady's temper had time to abate. Nevertheless, he kept a proprietary eye on her. Not by a flicker of an eyelash did Annabelle betray that she knew he was watching her. He might have been a piece of furniture, for all the notice she paid him. His own eyes followed her like the needle on a compass.

There wasn't any doubt in his mind that of all the ladies present, it was Annabelle who stood out of the crowd. Her gown was the color of a clear vintage claret. Very becoming, he thought, with its low-cut, square neckline, puffed sleeves, and rows of horizontal tucks down the bodice and back. It revealed just enough of her shapely, high-breasted figure to set a man's imagination on a riotous flight of fancy. He noted the flare of her lush hips and the length of her leg, and his brows slashed together. He'd heard of the current mode where certain ladies of fashion, the dashers, dampened their petticoats to make their skirts cling. Annabelle had taken the fashion one step further. He'd wager his last farthing that beneath the sheer silk of her gown, she wasn't wearing a stitch. The thought acted on him in a predictable fashion. He wanted to make love to her. He wanted to beat her.

He subdued the impulse to rush to her side and drag her away from all the men who were ogling her and forced his attention to his surroundings. Her house on Greek Street intrigued him almost as much as the lady herself. It was very small, all the public rooms being on the ground floor, but beautifully proportioned. Its most distinguished feature was the elaborate rococo plasterwork on the ceilings and around each lintel and archway, as well as the framed medallions picked out in white against the pale green walls. The carpets were also green and matched the walls and curtains. The few pieces of upholstery he had observed in the various rooms in use were either gold or white. Though the effect was Spartan, everything was chosen, as far as he could tell, with a meticulous eye to detail. Great vases of white calla lilies stood on the white marble mantels and on tables around the rooms. But it was Annabelle's choice of wall hangings which he found oddly revealing. On almost every wall was to be found the picture of a medieval knight in armor. The background was invariably white, but the knight, to Dalmar's untutored eye, was picked out either in gold leaf or in black ink. He chanced to mention it to someone and was told that the pictures were rubbings, a hobby in which Annabelle had indulged for a time. The house had Annabelle written all over it—spare, elegant, and with considerable dash. Apart from the gold and black knights which adorned her walls, her taste held no surprises for him. It was perfect, he thought. Too perfect. Just like Annabelle.

He spent the next half hour deliberately desecrating her perfect setting. It was easily managed—a few drops of wine spilled on her immaculate carpet; a bloom plucked from its vase and left hanging; a cushion tossed under a table; the elaborate folds of her draped curtains bunched into knots. He wasn't being unkind, he told himself. He just wanted to leave his mark on her in any way he could.

His thoughts wandered to his own cluttered rooms in St. James Street and he wondered if it was time to open up the house in Cavendish Square. Since his uncle's demise, the furniture had been kept under holland covers and the house left empty, with only a caretaker in residence. Should he give Annabelle a free hand to arrange things to suit herself, he was almost sure that she would begin by emptying the place. Perhaps that's what the old mausoleum needed, a new chapter in its history written by Annabelle. Truth to tell, he was hoping that it was a project to which he could persuade her.

He turned his attention upon her guests, relying on Murray, the man who had brought him, to make the introductions, since it was obvious that Annabelle had no intention of making things easy for him. They were a flamboyant lot and not the sort he would normally have given the time of day to—poets, writers and their patrons, and a sprinkling of academics, all of whom affected opinions which in a former era would have soon lost them their heads on the block. He absorbed everything but said little, and there was much that he might have said in rebuttal to the scathing criticism he heard on every side on Wellington's conduct of the war. It annoyed him to think that Annabelle shared the naïve opinions of such people.

His eyes came to rest on one of the footmen who was dispensing glasses of champagne from a silver salver, and his thoughts took a new direction. He had taken Somerset's warning seriously. If there was any danger to Annabelle, however remote, he wasn't taking chances. When he'd arrived in London the week before, he had been in a fever of impatience to find her and provide protection for her safety. He'd thought then that the task of finding her would be monumental. She could be anywhere in England, for all he knew. In point of fact, he'd discovered her direction the very day he'd arrived.

He'd dropped in on John Murray, the man who had brought him to Annabelle's party, and who had the distinction of being Lord Byron's publisher. He'd asked a few questions about Bailey's Press and in a matter of minutes was listening to a glowing encomium on the woman who had taken over the helm of the almost bankrupt company some years before.

"That's strong praise for a rival," he'd said. "Aren't you afraid of the competition?"

"Not a bit of it. We're not really competitors, you see. Longmans and I are the respectable academics of the business, so to speak. Minerva Press deals almost exclusively with romantic trivia."

"And Bailey's Press?"

"Annabelle has an eye for the exotic and unusual—anything that's like to stir up controversy."

"So I've heard."

"She's not really a lover of books so much as simply a first-class entrepreneur. It just so happens that Old Man Bailey left her a half interest in a book business. If it had been in coal mines or steel, she would have made her mark there. Well, she has a thing about trends, you see, and is always one step ahead of the competition."

"I don't think I follow you."

"She's got a bee in her bonnet that Raikes's Sunday Schools for the children of the poor have opened up a new market of readers. She's rather eloquent on the subject."

"And what of it?"

"They can't pay the going price of our books. They're poor. And their tastes are something of an unknown. Well, it stands to reason . . . they may have learned to read, but one can hardly call them educated. Annabelle has her eye on this market."

"Surely *The Confessions of a Footman* has limited appeal?"

"*The Confessions of an English Footman in India*," corrected Murray. "It outsold every book on the market, with the exception of the Bible. Stands to reason, it would. Until then, we at home had always imagined our poor chaps in India as leading a rather lonely existence. You know—sitting around drinking tea with their legs crossed. What an eye-opener that book was, I can tell you! But you can vouch for its veracity. You were there."

Dalmar looked to be slightly offended. "We did more than just hop into bed with the local women."

"So it was true! I thought as much. Don't look so savage. Not only did that book make a packet for Annabelle, but as I understand, it almost trebled the number of young men who rushed to enlist. Annabelle wasn't a bit pleased when I teased her about it. Can you imagine, she'd thought to give the public a disgust of the British aristocracy? She's rather an innocent, underneath that worldly exterior."

"You know, John, you've piqued my interest in the lady. Where am I like to meet her?"

Murray gave him a sideways glance. "She moves in your own circles, David. Somehow, I was under the impression that you knew of her. Don't get your hopes up. She has an antipathy to everything you stand for. Annabelle is very selective."

"What is that supposed to mean?"

"It means, old boy, that Tories and their supporters are given short shrift by Mrs. Annabelle Jocelyn." He chuckled. "There's as much chance of finding that breed in her elegantly appointed drawing room as there is a cockroach, yes, and they're as like to meet with as summary a fate. Take my word for it, you'll never get near her, not unless you're willing to sink to a little subterfuge."

It had been impossible to suppress the self-satisfied smile which had creased his face. He'd done a damn sight more than get near her! To divert the awkward questions which he sensed were coming, he had immediately asked, "What subterfuge?"

"She's giving a party for her latest protégé, a poet who sees himself as a cross between Robbie Burns and Lord Byron. Personally, I can't stand the fellow—too full of his own conceit by half. You know the type—he thinks he's an expert on everything. It's on Saturday. Come as my guest, why don't you? But don't come as a Tory."

"Thank you. I'll take you up on that. But tell me, what of the husband? Where does he stand in all of this? He sounds like a very complacent gentleman."

"Oh very," agreed Murray with a gleam in his eye. "But of course, he's been dead these number of years. A veritable war hero, as I understand. He fell at Badajoz. You were there, weren't you? Annabelle never speaks of him. There's a child— a son. I forget his name."

"A son," mused Dalmar. "A boy of five summers or so? His name is Richard?"

"I believe so," answered Murray. "From what I hear tell, Annabelle would do anything for that boy. By all accounts, it's Master Jocelyn who's dashed the hopes of many a suitor aspiring to the mother's hand. They've been known to go to extremes to try to win the boy over, but it seems the harder they try, the more they earn the boy's dislike."

Dalmar had gathered more background on the lady after one of his men had inveigled a position as a footman on her small staff, and another had joined Bailey's as a printer. For one thing, he'd learned that there was no hurry to stop publication on Monique Dupres's memoirs. The book's publication was not for several months. Also, something he had not considered, the girl's diaries were in French, and Annabelle was spending most of her time in laborious translation. Furthermore, his men had uncovered nothing which might lead him to believe that Annabelle stood in any danger. Somerset's suspicions were beginning to look as if they were groundless. All of which played right into Dalmar's hands. In his scale of priorities, the relationship between Annabelle and himself was prime. The last thing he needed, until that was settled, was the complication of the diaries. Once he had bound her to him irrevocably was time enough in which to persuade her to give up her prize. And he wasn't fool enough to expect it to happen without a show of resistance.

From one of the rooms on his left there came the sound of raised voices. Among them he detected Annabelle's, rather high pitched, and showing some signs of strain. He debated whether or not to go and investigate. Since the little contretemps with "The Milksop," he had been at some pains to keep his distance, reasoning that he had made his point and that his design would be best served by giving Annabelle time to reconcile herself to her fate. She had taken advantage, of course. That she would do so had been almost a forgone conclusion. As if testing the limits of his patience, she had flirted indiscriminately with every man present. He had observed it all with an indulgent eye. His time was coming, and they both knew it.

It was the sound of shattering glass which decided him. He shouldered his way through a press of men who looked to be three sheets to the wind—mentally noting that Annabelle dispensed her champagne far too freely—and came to a halt just inside the door.

Murray was there, and said in an amused undertone, "The guest of honor, Annabelle's poet. He's half-seas-over. This should be interesting."

A young fop of sanguine complexion, very much in the mode of Lord Byron, with a mop of dark curly locks artfully

91

disarrayed, stood swaying on his feet, nose-to-nose with Annabelle. Stretched out on a gold satin settee was the black-uniformed figure of a maid evidently just coming out of a swoon. Dalmar had been introduced earlier to the lady bending over her, vigorously slapping her wrists, a Mrs. Pendleton, as he remembered, and Annabelle's companion. On the floor was a silver tray and the shattered remains of several crystal glasses which it appeared the maid had let slip from her fingers.

In a voice that would have formed ice on the sun, Annabelle said, "My dear Mr. Cameron, of course I subscribe to the principle of freedom of speech. Can anyone here doubt it? Moreover, I regard myself as a woman of the world. It would take more than a naughty word or two to bring a blush to my cheeks. But as for my maids and servants, that is a different matter. Their sensibilities are more fragile. Kindly refrain from using such coarse expressions in their hearing."

The maid, Nancy, was by this time energetically blowing her nose into a large linen handkerchief. Her eyes full of reproach, she looked up at Annabelle and said, "No gentleman has ever said that word to me before. What the vicar would say if he knew I had been exposed to such an insult, and in your own home, does not bear thinking."

The girl's words seemed to arrest the poet's attention. He peered down at her. "If you truly were an innocent," he said, "the word would have meant nothing to you. Come now, my girl—admit it. You're not so shocked as you let on."

"What word?" asked Dalmar beneath his breath, addressing Murray.

"A four-letter Saxon word," was the amused rejoinder.

Dalmar's brows shot up. "Things must have changed dramatically since I was last in a lady's drawing room."

"No . . . they're the same as ever they were. But anything can happen at Annabelle's parties. The blight of boredom would not dare show its face here. Uh-oh! I think our poet has the look of a bull in a china shop. Things are just beginning to warm up. I wonder what tack Annabelle will take now? You wouldn't care to make a small wager, would you?"

"A wager?"

"I'm putting my money on Annabelle." Something in his companion's expression constrained Murray to hastily add, "Forget I said that. It was a joke, nothing more."

Dalmar balanced one broad shoulder against the door jamb. One word, one look from Annabelle, and he would soon settle the obnoxious jackanapes.

"It's a perfectly good word," protested the poet unsteadily, his glaring and slightly bleary eyes challenging the silent bystanders. A beatific smile slowly lit up his face. With growing relish, like a precocious infant testing the temper of his straitlaced elders, he proceeded to repeat the shocking word, over and over, till it rose in a crescendo to tremble on the air. That he was enjoying every minute of his dubious glory was never in doubt.

The next move was up to Annabelle. She seemed preoccupied, gazing steadfastly at the toes of her red patent shoes, which peeked from beneath the hem of her gown. When she looked up, Dalmar noted that her expression had softened. His own hardened. She batted her long, sooty lashes and said in a soft, suggestive undertone, "Why don't we discuss this at our leisure in some quiet nook?" She placed one hand on the sleeve of Cameron's dark superfine and smiled tremulously up at him. "I'll send for a bottle, and we can be private."

A sly, drunken leer slowly spread over Cameron's wine-coarsened features. He leaned into Annabelle. "That's not the only naughty word I know by a long shot," he told her. His speech was slurred, but perfectly audible to the avidly interested audience, which had fallen back a pace, the better to observe the spectacle. "Whatever your pleasure, my dear Mrs. Jocelyn, you have chosen the right man to be your tutor."

A gasp went up, and all eyes turned on Annabelle. Her smile scarcely wavered. As everyone in the room well knew, with the exception of Dalmar, there was scarcely a man alive who couldn't be cowed or turned up sweet by Annabelle Jocelyn when she put her mind to it. She opened her mouth to speak, but at that moment an incipient growl deep in Dalmar's chest erupted into a full-throated roar. His shoulder came away from the doorjamb, and in one long stride he was at Cameron's back. He made short work of the unsuspecting malefactor. Grabbing him by the scruff of the neck and the seat of his black pantaloons, he forced him from the room. A footman, smiling broadly, hastened ahead of the Earl to open the front door.

Cameron, bawling like a baby, was unceremoniously booted down the front steps. His hat and cane landed on the pavement beside him.

The befuddled poet, still on his knees, looked mournfully up at the Earl and said with as much dignity as he could muster, "Might I trouble you for my umbrella? I wouldn't ask, but it's raining, you see, and the damp will wash out my curls."

The spate of colorful expletives which fell from Dalmar's lips quite eclipsed anything the poet had ever heard in his life. There was a moment of stunned silence, then admiration leaped to the young man's eyes.

"I say," he said, when Dalmar paused for breath, "you have quite a way of stringing words together. It's an art, you know. You should write that down—for posterity."

Each obscenity that Dalmar uttered carried to all the corners of Annabelle's elegant salons. She heard the mighty crash of the front door as it was forcefully slammed. An uneasy pall descended on the party. Annabelle found that she was literally shaking in her shoes. The tall, broad-shouldered figure of the Earl appeared in the doorway. As if on cue, her guests began to take their leave of her, with many a sly wink and smothered chortle. She was conscious that Dalmar was on the prowl and hastening their tardy departure with challenging looks from eyes as stormy as a North Sea gale.

"Bertie," she appealed as that lady made to sweep past her, "you're not thinking of deserting me?"

Annabelle's companion cast one unquiet look in Dalmar's direction. "If he beats you, I'll send for Jerome," she said unfeelingly, and bobbed a hasty curtsy in the general direction of the Earl before making a fast exit.

Dalmar gently closed the double doors behind him and took a threatening step toward Annabelle. She looked around wildly. Nary a footman, lackey, or maid had had the gumption to remain at his post. She squared her shoulders. Damn if she would take a leaf out of Wellington's book! She'd let Napoleon be her mentor. Attack, she decided, was the best method of defense. It was hours later before she belatedly remembered that her mentor had gone down in ignominy in the face of Wellington's superior strategy.

Chapter Six

Shutting her mind against the vivid images of the chase which had plagued her all evening, Annabelle concentrated on projecting a semblance of her habitual worldly poise. She was Annabelle Jocelyn, a force to be reckoned with, and there wasn't a man born who could make her lose face.

Nevertheless, when Dalmar finally swooped down on her, she could not prevent herself from taking several quick backward steps.

His eyes searched hers, and the angry lines on his face gentled. "For God's sake, Annabelle, what do you think I mean to do to you? You must know I could never hurt you."

"There is more than one way of hurting someone," she said, and cautiously turned away. She settled herself on a small white satin settee and indicated that he was to take an adjacent chair.

Ignoring her outstretched hand and the careful distance she tried to set between them, Dalmar took the place beside her, crowding her against the armrest of the sofa. "What, that little contretemps with Temple? I let you off lightly, and you know it. What did you expect me to do when I finally caught up with you?"

"To be frank, I never thought our paths would cross again."

"You don't have to tell me that. If you had, you would have conducted yourself with a little more propriety."

It was evident that he did not plan to do her bodily harm. She peered at him curiously for a moment. Though she could not say why, she had the sudden conviction that the kind of threat he posed was far more subtle than she understood. She was not sure whether or not she should take comfort from that thought. While she was still trying to make up her mind, he repeated his observation on her lack of propriety, only this time at greater length.

She snorted. "I wasn't the one to air my dirty linen in public."

"No!" he shot back, his eyes sweeping over her, "and for a very good reason. You aren't wearing drawers or petticoats, as anybody with eyes in his head can see."

She faltered a little. "It's the fashion," she said lamely, and hoped that she was not blushing.

"Fashion be damned! Not another lady here this evening was half as bold, yes, and there were a few hussies in their number, if I'm not mistaken."

Stung, she cried out, "You had no complaints about how I dressed in Paris," and bit down on her tongue when she realized into what channels she had inadvertently turned his thoughts.

He flashed her a wicked grin. "Actually, I never noticed. You were wearing a pelisse over your gown. And when I found you in my bed, I thought you had removed your underthings to make it easy for me."

Refusing to be drawn into the subject of Paris and all that it might signify, she looked at him sternly and said, "You had no business to impinge my good name."

"To what?"

"You tried to ruin me!"

"How did I try to ruin you?"

"I think that would be obvious," she said, consciously coating her accents with all the sense of injury she had experienced in the last several hours.

As if reasoning with an unpredictable child, he said, "I was very careful to keep my voice down when I was in conversation with Temple, which is more than can be said for you. It was not by my design that anyone other than the Viscount should be made aware of our circumstances." He shrugged. "I shouldn't lose any sleep over it, if I were you. There may be speculation, but it's not as if you are a young debutante embarking on her first season. You're a widow. You're permitted a certain laxity in whom you see and in what you do. Though, to be frank, if tonight's soirée is anything to go by, I should think you'd gone your limit even by the prevailing modes of the Devonshire House set."

"The Devonshire House set no longer exists," she said, visibly bristling at the undeserved set-down. "And I take exception to being lumped with that iniquitous lot. I'm not a libertine. I don't gamble. There's never been a breath of scandal attached to my name."

"No. But as I hear tell, you've sailed pretty close to the wind on occasion."

"Yes, and never more so than tonight after your odious performance."

She was on her feet, and agitatedly pacing the floor. Dalmar stretched one arm along the back of the sofa and watched her perambulations from beneath half-hooded lids.

When she rounded on him, her eyes were sparkling. "Do you enjoy hurting people?" she demanded.

"To whom are you referring?"

"Lord Temple, Cameron, myself," she replied.

"Annabelle," he said, very gently. "I consider that I've done Lord Temple a service. It is not a kindness to encourage him when his suit is hopeless. And as for that jackanapes Cameron, the fellow is insufferable. Can he really write poetry?"

"People are willing to pay for it," replied Annabelle evasively.

"Now why doesn't that surprise me? If he puts on a performance like that again, perhaps I should consider breaking his fingers. It would be a favor to us all."

Her jaw sagged momentarily until she spied the laughter lurking in the depths of his eyes. She could not help the giggle which escaped her own lips. "Don't trouble," she said. "He'll only expect me to act as his scribe."

That one little giggle seemed to open the floodgates. First there was a choked laugh, and then another, until finally Annabelle threw herself into a chair and gave herself up to unbridled mirth.

At length she turned to Dalmar and said simply, "Nerves." When the laughter had finally subsided, she continued, "You're like someone out of a Greek drama, do you know?"

"Ouch!" said Dalmar. "Methinks the lady doth not take me seriously."

Annabelle flashed him a tolerant grin. "I'll give you full marks for trying," she said, suddenly feeling more in control of the situation. "No gentleman has ever adopted such a masterful manner with me before. Tell me, do you have much success when you take that tack with other ladies?"

"No. I've never taken the trouble to go to such lengths. You should be flattered."

"Well, truth to tell, I'm not," she answered with a quick, quelling frown. "It may be all a game to you, but I take leave to tell you that you've given me a few unquiet moments since you first descended on my doorstep. You know now that I'm not the woman you mistook me for in Paris. But on the slight chance that you are under some misapprehension, let me remind you that I am a respectable widow. I have a son. Did you know that? I would never do anything to hurt my son."

"Lucky boy," murmured Dalmar.

"Why do you say so?"

"Mmm? Oh, I was just thinking that with you as his mother he begins life with an enviable advantage."

The words were more revealing, Annabelle thought, than Dalmar knew. Somehow they touched her deeply. She wondered about his own childhood, but she feared to voice the questions which rose in her mind. "What a strange man you are," she remarked idly.

"Why? Because I won't take no for an answer?"

"That's not what I was thinking. But I'm truly interested. Why is it so hard for you to accept my refusal?"

"Because you don't mean it. If you could say it and make me believe it, I wouldn't be here now."

Annabelle blinked owlishly. "But I do mean it," she protested.

His eyes, Annabelle noted, had gone as soft as velvet again. She wondered if many women had been able to resist that bedroom look.

"What about Paris?" he asked softly.

She answered with feeling, "David, please, try to understand. You caught me in a weak moment. You were sedated. I had consumed a couple of brandies. The intimacy of our situation . . . the events leading up to that moment . . . what I mean to say is . . . I could not help myself. I did not wish it to happen. It just did. Nothing like that has ever happened to me before. In spite of all this," she went on, gesturing vaguely, "I'm not that sort of woman."

The tightly drawn lines around his mouth relaxed into a faint smile. "Oh, I think I know you better than you give me credit for," he told her, and reached out to grasp her wrist. He tugged gently till they were positioned knee to knee.

"David," she warned, "there can be no repetition of that night."

With one sharp jerk, he tumbled her into his lap. His arms came around her like iron manacles. "Do you intend to resist me?" he asked, laughter threading his voice.

"With my last breath," she avowed, the second before his lips made speech impossible.

She clenched her teeth so tightly it would have required a vise to pry them apart. What Dalmar could not effect by straight assault, however, he gained by diversionary tactics. His hand closed over the soft contour of a breast. Annabelle's lips opened to suck in air, and Dalmar's tongue swept in to make its first foray into forbidden territory. Swiftly rallying, Annabelle clamped her teeth on the brazen invader. For the space of several seconds, she savored the sweet thrill of victory. It was to be short lived. She felt the persistent graze of his thumb on one nipple, and she gave up her prize to voice her protest. Somewhere between thought and word, the protest translated into a whimper of reluctant pleasure.

That small, choked cry of mingled feminine distress and desire acted on Dalmar like a siren song. He shifted her in his arms, arching her back to expose the long column of her throat and softly swelling breasts.

Annabelle understood the peril of her position. Give the man an inch and he would take a mile! Drawing on reserves of feminine intuition she scarcely knew she possessed, she

101

resorted to a less adversarial approach.

"David, please, you're hurting me." The pressure of his arms eased a little, and on a more hopeful note she added, "This isn't going to prove anything, you know."

She thought for a moment he had not heard her, so intent was his gaze on her softly heaving bosom. For the space of five seconds she contrived to stop breathing. It was a mistake. It seemed only to increase his fascination with her anatomy. She felt the bodice of her gown dip as he lowered it, and a long shuddering breath was torn from her lungs.

"David, please! I wasn't quite truthful about Paris. All right! So I knew perfectly well what I was doing. Can't we talk about it?"

"You should have used those tactics earlier," he said, his voice darker than she had ever heard it. "I want a damn sight more from you now. Admit that you belong to me. Then and only then shall we discuss terms of surrender."

Feminine intuition, not one of Annabelle's strong suits, was immediately abandoned when she heard these inflammatory words. "Go to Hades!" she snarled, and did a little jig on Dalmar's lap in a vain attempt to free herself.

Very deftly, Dalmar used her movements to position her to his advantage. Through the sheer fabric of her gown, Annabelle became startlingly aware of his blatant state of arousal. She stilled. Their eyes locked, and the heat of his ardent expression seemed to melt the edges of her resolve.

"No," she breathed, but they both knew that her small exclamation of refusal was primitive in origin, the impulse of the more vulnerable female when her powerful mate claims her submission. For the first time in her life, Annabelle became conscious of the threat of the aroused male when thwarted.

"David," she said, a new wariness in her expression, "you would not force me, surely?"

"Oh no. That won't be necessary."

His answer was oblique and afforded little comfort. Through her teeth and with more spirit than wisdom, she taunted, "Only a cad touches a lady without her permission!"

Dalmar's mind was of a different persuasion. Though he, none better, knew of men who were brutes with women, these

102

he held in utmost contempt, deeming them lower than animals in the divine scheme of things. His own deliberate attempt at masculine aggression he did not view in the same light. Some few women, indeed, had refused his advances with no hard feelings on either side. Not for a moment did he think of extending this courtesy to Annabelle. From the first, he had made his design plain to her. Afterward, not only had she accepted his protection in the Palais Royal, but she had also sealed the pact with the surrender of her body. That her circumstances were other than he had surmised did not signify, in his opinion. She had accepted his claims once. She could be made to do so again. Brute force he eschewed. But seduction was a lesser weapon he did not hesitate to employ against her. In short, Annabelle was his woman, and he was willing to protect her from everything and everyone but himself.

He brushed one finger against the tip of a nipple as if he were testing fire. Annabelle felt that gossamer touch all through her body. He touched her again, and the peaks of her breasts tautened and throbbed into life. The hard, quick pounding of her heart was matched by the tempo of her breath, deep, labored, erratic.

"Swear to me now," he said roughly, "that you don't want this as much as I do," and he cupped the weight of one breast in the heat of his palm. Annabelle cried out softly and turned her head into his shoulder.

"Annabelle . . . Annabelle," he said, her name a mere breath of a whisper as his mouth began to explore the wildly beating pulse at the hollow of her throat.

She felt the stroke of his tongue as he laved first one aching peak, then the other. Her body jerked, and heat swept through her, sensitizing every pore, arousing her most secret places, tuning her senses to the anticipation of his possession.

"David . . ." Whether she meant the plea as a protest or a benediction she could not tell. She felt the soft pull at her breasts as he took full suckle, and everything that was feminine in her went liquid with longing.

When his lips claimed hers again, there was no way she could hide the depths of her arousal. He released her arms.

"Yes, sweetheart, yes, like this," he said, and wound her arms around his neck. "You belong to me. Show me that you know it."

This time when his tongue stormed the citadel of her mouth, she allowed him an easy conquest. It drove through the barrier of her teeth and set up a slow pulsating rhythm, the harbinger of things to come.

They seemed to catch fire from each other. His hands, palm open, rode the length of her body, straining her against him, as if he could fuse them into one. The hungry impatience of his onslaught fed the flames of Annabelle's desire.

When he drew back his head, she heard the harsh rasp of his breath as he tried to steady it. "Annabelle?" he said hoarsely. "I can't take you here. Come with me now, to my rooms. You can tell your servants that I'm escorting you to some party or other. I swear I'll get you back long before morning."

She stirred uneasily, unwilling to come to terms with this unwelcome intrusion of reality.

"Annabelle," he breathed, his lips brushing her eyelids. "Let me love you. It's what we both want."

To deny the wanting he had deliberately aroused in every cell of her body seemed too cruel to be borne. She wished that he had not put the onus on her to decide how far their lovemaking should go. She struggled to subdue her awakening conscience. She failed. Though she had once, in a weak moment, given in to temptation, she could not, with anything resembling equanimity, break the tenets by which she had been taught from childhood to order her life.

With a small sigh of regret, she curled herself against the wall of his chest. "No," she said softly.

He groaned, "Annabelle, yes!" and his fingers speared into her hair, sending pins flying. He raised her face and rained hot, silencing kisses on her mouth.

"No," she said against his lips, more sure of her power to deal with this man, and then with more finality, "No!"

Her confidence wavered a little when she came under the blazing silver of his eyes, but she braved his fury by repeating her refusal.

As uncompromising as she, he said, "Then you'd better be

104

prepared to talk terms, or I'm taking everything you were offering a moment ago here and now."

For some reason his harsh words amused her. She touched a finger to his lips to silence him. "Do you love me?" she asked softly.

If she'd thrown a basin of cold water in his face, his reaction could not have been more startled. She found herself pushed to a sitting position, and the bodice of her gown hauled up roughly to cover her nakedness. Thrown into confusion by this abrupt, unloverlike conduct, she turned to face him. His eyes had darkened and were as unfathomable as the gray of the ocean deep.

"Love," he said, not quite meeting her eyes. He laughed. "Love, I leave to the poets. Thankfully, that trite emotion and I are strangers to each other." Almost regretfully, he continued, "Annabelle, love is transitory. Only fools and romantics think otherwise. I am neither. But words are cheap. I can say them as well as the next man. Is that what you would have me do—swear to an emotion I put no stock in?"

His candor left her more disappointed than she would have thought possible. She herself was no stranger to love, and she knew from experience how treacherous a snare it was for the unwary. Having shunned its allure for any number of years, she ought to have felt some empathy for Dalmar's convictions on the subject. She did not. If anything, she felt deceived, and in some unspecified way, grossly insulted. She knew of at least a dozen men in London who professed to be madly in love with her. Why not he? She resolved in that moment that whatever the future held for them both, the subject of love would never again be raised by her.

Nothing of her feelings showed on her face when she finally said, "Of course I don't wish to hear any declarations of love. What could be more tedious? Nor shall I ever bore you with an expression of those same sentiments." The relief which showed plainly in his eyes goaded her to add, "One grand passion is enough for anyone's lifetime. Having experienced it once, I have no wish to experience it again. But perhaps you find yourself in the same position?" She let the question hang on the air.

"No," he said, frowning slightly. "But what I've seen of it, I don't like. Forgive me, but I understood from something you said that your marriage was not a happy one. Was I wrong?"

"Edgar made me very happy," said Annabelle. It wasn't exactly a lie, she reasoned. For a time she had been happy . . . and in love. And blissfully ignorant. And then had come the disillusionment. But she wasn't about to reveal the details of her private life to a comparative stranger, especially when that stranger had disavowed any romantic interest in her.

"Do you still love him?"

She was conscious of a vague desire to ruffle his feathers, and she wondered at a streak of spite which had never before manifested itself in her nature. "Oh, I shall always love Edgar a little," she said. "If it were not for him, I would not have my son."

After this exchange, their conversation became desultory, touching on any number of topics which could be safely broached before a whole roomful of people. Annabelle could scarcely credit that only moments before the man had acted like a passionate lover to whom she had almost surrendered everything. It occurred to her that such goings-on were mere commonplaces to Dalmar. His experience and expertise were far beyond anything she could claim. The thought that she had been easy prey for the Earl was the perfect antidote to the more tender feelings she had begun to entertain for him. In no time at all she was congratulating herself on a lucky escape. She had put him in his place and was glad of it.

It was his parting words which disabused her of the notion that she had inadvertently turned the tables on him.

"I shall wait on you tomorrow."

"Tomorrow? For what purpose?"

"Did you think that I'd forgotten? To discuss the terms of your surrender, of course."

She met his roguish grin with a faint but eloquent lift of her eyebrows. "You do that, Dalmar," she said. "But don't think to pick up any bargains. I think my price is more than even you can afford."

She ascended the stairs and went first to her son's room.

Richard, as was his wont, was tangled in bedclothes, as if he had been fighting an imaginary army. Smiling, Annabelle smoothed the eiderdown coverlet over his sleeping form and touched her hand to his dark head. Now here was a love, she thought, that was true and enduring. Her thoughts shifted to Dalmar, and she began to speculate again about his own childhood—not very happy, she decided, if she was the judge of anything.

In her own chamber, as she absently allowed a stony-faced, tight-lipped Nancy to disrobe her and prepare her for bed, her thoughts became desultory, drifted, and finally focused on the man who had been the instrument of bringing Richard into her life.

His name had been Edgar Jocelyn, and he'd ridden into Yorkshire as if he were young Lochinvar coming out of the West, or so she'd thought at the time. She first became aware of his covert interest during Sunday services at York Minister, of all places, and had been introduced to him at one of the assemblies. Of course, she'd fallen head over heels in love with him. What young woman wouldn't? He was like one of the knights on the rubbings she'd made of the brasses at various parish churches she'd visited with her father. The Black Prince, so she'd persuaded herself, could not have been more chivalrous than Edgar. At thirty he was in the flower of English manhood.

Within a month they were wed. She could scarcely take it in—that she, Annabelle Summers, only moderately pretty, painfully shy and past the first bloom of youth, had captured the heart of the dashing captain of dragoons. And they were in love. There could be no doubt of that. There was only a modest portion settled on her by her maternal grandfather, certainly nothing to attract a fortune hunter. And Edgar's circumstances had not been much better. He was a younger son and was expected, by and large, to make his own way in the world. In those days, in spite of lack of fortune, they had counted themselves rich in the things that mattered. They were deep in love. What could they lack?

Two months later Edgar was on his way to Portugal with Wellesley, and she was installed at his brother's house in town.

It was to be Annabelle's introduction into circles to which she had never thought to aspire. The Jocelyns, she discovered, moved in the higher reaches of polite society. Annabelle's debut into that brilliant world was not auspicious. She was too shy to make much of an impression, too nondescript to attract any notice. It troubled her in no wise. She was impatient with anyone and anything that kept her from Edgar.

Their separation was to be temporary. The wives of many officers followed their husbands, and she was to be no exception. And then the letters had arrived describing the hardships and danger. Her departure was delayed, and delayed again, and finally put off indefinitely.

To begin with, she had not questioned her husband's decision. In the early days of their marriage, her highest ambition was to be a conformable wife, one that Edgar would be proud to come home to. But as the years slipped by, she began to fear that her years of childbearing were slipping away also. She begged him to come home on furlough, or to permit her to join him, to no avail. It seemed that the joys of motherhood were never to be hers.

Ironically, her prayers were answered, though at the time she'd felt as if the bottom had fallen out of her world. She would never forget that cold January morning when her brother-in-law called her into his study. Poor Sir Charles! He had hemmed and hawed and tried to spare her feelings. So vague was his address that she had thought at first that her sister-in-law was again breeding, and had felt the familiar ache of envy. Henrietta and she were of an age, but Henrietta had been blessed with four thriving children. It was Charles's sad and solemn demeanor which had been her first inclination of impending disaster.

When all was revealed, she'd behaved with commendable restraint. In point of fact, she'd been in shock. She was to have her husband's child after all, it seemed, one that he had fathered on a Spanish girl. The mother had died. The child was barely a year old. Edgar was beside himself with worry over the child's welfare. The only solution that presented itself was to send his son home to the arms of one whose heart he knew was big enough to accept and forgive a husband's follies. And gullible enough, she'd thought at the time.

But that was before she'd seen Ricardo. Once the babe was in her arms, there was never any question that she would turn him over to her sister-in-law's care. Within months of his arrival, a bonding had taken place. She could not have loved the child more if she had been his natural mother.

Toward Ricardo's father, however, her feelings were otherwise. A child out of wedlock she could forgive. A string of women she could have forgiven. But what she could not forgive was that while she had moped in England, filling her time with useless occupations which held no interest for her, longing to be in her husband's arms, he had another family, a Spanish one, comfortably installed for his convenience. That was the reason why he had forbidden her presence in Spain, not out of any sentiment for her welfare. And while another woman had given him a child, she had been robbed of her chance at motherhood. As a result of her new insight, two things happened simultaneously. She became disenchanted with knights in shining armor and no longer included them when she sought out brasses for her hobby. And the role of conformable wife fell completely into disfavor.

At the age of twenty-six, Annabelle underwent a metamorphosis. She put away childish things and emerged as a woman in her own right. Her transformation was not to everyone's liking. It was one thing for Lady Jocelyn to have an extra pair of willing hands to help with her demanding brood of hopefuls, but quite another when a swarm of courtiers beat a path to her door for the privilege of kissing one of those same hands now delicately encased in fine kid leather. When Annabelle took to flaunting paint and powder—gilding the lily, as Lady Jocelyn derided it—Sir Charles was prevailed upon to lay down the law, a task which he evidently found little to his taste.

His first mistake was in appealing to Annabelle's sense of what was fitting as Edgar's wife. Finding that tack fruitless, he compounded his error by threatening to tighten the purse strings. By this time, however, Annabelle had a source of income which gave her a fair degree of independence. She'd fallen heir to a half share in Bailey's Press by the terms of the will of some distant relative on her mother's side. It provided the impetus she needed to strike out on her own. At the time, it seemed as if she were taking an awful chance. A husband's authority over a wife was far reaching. Whether or not Edgar ever got wind of what she was up to was never made clear. Shortly afterward, he was mortally wounded at Badajoz; and he died a few days later.

She'd been twenty-seven years old when she'd set up her own establishment on Greek Street. The house, just off Soho Square, suited her by virtue of its being close enough to Mayfair to be deemed fashionable, yet far enough distant to command only a moderate rent. Moreover, her comings and goings could not be so closely monitored by that close-knit, almost incestuous community which was quick to pounce on anything out of the way in a neighbor's conduct, especially if that neighbor happened to be a lady.

"The Worldly Widow," they called her behind her back, and, some few, to her face. Much she cared! On the contrary, the soubriquet rather gratified her vanity. Better that handle by far than "The Dowdy Drab," which was what she had been fast sinking to as unpaid drudge in her sister-in-law's household. Though, to be scrupulously fair to Henrietta, Annabelle had been no more drudge than any other unmarried or widowed lady of her acquaintance who was a pensioner in a benefactor's home. It was simply the way of the world. In some corner of her mind, she was aware that by making herself over and striking out on her own, she was engaging in an act of bravado. But whether she wished to thumb her nose at the world in general, or at her late husband in particular, was not clear to her. She scarcely gave it a thought.

Truth to tell, she had scarcely given her late husband a thought in the last number of years. It could not be otherwise. She had known him for all of three months before he had left England with the expedition to Portugal. She had not seen him in seven long years, and of those, she had been a widow for four. It was Dalmar who kept bringing Edgar to mind. She wondered why. Oh yes, something to do with the *grand passion*, the great love of her life. Not to be compared, of course, to the love she felt for her son. She would love Ricardo—Richard

110

now—till she drew her last breath.

Dalmar was right. Love between the sexes was a transitory thing at best, here today, gone tomorrow. Which led her to ponder why she had taken such offense when he had done nothing more than voice her own sentiments. The answer came to her in that estate which falls somewhere between wakefulness and slumber. It was true that Edgar had been the only love of her life, the man to whom she had surrendered her virginity, but it was Dalmar who had demanded and claimed her passion. How strange, she thought, that he, a man who professed not to love her, should be the one to bring her body to heights she had never suspected were possible for a woman. She was sure that there was an insult implicit in such a state of affairs. Her last coherent thought before sleep claimed her was that the man had such conceit that he probably thought he had done her a favor.

Chapter Seven

Annabelle's ears picked up the soft tread of footsteps as they made a stealthy approach to the door of her chamber. She quickly drew on her robe and scrambled beneath the covers of her unmade bed. The door opened, and she braced herself for the expected attack. A small body launched itself upon her. She fought back in a flurry of feather pillows and bedclothes.

"I'm the king of the castle, and you're the dirty rascal," a shrill voice sounded in her ear. "Yield or die!"

She let him have it full blast with her pillow. "Take that and that, you villain," she grunted. "I'll teach you to beard the dragon in his den," and she rolled, pulling her attacker beneath the full press of her weight. His struggles were unequal to her superior strength.

Her young son looked up at her with dark, shining eyes. Undaunted, he panted, "Yield, dragon, and I'll spare your life. Fight me, and I'll slay you with my knife."

"Not on your life, St. George! You yield, or I'll burn you to a cinder with my fiery breath." And she bared her small white teeth in a ferocious snarl.

"But Mama, that's not how the story goes," said the voice, turning petulant. "St. George always slays the dragon. Everybody knows that!"

"What I want to know," said Annabelle, throwing up her hands in the accepted mode of surrender, "is when it's my turn to be St. George. Or even better, why can't we change the story? What's to stop us letting the poor dragon win the

113

contest now and again? Wouldn't that be fun?"

The small body wriggled from beneath her weight. "It might be," said the child, considering her suggestion. After a moment's reflection, he concluded, "But it wouldn't be the same."

Annabelle sat on the edge of the bed as her son, a child of five summers or so, climbed onto her back in what was evidently a well-loved ritual. "Richard," she said, adjusting the small hands which clung tenaciously to her throat, "as always, your logic is impeccable."

"Is that good?" he asked, tightening his knees against his mother's sides.

"It's better than good," she answered, and was rewarded with sparkling eyes and a brilliant smile.

"*En avant*, Barcephalus," he urged, and put his imaginary spurs to the flanks of his equally imaginary horse.

Annabelle obligingly made a few turns around the room with her precious burden on her back and finally collapsed in laughter on the bed in a tangle of flying arms and knees.

From the open doorway, Mrs. Bertie Pendleton surveyed the domestic scene with something like wistfulness in her expression. When she spoke, however, her voice was crisp and cheerful.

"Annabelle, I must protest. 'Barcephalus' was not the name of St. George's horse."

"Oh we know *that*," said Annabelle, exchanging a who's-your-daft-friend look with her son. "But until we discover what it was, we've decided to name him for Alexander's famous steed."

"I like the name 'Barcephalus,'" said Richard, making a game of rearranging the sundry pots and dishes on top of his mother's dressing table.

"Really? Why?" asked Bertie.

"Because James can't say it and I can." The thought of besting his cousin, a boy who was older than he by a good twelvemonth, brought dimples flashing to his cheeks.

"Did you dress yourself this morning?" asked Annabelle, eyeing askance the mismatched buttons and buttonholes on her son's waist-length green velvet jacket.

114

"Why do you ask?"

There was the look of something in her son's eyes which stirred Annabelle's most tender feelings. "Because, imp," she said, twitching his nose, "you're not wearing your sash. Now go and put it on, and be downstairs for breakfast in five minutes. Hurry, or we'll be late for church."

Across the space of the small chamber, the two ladies took silent stock of each other. Annabelle's look was wary. In Mrs. Pendleton's eyes there was the glint of unabashed curiosity. Annabelle took note of that look, and for the first time in the two years since she'd taken Bertie as her companion, began to regret that she had always encouraged an easy converse between them.

From the moment they had met, there had been an instant attraction. Their acquaintances wondered at their friendship, for where Annabelle looked and acted the part of a dasher, Bertie was every inch the lady. Her carriage was graceful, her figure slender, and for one of such fair hair and complexion, her most distinguishing feature was a pair of startlingly brown eyes which observed the world with something like imperturbable patience. Many a man who had overstepped what was proper (and there were several of that breed hovering around Annabelle) had faltered before that stare.

It had been Sir Charles's fond hope, when Mrs. Pendleton first took up residence in Greek Street, that her influence would work a salutary change in his sister-in-law. In point of fact, appearances to the contrary, the two ladies were not so very dissimilar. Each had a history which left much to be desired. In some sense, each felt abused by the male of the species. But whilst Annabelle's mode was to strike out and dare the world to do its worst, Bertie, by temperament, was inclined to withdraw into her shell. It would have shocked Sir Chales to learn that, in Mrs. Pendleton's estimation, it was his scapegrace sister-in-law who had worked a salutary change in her.

By tacit agreement, Annabelle and her companion rarely discussed their respective late husbands. Each was content to draw a veil over what had evidently been an unhappy period in her life. It was otherwise with current events, hence

115

Annabelle's look of wariness and Bertie's frank curiosity.

Mrs. Pendleton advanced upon her friend. "Here, let me help you," she said as Annabelle made to slip out of her silk robe. Annabelle, clothed in her underthings, flashed a challenging look at her companion. Bertie eyed Annabelle's petticoats with marked favor. "There wouldn't be pantalettes hiding under those petticoats by any chance, would there?" she quizzed.

Annabelle, quickly lowering her lashes, signified that there were.

"May I ask what has brought about this change of heart?"

"Fashions change, Bertie," said Annabelle, and quickly thrust her arms into a dark blue dimity which her companion held for her. The bodice of the frock covered her from throat to wrist.

Mrs. Pendleton gave an unladylike snort. "But not betwixt Saturday night and Sunday morning. This is Dalmar's doing or my name isn't Beatrice Pendleton. Annabelle, I'm expiring with curiosity. Who is the man? How do you come to know him? Why does he have such a proprietary interest in you?"

Annabelle seated herself at her dressing table and began hunting for the pot of blacking her son had newly displaced. Her fingers were very steady as she applied the brush to her gold eyebrows and lashes. "He is the Earl of Dalmar. I met him in Paris. He was the man who saved my life in that melee I told you about in the Palais Royal. Because I was unchaperoned, and he found me in such a place and . . . well . . . everything else," she added vaguely, "he mistook me for a lady of easy virtue."

"I warned you that something of the kind might happen," said Bertie, appalled. "It was sheer foolishness to travel to Paris without me to chaperone you."

"There's no sense crying over spilt milk," said Annabelle, trying for an air which would depress further questions. "Someone had to remain behind with Richard. It was imperative that I be in Paris. I had my maids as chaperones and Lord Temple as an escort."

Annabelle chanced a quick look at her companion, and just as quickly looked away. "I don't see what more I could have

116

done," she added.

"You were very fortunate to come out of that little escapade with no harm done."

"Yes, wasn't I?" agreed Annabelle, studiously applying a dab of Denmark lotion across her cheekbones.

Mrs. Pendleton studied Annabelle's ingenuous and slightly abstracted expression in the reflection of the mirror. After a moment she observed, "Lord Dalmar must know by now that you're a respectable lady of quality."

"Certainly. But I'm a widow. To men of his kidney, that makes me fair game."

"The bounder!"

"Yes! Which is why I was very disappointed when you left me to his mercies yesterday evening. Well, you're a widow too. You know how some men, I won't say 'gentlemen,' think that that circumstance gives them license to treat us as if we were lightskirts."

"Annabelle . . . he didn't . . . you didn't?"

"Oh yes he did, and of course I didn't!"

"How awful! And to think I liked him on sight! Well, I'm sure that you sent him about his business with a flea in his ear."

"I tried to," said Annabelle, savagely drawing a comb through her tangled locks. "I might as well have tried to beat my fist against a brick wall. He won't take no for an answer."

Mrs. Pendleton took the comb from Annabelle's fingers and deftly wound the curtain of hair into a loose knot. Her eyes met Annabelle's in the mirror. Suppressing a smirk, she said, "I did not even think to hear you admit that there was a man you could not manage."

"There isn't!" said Annabelle, her teeth clamping together.

Bertie smiled but said nothing, and Annabelle burst out, "Anyone would think that you were hoping to see me get my just desserts."

Without haste, Bertie affixed several hair pins to the smooth chignon at Annabelle's neck. She surveyed her handiwork with a critical eye. "Fustian," she said at length. "You know better than that. But there is something about Dalmar which invites confidence, yes, even in a misanthrope such as myself. Why don't you give him a chance?"

"I don't believe my ears! You have no more reason to trust men than I do. You've never before displayed such partiality to any of the gentlemen of our acquaintance."

"No, and with good cause. You surround yourself with milksops and manikins. Dalmar is the first real man who's come close to you in an age. How did he manage it, I wonder?"

"Perhaps," said Annabelle through set teeth, "it was an act of God—you know, like earthquakes and natural disasters."

"Or the hand of fate," replied Bertie, her eyes twinkling.

They descended to the morning room without exchanging another word. Annabelle's lips were set in a straight line, and Bertie attempted without much success to emulate her employer's example. They found Richard at table, waiting on himself.

By virtue of the fact that it was Sunday, and therefore a day of rest, Annabelle saw no reason to discommode her servants if they had better things to do; and it seemed most of them had. Her small domestic staff of five was reduced to two, a footman and a maid-of-all-parts who did little more than set out and remove the cold collations which Cook had prepared the day before.

Mrs. Pendleton, in the two years that she had been Annabelle's companion, also availed herself of her employer's generosity. There was a cousin in Kensington, a Mrs. Black and her family, with whom she was in the habit of spending the day. Annabelle allowed her the use of her carriage to make the journey and sent it to fetch her very early the following morning. The routine never varied as long as they were in residence in Greek Street. After dropping Annabelle and Richard at the gates of St. James Church on Piccadilly, Mrs. Pendleton would continue on to Kensington and send the carriage back in time to pick up Annabelle and her son at the close of services.

Annabelle had never made the acquaintance of this cousin, but not from the want of trying. With almost boring regularity, she made it known to her companion that her house was always open to her friends and relations. Bertie never availed herself of the offer, and Annabelle, though curious, did not press the issue.

Almost as a matter of habit, she said, "My compliments to your cousin when you see her, Bertie, and be kind enough to remind her that my invitation still stands."

"Thank you, I shall. But I don't doubt that Lotty will remain in Kensington." Carefully buttering an edge of dry toast, she said by way of explanation, "She would never leave her husband to fend for himself even for a day or two."

"I thought she was a widow," said Annabelle, frowning. Her eyes followed the burly figure of the new footman who had entered the room bearing a pot of fresh tea.

"What? Oh no! What ever gave you that idea?"

"Something you said. I must have misunderstood. Thank you, Edwards," she said to the footman. He set the silver teapot at her elbow. Annabelle observed his rough, callused hands and wondered idly what his former occupation had been before joining her employment. She made a mental note to ask Jerome when the carriage was brought round.

"What about your niece, Amy?" asked Annabelle, pinning Richard with a fierce glare when the scamp used his fingers to clean the marmalade from his side plate. He desisted immediately and won an approving smile from his mother.

There was a moment's silence. "What about her?"

"I know you're very fond of her. Would your cousin permit her to accompany us when next we visit Rosedale? Or perhaps she's too young to make the journey?"

"No . . . no. She's four years old. Do you really mean it, Annabelle? And what about your good brother and good sister? Won't they object?"

"Of course I mean it, and you must be funning if you think they'll object. They have five boys. Henrietta will positively go into raptures over having a little girl under her roof for a week or so. And they're really very kind people at heart. It's only that . . ."

"Yes, I know. Your unconventional not to mention hoydenish conduct brings out the worst in them. Let's hope they don't hear about last night's escapade, or you may find yourself sent to Coventry."

"Careful," said Annabelle, pointedly glancing in her son's direction. "Little people have long ears."

"I'm not little, and I don't have long ears," said the object of her obliquity, clearly affronted. "May I be excused?"

"Yes, dear. There's a nip in the air, so better wear your warm woolen cap, the one that Grandpapa sent you from York."

When the two ladies were alone, Annabelle said, "Charles and Henrietta would never give me the cut direct. For one thing, I'm family. For another, Charles and I are Richard's joint guardians. At the most, I may expect a very long and boring lecture."

"I'm surprised that Sir Charles hasn't stooped to using Richard as a lever to reform your wicked ways."

"No," said Annabelle, refilling both empty cups from the teapot, "Edgar made it very plain that Richard was to be my responsibility. Naming Charles as co-guardian was in the nature of a formality. Charles would never go against Edgar's express wishes."

"You like them, don't you?"

"Of course. I like them both. Though I will admit that sometimes Henrietta is a little hard to take."

"Don't you know why?"

"Well it's obvious. She thinks I'm a hoyden."

"That's not the reason," said Mrs. Pendleton, and bit into a corner of toast to hide her smile.

For some reason, Annabelle did not wish to pursue the subject. "You will remember to ask your cousin," she said.

"I beg your pardon?"

"About Amy. I expect we shall receive our usual invitation to go to Rosedale the first week in November. The children will love it."

"Oh yes. It ends with Guy Fawkes Night at Lewes."

"You mustn't worry about Amy being frightened. You can keep her indoors if you think it will be too much for her."

"If I know Amy, nothing will keep her indoors, not even if she's terrified out of her wits."

"Yes, children are funny that way, aren't they?" said Annabelle. "They seem to thrive on excitement."

"Speaking of which," said Mrs. Pendleton meaningfully, "I expect we shall be seeing something of Lord Dalmar during the next month or so, whether we will or no. He said that he has a house in Cavendish Square and plans to open it up and take up residence until Christmas at least."

"Wonderful," said Annabelle, determined not to rise to the bait. "If you can pull it off, I'll give you a phaeton-and-pair as a wedding present."

"What?"

"You will let me know when I may wish you happy?"

Bertie laughed. "Oh Annabelle, something tells me that you will not be a gracious loser."

For the short time that it took to drive to Piccadilly, Annabelle chattered like a magpie, carefully avoiding the distressing subject of Lord Dalmar. And she was distressed, almost more than she was willing to admit. She might disclaim his proprietary interest in her with her last breath, but deep down she knew that she had made a fatal blunder. For whatever reason, she had given herself to him though every instinct had warned her that to do so would forge an unbreakable bond between them. She felt the inescapable pull of those bonds, and everything in her rebelled against it.

She entered the high-vaulted nave with its capacious galleries determined to banish him from her mind. For a time she was successful, for as her eyes roamed the impressive interior designed by Christopher Wren and richly embellished with the carvings of Grinling Gibbons, she could not but reflect that she knew more intimately than she would have liked many of the notable fashionables who graced the pews. Their names were to be found in the pages of Monique Dupres's diaries. Color heated her cheeks. She put her head down and led her son to their regular places in the Jocelyn family pew.

The organ prelude, normally wont to leading the worshipers to a time of quiet introspection before the service began, was on this occasion torture to Annabelle. Her head was filled with the vision of a pair of fine gray eyes flashing with the brilliance of silver, softening like the gray mists which floated up the Thames estuary, gentle and yet so cunningly misleading that the unwary might easily become lost in their depths.

It was the deep and melodious tones of the rector himself which finally brought her out of her reverie. Dean Gerrard Andrews delivered the sermon, and a very fine sermon it was, too. His text, from the Gospel of St. John, was "Let he who is without sin cast the first stone," and he dealt with the passage on the woman taken in adultery. And how Annabelle squirmed! It not only brought to mind a weakness with respect to Dalmar which she could not explain to herself, but also raised some doubts in her mind about whether or not publishing her latest acquisition was the Christian thing to do.

Her confusion on the subject did not last long. As the congregation filed out of the north door, where the rector had stationed himself to shake hands with his flock, she could not help the quick rise of indignation as she listened to the unguarded, sanctimonious comments of some of the male worshipers.

"That's telling 'em, Rector!"

"That's women for you! Agents of the devil, as we poor males know to our cost."

"Letting 'em off too light, Rector, letting 'em off too light. Fire and brimstone. That's what they want."

And *that*, thought Annabelle, bristling with annoyance, was from three members of Parliament who figured quite prominently in the pages of Monique Dupres's diaries!

Her look was direct, her hand was quite steady when she finally offered it to her priest. "I'll try not to break any glass windows," was her only comment before she followed the press of people into the walled churchyard.

After church, it was her wont to idle away a good half hour in exchanging commonplaces with her neighbors. On this day of all days, however, Annabelle did not wish to tarry. Lord Temple was a member of St. James and was almost certain to be present among the crowd. After what had passed between them the night before, she did not know how she could look him in the eye. Smiling and waving vaguely in the direction of some ladies who hailed her, she grasped her son's hand and made a beeline for the great domed stone archway which gave onto Piccadilly.

Lord Temple was lying in wait for her on the other side of the wall. She heard his voice at her back, and schooling her features, she turned to offer him her hand.

"Gerry," she said, making a fair attempt to appear natural.

From the corner of her eye, she caught a glimpse of her carriage across the street, outside the gates of Albany House.

"I want to go home," piped Richard, edging away from the approaching figure of the Viscount.

Though normally of a sunny disposition, young Richard could turn belligerent on occasion. It was no secret in Annabelle's household that the young master viewed his mother's suitors with marked disfavor. This display of jealousy was thought to be quaint and rather appealing among the servants. To Annabelle it proved something of a nuisance, and extremely embarrassing on more occasions than she cared to remember.

Without moving her lips she said, "Richard, I'm warning you. Be on your best behavior, or else . . ."

The Viscount was upon them, and Richard's brows drew together when he silently suffered the insult of having his curls ruffled as if he were an infant. To prevent further indignities, he jammed his cap upon his head.

"I collect it's nurse's day off," observed Lord Temple, taking in the mismatched buttons and buttonholes on Master Jocelyn's velvet jacket. Before Annabelle could make a move to prevent it, the Viscount deftly corrected the error.

Annabelle glanced in some trepidation at the gathering storm on her young son's face. There could be no doubt about it. His bottom lip projected in what could only be described as a pout. She knew that look well, and trembled.

The Viscount, having paid his unwelcome compliments to the son, turned his undivided attention upon the mother. Annabelle, clearly distracted, laid a warning hand on Richard's shoulder.

"Richard!" she pleaded.

Disregarding his mother's evident panic, in a clear carrying voice he piped, "What's an adulteress?" It was a question which had exercised his mind since Dean Andrews had first used the unfamiliar word during the sermon. Since then he had asked his mother to explain it at least a dozen times only to be bullied into silence. Naturally, after that, he'd memorized it and had added it to his store of not-nice words with which to astonish his cousins when he was next in Sussex. From the

123

Viscount's pained look and the prim set of his mother's lips, he deduced that it was more wicked than he had supposed. Calmly he waited for the explosion.

Annabelle threw an agonized look at the Viscount. "Richard, you will apologize at once for using that naughty word," she told her son with a dark meaningful look which promised retribution.

Carefully Richard used the toe of his black patent pump to position a small pebble which he'd found on the pavement. "Dean Andrews used the word, and he didn't apologize," he said. As if to prove his point, he added, "He read it from the Bible."

"Spare the rod, spoil the child," said Lord Temple darkly.

Annabelle was torn between umbrage at Lord Temple's patronizing tone and chagrin at being shown up as a parent who exercised little control over her child. Almost desperately she remembered how Lord Dalmar had handled a similar situation in her own drawing room the night before, and wondered what tack he would take in the present circumstances.

She exhaled slowly and bent her head to hiss in her son's ear, "You're quite right, Richard. 'Adulteress' is not a naughty word. And when we are in the carriage, I shall satisfy your curiosity. However, young man, you *thought* it was a naughty word and meant to shock Lord Temple. For that, you *will* apologize. This instant, Richard. And I mean it."

The game was beginning to bore the boy. He recognized that his mother had reached the end of her tether. Furthermore, she had inadvertently paid him a very high compliment. "Young man," she had called him. Though he did not like Lord Temple, nor indeed any of the gentlemen who courted his mother, it was not she that he wished to discomfit. He apologized very nicely. Looking from one to the other, he had the satisfaction of knowing that while he was once again in his mother's good graces, he still remained at outs with his lordship.

Honor satisfied, Annabelle was not about to test the limits of the fragile truce which she had secured. She moved resolutely to cross Piccadilly to her waiting carriage.

"Annabelle, please. I must talk to you," said Temple.

"Not now, Gerry," she answered, looking pointedly at her son and then at the knots of people who stood about on the pavement.

"It's important. It concerns Lord Dalmar. There are things about him you should know. It will take only a few minutes. Why don't I ride with you in your carriage?"

Lord Dalmar was a subject she did not wish to discuss with Temple, or anyone else, for that matter. For how could she explain to others what she herself did not understand?

"No. It's all been said. Leave it, Gerry, please, or we can never be friends."

"This has nothing to do with last night. Please, just a few minutes of your time? I'll wait on you this afternoon, if I may?"

"No, not this afternoon," she replied quickly. The Earl had promised to call on her that very afternoon, and the last thing she wanted was a repeat performance of the night before. "Tomorrow morning I'll be in my office. If you think it's really necessary, you'll find me there."

"Oh, it's necessary," he told her grimly. "Until you hear what I have to say, don't have any truck with the man. He's dangerous, Annabelle. I mean it."

Temple's words did not alarm Annabelle unduly. In the years since she had known the Viscount, it had been his practice to try to cut out his rivals by relaying some choice tidbit of scandal which he had ferreted out. Annabelle recognized the ploy for what it was. At one time she'd been amused by such obvious tactics. Of late she was coming to view them in a less charitable light. It occurred to her that she was becoming more and more disenchanted with Temple's doglike devotion. She grew impatient with herself. Time and time again Lord Temple had proved himself a worthy friend. That he had a few annoying traits went without saying. What man didn't? She herself was no paragon. It behooved her, of all people, to be more forgiving of a friend's foibles. And their friendship was of long standing. In spite of Dalmar's meddling, she hoped it would continue so.

At the thought of the Earl and his projected visit, butterflies began to stir in Annabelle's stomach. She barely tasted what she ate for luncheon, so occupied was her mind in arranging the coming interview to her advantage. Like a general on the eve of battle, she examined her strategy from all angles. He was intent on discussing terms of surrender—hers, of course. But she had discovered his Achilles heel. And she could not quite stifle a gleeful smile when she glanced at her small son—she had a secret weapon she had yet to unleash upon the unsuspecting Earl. All in all, she thought the balance of power tipped slightly in her favor. With someting like shock she realized that in spite of nervous tension and some misgivings, she was possessed of a strange and not altogether unpleasant humor. She was anticipating the coming confrontation with eagerness, if not downright relish. It had become her object to humble the man, and for the first time since she had met him, victory seemed to be within her grasp. The notion was heady.

She set the scene with meticulous care. The garden, she decided, would suit her purposes admirably, since it was in clear view of every window at the back of the house. And though Bertie was gone for the day, Annabelle did not doubt that her son would prove a formidable chaperone. If past events were anything to go by, he would not let his mother out of his sight when any man with the smell of "suitor" appeared on the horizon. And Richard had the nose of a bloodhound.

Though it was early October and there were few leaves on the trees, the weather was unseasonably mild. Not a breath of wind stirred. Wearing only a long-sleeved velvet spencer over her blue dimity, she settled herself on a bench overlooking a small fountain in a far corner of the garden. Nearby, sitting cross-legged on the flagstones, was Richard. From somewhere, he had procured a bag of clothes pegs and was setting them out in what appeared to be military order. Annabelle's brows drew together, but she kept her own counsel.

From time to time, mother and son exchanged a few desultory comments. After an interval, Annabelle picked up her needles and examined the work in progress. She was knitting a muffler for her son, a task in which she took little pleasure. She had always preferred to sew and had some talent as a seamstress. Though she was in the habit of sewing any number of fine lawn shirts, satin breeches, and fancy waistcoats for her son, he remained unimpressed. It seemed that some old crone of a nurse, a dab hand with knitting needles, was forever presenting his cousins with stockings and mufflers and suchlike, and nothing would do till Richard sported an almost identical article of clothing. Bertie had offered to relieve Annabelle of a chore which she obviously found little to her liking. But Annabelle knew her duty. As she told Bertie, a boy ought to be able to take for granted these small tributes of a mother's love and devotion. With great perseverance she attacked her knitting needles.

Half an hour later saw Annabelle yawn from sheer boredom. She counted her stitches and was relieved to discover that she had the same number as she had started with.

"Who says the age of miracles is over?" she said aloud, and had to explain the joke to her son.

They were both laughing when the maid announced Lord Dalmar. Annabelle could scarcely prevent herself from rubbing her hands together. "Well, go and fetch him, Mary, go and fetch him," she said, smiling a secret smile to herself. As was to be expected, Richard scowled. Under her breath, Annabelle murmured, "Don't fail me, son. Don't fail me."

Chapter Eight

Dalmar's eyes searched the small brick-walled garden and found her, almost immediately, seated in stately splendor beside a stone fountain that gushed water from a lion's snarling head. At his approach she turned slightly and elevated her chin. She looked, he thought, like some pagan warrior queen in her chariot, exuding confidence, poised to accept the tribute of one of her vassal yarls. She wore no bonnet, and the warm rays of the afternoon sun gilded her crown of neatly coiffed dark hair with threads of purest gold. It was no wonder, he thought, looking directly into eyes as clear and brilliant as a Portuguese sky, that men were constrained to worship from afar, as if she were a planet in some distant galaxy, mysterious, beckoning, and yet forever beyond their reach.

Not for the first time, he reminded himself that he had contrived, once before, to reach out and grasp the unattainable. Stars were known, on occasion, to fall to earth. And if, like Zeus on Mount Olympus, he had to shake the heavens himself, he would do it and force her into his orbit.

Why this woman, more than any other, had the power to stir the profoundest reaches of his male psyche was not clear to him. Her appeal was more than sensual, though he could not deny, in all conscience, that the pull on his senses was irresistible. No woman, simply by walking into his line of vision, had ever brought his senses to such a pitch. Annabelle sent his pulse surging like a tidal wave. He could feel the onset before his conscious mind registered that she was in his vicinity. Even the fine hairs on the back of his hands and on his neck seemed to be turned to her slightest gesture.

There had been many women in his life, but no one of any importance. His relationships had been transitory. He had preferred it that way. Women were weak. A man could easily hurt them if he had a mind to. Fragile women terrified him. His mother had been a fragile woman and no match for his father. In some ways, he was like his father. Or perhaps all men were the same. He liked to have things his own way. At times he could be intimidating. He did not think that any man could intimidate Annabelle Jocelyn.

He was thirty-four years old, and he had never shared more with a woman than a few hours' pleasure in bed. He had never wanted more. He wanted more now. For the first time he could envision a different kind of life for himself. At the center of that life was Annabelle. Suddenly everything seemed possible.

She was satin and steel, as innocent as a newborn babe, as sensuous as a kitten. She was like the kaleidoscope he had once treasured as a boy. When he looked at her, he saw all the colors of the rainbow. He had never met a woman like her and knew that he never would again. He craved her warmth and animation with a hunger which surprised him. She was everything that he had always wanted but never hoped to possess.

He'd been happy before, of course, but he now recognized that emotion for what it was. Not the presence of something, but its absence. As a boy, when his father left the house, he was happy. When he was sent away to school, out of his parents' orbit, he was happy. When he joined the army and left disgrace behind him in England, he was happy. It seemed to him at that moment that he had never asked for very much out of life. Annabelle Jocelyn had walked into his line of vision, and suddenly he wanted it all. He had tasted the sweet rapture of her surrender and would not rest until she had ceded him full title to all the mysteries of her femininity.

Base, Dalmar, he thought, *and so blatantly and unquestionably male.* But such was her effect on him. She had roused the sleeping beast of everything that was masculine in his nature, unconsciously inciting him to first possess and then protect the female of his choice. Only when she had accepted his claims to who and what she was would he be free to offer the generosity of the victor.

Strange, he thought, and so unlike anything he had ever experienced before in his relations with a woman. He lowered his eyelashes to veil the naked intent which he felt sure she would be able to read in his eyes. He had, perhaps, overplayed his hand, betraying too much too soon. *Gently, softly,* he cautioned himself, *lest your quarry take flight before you have tamed her to your hand.*

His eyes shifted to take in the stiff and trenchant figure of what was evidently Annabelle's self-appointed protector. The Queen's knight stood guard, so it seemed, and must be disarmed before he, Dalmar, could make his move to checkmate the Queen. As if he were, in truth, in the throes of battle, every instinct came alive, investing him with a sixth sense, alerting him to all the possibilities for success or failure in his mission.

His smile was lazy and carefully devoid of any overt show of confidence which might warn his two adversaries that he had divined their strategy. They could not know that he had received advance warning of how they would play the game.

Introductions were made and a few commonplaces exchanged. Annabelle invited the Earl to take the place beside her.

Both mother and son looked expectantly at the tin box the Earl carried under his arm. He made no move to satisfy their curiosity, but negligently placed it on the ground at his feet.

Annabelle became involved with her knitting, and under cover of counting her stitches, she surreptitiously took stock of the Earl. Apart from his exquisitely tailored, black cutaway coat, his attire was casual by Sabbath standards—tight-fitting beige pantaloons and hessians. Not that there was anything careless in his dress. Everything about him attested to his years of military service, from his carefully brushed crop of dark hair to the shine on his tassled hessians. He held himself well, and his proud carriage seemed only to enhance his broad shoulders and spare, muscular frame, hardened, she supposed, from endurance to the sort of life she could not even guess at. It was, however, that bedroom smile and those boudoir eyes which warned a lady not to take the gentleman at face value. Just looking at him made her feel that she had already given in to temptation. Her eyes traveled to her son. Her knight, she thought with a smile, would keep her to the straight and narrow.

Unbeknownst to his mother, however, Master Jocelyn was thrown off balance. For one thing, the Earl paid him not the slightest notice. For another, the tin box which Lord Dalmar unconsciously kicked with the toe of one foot looked remarkably similar to one belonging to his cousin James. In James's box there was a whole regiment of tin soldiers. That palatable thought was enough to divert young Richard from his purpose for a good five minutes.

At last he remembered himself. Thinking of his earlier success of that morning, à propos of nothing, he demanded, "Do you know what an adulteress is?"

"Yes," responded the Earl without batting an eyelash.

If Richard was disappointed with his lordship's show of indifference, he did not divulge it. He tried again, but this time, with more deliberate provocation. "I am not permitted to say the word *adulteress* in company. Mama forbids it."

Dalmar raised one sardonic eyebrow at this veiled insult and glanced at Annabelle's bent head. It was evident that there was to be no help from that quarter since the lady was assiduously counting stitches under her breath. The faint color across her cheekbones, however, betrayed an unquiet mind.

Dalmar looked directly into Master Jocelyn's challenging dark eyes and said negligently, "I should think not. A gentleman would not dream of embarrassing a lady by using such indelicate expressions in her hearing. And there are other words of that ilk with which a gentleman is careful to exercise a modicum of discretion." He sliced a hard look at Annabelle, but could not catch her eye. His voice droned slowly on. "Words such as *damn, bloody, hell, bastard* . . ."

"David!"

Dalmar's artless glance lifted to meet Annabelle's shocked stare. Hot color flooded her cheeks. "I beg your pardon," he said, "I was under the impression that your mind was elsewhere. If I had supposed that you had heard one word of this man-to-man conversation, I would have desisted at once. Richard, I am sure, would have done likewise."

For all that it was softly spoken, she felt the bite of his censure. Flustered, she stared at the Earl, then quickly glanced away and looked at her son. It was evident from the boy's expression that Dalmar's credit had risen perceptibly in his eyes. A few swear words and the Earl had practically won the boy over. She could not help but admire the man's technique. Her other beaux had set themselves to courting her son's favor and failed miserably. Dalmar, she thought, was too clever by half.

"You see how it is with loose speech," he said addressing Richard. "Between gentlemen, such talk is commonplace. With ladies, it is otherwise. Their sensibilities are easily ruffled. I think we both owe your mother an apology, don't you?"

Richard sat back on his heels and considered. "Man-to-man" were heady words for a boy who was going on five and a half, almost. Moreover, the Earl had included him in the exclusive fraternity of which he so much longed one day to be a member. "Between gentlemen," Lord Dalmar had said. Richard looked at his mother with pitying eyes. She could never aspire so high.

He did not hesitate to act the part of the gentleman and add his apology to Lord Dalmar's. Annabelle accepted them with something less than grace, mumbling an incoherent reply which set the boy to wondering.

When he next addressed himself to Lord Dalmar, there was less restraint in his manner. "Do you have a dog?"

"Yes," answered the Earl. "Several in fact. And you?"

"Oh no," answered Richard wistfully. "Mama doesn't like dogs."

"Oh?" said Dalmar, looking at Annabelle.

"I was attacked by a dog as a child," she explained. She sent her son a speaking look, knowing that the next predictable question was already forming on his lips. But Richard had eyes only for the Earl.

"Do you have a horse?" he asked.

"Of course," answered the Earl. "Doesn't everyone?"

"No, but I mean a real horse, one that you can ride. Not one to pull your carriage."

"Yes, I have a horse, a whole stableful of them. You're not going to tell me that your Mama doesn't allow you to ride?"

Annabelle quickly interposed, "Richard is only five years old. There's plenty of time for him to have his own mount."

"Five and a half," corrected Richard, frowning.

Dalmar flashed him a commiserating man-to-man look. "If you like, we could go riding in the park some morning before the paths are choked with carriages and so on. Naturally, I'll supply the mounts."

"Thank you. But I am afraid that is impossible," said Annabelle.

"Mama doesn't ride," said Richard.

"Don't tell me!" exclaimed Dalmar. "She was attacked by a horse when she was a child."

Richard chortled.

Annabelle glowered. "I was thrown by a horse," she said, as stiff as a board. When no one tendered any interest, she went on in an aggrieved tone, "My shoulder was dislocated. It was agony to have it put to rights."

"Quite," said the Earl. "When you come down to Gilcomston—that's my estate in Hampshire, by the by—I'll teach you both to ride."

"I don't want to learn to ride," said Annabelle, deliberately employing her best lecturing voice, the one that never failed to send her employees scurrying for cover.

The Earl was not intimidated. "Balderdash! Everyone should know how to ride. Even ladies. Isn't that so, Richard?"

The boy's eyes widened. He carefully avoided his mother's scrutiny. "She won't, though. Nobody can persuade her, not even Uncle Charles."

"Leave it to me," said Dalmar.

Annabelle caught the complacent and thoroughly masculine smile which Dalmar flashed at her son and, a moment later, the replica of that same smile on her son's lips. A little desperately, she insisted, "Nothing and no one is ever going to persuade me

134

to get on a horse again," and with great dignity she picked up her needles and dashed off a row of knitting, only to discover that she had dropped two stitches in her blind haste. She'd be damned if she would ever knit another thing again!

"Hell and damnation!" raged Annabelle. She slowly lifted her eyes, daring her startled companions to say one word in her dispraise.

It was Richard who first gave in to a bout of laughter. Dalmar soon followed. Annabelle began by glaring, but something in the situation tickled her fancy. She relented.

"Nobody's perfect," she said lamely, smiling, and bent her head to examine her handiwork. Slowly, stitch by stitch, she began to unpick her work.

It was then that Dalmar finally condescended to open the box which had occasioned so much curiosity when he had first walked into the garden.

"A knight," said Richard, and reverently held one up for his mother's inspection.

Annabelle glanced into the box. "I have no objection to knights," she said.

Richard explained the remark. "Mama doesn't like guns and war games."

With his eyes on the boy, Dalmar drawled, "Ladies seldom do. But then, we're not playing war games. These are yours, if you want them. They're not new, you'll observe. They were given to me by an uncle when I was just a little older than you are now. I told him, you see, that when I grew up I wanted to be a knight."

"Instead of which you became a soldier," interposed Annabelle with a smile, having resigned herself to the fact that her opinions weighed little in this masculine tête-à-tête.

"They're one and the same," said Dalmar. "A knight was first and foremost a warrior. His whole life was a preparation for the battlefield."

"Mama likes knights," said the boy.

"Yes, I gathered from the plethora of pictures on your walls that you had made a study of the subject."

"Rubbings," said Richard. "Mama does them from brasses on tombs."

135

"Rubbings?"

"It's an art form that comes from the East," said Annabelle. "I read about it in a book once." Throwing the Earl a sidelong glance, she went on, "It helps pass the time when everyone is out riding."

Ignoring the jibe, Dalmar said, "These are the English at the Battle of Poitiers." He slipped his hand into the box and withdrew one of the pieces. "And this is their commander, the Prince of Wales."

"The Black Prince," exclaimed the boy, holding out his hand for the knight.

"Why did you want to be a knight when you were a boy?" asked Annabelle. "Most boys want to be soldiers."

Dalmar turned a dazzling grin on Annabelle. "Perhaps it was the allure of saving maidens in distress, though to be sure, in these modern times, it's hard to come upon one of their number. They're almost extinct, you know."

"I don't doubt," she said dryly, "that saving maidens in distress is not all it's cracked up to be."

"You're wrong there," he said, and laughed when the sparks flew from her eyes. "No, really, there was something in the knight's code of chivalry that held me in thrall."

"Every morning, Mama and I play the game of St. George rescuing the damsel in distress," said Richard. On an afterthought, he added proudly, "I'm St. George."

"And naturally, your mother would be the damsel."

"The dragon," corrected the boy, "and then St. George's horse."

With a gravity that belied the smile in his eyes, the Earl remarked, "How remiss of me not to have guessed it. And how very appropriate."

"Yes," flashed Annabelle, "isn't it? And since I am on the receiving end of so much knightly chivalry, I can assure you that my opinion of it is not so high as it once was."

"But dragons represent everything that is evil," argued Dalmar. "It would be totally reprehensible for St. George to be merciful to the dragon unless the beast showed some evidence of reforming his character and way of life. Too much is at stake, you see, if you'll excuse the pun."

With a sudden flash of insight, she scoffed, "You're a romantic! I'll bet that's why you are a soldier! Tell me, Lord Dalmar," she asked archly, "do you really believe that you've given the best years of your life for king and country?" Belatedly, she realized that she had thrown out the very words that Temple had used the night before, and she could have bitten her tongue out.

Leveling a hard, impenetrable stare at her, Dalmar replied quietly, "I am not so naïve as to see everything in black and white. Nor am I so stupid as to think black is white or vice versa. It happens sometimes that a man is compelled to choose the lesser of two evils. It behooves him to pursue his course with honor. Yes, I believe I have been fighting to protect all that I hold dear. As for the best years of my life—who can say? However, I fervently hope that they are ahead of me, which is more than can be said for many of my comrades who paid the supreme price, willingly, for an ideal—life with honor." He shrugged, "Or king and country. It matters not how one calls it."

Into the charged silence, the boy said, "My father was a soldier."

Dalmar's expression instantly softened. "And a very fine soldier he was too, so I've been told."

"I have his spurs and saber. Would you care to see them, sir?"

"Thank you. It would be an honor."

"Mama?"

The look that Annabelle bestowed on Dalmar was compounded in equal parts of gratitude and apology. In her vanity, and wishing only to score points off the Earl, she had forgotten that her son was present. That the boy should think ill of his father because of any careless word that fell from her lips was insupportable. Wishing to make amends to both Dalmar and her son, she said, "You see how it is with us poor mothers, Lord Dalmar. Having lost a husband, I have no wish for my son to become a soldier. But if Richard turns out to be half the man his father was, I shall be very proud indeed."

Her eyes averted, she went on resolutely, "I'm sure I speak for my son when I say that we would consider it an honor if you

137

could be persuaded to join us for dinner, that is, if you are free?"

"Oh rather! Please, sir," seconded the boy.

She lifted her lashes and chanced a quick look at the Earl. The warmth which radiated from his eyes seemed to reach out and enfold her.

"Thank you," he said, "I should be delighted."

"We dine very early on Sunday," she said, smiling shyly. "And only on leftovers. Cold mutton and ham, and second-day gooseberry pie."

He gave an exaggerated groan and winked at Richard. "Now she tells me what's for dinner! And after I've already accepted the invitation! Your mother is a very devious woman, you know. Oh well, we knights never go back on our word. But next time she won't outwit me so easily."

Annabelle blinked and could not help wondering how she had come to such an about-face. If there was any outwitting going on, it certainly was not by her design. "Then that's settled," she said, slicing a suspicious look at the Earl. Turning to her son, Annabelle said, "Dinner will be on the table in half an hour. After dinner you may show Lord Dalmar Papa's spurs and saber."

Galvanzied into action by his mother's unlooked-for capitulation on all suits, he gathered the treasured box of knights into his arms. "Oh sir, this is the best present I've ever had in my life. I can't wait till James sees it. He doesn't have any knights in his collection."

"James?" asked Dalmar.

"My cousin. He's older than I," confided Richard.

"In that case, I'd better explain the armor and crests and so on. Why don't you set them out in the schoolroom somewhere and we'll look over them later?"

As if afraid that the grown-ups might change their minds given time to think, Richard made for the back of the house as fast as his short legs could carry him.

"He's a fine boy," remarked Dalmar.

"I think so," Annabelle concurred, and was surprised at the flash of pleasure his words had produced in her heart.

Dalmar walked to the flagstones where Richard had earlier

set out the clothes pegs. He became lost in thought.

"The Battle of Waterloo, if I'm not mistaken," he said, finally.

"What?"

"Your son. He has quite an imagination. You may forbid war games as much as you like, Annabelle, but you can't prevent boys from being boys. He's circumvented you. The child has set out these old clothes pegs as if they were whole divisions in Wellington's army."

"I should have guessed," she said. "And don't tell me I'm fighting a losing battle. I already know it. It's just—well, I don't want to raise my son to be a soldier."

He smiled the strangest bittersweet smile. She did not know what to make of it.

Abruptly he asked, "Your husband fell at Badajoz, as I understand?"

"Yes," said Annabelle without elaboration.

"What are you? Richard's stepmother?"

She was completely taken aback by the bald question. "I b-beg your pardon?" she stammered.

"Who was the child's mother? Not an English girl, if appearances are anything to go by."

"A Spanish girl," she said, frowning.

"Ah, that explains it!" He was remembering the galleries in the Palais Royal and how Annabelle had resisted purchasing the pair of Spanish combs. "What happened?"

"What is this, Dalmar, an inquisition?"

"I'm just curious. Please don't be angry. Are you saying that you've adopted the boy?"

"I'm Richard's guardian. Edgar sent Richard home to me when the boy's mother died. I don't see what this has to say to anything."

"Don't you?"

There was humor in his voice, but also a deep well of some emotion which melted Annabelle's incipient annoyance. With one hand she shaded her eyes against the light and peered up at him.

"You're a very generous woman, Mrs. Jocelyn," he said. "Not many wives would do as much as you've done."

She was tempted to leave him with his illusions. Something in her nature, however, caviled at this unmerited encomium. She sighed. "No, I'm not generous," she confessed. "I wanted children more than anything. It was impossible. Edgar was not here. I'll admit I was shocked, hurt—oh, you know what I mean—when I first heard about Richard. What wife wouldn't be? But it all worked out for the best. Oh dear, I didn't mean that the way it sounded. What I mean is . . ."

"Yes, I know what you mean." With one finger under her chin, he tipped her head back and held her eyes with his. "Nevertheless, you're afraid to take a chance on another man."

Giving him back stare for stare, she asked coolly, "What makes you say so?"

He let her go. Placing one foot on the bench, and bracing one arm against his knee, he leaned toward her. "It's as clear as the nose on your face," he told her, his eyes brimming with laughter. "Consider! As a child you were attacked by a dog, ergo no more dogs. When you were learning to ride, you were thrown by a horse, ergo no more horses. As a woman, you were hurt by a man, ergo no more men. Annabelle Jocelyn, appearances to the contrary, you are a coward!"

Her eyes widened, and she blinked rapidly, as if to dispel something from her lashes. "Coward?" she repeated. It was a novel idea and one that she had never before entertained. "Oh no," she said, "you must be mistaken. It's only that I know my strengths and weaknesses. I never take up anything I can't excel in."

"Coward!" he reiterated, his eyes compelling. "I wonder what more in life you will give up because the specter of failure terrifies you?"

She glanced at the knitting in her lap and could not help grinning. "I don't believe in attempting the impossible," she said demurely.

He laughed. "Don't despair. You'll soon be attempting any number of things you once thought were beyond you."

"What is that supposed to mean?" Her wariness returned in full force.

"It means, my love, that by the time I've finished with you, your life is going to be filled with dogs and horses, figuratively speaking, yes, and literally too."

"And men?" she asked coyly, her small teeth bared.

His eyes held hers for a long moment. "Only one," he said softly. "Yours truly, to be precise. And it follows, naturally, a houseful of babies."

Her jaw dropped. She said the first thing that came into her head. "I'll have you know that my father is a vicar."

A look of surprise crossed his face, but his only comment was, "So?"

"So," she expostulated, "so you must see that I could never become your mistress."

"Oh that!" he said with a dismissive gesture. "You're harking back to the Palais Royal. What else could I offer when I thought you already married and estranged from your husband?"

Shocked, she asked, "*Are* you offering marriage?"

"Yes," he replied.

She stared at him blindly. Again without thinking, she said, "You would turn my life upside down."

"No more than you would mine," he answered, his smile widening.

"But why? We scarcely know each other. You don't love me. I don't understand."

"Annabelle, I know you as intimately as a man can know a woman. We're lovers, for God's sake. I'm thirty-four years old. I've spent the last seventeen years with the army in foreign parts. As I once told you, I don't regard myself as a professional soldier. I know there's more to life than sleeping under hedgerows, forced marches, and cavalry charges. I'm ready for a different kind of life, and I want it all."

"What exactly do you want?" she asked, eyeing him curiously.

"The usual. A home, a wife, children—a personal stake in the future, and someone to share it with. Is that so hard to understand?"

It wasn't, of course. Hadn't she experienced the same kind of longing when she was younger? But that was eons ago. She was not the girl she once was. Still, something in his tone or his words or his serious expression touched her deeply. In some sense he seemed to be a rather lonely man, which surprised her. She could not imagine what it must be like to be a soldier for so many years and away from one's home and everything one held dear.

"What about your parents?" she asked. "You must have been just a boy when you joined the army. Didn't they object, or try to force you to sell out and return home?"

In a voice which warned her that she was trespassing, he said, "My father was dead. My mother had remarried. When she died, there was nothing to come home to."

"Oh," she said, and did not know what else to say. She lowered her eyelashes to screen her expression. A pair of impeccable hessians came into view.

Above her head she heard him say, "Annabelle, we could make a good life together. Just give me a chance and I'll prove it to you."

She was possessed of the strongest urge to give in to him. A moment's reflection was enough to steady her. Marriage was not one of the things at which she had excelled.

"Truly," she said, smiling up at him. "I don't wonder at your ambition. But I'm not the woman you should be talking to. I already have everything I want. There's nothing I would gain by marriage, and much that I might lose."

"What, for instance?"

"My property, for a start."

"You mean Bailey's, of course. Annabelle, there are ways and means of tying up a wife's property so that a husband can't get his hands on it. You could settle it on your son, for that matter."

"I'm aware of it. But even if I did, if I married, what's to stop my husband from managing my property to suit himself? He could do it, if he had a mind to, and there's not a blessed thing I could do about it. The law recognizes that as a single woman I have some intelligence to manage my own affairs. If I were to marry, the law suddenly decrees that I'm an imbecile and subject to the law of my husband."

"And if I swore to you that I would not, under any circumstances in my role as husband, make any attempt to

142

meddle in your business?"

"Would you go so far?"

"You have my word on it. However, I would expect a reciprocal promise on your part."

"What does that mean?"

His gray eyes moved from her bemused expression and gazed steadfastly away into the middle distance. "Supposing—theoretically speaking, you understand—that our business interests should come into conflict?"

"You mean, if we were to become competitors?" she interjected, amused.

"Something like that, or adversaries. Would you be prepared to offer me the same terms?"

"I don't think I understand."

"If we were competitors in business, would you expect me to suppress my own best interests simply by virtue of the fact that we were friends, or whatever?"

Enlightenment gradually dawned. It was Murray, the publisher, who had brought Dalmar to her party. It seemed obvious that the Earl had holdings in some publishing house or other. She laughed. "Dalmar, you don't know me very well. Competition is the spice of life. I thrive on it. You can try to best me at my own game, but I give you fair warning, in business, I always go for the jugular."

He finally looked at her. "In other words," he said, smiling, "do my worst?"

She shrugged. "If you get in my way, I'll mow you down."

"And I'm free to do the same to you?"

"You can try," she scoffed.

"And it won't make a jot of difference to our friendship?" he persisted. "Can I have your word on it?"

"Good grief," she exclaimed, "of course! What do you take me for? I'm not some silly, frivolous creature who breaks down in tears or has a fit of the vapors when things go against her. It's a man's world out there. I meet my business competitors on their terms. It's not only men who know how to take a spill and come up smiling. I'm not at outs with Murray or Longmans or a single one of my competitors, and yet *we've* tried to put each other to the wall on more occasions than I care to remember."

She paused for breath, and he interjected, "Careful, Annabelle. I may hold you to those words one of these days."

"Do," she rashly declared.

"It will never come to that, I hope," he instantly responded.

Her brow furrowed in thought as she took in his bland expression. "Have you bought into one of the houses, Dalmar?" Strange, she thought, that there had not been a whisper of anything coming on the market. Her mind did a quick inventory and came up with a blank.

"You're going too fast, Annabelle. We were talking in hypothetical terms, remember? The gist of what I am trying to say is this—our business and personal lives are to remain separate. What transpires in the one sphere is not to be transferred to the other. I gave you my word on it, and you gave me yours."

"Did I?" she murmured, suddenly uneasy. The thought occurred to her that Dalmar looked surprisingly like a replete jungle cat who had just risen from the table. She brushed away the absurd notion. She had done no more than promise to conduct herself as she habitually did. Even members of Parliament on opposite sides of the House were known to attack each other ferociously during debate and fraternize before and after in the lobby of the House of Commons. There was nothing personal in such rivalry. Then why, she asked herself, did she feel as if her hands had just been tied?

"Now that little matter has been disposed of," she heard him say, "what's to stop us getting married next week or even sooner?"

"My preference," she stated, knowing that the tartness in her tone was occasioned by the vague feeling of having been taken advantage of when her mind was elsewhere.

"But why?"

He seemed to be honestly at a loss. "Because," she said, trying not to antagonize him, "as I said before, I have everything I want—my business, my house, my son, my friends. A husband would just be an added distraction, and one I can well do without. Don't forget," she said roguishly, trying to take the sting out of her words, "I'm thirty years old—too

144

old to change my ways to suit any man."

"And what about passion?" he said, moving closer. "Where does that fit into your life?"

Rather primly, she retorted, "That's something ladies have no interest in."

Grinning devilishly, he replied, "That's what I thought until I met you. And to think I've steered clear of the breed since I was a greenhorn! If I'd known then what I know now, I wouldn't have been so averse to the thought of marriage. Annabelle, you're the most responsive woman it's ever been my pleasure to take to bed. I can't wait to repeat the experience."

She went as stiff as a poker when he sat down and crowded her to the edge of the bench. "It was very kind of you to give Richard a set of knights," she said, and raised her knitting needles in an involuntary defensive gesture.

"Was it?" he asked, smiling broadly, and prised the weapons from her fingers. "I love this mole." He brushed her cheek with his knuckles.

"I'm sure he'll have hours of fun playing with them," she went on, determined to steer the conversation into safer waters.

"Will he?" With his forefinger he gently traced the delicate arch of one dark brow.

Distracted, Annabelle babbled, "Actually, the Black Prince has never been one of my favorites. It's his brother, John of Gaunt, whom I've always admired."

"Mmm. You have the longest, silkiest eyelashes I've ever seen."

"In my opinion, he's never had the recognition that he deserves. What do you think?"

"What I think is that I love the way they quiver when I bring myself into your body."

Her eyes darted to the windows at the back of the house. "Please, David," she begged. "Someone will see us."

"I'm only talking," he said, his voice turning husky. "No one but you can hear what I'm saying."

His fingers brushed the nape of her neck, then lost themselves in her hair. Annabelle squirmed. "Don't!" she pleaded. Her skin felt as if it was melting where he touched it.

"Don't you like it?" he crooned. "Better get used to it, Annabelle. Next time I take you to bed, I won't be incapacitated because of injuries." His tone darkened, became liquid and overlaid with a masculine intent that was flagrant in its attempt to seduce. "I have a million fantasies I want to act out. There are ways I want to take you, things I want to do to you . . ."

Her breathing suddenly became lodged in her throat. "Please . . ."

"You're remembering, aren't you?" he whispered, and she felt the stroke of his tongue in her ear. "Good. I'm never going to let you forget how it was between us."

She tried to rise, but he prevented it by the simple expedient of stretching one arm along the back of the bench, confining her shoulders. "My son . . ." she groaned, trying to marshal her defenses.

". . . is occupied," he answered. "You can't breathe, can you? And your heart is pounding fit to burst. I know. I'm feeling it too." He captured her hand and brought it to his lips. "I'm not touching you in any way that counts, and yet you're burning with fever, aren't you? That's why we are right together. You don't feel this way with anyone else, and neither do I. Passion, Annabelle . . . it's important."

"No . . ." Her eyes were closed, her lips open, and he could feel the deep, shuddering breaths that lifted her shoulders.

"Give me more Annabelle," he whispered, his voice unsteady, hoarse. "I want those little sounds you make when I'm thrusting into you."

Her head angled back on his shoulder. "David . . . stop."

Words, hot and heedless, spilled from his mouth. "You don't want me to stop. Not really. I could take you now if I wanted to. If I stroked my fingers into you, I know what I would find. You're ready for me now, aren't you Annabelle? *Aren't you?*"

She cried out and curled into him, her fist clutching at the lapel of his jacket.

Relentlessly, as if driven by a demon, he pushed her. "You

want me as much as I want you. Say it. *Say it!*"

Bewildered more by the anger than by the passion in his voice and more confused still by the strength of the unfamiliar and unwelcome longings which swamped her, she began to weep.

Instantly contrite, he murmured, "I'm a brute! Hush, love!" He turned her face up and kissed away her tears.

"Why?" she asked, between sobs.

He angled her a droll look of mingled apology and reproach. "I never thought to see Annabelle Jocelyn reduced to tears. And here I was, hoping that you would throw yourself into my arms and kiss me into silence. You certainly know how to depress the pretensions of a man who is trying to make love to you."

She gave a very watery smile, followed in quick succession by several watery sniffs. "This isn't my usual mode," she carefully explained. "I never cry."

He laughed, a sound filled with delight and heartwarming tenderness. "You don't have to tell me that. No really, I expected you to box my ears. Though frankly, those tear-brimmed eyes are devastating—a secret weapon on a par with Congreve's rockets. See how you've taken the wind out of my sails?"

Between sniffs, she said, "I hate women who use tears as a weapon."

He produced a handkerchief and carefully dabbed her cheeks. "Better?" He gave her one of his unconsciously heart-stopping smiles which Annabelle had long ago decided was his own secret weapon in the war between the sexes.

"You didn't answer my question," she said, and lifted her eyes to look directly into his. "Why?"

"I wanted to prove something to you."

"That I'm a woman without morals?"

He was tempted to laugh, but he said gravely, "No. That you are a woman of passion, and that passion belongs to me. You made it so when you gave yourself to me that first night. We have something unique, and I'm not about to let you throw it away in your ignorance. And you *are* ignorant in the game of love, Annabelle—a veritable novice, if memory serves. Are you blushing?"

"No. I never blush," said Annabelle, blushing.

"Mmm. In the same way, I suppose, that you never cry. Annabelle, you'd argue with me on any and every triviality. But this fight is too important. I won't let you win it. Better make up your mind to it. I've tasted your passion, Annabelle Jocelyn, and I won't settle for anything less."

"But I don't *want* passion," she averred, as if he had just suggested that she harbor a felon in her bed. A secretive smile curved her lips. "You're not offering love, I notice, and frankly, *I'm* not interested in anything less."

Laughing, he said, "You would like that, wouldn't you—for me to fall in love with you? It would give you the upper hand, and we both know it. Annabelle, you may expect a soldier to know a few tricks when it comes to the art of self-preservation. Trust me. Love is a weapon that weakens even the strongest. I wouldn't wish it on my worst enemy." His smile widened. "How would you like it if I were to make you fall in love with me?"

"You could try,' she said, her eyes dancing at the thought of the challenge.

"No. I don't particularly want your love. I'm happy with what we've got. I've never wanted any woman as much as I've wanted you. And I know the feeling is mutual."

A gong sounded from within the house.

"Dinner," said Annabelle, patently relieved.

Ignoring the hint, Dalmar prevented her from rising. "I warn you, I'm not going to let up for a minute until you finally give in. And don't be so quick to turn up your nose at what I'm offering—a home, children, a father for your son, a husband whose fidelity and protection you can always count on, and . . ." his voice dropped to a husky whisper, "your nights filled with the sweet heat of passion."

His eyes were too bold, his grin too knowing for comfort, thought Annabelle. Her own feeble smile and evasive glances lacked something in comparison. Squaring her shoulders, she said in the most confident voice she could muster, "I'll think about it, Dalmar, and that's a promise."

Inwardly, she told herself there was nothing to think about.

Still, it left her wondering about the delicious feeling of anticipation which seemed to bring every sense and faculty alive in his presence. The emotion was not unlike those she had experienced when she'd first taken over the reins of Bailey's and faced down an officeful of hostile employees. And now she had them all eating out of her hand. The thought was positively tantalizing.

Chapter Nine

From her house on Greek Street, traversing the south side of Soho Square, to her offices in Frith Street took Annabelle all of ten minutes on foot. She had always had a fondness for this cosmopolitan corner of the city. Émigrés and their descendents, refugees from persecution in their own countries, Greek, Portuguese, Dutch, French Huguenots and, more recently, victims of the French Terror—all were to be found in and around Soho Square. For the most part they were prosperous artisans and found a ready market for their skills and wares. Shop windows displayed a plethora of goods—fine lace, hand-crafted violins, delicately wrought silverware, elaborately carved furniture, and, Annabelle's particular temptation, bolts of the finest kerseymeres and satins skillfully dyed in a profusion of colors. Annabelle, wise to her vices, made it a rule never to arrive at her office before ten of the clock, the hour when shutters came down and shopkeepers opened their doors. Nevertheless, street hawkers, selling everything from eels to eyeglasses, were already peddling their wares, and their raucous cries as they tried to din each other out rose, on occasion, to an alarming pitch.

Annabelle, with footman in tow—a tiresome convention, in her opinion—observed the scene with a spring in her step and a sparkle in her eye. It seemed to her on this particular fine Monday morning that colors were inexplicably brighter, the air crisper, the birds chirpier, the pedestrians happier, the sights and sounds around her more lively than she could ever remember. Humming tunelessly under her breath, she purchased a small posy of daisies from one of the young coster girls who habituated the area and she swept into the imposing brick premises of Bailey's Press, Booksellers and Publisher.

On the ground floor, fronting the street, to the right of the entrance, three rooms were given over to the bookselling part of the business. Annabelle called out a cheery greeting to the manager and sales assistants, who were folding away dust sheets and plying feather dusters along shelves and flat counters set out with books. She entered the door on her left and stepped into the printing shop.

Annabelle's eyes flicked over her fleet of new printing presses and the small army of leather-aproned pressmen and printers who serviced the tools of their trade like any well-trained corps of artillery gunners on the field of battle. As it always did when she entered this hive of activity, Annabelle's heart beat just a little faster. Only the *Times* in Fleet Street could boast a more modern facility. The cost to replace the old temperamental wooden presses with the Earl of Stanhope's more expensive cast-iron models had seemed, at the time, exorbitant, though to be sure, when his lordship had first broached the subject at one of Lady Bessborough's soirées, Annabelle had thought the old boy merely an endearing eccentric known for a quaint predilection to inventing things. Her foreman had soon disabused her of that notion.

Though Douglas had talked in technicalities which Annabelle could not fathom, she had understood enough to grasp that the Earl's latest invention, an improvement on the first Stanhope Press, promised a clearer impression and a relatively trouble-free operation. In the two years since the presses had been installed, Bailey's titles had increased from a modest thirty per annum to almost double that number. Not that the Earl's presses could be given sole credit for that achievement. By Annabelle's design, Bailey's books had become considerably thinner over the years. Thinner, cheaper, and highly competitive.

With the scent of the printers' ink in her nostrils, a pleasant odor which invariably lifted her spirits, Annabelle made for the stairs which led to the offices above and the rooms reserved for the bookbinding part of her enterprise. Her secretary and clerk, a fresh-complexioned young man in his late twenties, was there before her, filling two china cups from an earthen teapot on her desk.

Albert Sommerville had joined Bailey's at fourteen years as a printer's devil, and long before Annabelle had taken over at the helm. There wasn't a facet of the business the young man did not know. There wasn't a job he could not do. He was self-educated, articulate, and ambitious. But there was one talent he possessed which Annabelle admired above all others. He wasn't afraid to try something new. And when the going got rough, he wasn't afraid to roll up his sleeves and pitch in to see a job through. Annabelle intended to reward Sommerville's industry by giving him his own domain to preside over. Very soon Bailey's would need its own representative in the highly populated Midlands to find and open up new arteries of distribution for their books. At present, Bailey's normally printed ten thousand copies of every title. Annabelle wanted to double that number. Sommerville was the man to help her achieve her ambition.

There was a twinkle in his eye as he waited patiently for Annabelle to remove her high poke bonnet and green velvet pelisse. Annabelle dismissed her footman, having first accepted a decrepit-looking handgrip which he had dutifully transported all the way from Greek Street.

"The memoirs," she said to her secretary, sinking gracefully into the chair he held for her. "Good morning, Albert. I see from your smirk that you're about to tell me 'I told you so,' or congratulate me on my astute business acumen. Give me a minute, will you, till I have my first infusion of the day."

Wordlessly and with great deliberation Sommerville laid a calf-bound volume on the cluttered desk top in front of Annabelle. She studied it silently for some few minutes, and, her curiosity notwithstanding, continued to sip the strong brew of hot tea until her cup was drained. Only then did she set cup and saucer aside and open the book to the frontispiece. She read the title page and let out an unholy squeal of delight. *More Tales of the Settlers*, she breathed, and reverently fingered the pages of the volume.

"These arrived Friday, not long after you left," said Albert, smiling broadly.

"How many did they send us?"

"Five thousand, most of which have already been dispatched to our various outlets."

"How many did you set aside for Bailey's?"

"Forty copies, as per instructed. Of course, there's only thirty-nine, now that I snitched one for you." Referring to the manager of the bookshop, he went on, "Armstrong told me to tell you that you owe him ten shillings."

"It's worth it," said Annabelle, skimming through the pages as if she would devour the book whole. "This stuff is absolutely authentic."

"How do you know?" He was quizzing her.

"I can feel it in my bones when I read it."

"What? Do you believe all that nonsense about shooting the rapids, building log cabins, and fighting off Indian attacks? It's my surmise the author, what's-his-name, has a nice safe desk job in the heart of the city. He's probably never seen a blade of grass, let alone an Indian."

"I don't care if it is all imagination," said Annabelle, her defenses aroused. "It's like stepping into another world. Besides, they're published in New York and widely read there. If it weren't authentic, the Americans would know. Trust me, Albert. In another year or two, this author is going to have an enormous following on both sides of the Atlantic. And I," she said, preening a little, "have the patents to publish his next work in the British Isles."

"What if nobody cares for that sort of thing?" he goaded.

"They will, they will," she said, and sliced him a faintly annoyed look. "At least, anyone with an ounce of imagination will. Don't disparage what you don't know Albert. The least you can do is read the darned thing before passing judgment."

"D'you know what I think?"

"What?"

"That only highborn gentlemen and ladies who never get

154

their hands soiled are going to go into transports over the hardships these first settlers in the New World endured."

Sommerville's approach to his employer might have been thought in the eyes of some to come just short of impertinence. Annabelle did not see it in that light. He was too intelligent and resourceful to offer a blind obedience. From the very first, he had questioned every innovation she had tried to introduce. Some she had discarded at his persuasion. Those that were adopted, he threw himself behind unstintingly. In short, he was one of the few employees who was not intimidated by her, and no one lost favor in Annabelle's eyes by standing up to her.

"Don't think! Work!" she said. She reached into the grip at her feet, removed a sheaf of closely written papers, and slapped them down on her desk.

"The latest chapter?"

"Yes. We're in Brussels now. Frankly, this is the first episode I've found to be really diverting. And the first time to date that I have not been able to penetrate the identity of one of Monique Dupres's characters. She calls him 'Sir Spider,' but why this should be so, I haven't an inkling."

"What happens?"

"Read it and you'll find out. Did you get those chapbooks for me?"

"They're over there," he said, indicating a table along one wall.

"And what about the samples of paper and cloth covers?"

"I talked to Delancey. He's made up your samples for you, but he's not sold on the idea."

"That doesn't surprise me. He's a bookbinder who takes pride in his work. The trouble is, he wants his work to last till doomsday. Some books just aren't written for posterity. Their appeal is for the here and now. Paper-and-cloth bindings, if viable, are all that they deserve."

"Yes, and some books deserve to be stillborn," he said meaningfully, retrieving the pages of Monique Dupres's diaries which Annabelle had slapped on her desk.

He made a quick exit before Annabelle could deliver her predictable lecture on the policy prevailing at Bailey's with respect to the publication of works of dubious content. Frowning ,she gazed at the closed door between their offices. After a moment, she bent over her desk and began her day as she usually did, with correspondence.

The morning was half over before she had her first visitor. In that time, she had already made her rounds, conferring with the foreman in each department. She was back in her office, at her desk, reviewing the more polished and literary prose with which Albert had imbued her rather stark translation of the latest chapter of Monique Dupres's memoirs when Lord Temple was shown in.

"Gerry," she said, rising and offering him her hand.

Tea was sent for. They spent a good ten minutes talking in circles. Annabelle became restive. Though she had no real wish to hear any scandal relating to Dalmar's past or present, she was anxious for the interview to be over so that she could get back to her work. When Annabelle became involved in a task, she could scarcely tolerate interruptions, as her staff well knew. On one level, her mind framed appropriate replies to Temple's spate of chit-chat; on another level, her thoughts were occupied with the mysterious "Sir Spider" whom Albert's prose had imbued with a certain devil-may-care charm. She thought of the scapegrace knight and his barefaced effrontery, and a laugh was startled out of her.

"I beg your pardon," she said, and laughed again. Of course, after that, she was forced to share the joke.

Unsmiling, Temple observed, "You're still resolved to publish these diaries?" He picked up the pages Annabelle had been studying and looked through them idly.

"Adamantly," she assured him.

"Mark my words, before the ink is dry, Bailey's Press will be up to its neck in lawsuits. I must have been insane to give you escort to Paris."

"Why did you?"

He took a moment or two to reply to her question, but whether it was because something on the page he was reading had caught his interest or because he was choosing his words with care was not clear to Annabelle.

156

Finally, he looked up and said, "Because, my dear, you would simply have found someone else to escort you, or worse, relied on your grooms for protection. I know you to be a resourceful lady. I had hopes, of course, that given time, you would see how utterly impossible it is to even think of publishing this material. Annabelle, destroy these diaries before you get hurt. These men are powerful figures both in Court and in government circles. They won't let you get away with this."

"In a court of law . . ."

"It will never come to that. I'll wager anything you like that right this minute someone is hot on your trail. How many people know about the diaries? How long do you think it will be before they're tracked down to Bailey's Press?"

Visibly shaken, she said, "This is England. There are laws to protect the innocent. I've done nothing wrong." He shook his head, but before he could remonstrate, she cut him off. "Gerry, was there some point to this visit? If not, there are any number of things which need my attention."

If her abruptness annoyed him, he covered it well. He took a few halting steps around the room before turning on his heel to face her.

"We've been friends for a long time," he said simply.

Her expression softened. "Yes."

"I've always looked out for your interests."

"Without fail," she agreed.

His voice lowered, became husky. "Give up Dalmar, Annabelle. The man is dangerous. He isn't for you."

"You've said that before. What does it mean?"

"He's a suspected murderer."

Her response was quick and automatic, but for all that, she meant every word. "I don't believe it! It's not in the man to be a murderer. Besides, I always understood that murderers went to the gallows."

"He's clever, I'll give you that. He was cleared at the inquest, but only because his mother and younger brother testified on his behalf. It was widely known that there was never any love lost between Dalmar and his father."

"Is that whom he is supposed to have killed—his father?"

"Oh, there's no question that his was the hand that struck the blow. He claimed it was an accident, but no one who knew his family believed him. His father hated him. His mother was indifferent."

"But . . ."

"Yes?"

"From what he said, he must have been only a boy when his father died."

"Just short of seventeen. Old enough to run away to the army. Well, where else was he to go with such a stigma attached to his name? If he'd stayed in England, he would have been completely ostracized. And even supposing he's fallen heir to his uncle's title and fortune, I make no doubt that there will still be some doors that are barred against him."

Speechless, she stared at him, shock clearly registering in her expression. Almost to herself she murmured, "Dear God! What a waste!" She was thinking that a boy should have the chance to do a few foolish things, get into a few wild scrapes, before he was asked to take on the responsibilities of a man. Hard on that thought came a rush of anger for the parents who had failed him, and a society which had carelessly thrust him beyond the pale. In some obscure way, she recognized that her feelings were inextricably bound up with the fierce, protective emotions she experienced for her son. No child should ever be alone and unloved and left to fend for himself.

Aloud, she said, "He deserves . . ." Her voice trailed off. She could not think of a single thing that would recompense him for so much lost time—in truth, the best years of his life. She remembered her taunt in the garden and was ashamed.

A voice from the open doorway quietly drawled, "Yes, Annabelle, what do I deserve? Pray continue."

She spun to face him, and a slow, guilty flush stole under her skin from throat to hairline. "Dalmar," she said, and fell silent.

She swallowed with difficulty. Across the short space that divided them, his eyes locked with hers. She was aware that Temple had made some noncommittal remark, but he might as

158

well not have been there for all the attention Dalmar paid him. Dalmar's eyes held hers, and he repeated the question.

Her lips felt dry. She wet them with the tip of her tongue. Into the silence she said, "You deserve . . . you deserve some happiness for what you lost when you were a boy. I hope you find it."

"Thank you." The tension across his shoulders visibly relaxed.

Though she covered it well, Annabelle was self-conscious to a degree and was excessively glad that, on this occasion at least, Dalmar and Temple conducted themselves with commendable civility. When Lord Temple finally took his leave, there was nothing to show that there was any awkwardness between the two men. On the contrary, they gave every appearance of having enjoyed the encounter.

The minutes passed. Dalmar said nothing, but Annabelle could detect a waiting quality in him.

When it became evident that he would not be the one to break the silence between them, she said, "How much did you hear?"

"More than enough," he replied, his look unfathomable.

"I wasn't prying."

"I don't care if you were. But if you want to know anything, come to me."

She became conscious that they were both standing. Seating herself, she invited him to do the same. His eyes traveled the cluttered room, touching on the untidy stacks of books piled every which way on the floor, tables strewn with broadsheets and chapbooks, her desk littered with layer upon layer of manuscripts and papers. Finally his eyes came to rest on her.

He pulled his chair closer. "How can you ever find anything in this chaos?"

"Organized chaos," she said, smiling. "As each task is completed, I tidy things away."

He quirked one brow. "You must be working on a hundred different things at once." Abruptly, his tone changed. "It was self-defense, you know."

"What?"

"My father. I killed him in a duel. Temple was right. It wasn't an accident. But it wasn't murder either. It was self-defense." As he continued to speak, an edge of bitterness crept into his voice. "Not unnaturally, my mother wanted to protect the family name. To admit that her husband tragically lost his life in a mock duel while demonstrating the finer points of the sport to his son was more acceptable than to have our private scandals become common knowledge."

When it was evident that he was not about to elaborate, she said simply, "I'm sorry," and wished that she could find the words to adequately express everything she was feeling. It was the boy she pitied, she told herself. The man he had grown into invited any number of emotions, none of them remotely resembling pity. Still . . .

"I assure you, my scars have healed nicely."

"Ah," she replied, equally casual. "You've read my thoughts. I shall have to watch that tendency in future."

He laughed. "You believe me, don't you?"

"That your scars have healed nicely?"

"No. Don't play with me, Annabelle!"

She saw that he had turned very grave, and she quickly replied, "Yes, I believe you."

"Why?"

The question jarred her. She gazed at him for a long interval. Behind her blind stare, pictures, impressions, and fragments of conversations jostled each other in her mind. Taken together, to her way of thinking, they made a solid foundation for trusting the man, at least on one level. Dalmar would do whatever he thought was right, by his lights. Somehow, the thought was not comforting.

"Well?"

"Because," she said, flashing him a look of pure coquetry. "I believe that you are, appearances to the contrary, a man of honor, courage, and kindness itself, and quite without rancor."

"Appearances to the contrary!" he exclaimed, looking at her askance. "What does that mean, may I ask?"

"It means, Dalmar, that on first glance you might easily be

mistaken for a rogue." A thought occurred to her, and she grinned.

"What?" he asked, a matching grin softening the rugged lines of his face.

"When I first saw you I thought you were a pirate, or at the very least, a bandit. I prayed our paths would never cross."

"And now?"

Still smiling, she said, "Don't press your luck. You're here for a reason, I presume. May I know what it is?"

For a moment he looked as if he might argue the point. Suddenly capitulating, he offered with a crooked smile, "Vulgar curiosity. I called in at Greek Street, you see, and Richard told me that I could find you here. I got the impression that he had let the cat out of the bag. Was I wrong?"

"I shall have to talk to that boy," she said, her eyes and fingers suddenly busying themselves with the manuscript which lay conveniently at hand.

"So that's it! I thought as much. You're ashamed of what you do! Are you afraid that the taint of 'shop' will have you thrown out of London's most prestigious drawing rooms? Is that why it's not generally known that you are the driving force behind Bailey's? Somehow I thought you wouldn't give a brass button for the opinions of others."

During this cajolery, Annabelle's head came up. Her eyes flashed. Majestically she rose to her feet. She looked down the length of her unquestionably patrician nose.

Dalmar's lazy grin grew even wider. "Stubble it!" he told her. "I didn't come here to argue. Don't worry, your secret is safe with me. Now show me your little empire."

She was tempted to show him the door, but before the words could form on her lips, he was on the move, pacing about her office, touching everything, shooting questions at her in rapid succession. She could scarcely keep up with him. Without a by-your-leave, he took off on a tour of the building, Annabelle trotting hard at his heels. He had done his homework, she noted, for there wasn't one department from front desk to dispatch where he didn't make a few intelligent observations or flatter her "gaffers" with gratifying interest. By the time they returned to her office, Annabelle was out of breath.

Dalmar was as much fascinated by the change in Annabelle as he had been by the tour of Bailey's. For a solid hour they'd talked nothing but business. By degrees her pose of aloofness had dissipated, leaving in its wake something more resembling a childlike eagerness to share a secret with a cherished friend. He'd seen her flush with pleasure every time he had uttered some mild words of praise. She could deny it to her dying breath, but he knew now that his appeal for the lady was based on more than mere physical attraction. Until then, he had wondered. Something inside him seemed to dissolve. Everything was going to be fine. Soon all that spirit and intelligence, all that warmth and softness which lay just beneath the surface were going to be his. He needed them as much as he needed her passion, if not more. In return he would cherish and protect her, even if it meant protecting her from herself. Especially if it meant protecting her from herself.

Annabelle shut the door softly and leaned back against it, watching him through narrowed eyes. He was at her desk, leafing through the loose pages of Monique Dupres's memoirs, just as Temple had earlier done.

"It's Minerva Press, isn't it?" she said, slanting him a sly look.

He glanced over his shoulder. "Minerva Press?" he repeated slowly, trying to look intelligent.

She pushed away from the door. "Oh, don't look so stupid! You know what I'm talking about. The house that you're trying to buy into—it has to be William Lane's company. I've racked and racked my brains, and it's the only one I can come up with."

"It's not Minerva Press."

"Is it Thomas Kelly then? Is he up to something?"

"Who?"

"Oh, don't give me that innocent look! You know who I mean. Kelly of Paternoster Row, the one who's making money hand over fist by selling the Bible off in installments."

"Annabelle, I haven't an inkling of what you're talking about. But don't stop. I'm intrigued. How is it possible to make

162

money by selling the Bible piece by piece?"

"Copyright," she said, "as if you didn't know."

He sat down in her chair, crossed one booted foot over the other, and made a steeple with his fingers. "I'm burning with curiosity," he told her. "Sit down and explain it to me."

She did. "There's no copyright on the Bible. Hence, no author's advances or royalties."

"I get it. Therefore, there are more profits to be made for the publishing house?"

"Precisely."

"But who would want to buy a Bible? Surely every home has one already?"

"Only the moneyed classes can afford to buy books. There's a whole new reading public out there who are just beginning to show an interest. Only they haven't the money. That's the beauty of Kelly's scheme, you see. They can't afford to buy the Bible at one go. So he's making it easy for them. They buy it piece by piece, and at a price they can afford."

"Fascinating. And there's money to be made from this? Then why isn't everybody doing it?"

"We do, to a greater or lesser degree. But even supposing that we print the odd book where the copyright has run out— that's twenty-eight years after first printing, by the way—our product is still too costly for most people."

"But Annabelle Jocelyn has figured a way to change all that. Am I right?"

She looked, he thought, like Joan of Arc must have looked when she was tied to the stake. Her eyes burned with an almost fanatical light, her breathing quickened, and her skin took on a glow. When she opened her lips to speak, he half expected to hear the ringing tones of a preacher bent on saving the world from damnation.

Her expression suddenly changed, and she said contritely, "I'll only bore you," then quickly sliced him an adorably eager look which invited him to contradict her.

He couldn't resist that look. "Annabelle," he said, "nothing about you could ever bore me. You could recite recipes for all I care and they would be as sweet to my ears as the sonnets

163

of Shakespeare."

"You're sure you want to hear?"

"Positively." He sat back and watched her through the veil of half-lowered lashes. "Go on," he encouraged.

"Earlier, you were asking me about those broadsheets and chapbooks." She gestured to the table along the wall where an assortment of thin picture books and single-page broadsheets were set out.

"And you told me that these scurrilous bits of nonsense were a gold mine for their originators."

Frowning, she said, "Don't be so top-lofty about something you know nothing about. Chapbooks may not be for the man or woman of a more exalted palette, but . . ."

"Annabelle," he scoffed, "I wouldn't let a child get hold of that piffle."

Her lips thinned. "Oh? And what kind of books do you read, Lord Dalmar?"

He shifted uncomfortably under her hard stare. "I haven't had much time for reading lately," he said cautiously.

"Mmm," she mused, "another non-reader, and therefore a potential market for my product. But that's another story. If you're going to get into publishing, Dalmar, you'd better make it your business to learn a thing or two about your readers. I have, and I'll let you into a little secret: I don't care if we're talking about those who read the so-called scurrilous chapbooks or a leatherbound volume authored by Walter Scott, we readers are all captivated by the same thing, more or less."

Though he was not persuaded, he did not know enough to contradict her. He waited patiently as she rose and moved gracefully to the tabletop collection of chapbooks and broadsheets he had earlier perused. After a moment he joined her.

"Look at these titles," she said, "'The King and the Cobbler,' 'St. George and the Dragon,' 'Jack the Giant-Killer.' Doesn't that suggest something to you?"

"What?"

"The old myths and legends, that's what! There's something

164

about them which appeals to everyone. If you're a literary type, you'll go for the ones which are dressed up in a suit of new clothes, you know—Walter Scott's romances, for instance. What do you think all these gothics which women read are? They're the story of St. George and the Dragon, suitably disguised, of course."

"And what about this tripe?" he asked, waving a broadsheet under her nose. "I ask you, Annabelle, 'Shocking Rape and Murder of Two Lovers!' It's a dreadful tale."

"Did you read it?"

"Yes."

"Did you read any of the others?"

"No."

"Aha! I'm onto you," she said, like a cat pouncing on a mouse. "You've betrayed the myth that appeals to you most. I'll wager the only books in your library which you read are those horrid, shocking tales of the old Greek dramatists. Am I right?"

He smiled ruefully. "Yes, but . . ."

"In a broadsheet, these stories would have lurid titles—nothing subtle about them. Let's see now. 'Medea' would be 'Mother Murders Two Innocent Children,' for 'Electra' read 'Dastardly Matricide in Royal Palace,' and for 'Iphigenia,' how about, 'Father Practices Child Sacrifice on Lonely Moor'? The sequel might easily be entitled 'A Mother's Revenge.'"

He laughed. "You've made your point. But surely you're not thinking of getting into chapbooks and broadsheets? I thought Bailey's was a cut above that. Don't you publish books of poetry and essays and so on?"

"We do. But so does every other publisher. There's slim pickings to be had there. Dalmar, let me give you a word of advice: don't try to copy anyone. If Bailey's was to try and become another Longmans, we'd fail miserably. They're good at what they do. Find something that nobody else is doing, or a market that has yet to be tapped. As for chapbooks and broadsheets, I think they've had their day. No, the point I wish to make is this: there are two reasons why this form of literature is doing well. The first is that more people can afford it. The second is that it is widely distributed."

"By street hawkers and peddlers."

"Yes. Quite an impracticable way to sell books. But believe me, Dalmar, for the publisher who comes up with a cheaper product and a better means of distribution than we have at present, the profits are likely to be enormous."

"And you think you have solved the problem?"

"I may have." Her smile was faintly self-congratulatory.

"And?"

"Oh no! I'm not telling you *all* my secrets until I know what you're up to. You might steal a march on me. I've told you more than enough as it is."

His eyes dropped to the pages in his hand. "I would never do anything to hurt you," he said quietly.

"Hurt me?" His words seemed to amuse her. "Dalmar, this is business." She shook her head as if she could not quite believe that anyone could be so naïve. "It's not a question of hurting anyone. We're competitors. You do your best; I'll do mine. If you're going to make a success in this business, you must . . . well . . . forget about the ties of friendship and so on. We've had this discussion before. I thought you understood. Hurting a competitor, even supposing that competitor is a friend, is not the same thing as betraying a friendship. In the marketplace, it's every man for himself."

"Is that your philosophy? No quarter asked or given?"

"Not generally, of course. But . . ."

"Yes, I know. Business is business." He returned her hard, suspicious scrutiny with innocent eyes and a bland smile.

"I'd love to help you get started," she said finally in a conciliatory tone. "If you'd only tell me a little more."

"Nothing's settled, and I would not want a competitor to steal a march on me," he returned suavely.

She tilted her head and looked up at him with reproach in her eyes. "David! I would never do anything unethical!"

"Wouldn't you? What about this stuff?" he asked and he strode to her desk and held out the loose pages of Monique Dupres's memoirs.

Annabelle snatched them out of his hands and clutched

them to her bosom. "You were eavesdropping!" she accused. "You overheard Lord Temple!"

He did not deny it.

With color high on her cheekbones, she stalked to a large oak escritoire, unlocked the bottom drawer, and thrust the manuscript inside. She locked the drawer and pocketed the key. Only then did she turn to face him.

Before she could rail at him, he interjected, "Publish that particular work, and I can promise you a rash of lawsuits."

"Let them sue," she said disparagingly. "It will more than triple the sales I'm expecting to make. But you're wrong. They won't take Bailey's to court. They'd only lose, and they know it."

"There's more at stake than Bailey's Press. There's your own reputation to consider. Publish that manuscript and every door in London will be closed to you."

"You're making a mountain out of a molehill," she protested. "Besides, I'm not publishing anyone's name. I've changed them all to protect the guilty. Take today's chapter, which I've just translated, for example. 'Sir Spider,' Monique calls one of her admirers. In my edition, I shall change his name to 'Sir Beetle.'"

"That's not much of a change," he pointed out.

She laughed. "No. But 'Sir Spider' won't be able to sue me for libel in a court of law. That's all I care about."

"Who is the fellow? Do you know?" he asked casually.

"I haven't a clue. But he's certainly one of Monique's more colorful characters."

He became absorbed staring at the inkpot on Annabelle's desk. "I suppose he's a bit of a libertine," he finally offered.

"Well of course. Otherwise he wouldn't be in the girl's diaries."

"What does she have to say about him?"

"Plenty. And not anything that a lady would repeat to a gentleman. You'll just have to wait until the thing is published, if you're really interested."

He smiled weakly. "You've developed a thorough disgust for him, I presume."

"Certainly not. In fact, he's an attractive rogue with no malice in him, in spite of his amorous adventures, which according to Monique are legion."

"She was probably exaggerating. They do, you know."

Annabelle slanted him a keen look. "You know his identity! That's it, isn't it?"

"No, no! Really, I don't."

"If I didn't know better," she mused, "I'd suspect that you and 'Sir Spider' were one and the same person. However . . ."

"Yes?" He seemed to be hanging on her next words.

"Sir Spider has a penchant for beautiful though feather-brained widgeons. So I knew he could not be you."

Swallowing a sigh, Dalmar said, "Will you be having any lunch?"

It took a minute for it to register in Annabelle's brain that Dalmar had changed the subject. "Lunch," she repeated blankly. "Oh, I always go home and eat with my son."

"I'll come with you," he returned in a voice that brooked no argument. "Get your hat and coat."

They were in the outer office before she turned on him and asked, apropos of nothing, "How do you feel about Homer's *Odyssey*?"

Cautiously, he answered, "Like most boys, I loved it. Why?"

Her eyes lit up with that fanatical gleam he was coming to know so well. "I've got just the book for you," she exclaimed, and darted back into her office. In a moment she returned and held out a slim volume bound in maroon calfskin.

"*More Tales of the Settlers*," he read from the cover, "and published in New York, of all places. What has this got to do with Homer's *Odyssey*?"

"Think, Dalmar—adventurers in uncharted territory with horrendous, hair-raising trials and tribulations to overcome before they find what they're after. It's an old legend but . . ."

". . . dressed up in a suit of new clothes," he finished for her.

She threw him a brilliant smile. "I think you've got the makings of a publisher," she told him, and held out her gloved hand, palm up.

"What?" he asked at a loss, examining the proffered hand.

Saucily, she answered, "You owe me ten shillings. That's the price of the book, and I ought to warn you, at Bailey's there's no haggling the price down."

He could not help himself. With a great whoop of laughter, he dragged her into his arms and kissed her swiftly and hard. "Now I know why I want to marry you, Annabelle Jocelyn. By the time I'm forty, you'll have made me a millionaire."

Annabelle was flustered, but not so flustered that she forgot about the ten shillings. He paid up without demur.

It was hours later before it occurred to her that Dalmar had shown a remarkable awareness of Monique Dupres's diaries. She herself had never mentioned them to him. Assuming that Albert had let slip something when her attention had been engaged elsewhere, she dismissed the matter from her mind.

Chapter Ten

Three weeks later, as October drew to a close, Annabelle held out her left hand for the inspection of her good friend and companion Mrs. Beatrice Pendleton. On her third finger glittered a ruby and pearl betrothal ring which Lord Dalmar had given her the night before.

"When and where will the marriage take place?" asked Bertie, her eyes lifting to slant her employer a brazen I-told-you-so look.

"December," said Annabelle emphatically, "and in York, with my father officiating."

"You surprise me. Somehow I thought Dalmar would procure a special license and have the thing done before you had time to change the garters on your stockings."

Annabelle smiled at her friend's perspicacity. In truth, it had taken every ounce of her logic to persuade the Earl to a more moderate course. Even the betrothal ring was a little precipitous, in her opinion. Apart from their immediate family, there had been little time to inform their acquaintances of their intentions. For most of them, their first intelligence of what was afoot would come that very evening at a ball which Lord Dalmar was hosting in his newly refurbished house in Cavendish Square.

Annabelle absently stirred the small silver spoon in the third cup of tea she had poured for herself that morning. "Patience is a virtue that Dalmar is going to have to learn." Carefully she began to enumerate the reasons she had given the Earl for the

171

delay in their marriage. "To begin with, my father can't drop everything and come to London. Nor can I drop everything and go to York. There are things happening at Bailey's, critical things which cannot be left in abeyance at this moment. And there's no question of having some other priest perform the ceremony. Good grief, I'm a vicar's daughter. My father would never understand such unseemly haste. By Christmas or the new year, things at Bailey's should be on a more even keel. Plenty of time then to think of getting married."

Bertie darted her friend a troubled look. Very gently she said, "Are you sure, my dear?"

"I beg your pardon?"

Choosing her words carefully, Annabelle's companion observed, "Are you sure you won't find some other excuse to put off the wedding once Christmas is upon us? Forgive me, Annabelle, I know that I've all but pushed you into this step in the last number of weeks, but if you're not absolutely certain . . ."

Annabelle chuckled. "You're beginning to sound like Dalmar. I'll tell you what I told him. This isn't a delaying tactic. Albert is already in Manchester. The presses are going night and day. The bookbinders have cleared the decks. Bailey's first cheap edition of a work of fiction is almost ready for dispatch. I can't be expected to drop everything now. Put your mind at rest, Bertie. I said I would marry Dalmar, and I shall."

Leaning forward across the small breakfast table, Bertie asked, "Why *are* you marrying him, Annabelle?"

Annabelle's eyes widened a fraction. "Why, for all the reasons you gave me, Bertie, and a few that you didn't. Richard needs a father, and Dalmar, for some reason I can't fathom, has the boy in his pocket."

"Yes, the Earl has worked a wonderful change in Richard in the last number of weeks. If you ask me, the boy was too old for his years. Dalmar knows how to shake the child out of himself. I don't think I've heard Richard laugh so much in the two years since I've been with you. I should think that Dalmar will make a wonderful father."

Annabelle's artfully rouged cheeks deepened a shade. With

head averted, she said, "Yes, well, I was an only child myself. It's my hope that Richard will have a few siblings before he's very much older, if only to take him down a peg or two. Moreover, Dalmar is persuaded that Richard suffers from a surfeit of petticoats. I daresay there's something in what he says."

"Surely you're not marrying the man merely to provide a father for Richard?"

"Of course not," disclaimed Annabelle calmly. "If that were the case, I would have married long since. I think I told you that Dalmar has promised that once we're wed, he'll allow me to pursue my publishing interests without interference? There's not many men who would do as much, I don't mind telling you."

Skeptically, Bertie asked, "Do you trust him to keep his word?"

"Implicitly," answered Annabelle.

It was a question she did not have to think twice about. As one week had slipped into the next, she'd begun to understand something of the Earl's character. He never made promises he could not keep, and he expected as much from those who were close to him. The small white lies which were woven into the fabric of polite social intercourse he eschewed as if they had been the invention of the devil (which Annabelle, as a daughter of the manse, knew perfectly well they were). Unthinkingly, since leaving her father's roof, she had picked up the habit, something which Dalmar warned her he would not tolerate under any circumstances.

"Do you love him?"

The question startled Annabelle. The delicate teacup which she'd been holding to her lips jerked, sending droplets of tea over the white linen table cover.

Flustered, Bertie said, "I beg your pardon. I had no right to ask such a question."

Annabelle carefully used her table napkin to dab the front of her pomona green silk. Her lashes lifted, and her blue eyes, faintly hooded, regarded her friend's flushed cheeks.

"Bertie," said Annabelle quietly, "I married for love once before, remember? I'm not like to make the same mistake

173

twice. I'm very fond of Dalmar. One might even go so far as to say I admire the man. We understand each other. When he makes those vows to me in front of witnesses, you may be sure that he'll keep them. He's not the sort of man to humiliate his wife by flaunting his ladybirds in public. Richard likes him. You said yourself that Dalmar will make a wonderful father. I would not marry him if I did not believe he would make an excellent husband. What more could a woman ask for?"

"Nothing, I suppose," answered Bertie, studiously involved in buttering a slice of dry toast.

There was another, more compelling reason for her marriage to Dalmar which Annabelle chose not to reveal to her companion. Quite bluntly, David Falconer had proved to be something of a nemesis.

For years she'd listened to sermons from the pulpit on the boring topic of the sins of the flesh. Obviously she had not been paying attention. For some obscure reason, she had always supposed that she was immune to that particular temptation . . . until the Palais Royal. And in the weeks following her shocking fall from grace, she had persuaded herself that she had been the victim of a set of circumstances which could never again be repeated. Annabelle Jocelyn just wasn't that sort of girl! She could not have been more mistaken. Where David Falconer was concerned, as he was at some pains to prove to her, Annabelle Jocelyn was *exactly* that sort of girl. When he had been sedated almost senseless, his appeal had been powerful. In full possession of all his faculties, the man was irresistible. It was either marry the rogue or burn. He left her no alternative.

For all that she'd been a married woman and madly in love with her husband, she was totally confused by the lush sensations and achy feelings Dalmar could evoke so effortlessly with one word, one soft look, an accidental touch that wasn't accidental. She'd had words, looks, and touches—dozens of 'em in her day, and not one had done more than gratify her feminine vanity. Dalmar was different.

David Falconer was a walking, talking, living, breathing invitation to a rocky road that led straight to hell—or heaven, as he would have it. Need, naked and unashamed, blazed at her from eyes that were endlessly gray, endless with wanting. Not in a hundred years could she explain even to herself the conflicting images which haunted her. He was the lazy lion surreptitiously stalking his prey. He was the stray lamb, defenseless and lonely, in search of a refuge. Every logical cell in her brain urged her to pull up the drawbridge and man the defenses; every feminine instinct in her body coaxed her to wrap him in her arms and protect him from a cruel world.

Pushing thoughts of Dalmar to the back of her mind, she concentrated on what her companion was saying. "Diaries?" she asked.

"Yes. How far along with them are you?"

Annabelle grimaced. "I've finished the translation, thank heavens. And what a beastly bore it was!"

"You surprise me. If it's boring, how do you expect people to buy the book when it's published?"

"It's not the content of the book that's boring, Bertie. It's only that I scarcely know what I'm reading when I'm in the throes of translation. Once Albert polishes my prose and puts the finishing touches to it, it will be quite racy. I should be thankful that it's not his version of the manuscript that marches through my mind when I go to bed or I'd be up all night." Observing her friend's blank look, Annabelle went on to explain. "I've given up counting sheep—or perhaps it's the other way round. They've given me up. What I mean to say is, my head scarcely touches the pillow, but page by page, my brain sifts through every word in Monique Dupres's horrid manuscript."

"In French?"

"Oh yes. In the original. It's more effective than a sleeping draught, I can tell you."

Bertie laughed. "And to think I always envied you your prodigious memory."

"As I've told you before, it's not exactly memory," explained Annabelle patiently. "I'm as like to forget a name or an appointment as you are."

"But not if it's written down."

"Something like that."

"And you can recall a whole book at one go, I think I once

175

heard you mention."

"Only if I study it."

"You must have walked off with all the prizes at school, you horrid girl!"

"Oh I never went to school. My father tutored me at home."

"Just as well! You would have been the most unpopular girl in class."

Faintly uncomfortable with this turn in the conversation, Annabelle observed, "Yes, well, when Albert returns from Manchester, the manuscript should be ready to go to press."

"Ah," said Bertie noncommittally, and carefully adjusted the cuff of her blue kerseymere spencer.

After an interval, Annabelle said wryly, "Not you too, Bertie!"

Bertie's brow elevated a trifle. "I never said a word," she averred.

"Your look spoke volumes!"

"Well, since you're asking for my advice . . ."

"I never said so . . ."

". . . I wish you would reconsider your decision to publish this particular work."

"Oh? You've suddenly become an expert on publishing too, have you?" said Annabelle without malice.

"No! But I trust Lord Dalmar's opinion. And Lord Temple also said something which made me feel that in this instance you are not being very wise."

With the merest trace of exasperation, Annabelle exclaimed, "I don't know why we bother developing policies if they are only going to be broken at the first real test. It's not as though we are unscrupulous at Bailey's, you know. We would never publish anything as gospel if we knew it was fabrication."

"Yes, dear," soothed Bertie. "You've told me before that these policies are meant to make your business run more smoothly. But . . ."

"I know! I've heard it ad nauseam—lawsuits, personal vendettas, threat to life and limb—Dalmar has been very eloquent on the subject." After a considering silence, Annabelle let out a telling sigh. "Frankly, though it goes against the grain, I don't mind admitting I've been having second thoughts." From the corner of her eye, she caught her friend's quickly suppressed grin. With a quelling frown, Annabelle went on, "You needn't think that Dalmar's opinion weighs with me. He's still a greenhorn as far as publishing goes, though I own he is a fast learner. No, it was Albert who pointed out that we have too many irons in the fire at present to take any chances. It's not that I've given up the idea of publishing the memoirs, you understand. It's just that I'm considering delaying the date of publication."

"Would you be so kind as to pour me another cup of tea?" said Bertie sweetly.

Annabelle obliged.

Beatrice Pendleton knew her friend too well to press her advantage. Where Bailey's was concerned, Annabelle never took advice gracefully from outsiders. Time to let well enough alone, decided Bertie. Abruptly changing the subject, she asked, "What are you wearing to Dalmar's ball this evening?"

"Something demure," said Annabelle, grinning broadly. "Don't look so shocked, Bertie. I want to make a good impression on Dalmar's friends and relatives. His younger brother will be there. Also, my own relations, Sir Charles and Henrietta."

"I heard something . . ."

"Yes?"

"Is it true that Dalmar has invited all your past and present beaux to this ball? He mentioned something of the kind, but I thought he must be funning."

Laughing, Annabelle said, "It's no joke. He's determined that they get the message loud and clear that Mrs. Annabelle Jocelyn is no longer in circulation."

"It should make for an interesting evening," murmured Bertie dryly.

"Yes. I daresay. Richard is beside himself because he can't attend. Which reminds me: you were going to give me a progress report on the scamp or some such thing."

Mrs. Pendleton's position in the household was ambiguous. Though always referred to as Annabelle's "companion"— Annabelle would never admit to the title "chaperone"—she shared with her employer the responsibility for the education of Annabelle's son. In this instance, she briefly outlined the curriculum she would be following in the next several weeks. From there the conversation moved to Rosedale and the upcoming house party which was to begin later that week and terminate with Guy Fawkes' night on November fifth.

"Have you spoken with your cousin?" asked Annabelle, deliberately casual.

"You mean about Amy? Yes. It's all arranged, thank you. Amy is counting the days till we leave."

The ladies rose from the table and made for the front foyer. "I've been thinking," said Annabelle. Bertie helped her into her claret velvet redingote.

"Yes?"

Annabelle carefully eased her fine kid gloves over long, slender fingers. "I don't suppose it's worth mentioning, but if your cousin could be persuaded . . . what I mean to say is . . . Richard is a lonely child so much of the time . . . that is, Amy and he are almost of an age . . ." She was getting into difficulty and trailed to a halt. She chanced a quick glance at her companion. Emboldened by what she read in the other's expression, she said, "There's no reason why Amy should not come to live here with us. It would do Richard a world of good. I know what you're going to say. But really, Bertie, my marriage won't make a jot of difference. Richard is going to need a governess for some years to come. Two children are scarcely more work than one. But I leave it up to you. Just remember, I'm only thinking of what's best for me and mine."

She turned on her heel and made for the front door. Before it could be opened, she felt a restraining hand on her sleeve.

Bertie's voice was as liquid as the brown eyes which were turned upon Annabelle. "You know, don't you?" she asked softly.

Expelling a breath she did not know she was holding, Annabelle said, "I don't know anything. Not really. But I'm not blind either. I suppose I've been putting two and two together without consciously thinking about it. I may have jumped to the wrong conclusion."

"Amy is my daughter." There was a wealth of pain and longing behind the simple statement.

178

"Yes," said Annabelle, and tentatively patted her friend on the shoulder.

Bertie smiled.

Annabelle smiled.

Everything was going to be all right.

It was Annabelle who broke the silence. Almost gaily, she said, "Tell Nancy to look through my wardrobe for the plainest ladylike frock I own. She can give it a good airing for Dalmar's ball this evening."

Equally gay, Bertie responded, "Annabelle Jocelyn, you don't own a stitch that could possibly pass for 'ladylike,' and you know it."

"Then I'll just have to borrow something of yours, won't I, Miss Prim and Proper?" was Annabelle's parting shot.

The carriage was waiting for her just outside the front door. A fine drizzle had been falling intermittently for the last number of days, typical weather for October. She settled herself against the squabs and thought fleetingly of the children in every hamlet and town who had been gathering fodder for the bonfires which would blaze throughout the length of Great Britain to mark the anniversary of the Gunpowder Plot. Canny housewives and shopkeepers were known to nail down or lock up anything flammable and movable in an attempt to foil the gangs of children who roamed the streets like the troops of a well-organized army foraging for supplies. Rain, sleet, or snow notwithstanding, nearly every common would blaze with its own bonfire and effigies of Guy Fawkes, the man who almost succeeded in blowing up the House of Lords more than two hundred years before.

Her thoughts turned from children in general to one particular little girl, Amy, four years old. Bertie had given out that she had been a widow for six years or more. Annabelle could not help speculating on who the child's father was, or what had prevented the parents from marrying. Amy's existence explained Bertie's reticence with members of the opposite sex. She was a handsome woman and had attracted her share of attention. But Bertie had never been attracted to anyone as far as Annabelle could remember. She felt a twinge of regret, as if her own forthcoming marriage was in some sort a betrayal of their friendship. She had thought not so very long ago that she and Bertie would go on as they were for years to come. The prospect had been a pleasing one. But that was before Dalmar.

She made a small moue of impatience. Just as all roads led to Rome, all Annabelle Jocelyn's thoughts, of late, led straight to the Earl. It wasn't, she assured herself, that she was in love with the man, or suffered from a schoolgirl infatuation, or anything of that ilk. There were things about Dalmar she could not like. He took far too many liberties, stole kisses in broad daylight, and whispered the most outrageous things at the most inopportune moments, causing her untold agonies of embarrassment. No one would believe, to look at the man, with his grave expression and that level stare from intelligent gray eyes, that he was capable of such utterly ungentlemanly conduct. He was a knave! A scapegrace! A rascal! And she was sure she could not explain even to herself why she was shaking with laughter.

He was like no other man she had ever known. No gentleman of her acquaintance ever tried to draw a lady into a conversation on politics, or religion, or commerce. It was as if the Earl actually admired a woman of intelligence, a woman who wasn't afraid to take a stand and argue her point of view with vigor. And his interest in Bailey's was gratifying, to say the least. There was no facet of its operation that did not seem to fascinate him. And she had never talked so much in her whole life.

In one month he'd wormed all her secrets out of her, and she was not sure how he'd managed it. About his own life he was reticent. He made light of his experiences in the army, told her amusing tales about his school days at Eton, and had shared the odd anecdote about scrapes he had fallen into with his younger brother when they were boys. But over anything that touched on his life with his parents he had drawn an impenetrable veil. Not that he had not mentioned them in passing. But what little he had told her she could quite easily have written on the head of a thimble.

She was not one to intrude on another's privacy uninvited. Pride was something she understood only too well. A facile

180

sympathy he would have scorned. She respected that. But it was the loneliness at his core which drew her like a river to the ocean. She sensed that he reached out to her in ways that he had never reached out to anyone. He'd told her often enough that he wanted a home, a wife, children. But he had never adequately explained why he had chosen her to be his mate. Not that it mattered . . . there was something in her own feminine psyche that responded to all the unexpressed needs of the man. What she felt was not love. She'd been in love once before. Annabelle Jocelyn never made the same mistake twice. She and Dalmar both wanted the same things. In her opinion, that was a better basis for marriage than love could ever be.

By degrees she became aware that they were approaching their destination. It was an excursion which Annabelle was in the habit of making twice a year. On this occasion her journey was not part of her normal schedule. Her errand was of a particular and pressing nature.

Annabelle did not own Bailey's Press outright. Her partner, a certain Mrs. Dobie, was half-owner and had her house in the village of Hampstead. Their arrangement was an amicable one. Decisions affecting the operation of the business were left entirely to Annabelle's discretion. Mrs. Dobie was content merely to share in the profits and accept Annabelle's verbal report in January and June of every year. This was October. Bailey's was on the verge of a new enterprise. With one thing and another, cash reserves were at an all-time low. It was imperative that Annabelle discuss her solution to the problem with her partner.

The carriage rolled to a halt in front of a small stuccoed villa which nestled in a grove of plum trees behind a brick wall. In a matter of minutes Annabelle was ushered inside the vestibule by a young maid. Her wraps were removed, and she was shown into a very feminine parlor displaying every kind of bric-á-brac and where a cheery coal fire blazed a welcome.

Mrs. Dobie, a small stout lady on the wrong side of fifty, had always displayed a natural reserve in Annabelle's presence. On this occasion a spate of effusive words gushed from her lips. Annabelle found herself clasped to the lady's ample bosom, and a smacking kiss was placed squarely on her cheek. Surprise was gradually overtaken by enlightenment.

Moving toward one of the blue velvet upholstered Queen Anne chairs which flanked the fireplace, Annabelle said, "Oh, you noticed the ring Lord Dalmar gave me."

"My dear, I couldn't be more happy for you."

Mrs. Dobie opened the doors of a squat mahogany bureau and removed a decanter of sherry and two small crystal glasses. The ritual was as familiar to Annabelle as it was welcome. The decanter and glasses were placed on a small side table at Annabelle's elbow. It was always she who did the honors, since her companion averred that her eyesight was not what it once had been.

The two ladies sipped their sherries in companionable silence. Not till the second glass was broached would Mrs. Dobie hear of any business being introduced into the conversation. Annabelle answered and parried a number of questions all of which revolved around Dalmar and her projected nuptials. In her turn, she enquired after the health of the lady's only living relatives, some distant cousins who were domiciled in Wales. After an interval, she raised the matter which had brought her so far out of her way.

Though she had absolutely no interest in books or publishing, Mrs. Dobie always listened to Annabelle in rapt silence, occasionally throwing out a neutral "Really?" or "You don't say!" Annabelle could never disabuse herself of the notion that her partner viewed her as if she were some unusual specimen of butterfly that she would dearly love to net and pin in her collection. In point of fact, Mrs. Dobie viewed Annabelle as something of an Amazon and went very much in awe of her.

Annabelle never went into a business meeting without rehearsing in her mind exactly what she wished to say and what objective she wished to reach. She began by outlining her plans to open up new avenues of distribution for the inexpensive line of books Bailey's had begun to produce. She spoke of a new reading public which nothing could induce to step inside the doors of a regular bookshop. She mentioned Longmans and their growing investment in advertising so that a demand for their product was created as the books came off the presses.

She reminded her partner of the fleet of Stanhope presses which were still to be paid for. She spoke of authors and their advances, wages, upkeep, and taxes. In short, she spoke of everything that would persuade her partner that, though business was thriving, a shortage of capital at this particular juncture would be a crippling handicap from which Bailey's might never recover.

Like a sponge, Mrs. Dobie absorbed every word that fell from Annabelle's lips. When Annabelle reached the end of her monologue, her companion looked suitably impressed.

"What it comes down to," said Annabelle, flashing the older woman a rueful grin, "is this: every spare penny must be plowed back into the business, at least for the foreseeable future. Do you agree?"

"Oh, I think so," was the cautious rejoinder.

"I won't be paying myself a penny in wages for a good twelvemonth or more."

"Don't let that trouble you," said Mrs. Dobie consolingly. "I'm sure your husband will pick up your expenses."

Swallowing back a retort about Bailey's Press having *nothing* to do with her husband, Annabelle asked baldly, "How much do you need to get by on? And I'm talking the bare minimum, mind you."

"I beg your pardon?"

Mrs. Dobie was not generally so obtuse. Striving for a patient tone, Annabelle persisted, "If you forgo your half-yearly checks for the next two years or so, I can almost promise that you'll be making double what you're earning now once they resume."

In quick succession the emotions of surprise, amusement, and finally consternation chased themselves across the older woman's plump face. Hesitantly, she offered, "Lord Dalmar *did* tell you about our arrangement?"

Frowning, Annabelle demanded, "What arrangement?"

"My dear, I sold him my interest in Bailey's . . . oh . . . weeks ago."

If a brick wall had fallen on Annabelle, she could not have felt more stunned. Though her first impulse was to vehemently deny the truth of Mrs. Dobie's statement, everything suddenly

183

came into focus with blinding clarity. Dalmar's interest in Bailey's was instantly explained. It was no sham! Nor was it to gratify any whim of hers that he had delved into every facet of her business. He'd made himself at home in her office, was on a first-name basis with all her employees, and had picked her brains unmercifully till he knew everything there was to know about the day-to-day operation of what he always teasingly referred to as her "little empire."

From the very outset, it had been *her* company that he was determined to buy into. No wonder he'd been so close-mouthed about his plans. And like an idiot, she had taken the viper to her bosom.

Drawing in a deep, steadying breath, she managed in a creditably calm voice, "You and I had an understanding, Mrs. Dobie. I was to be given first refusal if ever you decided to sell."

The lady's answer did not surprise Annabelle. She could almost picture the scene: Lord Dalmar, oozing charm as only he could, persuading the lady, in spite of her scruples, that since he was Annabelle's intended, there could be no disloyalty in selling to him. And Mrs. Dobie, as Annabelle well knew, had never put much credence in the stability of a mere publishing house. No doubt her capital was now safely deposited in the impregnable vaults of the Bank of England.

Whatever her thoughts, Annabelle managed finally to breeze out of the house as if the intelligence of her fiancé's duplicity had been a rare joke. In the confines of her carriage she was not so sanguine.

Fury, hot and heedless, ripped through Annabelle. At all her pulse points, her blood beat out a tattoo in double quick time. Her skin grew cold and hot by turns. She knew that her thoughts were spinning off in every direction and that if she made the attempt to speak, her words would be completely incomprehensible. She was shaking like a leaf. She curled herself into a ball and touched her trembling fingers to her brow to stop the dizziness. Think . . . she must think.

Dalmar had stolen a march on her. She'd been duped, hoodwinked, lulled into trusting him. She swore that she would never trust him again. Like a fool, she had bragged of Bailey's potential, flaunted her successes, revealed secrets she had no business revealing. With almost laughable naïvety, she had even given him advice—she, the lamb, trying to teach the lion how to be a predator! How he must have laughed at her! He would never laugh at her again.

Blindly she stared out the carriage window, seeing nothing. Dalmar was now her partner, and she did not think for a minute that he would be willing to assume the role which Mrs. Dobie had assumed. The man would be into everything, questioning her decisions, usurping her authority. Only one hand could be at the helm. *She* was the one who had earned the right to steer the ship. It was *her* business acumen which had turned Bailey's from its rocky course, *her* intuitive grasp of markets and trends which had propelled Bailey's into the forefront of the publishing world. Nothing would make her relinquish her place to an underhanded, unethical, unprincipled scoundrel! Nothing!

Try as she might, she could not fathom his game. The man was an aristocrat, a peer of the realm. His proper place was at Court, or managing his estates, or in politics. Unlike Lord Stanhope, few noblemen showed the slightest inclination to soil their hands in anything that resembled trade. They had turned their backs on the merchant classes, where, if truth were told, many of them could trace their origins. But then, Dalmar would never fit any preconceived mold. After seventeen years in His Majesty's Service, perhaps the quiet life of a gentleman seemed too tame by half for him. Then let him try his hand at gaming, or horse racing, or anything else, for that matter. She was sure she did not care. Just so long as he kept out of *her* domain.

She felt like such an idiot! And she had no one to blame but herself. She'd broken one of her own cardinal rules—never to make the same mistake twice. She'd listened to one man and had been robbed of her chance of having children. She'd listened to Dalmar and he had practically stolen her baby from under her nose. Bailey's! She loved it with more passion than she could ever feel for a mere mortal man. Next to her son,

Bailey's was everything to her.

It was some time before she realized that her cheeks were wet with tears. She groped for her handkerchief and dabbed at them furiously. That a man should reduce her to such straits! Intolerable! But then, Dalmar wasn't just any man. He was a devil! He'd managed to cozen every member of her household, every servant, every employee, till he had them all eating out of his hand. Damn it! He had *her* eating out of his hand! It wasn't just Bailey's. It was personal. He'd stirred longings, dreams, feelings about herself as a woman that she had long since repressed. After Edgar, she'd never put her trust in anyone, not really. Oh, the world viewed her a gregarious butterfly, but in reality she never allowed herself to get too close to anyone. Even with Bertie there was a natural reserve. But Dalmar had breezed into her life, and she had suddenly begun to trust again, see other possibilities for her life. More than anything, she had wanted him for a *friend. Liar,* a little voice whispered inside her head. *You wanted him for your lover, the father of your children. You wanted his love.*

"I am *not* in love with him," she cried aloud, and slammed her reticule into the opposite seat of her coach.

Humiliation, betrayal, rage—she nursed her grievances as she made several stops before her coachman finally delivered her to Cavendish Square. She had promised the Earl that she would oversee the preparations for the ball where the announcement of their engagement was to be made public. Though every nerve in her body screamed at her to vent her spleen on her tormentor, Annabelle was too experienced an opponent to show her hand in a moment of weakness. She had weathered a few storms in her time. Nothing was to be gained by throwing a child's temper tantrum. Lion he might be, but she was resolved that by the time she had finished with him, Lord Dalmar would know that he had tangled with a tigress.

He came out of the library to meet her before his butler had a chance to announce her.

"You're shaking," he said, gray eyes quickly scanning her frozen expression.

"There's a nip in the air," she temporized, looking around

her with interest.

Warm lips brushed her cheek in a proprietary caress. "Don't fret! The painters and plasterers cleared out days ago. Everything is just as you wished."

And it was. It had been a pleasure to do over Dalmar's house . . . not that there had been much room for improvement. The beautifully proportioned foyer with its arched Venetian window on the first landing and the elegant sweep of white marble stairs was a picture in symmetry. Through the well of the double staircase two floors above one could catch the light from the glass dome in the white and gilt coffered ceiling. The adjoining salons were a perfect complement to the gracious entrance hall. A new coat of paint and a lick of polish had worked a remarkable change in the place. Though she'd offered to have the interior done in restrained blues and greens, colors she felt sure were more comfortable for the Earl, he had insisted that she use the warmer hues which she preferred, reminding her that the house would be home for both of them.

In the end she had compromised. She had kept the pearl gray damask which was already on the walls, but where there were carpets laid, on the stairs and in the main salons, she had chosen a maroon Axminster with a small gold fleur-de-lis design. On the long windows, in matching damask, were reefed curtains lined with taffy. The upholstered pieces, like most of the mellow walnut furniture, was from a former era, and now recovered in shades of either gold, crimson, or gray.

"Are you pleased with your handiwork?" he murmured, leading her firmly into the ground floor book room.

Smiling easily, she responded, "You're the one who has to live with it. You tell me."

He turned her slowly to face him. She almost faltered when she came under his searching scrutiny. "What is it? What's wrong?" he asked softly.

His solicitous tone, played to perfection, grated on her nerves. Summoning a weak smile, she playfully essayed, "I did not come here today so that you could seduce me, Dalmar. I have work to do, or had you forgotten?"

His intent look relaxed, and he flashed her one of his special cozening grins, which never failed to do peculiar things to her heart. Evidently her heart had petrified, for it did not so much as tremble.

"So that's why you're nervous. How can you think it? I brought you in here merely to show you my uncle's library." His eyes lightened in amusement. "I thought you might give me your professional opinion of it. But now that you mention it, surely one little kiss . . ."

Carefully stepping away from him, she said over her shoulder, "You seem to have developed quite an interest in the subject of books." She made a pretense of examining a shelf of leatherbound volumes, her fingers deftly skimming over their spines. He was watching her with a hooded expression. She selected a book and opened it. Seconds later she slammed it shut and said brightly, "What a disappointment! Ah well, let that be a lesson to me. One should never judge a book by its cover."

"What did you select?" he asked, moving closer.

"A book on horses, a subject in which I have not one iota of interest."

He smiled lazily. "And as I told you, I intend to change your petty aversion to horses and dogs and so on."

"Ah yes, your personal crusade. You just won't believe that I refuse to make the same mistake twice. You'll never learn." She hoped that the sugary smile she bestowed on him blunted the sharp edge of her words.

As she tried to push past him toward the door, he captured her wrist. "Why is it I feel you are being deliberately obscure?" he asked.

Her smile slipped and her lashes lowered to lie like fans across her cheeks.

"Annabelle?"

Her chin was tipped up. "You were right before. I'm nervous," she told him truthfully. "It's just that I want our first ball to be a memorable occasion."

His eyes moved leisurely over her face. Apparently satisfied with what he read, he let her go. "I have every confidence in your ability to achieve whatever you set out to do," he told her gravely.

"Oh, I do hope so," she said, patting his cheek with one long finger. "Oh, by the by. Promise you won't peek into the supper rooms? I'm planning a surprise for you. Your engagement present."

"There's no need . . ."

"There's every need. Believe me, you deserve it."

His eyes were thoughtful as she closed the door.

Chapter Eleven

Colonel Ransome replaced his snuffbox in his coat pocket. His eyes absently roved the room, finally coming to rest on the tall figure of the Earl. Dalmar, formally resplendent in white satin breeches and dark evening coat, was replenishing two glasses from an opened bottle of hock which stood on a satinwood console table.

"What was all the hammering about?" asked Ransome, edging himself more comfortably into the commodious armchair which was drawn close to the grate for warmth.

Dalmar looked up. "Hammering? Oh, you mean this afternoon? That was Annabelle's doing. At supper tonight she's going to present me, publicly, mind you, with my engagement present. It's all a big secret. Well, you know women."

"It didn't sound like much of a secret."

"It isn't really," allowed Dalmar. "She's had upholsterers hang curtains against one of the walls. It doesn't take much imagination to guess what's concealed behind them."

"Her portrait," drawled Ransome ironically.

Dalmar's lips flashed a quick, enigmatic smile. "I don't doubt it," he murmured.

"Women are so unimaginative. Why don't they ever think to give us precious gems or furs? It's what they expect from us. I don't think I shall ever understand their thought processes."

"Annabelle doesn't lack imagination. I don't think you'll be disappointed." Again, that secretive smile came and went on the corners of Dalmar's mouth.

"Mmm," said Ransome, unconvinced, his gaze narrowing on his friend's suspiciously bland expression. After a considering moment, he went on, "I shouldn't have descended on you unannounced. To be frank, I'd feel more comfortable taking myself off to Grillons or the Pulteney. Don't get me wrong, David. I'm honored for the invitation, but if it's all the same to you, I'll skip the family dinner and come back for the ball."

"You're staying, and that's flat," answered Dalmar. "I need all the moral support I can get."

"Odd! I never took you for a coward," mused Ransome.

"You're thinking of the battlefield. I'm at home with cannon and saber. This is different."

Ransome raised one questioning brow as he accepted the long-stemmed glass which was thrust into his hand.

Gravely Dalmar explained, "I expect to come under fire from a score of disappointed suitors and, if I'm not mistaken, my credentials are going to be thoroughly vetted by the lady's relations. I'm counting on you, for old time's sake, to put in a good word for me. In other words, lie like blazes!"

Chuckling, Ransome asked, "What's she like?"

"You're mad if you think I'm going to sing the lady's praises to you. I have a long memory, Paul."

"You are referring, I collect, to that unfortunate episode in Madrid?"

"I'd forgotten her. What was her name? Not that it matters. No, I was thinking of the girl in Paris."

"You've only yourself to blame if Mimi preferred me to you." Ransome raised his glass in a taunting salute. "As I recall, your affections were very fickle. You never made the least push to hang onto your *chères amies.*"

Slightly uncomfortable, Dalmar interposed, "Yes, well, this isn't a fit conversation for a gentleman who has just become engaged." He settled himself in a leather upholstered armchair and took a long swallow from the glass in his hand. "How long will you be in town?" he asked, abruptly changing the subject.

"That depends. I have taken a month's leave. There are relatives near Salisbury whom I ought to look in on. Truth to tell, there's nothing pressing. I'm at rather a loose end this time around."

Dalmar had a vague recollection of the last time they had spent a furlough together in England. Though the two men had only a nodding acquaintance at that time, they'd been drawn to each other by mutual antipathy to the whole race of women, Dalmar because his engagement had been abruptly terminated, and Ransome for reasons which he had never disclosed. The Earl had since heard that Ransome's wife, who had died in a carriage accident two years before, had been something of a harridan.

"That settles it then," said Dalmar. "You'll be my guest for as long as you're in town. You'll meet my brother in a moment. I can't think what's keeping him."

"He's younger than you by quite a few years, I think you once told me?"

"Five years."

"I thought it was more."

"No. What made you think so?"

Ransome shrugged. "I don't know. This and that. I had the impression that you were something of a mother hen where your brother was concerned. You always found time to write to him even when we were on the move, which is more than many men did with their wives."

Dalmar's lazy glance lifted to meet his friend's considering stare. He said casually, "Scarcely a mother hen. In spite of my years of absence, we've always been close. That is all."

Ransome, sensing the other man's reticence, allowed the comment to pass unchallenged. After a pause, he remarked, "I take it the business with Monique Dupres has been amicably settled? Oh, don't look at me as if I'm trespassing on private property. It didn't take much to put two and two together."

"And you came up with?"

"Your betrothed."

Dalmar's brows went up and Ransome gave an unrepentant chortle.

"David, this is my line of work, remember? Once I discovered that Monique Dupres had been keeping journals, foolish woman, especially in *her* line of work, it did not take me long to figure out where Mrs. Annabelle Jocelyn, owner of one Bailey's Press, fitted the puzzle."

"Remarkable!" said the Earl noncommittally.

"Well?"

"Well what?"

"Have you got the diaries?"

Ransome's persistence startled a reluctant laugh out of the Earl. Shaking his head, he confided, "No, but I'm not worried. For one thing, Annabelle trusts my judgment. She may not admit to it yet, but I've already persuaded her that it's against her best interests to publish them."

"Clever," said Ransome with exaggerated respect. "How much have you told her?"

"Nothing. And with good reason. Annabelle would never adopt a course of action simply to oblige His Majesty's Government. Moreover . . ."

"Yes, I know. Once she becomes your wife, you'll do as you like with Bailey's."

"No! That has nothing to do with it. I was going to say that moreover, I've outflanked the lady, though she doesn't know it yet. Annabelle admires astute men of business. She'll have to admit that I've been one step ahead of her all the way."

"You think she'll congratulate you? Most women wouldn't."

"Well, not precisely 'congratulate.' She may not like it, but she'll accept it, given time. There's nothing womanish about Annabelle."

"Your confidence is staggering," said Ransome dryly.

The door to the library opened to admit a young man whose physical resemblance to the Earl was marked. Intelligent gray eyes appraised Ransome momentarily before the newcomer crossed the distance that separated him from his companions. He walked with a slight limp, Ransome observed interestedly.

John Falconer was a year or two shy of thirty. To Ransome he appeared much younger. Five minutes into the conversation and he had deduced why this should be so. It wasn't precisely because Falconer was of a retiring disposition. As Ransome closely observed, the two brothers' relationship came back in full force. Dalmar, affectionate, considerate, respectful, gave every appearance of having just taken a young fledgling under his wing.

Ransome was a trained observer. He sensed that the young man's life had been touched by the finger of tragedy or by some devastating misadventure. He'd heard, of course, of the gossip surrounding the death of Dalmar's father. It seemed to him in that moment that it was highly probable that John Falconer had played some significant part in that old scandal. On reflection it scarcely seemed possible. The man would have been no more than a boy of ten or eleven when he had witnessed the duel between his brother and his father. There was a mystery there that begged to be solved. Ransome grew impatient with himself. Every man had a few skeletons in his cupboard. He himself was no exception. Resolutely he turned his thoughts from unprofitable speculation.

"Is she a termagant, then?" he heard Falconer ask of his brother with a look that was a comical compound of genuine dismay and halfhearted cajolery.

Laughing, Dalmar answered, "Never say I said so! No, no, John, really, that description does not do justice to Annabelle. She's spirited, I'll give you that. But in other respects, she has a decidedly craven streak in her nature."

"Oh?" asked Ransome, interested.

"She's afraid of dogs and horses," explained Dalmar. Something in his brother's expression provoked him to add, "John, I assure you, Annabelle is quite human."

"Is she anything like . . ."

"Yes?"

"Lady Diana?"

Colonel Ransome became alert. Lady Diana Merril was the lady whose family had broken off her engagement to the Earl. Shortly afterward, she had been forced to marry a wealthy gentleman more than twice her age. Now a wealthy widow and no longer under her mother's thumb, rumor had it that she was on the hunt for a husband.

"There's no comparison," said Dalmar. "You'll love Annabelle, you'll see. She's just . . . different from the common run, that's all. I know how fond you were of Diana. Well, so was I. I still am. She'll be here this evening, by the by. So you'll have a chance to renew an old acquaintance."

195

Falconer surprised both his companions by saying obscurely, "I'm glad she's not like Diana."

Before Dalmar could ask him to explain his cryptic remark, a lackey entered with the intelligence that Mrs. Jocelyn and her party had arrived. Dalmar excused himself and went to greet his guests.

In the foyer, four people were being helped out of their wraps. Annabelle was flanked by Bertie Pendleton and a diminutive, dark-haired lady whose bright, birdlike eyes darted about her with keen interest. Their escort, a gentleman in his early forties, distinguished, with silver wings threading his short crop of brown hair, stiffened imperceptibly at the Earl's approach.

Dalmar's eyes were drawn to Annabelle. Her gown of diaphanous silk net was the color of rubies and was heavily embroidered along the borders of the bodice and hem with chenille garlands of pink roses. The skirt of her gown, though gored and slightly fuller than was fashionable, left nothing to the imagination. It was evident to Dalmar that Annabelle had reverted to her former habit of wearing not a stitch of underclothing. Her dark hair was swept high on the crown of her head in the classic manner, and a mass of tiny curls, like goose-down feathers, framed her face. Her blue eyes flashed like crystal prisms. Magnificent, he thought, and before she could take evasive action, he was at her side and had claimed a swift, proprietary kiss.

Under his breath he said, "This had better be for my benefit, or I'll want to know the reason why."

His smile was lazy.

Hers was brilliant.

The introductions were soon made. Lady Jocelyn was effusive in her praise of the Earl's house. Sir Charles was coolly polite, remote, and faintly challenging. Lord Dalmar, an uneasy suspicion taking hold in his mind, led the way to the book room.

Initially conversation was somewhat stilted, which was to be expected, given the circumstances. By degrees a slight thawing took place, and Dalmar, in his role as host, moved about freely, observing everything with a deceptively detached interest.

196

More guests began to arrive, for there were twenty invited to sit down to dinner and another sixty or so for the ball. Annabelle, radiant, played her part as the Earl's hostess as if she had been born to the role. That most of the men were under her spell came as no surprise to Dalmar. But by the time the last sugared fruit and roasted nut had been passed and the ladies were on the point of retiring to the cloakroom to repair for the ball, his first unquiet suspicion had hardened into a solid conviction. Sir Charles was besotted with Annabelle. His wife was fully cognizant of this fact, though she hid it well. Annabelle, with her customary carelessness, was ignorant of or indifferent to the passions which fermented just below the surface.

Nor had Ransome's attentions to Bertie Pendleton escaped the Earl's eye. Nor the lady's evident aversion to his friend. Dalmar could not think what had come over Ransome. He had never seen him so persistent where his attentions were not wanted. He watched covertly as Ransome laid a restraining hand on Mrs. Pendleton's arm. She turned back and said something in an undertone. Ransome dropped her arm as if it were a scorching-hot poker, and the lady swept past him.

Dalmar's eyes shifted to Sir Charles. That gentleman's attention was diverted to Annabelle. Each time he looked at her his expression softened. The reason for Annabelle's unconventional mode of living became very clear to Dalmar. She twisted men around her thumb as if they were threads of silk. He knew that no man, least of all the men who should have had some ordering of her life, her father, her deceased husband, and her brother-in-law, had ever faced her down when she was determined to have her own way. David Falconer was one man, he determined, who would never submit to being treated as a cypher by the headstrong lady.

Not that he had any wish to break her spirit. Far from it. He'd been drawn to her from the first by those fearless blue eyes which had looked at the world with a coolly challenging stare. Annabelle Jocelyn was her own person and judged the world on its merits. Not for her the place society assigned the female of the species.

He remembered that he'd found her in a Parisian brothel. He

recalled the riot in the Palais Royal, and the fatal duel where Annabelle's presence of mind had saved him from the sharp edge of Livry's blade. He thought of her at Bailey's and how she had made her mark in the publishing world. But most of all he thought of her sweet surrender in his bed.

God, she was perfect for him! No other woman could satisfy the passion she excited. No other woman could provoke this longing to possess her until she surrendered everything to him. He could never, now, shackle himself to some docile, proper lady who would defer to his wishes as if he were some deity. His mother had been that sort of woman. And he and his brother had paid the price for her docility.

Childhood memories, long suppressed, surfaced in his mind. A pulse began to tick in his temple. After a moment, a long, weary sigh fell from his lips.

Annabelle was not like his mother, he reminded himself. She would never allow herself to become the victim of any man. Her children would never be submitted to what he and his brother John had endured for years. He had always had a terror that one day his control would slip and he would become the animal his father had been. The thought had haunted him. In his relationships with women, he had never felt free to relax his guard, had, in fact, in spite of his thankfully short engagement to Lady Diana, shied away from committing himself to any one woman. In transitory affairs, there was safety for a man of his unhappy background.

He shook his head as if to clear his mind of painful memories. He was not like his father. He would make it so. Never once, when Annabelle had thwarted him, had he been tempted to do more than wallop her exquisite derriere. He tried to imagine what tack she would take when he finally wrested Monique Dupres's diaries away from her.

Ransome offered him the brandy decanter, and Dalmar shrugged off further unprofitable speculation.

In the downstairs cloakroom, Annabelle took in the white face and trembling fingers of her companion.

"Bertie, are you all right?" she asked, and put out a gloved hand to touch her friend solicitously on the shoulder. "You're shaking!"

198

"I think I'm coming down with something," admitted Bertie, her cheeks coloring.

Lady Jocelyn looked up from adjusting the folds of her skirt. Her quick eyes fastened on the heightened color of Annabelle's companion. She laughed and said archly, "Colonel Ransome is a very presentable gentleman, wouldn't you say, Mrs. Pendleton? In your place, I'd snap him up before some other lady takes a fancy to him. Oh, you needn't look daggers at me. Anyone with eyes in his head must have seen that he was more than a little civil to you. Though why *that* should ruffle your feathers is something of a mystery."

There was an embarrassed silence. Annabelle had no recollection of Colonel Ransome paying her friend more attention than he had paid any other lady. Of course, her mind had been preoccupied with other things. Slicing a chilling glance at her sister-in-law, she said, "Bertie, did that gentleman say something to upset you?"

"No! No, really. What gave you that idea? We were merely asking after mutual friends."

"Oh, you know him from before?" asked Henrietta.

"I met him a time or two in town, oh, years ago. Look, Annabelle, this has nothing to do with Colonel Ransome. Really, I'm not feeling well. Would you mind terribly if I took the carriage home and sent it back for you? You know I wouldn't miss your ball for the world, but I just cannot . . . oh . . . what should I do?"

Annabelle was all for sending for the Earl, but at this suggestion Bertie became even more agitated. Soothingly, Annabelle promised that her friend should effect her escape (for that was how Annabelle had come to think of it) before any of the gentlemen could be apprised of what was afoot. A maid was sent to order the coach round and accompany Bertie to Greek Street. Since the cloakroom was on the ground floor and the gentlemen were in the upstairs dining room, the thing was accomplished very easily.

"You're sure you'll be all right?" asked Annabelle. She had walked Bertie to the front door.

"Yes, dear. Don't worry. I'll see you tomorrow at breakfast. I'll be as right as a trivet by then, if I'm not mistaken. My one regret is that I shall miss the surprise you've arranged for the Earl. You must tell me all about it tomorrow."

Later, in the receiving line, Annabelle asked Dalmar a few pointed questions about his friend Colonel Ransome.

Having told her what she wished to know, he murmured, "Why do you ask?"

Frowning, Annabelle replied, "There's been some talk. It seems he monopolized Bertie's society from the moment she stepped over your threshold. I don't like it."

Mildly he reproved, "My dear Annabelle, whether you like it or not has nothing to say to anything. Mrs. Pendleton is of age. If she doesn't care for Ransome's attentions, let her tell him so. You keep out of it, d'you understand?"

Bristling, Annabelle turned on him, but at that moment one of the last of the guests to arrive had caught her eye as she ascended the wide sweep of the stairs with her escort, and the retort died on Annabelle's lips.

The lady, a child really, thought Annabelle, was exquisite and as perfect as a china doll. There was no art to those becomingly flushed cheeks and soft, rose-petal lips. And such hair—a glorious profusion of guinea-gold ringlets. Blue eyes like saucers, rimmed with soot, regarded Annabelle unblinkingly. The sweetest smile trembled on her lips.

"Lady Diana Merril," the majordomo announced.

At the name Annabelle's smile slipped a smidgen. She'd heard tell of Dalmar's former fiancée. It did not seem possible that this angel in a confection of pink satin, surely no older than eighteen or nineteen, could possibly be the lady in question. In her ignorance, she had supposed that Lady Diana was of an age with herself. But even the voice which murmured a polite greeting was girlishly high and husky. In comparison, her own response, two octaves lower, seemed as if it had been articulated by the voice box of a bass-baritone. Annabelle cleared her throat.

Lady Diana passed down the line. From the corner of her eye Annabelle observed the warm welcome the girl received first from Dalmar himself and then from his brother.

At her ear, Henrietta's voice, edged with acid sweetness,

intoned, "She's been the toast of the town since her first season."

"*I've* never met her before," said Annabelle, sniffing.

"My dear, we're talking Court circles. We're small fry in comparison. She's very young looking, isn't she?"

"Very," said Annabelle. "She doesn't look a day over thirty."

They entered the ballroom, which was normally the picture gallery, only minutes later. The great room was a blaze of lights. Though the announcement had yet to be official, there wasn't a soul present who had not heard the report of their engagement. Well-wishers greeted them from every side.

Annabelle was more than a little surprised to see how cordially Dalmar was received. Evidently, the *ton* had finally forgotten the old scandal. He led her out in the first waltz. She should have been savoring the moment of triumph which was to come. Instead, she could not stifle the first faint pangs of guilt. Annoyed with herself, and wondering at Dalmar's preoccupation, she kept up an unending stream of chitchat. It was a relief when the dance finally came to an end.

Her curiosity about Lady Diana was not to be satisfied until well into the evening. It was Lord Temple who volunteered what Annabelle wished to know. "She was twenty or so when she became engaged to Dalmar. It was his uncle, the Earl, who pushed for the marriage. But once the old scandal was resurrected, her father forced her to break it off and marry some old codger who left her a wealthy widow by the time she was two-and-twenty."

"They seem to be on the best of terms," murmured Annabelle. Her wandering glance came to rest on the couple who were the cynosure of all eyes. She could not fail to notice how well Dalmar and Lady Diana moved to the rhythm of the waltz. Her own partner, Lord Temple, was stiff and unyielding, his steps carefully executed. She felt a rush of remorse for the uncharitable comparison, knowing how great a price the Viscount paid to appear as normal as the next man. Though he rarely spoke of his injuries, it was her understanding that a bullet or a piece of shrapnel was still lodged close to his spine.

201

Without his daily dose of laudanum to dull the pain, he would be reduced to spending his life as an invalid, more or less.

"Diana is on the best of terms with everyone," said Lord Temple, his eyes lightening in amusement. "She's a charming girl. You'll love her."

"I'm sure I shall," said Annabelle mendaciously. Trying to feign indifference, she added, "I hear she's looking for a husband?"

"If that's true, there will be no end of applicants for the position. She's young, beautiful, and sinfully rich, if you'll pardon the expression. What more could a man want?"

Annabelle strained back slightly to catch Temple's expression. "Are you thinking of applying for the position, Gerry?"

He laughed. "I've given it some thought," he admitted. "It's time I was shackled. Unfortunately, Lady Diana lacks something of . . . well . . . spark. She's a clinging vine. Definitely not my style. I'm afraid you've spoiled me for other women, Annabelle."

Annabelle caught the quirk at the corner of his lips and smiled back. His words left her feeling more relieved than flattered. He was teasing her. It had been some time since their converse had been so free and easy. For months past, and long before Dalmar had come on the scene, the Viscount had turned possessive and sometimes truculent, as if he could bully her into marriage. It suddenly occurred to her that by not discouraging his attentions with more vigor she had done him a great disservice. Suddenly disliking the turn of her ruminations, she said, "Spark! I'm not sure that's a compliment."

"In moderation, it's an asset," said Temple with a twinkle. "However, there are some ladies, mentioning no names, who have more spark than a bolt of lightning. It's a brave man who thinks to channel so much fire. I wish Dalmar success where I have failed."

"He can try," she scoffed. She caught his sardonic look and was moved to exclaim, "I mean it, Gerry. No man is going to tell Annabelle Jocelyn what to do."

How it quite came about, Annabelle was never able to determine afterward, but from that point on, their conversation degenerated into an argument about whether or not Bailey's Press would publish the diaries of Monique Dupres. That Dalmar had boasted to the Viscount that there was not the least likelihood of such an event coming to pass provoked Annabelle to the point of rashness. By the time the dance came to an end, she had let Temple know in no uncertain terms that the diaries would be published come hell or high water.

Across the room, she met Dalmar's stare. His eyes blazed into hers. Endless seconds seemed to pass before he released her and turned away. She wondered what it might mean.

She was more than a little insulted. For a start, the Earl had engaged her for only the opening dance of the ball and had scarcely spoken two words to her all evening. For another thing, it was evident that his tongue had been running a malicious course. On every side she was mercilessly cajoled about her aversion to dogs and horses. The intelligence from Lord Temple respecting Dalmar's confidence that the diaries would not be published was one more faggot to add to the fire. Well, she had planned a fine revenge for my Lord Arrogance, and she refused to entertain the misgivings which had begun to gnaw at her conscience.

She marched off the dance floor determined to search out more congenial companionship. Her purpose was deflected when she caught sight of Dalmar's brother. He was on the sidelines, looking a little lost and sampling champagne from a long-stemmed glass.

He looked up at her approach, and something like alarm crossed his face before he quickly masked his expression.

"I don't bite, you know," said Annabelle, determinedly settling herself beside the young man.

His laugh lacked something of conviction. "Forgive me," he said, "I'm not used to town parties. In the country, everybody knows everyone else."

Snatching a glass of champagne from the silver salver of one of Dalmar's footmen, Annabelle remarked, "You don't much care for town, then?"

"No. I like the solitude of the country."

"With me it's the other way round," confided Annabelle. "I

can never find anything to do in the country."

"There are a million things to do in the country," protested Falconer.

"Name one," challenged Annabelle.

A good ten minutes went by before John Falconer realized that for the first time in memory he was talking to a vivacious lady without tying himself in knots. He could not think what possessed him to reveal so much about his likes and dislikes. He looked at his champagne glass and tried to remember how much he had consumed during the evening. He did not think it could be more than a couple of glasses. This saucy girl, either by accident or design, had provoked him into forgetting himself. More. She was flirting with him, and he was flirting back. He laughed, a truly spontaneous sound.

Glancing down, he saw that Annabelle was patiently waiting for him to respond to something she had said. "Your pardon," he apologized, smiling easily. "I was woolgathering. But I disagree with you. Of course you must learn to ride. It's no wonder you haven't taken to country life if you're afraid of horses."

"I know scores of ladies who don't ride," said Annabelle.

"Who, for instance?" asked her companion, relishing their thrust and parry.

Annabelle's eyes flicked to the lady who had evidently become the belle of the ball. Lady Diana was surrounded by a swarm of admirers.

Following her gaze, Falconer murmured, "Diana may look fragile, but I assure you, she rides as if she were born in the saddle." Keeping his lips grave, he commiserated, "Don't repine. In a hundred years or so, you'll be almost as good as she. Dalmar and I shall see to it."

"Horrid man!" said Annabelle, tossing her head. "Tell me, are all the Falconer men so disgustingly domineering?"

A shadow came and went in his eyes. When he spoke, the hesitation was back in his voice. "Y . . . yes. Awful, ain't it?"

Her smile faded. After a moment she laid her hand on his sleeve and said, "Don't take it to heart, John. I can handle domineering men. Ask anyone."

Her own words sobered her. She could not think why she

had allowed herself to be deflected from her purpose even for a moment. It was so totally out of character. Yet she had spent the last number of hours acting as if she were truly to become Dalmar's consort. It was not her business to charm his younger brother, no matter how strong the temptation to banish the shadows from his eyes. And as for the slight—very slight—pang of envy she had suffered when she'd first set eyes on the Earl's former betrothed, it was positively ludicrous. By morning Dalmar would be free to pursue Lady Diana without restraint. By the looks of it, the chase had already started. Well, let him. Her one wish was to go back to a time when she'd never heard of the Earl of Dalmar.

In another hour, she would be shot of him. It was what she wanted. No one took advantage of Annabelle Jocelyn with impunity. It galled her to think how easily she had become his dupe. Well, he was about to learn a lesson he would not soon forget. She did not think that he would resort to violence when her gift to him was unveiled, but she was taking no chances. She intended to make herself scarce the moment his hand pulled the cord to draw back the curtains. Only one hour to go, and it would all be over. She refused to be flustered by last-minute nerves.

The hour sped by in double quick time. When Dalmar came to lead her in to supper, Annabelle could not believe that the clock had already struck midnight.

"Just one more dance," she implored, her voice sounding strange and breathless.

"Annabelle, you've danced the feet of half the gentlemen here tonight. You're not having second thoughts, are you?"

"What?" Her eyes were enormous.

He tucked her hand into the crook of his arm. "Our engagement. It's too late to back out now."

She looked around frantically, as if seeking help from some quarter.

Dalmar chuckled. "Come along, dear! Don't be bashful. I'm quite certain you've arranged things just as you ought."

"David, truly I'm not hungry. I couldn't eat a bite!"

He looked at her oddly. "You *are* nervous, aren't you? Are you afraid I won't like my engagement present? Is there some reason I shouldn't?"

Almost desperately she said, "I think I should go home. I'm not feeling very well."

Her protestations went unheeded. Her elbow was gripped in a firm clasp, and she was propelled through the doors and down the marble staircase to the rooms which had been reserved for supper.

Her eyes were involuntarily drawn to the red velvet curtain which concealed her gift from curious eyes. When the guests were assembled, through a haze, she heard Dalmar's voice, deep and resonant, make the announcement of their engagement. She was dimly aware of accepting a glass of champagne from his hand and of the many expressions of congratulations which were tendered. The moment that Dalmar laid his hand to the cord which would unveil her gift, however, her senses sharpened and her instinct for self-preservation took over. She set down her glass of champagne and edged her way toward the exit. Colonel Ransome was stationed at the doors. He refused to let her pass.

"Lord Dalmar's orders," he said, and smiled apologetically.

Annabelle whirled to face the Earl. She thought his expression was very grim as his eyes burned into hers. In that moment, she knew that she did not wish to humiliate him before his peers. He deserved to be taken down a peg or two. That was indisputable. But what she had planned for him was worse than infamous. She could not be so cruel. At least not in public.

She gave an anguished cry. "David! Don't touch those drapes!"

He returned a cool, dispassionate smile and pulled on the cord. The curtains swished back. Annabelle could not bear to look. An awful silence descended. Then, in every part of the room, uproarious laughter broke out.

"She's a great gun!"

"What a sport!"

"Three cheers for Annie."

Annabelle chanced a quick look. Her eyes became riveted. The oversized satirical cartoon which was revealed was not the one she had commissioned that very afternoon by one of the famed Cruickshank brothers. The first flush of relief was instantly swamped by the rising tide of temper. It was a portrait of herself. The cartoonist had made her appear all eyes and chin. Her teeth, looking like the white cliffs of Dover, were bared in a travesty of a smile. At her heels were wicked spurs with which she was ferociously prodding the flanks of the most dejected-looking flea-bitten nag she had ever beheld. A pack of hounds, their tails between their legs, were slinking away from the lash of the whip in her uppraised arm. The caption infuriated her. "Annie Reformed," she read.

She forced a smile, her eyes all the while shooting sparks at the Earl. He held out his hand. There was nothing for it but to go to him. The applause was thunderous.

For his ears only, she said, "You didn't like my engagement present, I take it?"

She did not trust the smile he gave her. "I adored it," he said. "But I prefer not to be cut dead by all my friends on the morrow, if it's all the same to you."

His long fingers clamped over her small hand like a steel manacle, a warning of things to come.

Chapter Twelve

The last guest had finally gone home. The servants were all dismissed. Falconer and Ransome had long since mounted the stairs to their beds. Annabelle and Dalmar were alone in the book room.

"What became of the original cartoon?" she asked, her eyes wary as the Earl approached. Silently she accepted the glass of amber liquid he held out to her. Her nose wrinkled. She preferred sherry to brandy, but in that moment, nothing would have made her say so.

He remained standing, his back to the mantel. Annabelle did not demean herself by craning her neck to look up at him. She gazed blindly at the glass in her hand.

"Destroyed," he finally answered, cool eyes raking her. "I could not take the chance that it might fall into the wrong hands."

She gave him a smile hinting of insolence. "I thought it was one of Cruickshank's more memorable efforts," she taunted. "He caught your friends' likenesses to a tee."

Brusquely, he answered, "You're playing with fire, Annabelle. What do you imagine would have happened on the morrow when some of the foremost peers in the realm discovered themselves to be the butt of your malicious wit?"

"Don't forget Monique Dupres," she reminded him airily. "I thought Cruickshank did a fair likeness of her too—not to mention yourself—considering he had only my description to go on."

"And in their nightclothes."

Annabelle's eyes widened. "Well, I could scarcely have permitted them to be portrayed as naked as the day they were born, though to be sure, the thought did occur to me. D'you think I was craven to insist that they were covered, at least to their knees?"

"What I think," said Dalmar, "is that you've had a near escape. That cartoon was more than offensive. It was libelous. To portray Wellington, Worcester, Argyle, and so on like a pack of rutting dogs on the tail of a bitch in heat is enough to ruin us both for eternity and beyond."

Dryly she answered, "You don't think it would have ruined the gentlemen in question? Perhaps you are right. But you missed the whole point of the exercise, Dalmar. In her hand Monique was carrying her memoirs, and she was running to you." She tipped her head up and said softly, "I only thought to reveal your interest in Bailey's." There was a silence, and she added for effect, "Partner."

He stared at her for a long moment. Her eyes never wavered from his. "So that's it," he said, and quickly drained the glass in his hand.

"Yes, that's it," she said, and tried to emulate his example. After one swallow and several mortifying coughs, she rose to her feet and slammed the glass of brandy onto a side table. "I trusted you . . ." she began.

He cut her off without a qualm. "And I heeded your advice. In business, friendship counts for nothing. Those were your very words, Annabelle."

She came to stand a pace away from him, her head held stiffly. "I remember other words, something to the effect that you would never meddle in my business. Or have you forgotten your promise to me?"

He made a gesture of impatience. "You weren't listening. I tell you now what I told you then, I will not use my position as your *husband* to enforce my will. As your business partner, however, I claim the right to have some say in how things are managed. I have not broken my promise to you. If you remember, *I* was the one who questioned your lack of scruples, and *you* were the one who assured me that in business, no quarter should be asked or given."

"Scruples!" she flung at him. "Was it scrupulous to approach my partner and trick her into selling her half of the business when she and I had an agreement to give the other first refusal on it?"

Unperturbed, he readily agreed. "Not scrupulous at all, at least not by my lights. But that was before you gave me advice on how to conduct myself in the world of commerce. Admit it! You've been hoisted on your own petard."

She could not like his levity. And the twinkle in his eyes set her teeth on edge. There had been times, naturally, when she'd taken a tumble and had to cut her losses. And times when competitors had fought her to a standstill. But oh, she'd never felt this sense of betrayal with them.

She felt compelled to drop her lashes to check the wet sting of incipient tears. After a moment she turned aside and moved to the window, where she stationed herself, gazing out on the square as if she could see more than the dark, cavernous night, with only the odd lantern swinging from wrought-iron grilles to chase the shadows away.

When she turned back, she had herself well in hand. Her voice as level as she could make it, she said, "I think I once told you that if you got in my way, I would mow you down."

"Something of the sort," he said, and turned away to hide a grin.

"I'm the one who makes the decisions at Bailey's Press," she told him, in deadly earnest.

He folded his arms across his chest. "I'm prepared to give you a fairly loose rein. In most things, I trust your judgment. When occasion demands, I'll pull on the bit. I think we shall deal very well together, Annabelle."

"With you holding the reins? I think not. I don't take direction from anyone."

He was very relaxed and even more amused. "It's about time you learned to, my girl. That's been your problem all along."

She managed a convincing laugh. "Good God! You're just like all the others. You see me as a challenge. And I thought you were different! Give it up, Dalmar. Better men than you have tried to save me from myself."

"Ah, but I mean only to reform you."

His unfortunate choice of words brought to mind the caption of the cartoon. Again she laughed, though this time it sounded forced. "Annabelle reformed," she jeered. "I don't wish to be reformed."

"*Annie* reformed," he corrected, "and your wishes have nothing to do with it."

"There's no point in talking to you," she said, turning up her nose, and she made to leave the room.

Laughing, he grabbed hold of her arms and shook her gently. "Where's your sense of humor?" he demanded, and forced her to the chair she had recently vacated. "I know you haven't finished with me yet. Nor have I with you. Why don't you get it all off your chest—clear the air—and after, we'll see where we stand?"

She forced herself to draw several deep, calming breaths. When he saw that she had herself under control, he moved away, giving her breathing room.

Calmly, clasping her hands together, she said, "What I can't understand is why in heaven's name you would want to buy into a publishing house. There are other enterprises which are far more lucrative for a man of your wealth. Tin or coal, for instance." She was thinking that perhaps she could shame him into selling her his half of Bailey's, or at the very least, convince him that his money could be more wisely invested. His next words disabused her of the notion.

"I thought I'd explained that. I needed a hold over you, something that would give me an advantage. Did you really think that you could go on as you are? I'm even more convinced, having met your brother-in-law, that it needs a strong man with his wits about him to manage a woman of your temperament. I did what I thought was necessary."

"You tricked me!"

"No. I followed your advice. You left me no option once I gave my word that I would not exercise my rights as your husband—rights the law confers—to temper your conduct."

Passionately she cried out, "Thank God I discovered the truth about you in time. If I'd married you, your power over me would have been absolute. Let me tell you something,

Dalmar. I've been my own mistress for a good number of years. I'm not about to trade my freedom for an uncertain bondage as any man's chattel. I should be grateful to you, I suppose, for having taught me a lesson I needed to remember. Matrimony is a snare to entrap unwary females. Well, thank God I've come to my senses."

His voice as soft as satin, Dalmar said, "I wondered when it would come to this. So! You mean to break off the engagement."

"Can you doubt it?"

"You gave me your word."

"Under false pretenses! If I'd known then what I know now, I wouldn't have given you the time of day. It's finished, Dalmar. Over."

Something awful seemed to have been unleashed in the room. Annabelle clasped her hands more tightly together and braced herself for the storm.

Dangerously calm, Dalmar said, "You're angry now, like a child having a temper tantrum. I should have expected it. That will pass. You need time to accustom yourself to the idea that there's a man in your life who means to exercise some control over you."

She blinked, and blinked again. It seemed to her that the man was like a block of granite, impervious and unshakable. Acidly sweet, she inquired, "You mean you'll be the puppeteer and I'll be the puppet?"

The harsh lines of his features relaxed into a grin. Chuckling, he said, "Nothing so obvious, Annabelle. I was thinking more on the lines of leading strings. Most of the time you won't even know they are there. I promise to pull on them only when I think you're stepping into deep water."

The picture his words evoked was highly insulting. Leading strings were for nursery children who were too immature to understand that the world was a dangerous place which could hurt them. Nurses and mothers kept their young charges in check by tying them with long strings either to themselves or to some heavy immovable object.

As if reading her mind, he said, "You'll have more freedom than most wives."

"Dalmar, *dogs* have more freedom than most wives."

He laughed and shook his head. "There's something in what you say, but it won't be like that with us. I only want to protect you from yourself, like tonight, for example, when I switched pictures."

"Should I thank you?"

"Should I beat you? That's how some men keep their wives in check. Since I don't subscribe to those methods, I have to rely on my ingenuity. All things considered, I think I turned the tables on you rather adroitly, wouldn't you say?"

It had been in her mind to apologize for the embarrassment she had intended to cause him with Cruickshank's clever cartoon. She knew herself to have been grossly in the wrong even to think of shaming him before his peers. At these polemic remarks, however, her good intentions evaporated.

"You deserved a set-down," was all she could say.

"Public humiliation is not a set-down, Annabelle, as your own conscience should tell you."

There was a silence. Her conscience dutifully prodded her. 'I beg your pardon," she said, though the words almost choked her. But just to make sure that he understood, though she was sorry for the harm she had meant to do him, she had not forgiven him for stealing her business from under her nose, she added for good measure, "But what *you* did was unforgivable!"

After an interval his eyebrows rose. "And that is all the apology you think I deserve?"

"No harm was done," she pointed out, on the defensive.

"Through no thanks to you. Moreover, you gave me your promise that what happened between us in the world of business would be kept separate from our private lives. You broke that promise, or tried to."

His softly spoken words acted on her like a scourge. She could scarcely believe that she was her father's daughter. That she, Annabelle Summers Jocelyn, in a fit of temper, should stoop to such a level merely to revenge herself for his backhanded turn was a lowering thought. She'd considered herself, once, above such pettiness. But oh, the man was clever! He'd fenced her in at every turn. The truth of the matter was that she'd never expected that Dalmar, a mere novice, could best her in her own game.

"I wouldn't have gone through with it," she said. "I tried to stop you, but you ignored my warning. You, on the other hand, had no scruples about shaming me in public."

"Nonsense! Your credit has climbed. People always admire those who poke fun at themselves."

"Only I wasn't poking fun at myself!" she cried out.

"Ah. That stung, did it? Should I feel sorry for you after what you tried to do to me?"

Something in his voice, some emotion, arrested her. She darted a quick glance at him, then looked away. "I never meant to hurt you," she said miserably. "I only meant to take you down a peg or two. Won't you let it go at that?"

"No. I won't," he said, and smiled the strangest smile.

After a moment, Annabelle rose to her feet. "Nothing more can be served by this conversation," she said. "I'd be obliged if you would send the notice to *The Gazette* terminating our engagement. If you wish to delay a week or two, for appearances' sake, I have no objection."

She began to remove his engagement ring, but he prevented it. "Annabelle," he said so softly that she had to strain to hear him, "don't make me lose my patience."

He'd thought himself so very clever in extracting a promise from her that what happened in the sphere of business was to be kept separate from their personal lives. He'd miscalculated. Evidently Annabelle had no intention of honoring that promise. And he had no intention of letting her break it. An appeal to her sense of fair play had failed to sway her. She was leaving him no option but to use the only other tactic he held in reserve.

"You do want to marry me," he said softly. "I'll prove it to you."

She swallowed hard and tried to back away from him. His arms circled her waist and tightened. "Don't!" she said in a hoarse whisper.

Annabelle had been living on nerves for the better part of that long, interminable day. In the last several hours, one emotion after the other, in quick succession, had held her in its grip—fury at Dalmar's duplicity; self-disgust at her own gullibility; shame at the paltry revenge she had meant to exact, and finally an emotion which she abhorred—self-pity. Through it all she had managed to project her habitual air of composure. That composure was very close to disintegrating. All she wanted, she thought, was a quiet hole she could crawl into, where she might lick her wounds in private. She was very close to tears. Dalmar's arms closed around her. She halfheartedly made a move to escape, then the feel of those strong, comforting arms was too much to resist. She melted against him.

His hand cupped her head, and he used his lips and tongue to evoke memories of the time she had surrendered everything to him. He wasn't going to take her all the way, he decided. But when he was done with her, she would never again deny that she belonged to him.

He'd forgotten how sweet she tasted, how soft she was in his arms. She wasn't supposed to open her lips to get more of him; she wasn't supposed to melt against him like warm honey. And when she made that familiar, low moan of surrender at the back of her throat, he wasn't supposed to go mad with wanting her.

His hands were desperate to relearn every intimate secret of her body. It had been so long, so damned long, since he'd taken her, and for months he had been living the life of a monk. Oh God, he should have known that once he put his hands on her, there could be no turning back.

Her body was trembling, her desire rising to match his own. He could taste it in her mouth, feel it as she arched instinctively into each caress of his hands. Lifting his head, he looked down at her.

Her lips were parted and red and swollen from his kisses, her eyes dark and dreamy. He could tell by looking at her that her body was ready to receive him. His hands slid to her hips, and he dragged her into the cradle of his thighs, showing her that he was ready for her too.

"David," she gasped softly. "Oh David."

"Don't tell me to stop now," he groaned. "I don't think I can. And you don't want me to." And he hungrily kissed away the last shreds of her resistance. "Oh God, Annabelle, I need you so damn much."

His chest was heaving when he finally pulled away from her. 'You're coming with me," he said, "and I'm not taking no for an answer."

She knew, in the carriage, that he had no intentions of taking her home. She might have pleaded with him, or done any number of things to make him change his mind. She didn't do a single thing. She didn't want to.

It wasn't his skillful, passionate lovemaking that had seduced her, she thought, but that overwhelming need she always sensed in him whenever he took her into his arms. More than the pleasure of her body, this lonely, contradictory man needed a woman's loving. It was an appeal that never failed to work on her. He could be infuriating. And he could be so irresistibly vulnerable.

He'd told her once, in passing, and as if it were of no moment, that the happiest years of his life had been spent with Wellington. It didn't take much intelligence to deduce that he had never enjoyed the comforts and security of an ordinary home. He'd had to grow up too fast and too soon. She couldn't imagine it. All her life she'd had to struggle against the suffocating restraints imposed by those who loved her in order to gain a modicum of independence. He'd been a boy when manhood had been thrust upon him. And she ached for the pity of it.

Sighing, confused by a press of conflicting emotions, she stared at him wordlessly and waited for events to unfold.

The house he brought her to was in Kensington. Without saying a word, she allowed him to escort her over the threshold.

"It's not really mine," he told her, the first words he had spoken since they'd left Cavendish Square. "It belonged to my uncle. He was a bachelor. Once, before I met you, I thought I might have a use for it. Now it's up for sale."

He left her in the small dark hallway whilst he went away to inform the caretakers of his presence. He returned with a brace of candles.

"David . . . I never meant . . ." The rest of her words were

217

said to his chest. He crushed her to him with his free arm, half supporting her as he swept her up the narrow staircase.

In the bedroom, he left her to light several candles about the room. Finally, he threw his greatcoat over the back of a chair and sat down on the bed.

He held out a hand to her. "Come to me," he said in a voice so low, so indistinct, she scarcely recognized it.

Annabelle stayed where she was. At the moment of truth, she was plagued by second thoughts. She knew that if she surrendered herself to him, there would be no going back. And though her heart urged her to give in to him, vestiges of common sense held her in check. Dalmar wanted a woman he could control. She would never permit anyone to order her conduct. If they married, she could foresee endless battles ahead of them.

"Annabelle," he said slowly, patiently, "come to me."

"Can't we just talk about it?" she prevaricated, and came one step closer.

"Words just get in the way. And you don't want to talk any more than I do."

She stared at those silver eyes unblinkingly. "David," she said again, earnestly, sincerely, "breaking an engagement isn't so serious a thing. Scores of people have done it. In the morning, you'll see things differently. You'll be glad that you're not marrying a hoyden. Just look at me!" As if to make her point, she slipped her mantle from her shoulders.

"Annabelle!" he commanded, losing patience.

"I use rouge. I darken my lashes and brows. I dye my hair. Did you know that? I almost never wear drawers or petticoats. And I'm not going to change for any man. You should marry someone like Lady Diana. She's young, beautiful, proper, and just perfect for you. Think about it, David. I'll make your life miserable." She choked back a betraying sob.

He threw himself down on the bed and flung the back of one hand over his eyes. "Annabelle," he gritted, "will you get the hell over here?"

"Oh Devil!" she said, weeping, and threw herself into his arms.

Those strong arms clamped around her and rolled her under

218

him. One by one he removed the pins from her hair and tossed them onto the floor. Long fingers combed through her hair, then brought her face up for his kiss.

His eyes traveled her face and the laughter in them gradually faded. "Sweet," he said. "You're so sweet. Don't you know I love you just the way you are?" And he kissed her tears away.

His lips claimed hers, and she wondered that so much hunger, so deep a longing, could be contained in one kiss.

"I shouldn't," he groaned. "But I can't help myself." And his mouth slammed onto hers, as if to cut off any protest she might think to make.

Though she'd been married once, Annabelle's experience was very limited. She thought she might be as awkward as a green girl. But everything seemed so natural. She loved the feel of those broad shoulders beneath the sensitive pads of her fingers. She loved his taut waist and slim flanks. She loved the crisp texture of his hair. She wrapped her arms around him and answered the demand in his kiss.

He dragged his mouth from hers. His breathing was ragged. "I'm not forcing you," he said.

Annabelle smiled. She thought it would be easier to part the Red Sea as deflect the man from his purpose. "No, you're not forcing me," she murmured.

He kissed her again.

He grew impatient with the restriction of their clothes. He pulled her up to sit on the edge of the bed and knelt before her, slowly, sensually, peeling the silk stockings from her legs, then removing her gown, her stays, and her chemise. When she was bared to his eyes, she felt suddenly shy, and even more shy when he stripped off his own clothes. No man had ever seen her naked before. Nor had she ever seen a naked man. She did not know where to look, and she veiled her gaze with her lashes. "David, the candles," she whispered.

There was no response. She chanced a look at him. He was totally absorbed, his eyes slowly traversing her from the crown of her head to the tips of her toes. Without thinking, she shook her hair forward like a curtain shielding her body.

"Not this time," he told her, and brushed her hair back. "That one time I had you, in the Palais Royal—it always

219

seemed like a dream. I remember so little. This time I won't be cheated of anything. And neither will you."

Slowly he straightened. "Annabelle, sweetheart, don't turn your head away. Look at me. I'm only a man. Don't be afraid."

She looked her fill, and little tremors began to shake deep inside her. He might be only a man, but he was a formidable animal. So much strength and power in that hard, masculine body! She felt the tiniest flame of fear, something primal and entirely feminine in nature. He was the male animal, dominant and infinitely more powerful than she.

"No," he groaned, and came down beside her, covering her protectively. "I'm harmless, I swear it! You're the one who's in control. You're the one with all the power. I won't take a thing you're not willing to give."

She touched him, shyly, boldly, and desire shimmered through her. She'd never felt more of a woman in her life. With mouth open, she drew his head down, and claimed him with her kiss, playing his game, tongues mating, surging, receding. She laughed deep in her throat. It was easy to love him. Almost as easy as it had been in the Palais Royal when he'd been dazed and sedated with laudanum. How curious that she should think that he would be more man than she could manage. He was a perfect dear, tender, gentling her of her fears. She loved the way he cradled her in his arms; loved the whisper of his breath at her throat, her eyes, her temples; loved the way he made her feel like the most precious, fragile porcelain. Recklessly, with more abandon, she lavished him with affectionate, grateful kisses, and all unknowingly, tested the limits of his self-control.

She heard the hiss of his breath, and suddenly his hands were everywhere at once. He shifted, and his tongue followed the path of his hands, playing at the pulse in her throat, the hollow of her shoulder, slowly, excruciatingly bathing the heavy, swollen buds of her nipples before his lips closed over them, teasing, wooing and then devouring.

"David . . . I . . ."

He didn't give her time to think. His hand brought her leg up. He cupped her, stroked her, and probed gently through the delicate folds of her femininity to her secret core. He felt her

220

body shudder, heard her moan. When she arched against his fingers, he stopped trying to control his breathing.

"Yes, love, like this," he coaxed. "I've thought of you so many times like this. Wild and sweet for me. And wet with wanting me."

"David, I can't think when . . ."

He eased his fingers deeper, nudging her legs further apart. Her sweet woman-scent drove him to breaking point. He heard the change in her breathing, the involuntary whispers that stole from her lips, and he grunted his satisfaction. He'd never wanted anything so much in his life. Not her woman's body, but her response to him. Unfettered. Uncontrolled. Her female to his male.

Abruptly he scooped her up till their positions were reversed. He grasped her shoulders to keep her from falling. Her eyes were all pupil, dark and unfocused, her gloriously dark hair cascading like a waterfall about them both. Her hands clamped around his arms to steady herself.

He saw everything he wanted to see; everything he hoped for; things she would try to conceal from him in her saner moments. She was such a joy to him, this innocent, vulnerable, fiery virago who had to be always in control. There was no sign of that control now. In his arms, she turned wanton. He wondered if she would forgive him for it in the morning.

He hadn't meant to take her again before their wedding night. For weeks he'd endured the bite of his ardor; stifled it, mastered it. The prize had been too precious to jeopardize by taking unnecessary risks. Everything had changed the moment she had tried to give him back his ring. He was angry with himself. And more angry with her. He felt shaken. Honor meant nothing to him when he thought of the emptiness she meant to consign him to. Once, he thought he might survive without her. But that was months ago. He couldn't live with her on her terms. But he wouldn't give her up without trying every trick he knew. He was doing it as much for her as he was for himself. It was the truth. It was a lie.

He began to murmur all sorts of loverlike endearments. He meant every word. She was like sunshine to his dark soul, he told her as his lips skimmed fleetingly over her face. She was

221

sweet, so unbelievably sweet, and soft and feminine. He claimed those things for himself and dared her, on pain of death or worse, to reveal them to any other male.

Incredibly, she answered him in kind, returning kiss for kiss, touch for touch. He thought his heart would burst with happiness.

He eased her astride his thighs. Her openness and vulnerability to him was more intoxicating than the sweetest wine. A frantic hunger to possess her tore through him. Roughly, urgently, he covered her shoulders and breasts with kisses, and she flung her head back. His fingers found her, delved, and began a rhythmic stroking. She brought her head down to his shoulder to muffle her cry.

Panting, she gasped, "David . . . please, I'm not myself."

"You're more yourself than you know. Passionate, giving, my woman, Annabelle." Deliberately, fiercely, he murmured dark, sensual words in her ear. He sensed the moment her crisis was upon her even before he felt her hands clutching convulsively at his shoulders.

He surged into her, taking her cries into his mouth, cupping her buttocks, compelling her to his rhythm. Again and again he filled her with himself, spilling his seed deep in her body. He heard her sigh as she stilled, and again he thrust deeply, emptying himself.

With heart clamoring, he held her to him for long moments, savoring her closeness. Tenderly, reverently, he unwrapped the silken tendrils of hair from his neck and arms and laid her on the mattress, half covering her with his body. He pulled the coverlet over her shoulders. They dozed in each other's arms.

Annabelle sighed. Languidly, like a lazy kitten, she stretched. Wide-eyed, she turned her head to look at her lover. "Are you all right?" she asked softly.

Dalmar raised on one elbow and reached out to smooth back the tangle of her hair. In the aftermath of love, she didn't look a bit like the Annabelle Jocelyn who terrorized the ton and ruled Bailey's with an iron fist. My woman, he thought again, and smiled slowly. They would have a wonderful life together. Nothing could convince him otherwise. "Why shouldn't I be all right?" he asked.

Her lashes lowered though she returned his smile. "It's not important," she said.

He raised himself farther. "What's not important?"

She pulled herself to a sitting position. Uncertainly she stammered, "I said things . . . look . . . I just want you to know I'm sorry about what happened tonight and what I said. All right?"

Impatience started to build in him. "Are you saying that's why you came with me tonight without a murmur? That you felt you owed me something?"

She could not understand why he was being so difficult. "I wanted to make it up to you," she temporized. "And talk to you. You were so . . ." Her voice tapered off. "I wanted to come with you," she said simply.

His eyes searched her face. "And am I forgiven for becoming your partner at Bailey's, uninvited?"

"Oh no," she said, serious for all the playfulness in her manner. "I may have played the good samaritan for you tonight, but when it comes to business, you'll discover that I'm a veritable shark. Be warned, Dalmar! In spite of your consequence, in my world you're just a little fish. And I eat little fishes for breakfast."

He swore under his breath. She had given him his title and not his name. He was inclined to take that carelessly spoken "Dalmar" and blister her backside with it. Instead, he seized upon the more telling slip of her tongue. "Good samaritan? Is that what you thought you were? And I suppose that would make me the object of your charity?"

Wordlessly she stared at him. She shook her head.

His hands reached for her and wrapped themselves in her hair. He pulled her face down till her lips were only inches from his. "As I remember, the Good Samaritan was generous to a fault. Correct me if I'm wrong."

She swallowed. "Very generous," she whispered.

"Show me," he commanded.

She discovered that his need was like a bottomless pit.

He learned that her generosity was like an everlasting fountain. He slaked his thirst but could not get enough. He wanted to drown in her.

Get 4 FREE Books!

We created our convenient Home Subscription Service so you'll be sure to have the hottest new romances delivered each month right to your doorstep—usually before they are available in book stores. Just to show you how convenient the Zebra Home Subscription Service is, we would like to send you 4 FREE Kensington Choice Historical Romances. The books are worth up to $24.96, but you only pay $1.99 for shipping and handling. There's no obligation to buy additional books—ever!

Save Up To 30% With Home Delivery!

Accept your FREE books and each month we'll deliver 4 brand new titles as soon as they are published. They'll be yours to examine FREE for 10 days. Then if you decide to keep the books, you'll pay the preferred subscriber's price (up to 30% off the cover price!), plus shipping and handling. Remember, you are under no obligation to buy any of these books at any time! If you are not delighted with them, simply return them and owe nothing. But if you enjoy Kensington Choice Historical Romances as much as we think you will, pay the special preferred subscriber rate and save over $8.00 off the cover price!

We have 4 FREE BOOKS for you as your introduction to
KENSINGTON CHOICE!
To get your FREE BOOKS, worth up to \$24.96, mail the card below or call TOLL-FREE 1-800-770-1963.
Visit our website at www.kensingtonbooks.com.

Get 4 FREE Kensington Choice Historical Romances!

💟 **YES!** Please send me my 4 FREE KENSINGTON CHOICE HISTORICAL ROMANCES (without obligation to purchase other books). I only pay \$1.99 for shipping and handling. Unless you hear from me after I receive my 4 FREE BOOKS, you may send me 4 new novels—as soon as they are published—to preview each month FREE for 10 days. If I am not satisfied, I may return them and owe nothing. Otherwise, I will pay the money-saving preferred subscriber's price (over \$8.00 off the cover price), plus shipping and handling. I may return any shipment within 10 days and owe nothing, and I may cancel any time I wish. In any case the 4 FREE books will be mine to keep.

Name _____

Address _____ Apt. _____

City _____ State _____ Zip _____

Telephone (____) _____

Signature _____

(If under 18, parent or guardian must sign)

Offer limited to one per household and not to current subscribers. Terms, offer and prices subject to change. Orders subject to acceptance by Kensington Choice Book Club.
Offer Valid in the U.S. only.

KN044A

PLACE
STAMP
HERE

IIı.ıı.IIlı.ııı.IIıl.ıl.ılı.ıl.ıIIlı.ıl.ıIIlı.ıl

KENSINGTON CHOICE
Zebra Home Subscription Service, Inc.
P.O. Box 5214
Clifton NJ 07015-5214

Chapter Thirteen

Annabelle did not break her engagement to the Earl. Though she had some misgivings about how she would manage such a strong-willed gentleman after their nuptials, she did not dwell on them. Her waking thoughts were filled with the vivid memories of the hours they had spent in the little house in Kensington. She remembered the texture of his hair and skin under her fingers; she thought of his whispered endearments as he had kissed every naked inch of her; and most of all she recalled the look in his eyes as they had blazed from tenderness to passion. Even the memories made her heart begin a rapid beat. She could not wait to repeat the experience and had no notion now of holding herself from her lover for the six or seven weeks that remained till they could be married by her father in York. In short, at thirty years old, Annabelle was a woman newly awakened to passion and, like a child offered carte blanche in a sweetshop, she was impatient to sample all of its delights.

Having admitted as much to herself, she waited for the first pangs of conscience to strike. Nothing happened. She delved a little deeper. Though she discovered her conscience to be as lively as ever it was in most matters, on the subject of Dalmar it was surprisingly (and thankfully) mute. She delved no further.

With Dalmar it was otherwise. His conscience scourged him. He'd taken Annabelle first in the Palais Royal when he had assumed she was fair game. There had been some excuse for his misconduct then. In the weeks since he had been courting her, however, it had been borne in upon him that in spite of her worldly airs and previous marriage, Annabelle was as unfledged and untried as a newly hatched nestling. And he had played on that inexperience, awakening her dormant sensuality with stolen kisses, bold caresses, and words that would have brought a blush to the cheeks of a hardened rake, till he had her panting for their marriage bed. He'd done it deliberately, exploiting the one hold he knew he had over her. Annabelle was attracted to him. He courted that attraction, fed it, fanned it, and counted on it to overcome any and every objection to the estate of matrimony his misguided lady might entertain. He'd never meant to go so far as to anticipate their wedding night.

Yet he'd seduced her. Worse he'd taken her in a house and on a bed where other females, not fit to touch the hem of Annabelle's gown, had played out their carnal lusts for monetary gain. Annabelle deserved so much better than that sordid little house in Kensington.

But he'd been helpless to stop himself once she had spoken the fatal words that would sever their relationship. Hurt, fury, desperation, and a host of other emotions had made him their victim. He'd felt compelled to reestablish his hold over her in a thoroughly primitive and masculine fashion. Lust had nothing to do with it. He had wanted to dominate her, impose his will on her, force her to submit to his claims. Nothing short of total and unconditional surrender was acceptable in that moment when she had tested him to his limits.

In his saner moments, he could scarcely recognize himself in the man who had used her so unscrupulously. His own frightful background where a brutish father had wreaked his will on his defenseless family had shaped him to a different course. He was sure that no woman before Annabelle could claim that he had ever been wanting in consideration. By and large, he treated the softer sex with chivalry. Only Annabelle brought out the worst in him as well as the best.

With respect to their business relationship, he felt on a firmer footing. Annabelle had laid down the rules and it suited his purpose to make her play by them. He did not imagine for a minute that he would have everything his own way. But on

226

some things, he was determined not to give ground.

In such a frame of mind, he entered Bailey's to meet with his betrothed for the first time since the night of his ball. Though outwardly he was the epitome of self-confidence, inwardly he felt as nervous as a thoroughbred. He did not know how he should answer Annabelle if she met him with a litany of reproaches for what he had done to her.

He found her at her desk. She looked up at his entrance. Her eyes were soft and dreamy, her smile shy; a faint blush lay across her cheekbones. Dalmar almost groaned his frustration. He could take her anytime. That much was obvious. Silently he cursed the fates for the gross injustice of making the woman he desired above all others available to him when he had made up his mind to play the gentleman. Hardening his resolve, he adopted a brusque air.

Annabelle noted the strangely sober expression, the offhand tone, the impersonal greeting, and gradually her smile died. She'd heard often enough that gentlemen despised foolish women who yielded themselves too readily to their advances, but logic had always rejected that myth as pure fiction. By her reckoning, it was the woman they had wronged who had the right to complain of it.

In quick succession, hurt, bewilderment, and mortification unfurled in her breast. Pride soon held sway. It made her a little reckless. By the time she had responded to the Earl's greeting, she had reverted to her habitual worldly pose.

She poured two cups of tea and held one out to Dalmar. "Now that we have dispensed with the amenities," she said pleasantly, "tell me, what brings you to Bailey's?" She had a good idea what it was, and wanted only the opportunity to put the man in his place.

"You mean, apart from the fact that I'm half owner and can walk in here anytime I choose?"

She inclined her head in acknowledgment of the mild reproof and kept her tongue firmly between her teeth.

"For a start, it would be more professional, when we are at Bailey's, if you would address me as Lord Dalmar, Mrs. Jocelyn." He wanted everything that happened between them in the business arena to be completely divorced from their private lives. He would not permit Annabelle to transfer, outside the walls of Bailey's, the anger and frustration he was sure he was about to provoke.

Annabelle lifted her head a notch. "As you wish, Lord Dalmar," she said, looking down the length of her intimidating nose.

"Furthermore, let me remind you of your promise not to confuse our professional and private lives. They're quite separate, Annabelle, and I'm going to hold you to that."

"Mrs. Jocelyn," she corrected.

"I beg your pardon?"

"It's more professional if you address me as Mrs. Jocelyn."

"Oh. Quite."

There was an awkward pause. It seemed to Annabelle that the Earl was gathering himself for something.

"About Monique Dupres's diaries . . ."

"Yes?" purred Annabelle.

"I've been giving the matter some serious thought . . ."

"What I think," said Annabelle with relish, bestowing on the Earl a smile which he highly distrusted, "is that the covers should be in purple calfskin and tooled in gold leaf at each corner with the crests of the great houses represented by her lovers—nothing below a marquess, of course—Beaufort, Anglesey, Wellington . . ."

"As you very well know," he cut in, "I'm here for one purpose only—to take those damned diaries away from you."

She bit back a furious retort and said with assumed calm, "I'm afraid I can't allow you to do that."

His eyes bored into hers. "If you know what's good for you, you will."

"Threats, Lord Dalmar?" she asked, and studiously went through the motions of drinking her tea.

"Be a good girl and just get the diaries for me."

Annabelle matched that patronizing tone exactly when she replied, "You've been laboring under a misapprehension, Lord Dalmar. The diaries don't belong to Bailey's. They're private property."

"What?" He sat bolt upright.

She savored her moment of triumph. "They're mine, Dalmar, paid for by my own money!"

"I don't believe it!" But even as he said the words, he remembered that the bank draft found among Monique Dupres's belongings in the Palais Royal had borne the signature of Mrs. Annabelle Jocelyn. "What about patents, and so on? Doesn't Bailey's have the rights to publish the damned things?"

"Now that was very remiss of me," she said, smiling with cloying sweetness. "There was no rush that I could see. It was left in abeyance. Of course, the moment I discovered I had a new partner, I rushed down to the Patent Office and registered the copyright. It's perfectly legal. I, Mrs. Annabelle Jocelyn, have the rights to publish the *damned* things if and when I want."

The gloves were off. Both sat like statues glaring at one another.

"Annabelle, I'm warning you, I shall not permit you to publish them. I'm a full partner here, and I say that Bailey's won't touch them with a barge pole."

She made a show of examining her manicure. "There are plenty of jobbing printers who will be glad of the work."

"No!" he roared. "I absolutely forbid it!"

"Anyone would think," she said, "that you had something to hide. You're not mentioned in them. What do you care?"

He gave a start and looked at her queerly for a moment. But his expression soon hardened, and Annabelle wondered if she had imagined the look.

Reasonably, patiently, he explained, "You'll make powerful enemies. There could be lawsuits. I've told you all this before."

"Yes," she said consideringly, "but that's not why you want to get your hands on the diaries."

His brows shot up. "What other reason could there be?"

"I don't know yet. But I mean to find out."

He was on his feet, looming over her like a huge bird of prey. "You're talking nonsense. Understand this, Annabelle. One way or another, I'm going to get those diaries. You think you are onto every trick. My dear, you're just a greenhorn pitting yourself against a seasoned campaigner. Give it up now and save us both a spot of bother."

229

"I'd be obliged if you would address me as Mrs. Jocelyn when we're at Bailey's," she said calmly.

"You won't like my methods," he warned her.

"Tell me something I don't know," she needled.

"You're asking to have your backside blistered!" he shouted.

"Lord Dalmar, that doesn't sound very professional," she pointed out, smiling gleefully at this show of temper.

"No. But I make no doubt it would give me a great deal of satisfaction."

He saw at once that Annabelle's humor was intractable, and the subject of the diaries dropped. For the next hour, Dalmar shot a barrage of questions at Annabelle. She could not help but admit that in the preceding weeks he had made himself thoroughly (though covertly) familiar with every operation at Bailey's. He won a reluctant admiration from her which she did not deign to articulate.

On the subject of the policies prevailing at Bailey's, they were again at loggerheads.

"Policies are essential for a smooth-running day-to-day operation," Annabelle insisted. By this time she and Dalmar had changed places. He was seated at her desk, leafing through a mountain of paper which one of Annabelle's clerks had set down five minutes before.

"Good God, woman!" he exclaimed. "How can anyone ever get anything done with so much verbiage to wade through? It will take me a month of Sundays to digest this piffle."

Annabelle peered over his shoulder as the Earl quickly thumbed through each offensive policy paper. "It does look like rather a lot when they're all together," she allowed.

He snorted. "Policies on punctuation and grammar—that I will permit. A policy in case of fire—well, perhaps that is prudent. But," his voice rose in incredulity, "a policy on the frequency of water-closet breaks? I ask you, Annabelle, is that really necessary?"

Her lips pursed together. "Some of the apprentices were taking advantage," she answered, clearly nettled.

"Then let their foreman settle them." He noted the slight pout of her lower lip and offered placatingly, "I daresay we can salvage the odd one. We'll work on them together at the end of the week when we go to your brother-in-law's place."

"I'm not erasing one iota of what's on those policy papers," she told him. "Dalmar, it's the only way to run a business."

"I can't work like that."

"And I can't work any other way."

He quirked one brow. "We could compromise."

"How?"

"Simple. You hand over Monique Dupres's diaries, and I leave your policies intact."

Furious, she told him what she thought of that idea.

"Plus three thousand pounds?" he threw in for good measure.

"What?"

"You heard me. That's one thousand clear profit. Take it or leave it, Annabelle. But just remember this: once I walk through that door, that's it. When I return, there will be no holds barred. Annabelle, you can't win this fight. Give it up."

Thin-lipped, she fetched his hat and gloves.

"I'll make it guineas," were the last words he said before she shut the door in his face.

Hours later Annabelle was still smarting from the encounter. Arrogant man! And unethical too! It wasn't Bailey's he was interested in, but only those diaries. Three thousand guineas was no mean bribe. Belatedly it occurred to her that Dalmar knew the exact sum she had paid over to Monique Dupres. It was possible that the French girl had confided in the Earl, but somehow Annabelle did not think it likely. It left her wondering how he had come by the information and why he was prepared to go to such lengths to lay his hands on the diaries.

In the drawing room after dinner, she appeared to be pre-occupied. If Bertie noticed anything amiss, she wisely kept it to herself. Since Annabelle was toiling at her knitting, Richard thought little of his mother's abstracted look. He was full of the projected trip to Rosedale. In front of the fire, he set out his knights in battle order and chattered incessantly of his cousins and all the things he was going to do with Lord Dalmar once they got there. He was in the throes of explaining the finer points of a horse's head (almost verbatim from the Earl's mouth) when Annabelle suddenly jumped to her feet.

"He's in those damned diaries, that's what!"

"Dear?" said Bertie, startled.

Annabelle was already making for the door. "Don't hold the tea tray for me. I have an errand to run. I shouldn't be more than half an hour."

"But where are you off to?" cried Bertie.

"Bailey's—to get the diaries."

She sent a footman to fetch a hackney. In the coach she got her keys ready. It took only minutes to get to her destination, and though it was dark, Annabelle dismissed the carriage. There were plenty of people about in the streets and in Soho Square. And there was a night watchman in attendance at Bailey's. She did not see what harm could come to her.

She pushed through the front entrance. "It's me, Mrs. Jocelyn," she called out to alert the night watchman of her presence.

Overhead, she heard a board creak. "Joe, are you there?" she called again, and made for the stairs.

In the upstairs landing she halted. The only wall lantern had gone out. Annabelle frowned. She presumed that one of her employees had omitted to trim the wick or refill the bowl with whale oil. Clucking to herself, she moved slowly through the blanket of darkness toward her office, holding her hands out in front of her. In one of her desk drawers she kept candles and flint for just such an emergency. She reached a hand for the drawer handle and froze.

"Who's there?" she called out, and instinctively sidestepped, evading the blow just as it fell.

Something heavy shattered against her desk. Annabelle emitted one shrill scream and bolted. She thundered down the stairs, raced out the front door, and careered straight into a passerby. Strong arms enfolded her. She screamed again.

"Annabelle? What the devil!"

She almost fainted with relief. "Gerry, is it you?" She saw that it was Lord Temple, and clung to him like a limpet. "Someone tried to murder me," she sobbed out.

It took several minutes to calm her. Lord Temple patiently

232

listened to her incoherent explanation, and by dint of careful questioning got the story out of her. He called a passing hackney, handed her in, and instructed her to wait for him.

She saw that he meant to enter Bailey's and called out, "Gerry, for heaven's sake, don't go in there alone! At least let me call the night watch!"

He waved her to silence and disappeared through the door. After several minutes, Annabelle observed a light in her office. Several more minutes were to pass before Lord Temple came out of the building.

"Burglars," he told her. "They've knocked out your night watchman. Don't worry! He's coming round. Why don't you go home, and I'll look after things here."

"Oh, thank God, Joe is all right," said Annabelle, then. "Burglars? But what . . . ?" Suddenly everything became clear.

"I can't see that they've taken anything," began Lord Temple, looking anxiously at Annabelle's set face, which had turned chalk white.

"Oh, I think I know what they were after," she said, and insisted on going back into the building.

Her first care was for the night watchman. Apart from the lump on the top of his head, he had no other injuries. Though he was dazed, several long swallows from Lord Temple's silver flask brought him out of his stupor. It appeared that he himself had opened the door to his attackers when one of them had identified himself as Annabelle's head printer. The ruse was simple but effective.

Upstairs, Annabelle found things just as she surmised.

"What's missing?" asked Lord Temple, his eyes traveling the small room.

The drawer had been forced. With candle in hand, Annabelle knelt down and opened it. "Only the diaries," she said in a strangely subdued voice.

Lord Temple knew at once to what she referred to. It provoked a lecture and a tongue lashing which made Annabelle wince.

"You've made your point," she said finally when he paused for breath.

"You've had a lucky escape," he told her severely. "I

warned you that something like this might happen." His tone gentled. "I don't suppose we shall ever discover who was behind the theft, but we'd better report it to the authorities."

Annabelle slammed the drawer shut and rose to her feet. "Oh, I think I know who was behind it," she said, unable to hide her bile. "And if you don't mind, Gerry, I prefer to keep the whole episode quiet."

No amount of remonstrating on Lord Temple's part could shake Annabelle of her resolve. At length he gave up trying to persuade her to call in Bow Street. As if reading her mind, he said, "I don't think this was the work of Dalmar, Annabelle. In the last number of weeks, I've observed the man. Whatever he was in his youth, it's not in him now to behave in so shabby a manner."

"Oh, do you think so?" she asked noncommittally. She was remembering Dalmar's words spoken only hours before. *Once I return, there'll be no holds barred.*

They locked up the building and took the night watchman home in their hired hackney. The drive to Greek Street was made in silence. On the front steps Annabelle seemed to come to herself and was profuse in her thanks for Lord Temple's assistance.

"Think nothing of it," he said. "It was sheer luck that I was passing by. I was on my way to call on you, as it happened, to ask if you would like my escort to Rosedale on Thursday."

"Thank you for the thought, Gerry, but Lord Dalmar has already made the offer, and I have accepted."

She made to move past him. "Annabelle," he said, detaining her with a hand on her sleeve, "I'm not sorry that the diaries have gone. At least now I'll rest easy knowing you're safe in your bed."

"Oh, the diaries haven't gone," she replied.

"What? Did you make a copy, then?"

"Only in a manner of speaking." Seeing his look compounded of disbelief and shock, she went on, "They're in my head. It may take me some weeks to regurgitate them, but you may be sure that every word Monique Dupres wrote in those diaries will come to me eventually."

"That's impossible!"

234

"Oh no, Gerry. That's a promise. And short of murder, there's not a thing anyone can do to stop me."

Once inside the house, she made for her chamber and immediately wrote a letter to the French girl advising her of what had happened and warning her to be on her guard. Though it was true that Annabelle could, with very little difficulty, reconstruct the diaries page by page, it was a tedious business and one she was not eager to begin upon. Thinking that Monique Dupres might have a copy in her possession, she requested that it be sent as soon as possible.

Until that moment, she had no real thought of publishing the diaries. In point of fact, it had wanted only Dalmar's capitulation and she would have surrendered them without a murmur. In her opinion, to allow the Earl to begin by setting such a precedent was sheer folly. It was the principle of the thing which had made her dig in her heels. Now everything was changed.

In her mind's eye she examined everything she knew about Dalmar, beginning with their first encounter at the Palais Royal. She wondered if, even then, it had been in his mind to take the diaries from her. Perhaps he had been prevented by the wounds he'd suffered in the riot. Her thoughts drifted to his more recent courtship, and she squirmed in mortification.

How could she have been so blind to his real object? To Dalmar, the diaries were paramount. And she had a shrewd idea of why this was so. *He* was the scapegrace Monique Dupres referred to only as "Sir Spider," that devil-may-care Don Juan who changed ladybirds as often as he changed cravats. In all probability, "Sir Spider" was a nickname he'd picked up at school. It was his own skin he was trying to save by suppressing the diaries. Though she herself had not at first recognized him, she was certain that his nickname would instantly betray him to his contemporaries. He would be a laughing stock, and he would not suffer such a fate without doing everything in his power to avert it. He'd proved that already by his conduct on the night of his ball. He'd switched cartoons, and she was the one who had ended up an object of ridicule.

"Oh Annabelle, how could you give your heart to such a man?" she wailed aloud to the four walls of her chamber.

When first she had met "Sir Spider" in the pages of the diaries, she'd thought him an attractive, chivalrous scamp for a lecher. How differently she viewed his past indiscretions now that she had penetrated the mystery of his identity. And he was the man she was promised to marry!

"I wouldn't marry you if you were the last man on earth," she said to the silence, and impotently beat her fists against the feather bolster on her bed. After a bout of weeping, it occurred to her that Dalmar never had any intention of going through with the wedding once he had the diaries. This shocking piece of deduction was, perversely, more enraging than the thought that she would be forced to accept him as her husband.

"Oh, where were you when I needed you?" she railed passionately, now addressing herself to her conscience. "Hussy! Betrayer! Sloth! You could have prevented my going to that den of iniquity in Kensington. For shame to put it into my head that I was compelled out of charity to give myself to the man." After a moment's reflection, she said in a more subdued tone, "Oh, he's an agent of the devil, that one. I see what it was now. We were both taken in. First he lulled you to sleep, and then he seduced me. How else are we to explain our fall from grace?" Evidently Annabelle's conscience said something in reply, for after a moment she hung her head and gave up trying to apportion blame for the fate which had overtaken her.

It was hours before Annabelle could think of the Earl with anything like equanimity. She'd been humbled once before when she'd learned of her husband's perfidy. She was humbled again, but not for the world would she wear her heart on her sleeve. She spent the hours before she finally dropped off to sleep rehearsing in her mind exactly how she would depress the pretensions of the man who thought he had got the better of her.

A week later, in the British embassy in Paris, Mr. James Somerset, attaché to the ambassador, smoothed the pages of two letters he had received that morning by diplomatic pouch. One was from Lord Dalmar and addressed to himself. The other was from Mrs. Annabelle Jocelyn and was addressed to Monique Dupres.

A frown clouded his brow. He picked up Dalmar's letter and carefully scrutinized it for the third time since it had been put into his hand. According to the Earl, though he did not have the diaries in his possession, he was perfectly sure that it was only a matter of days before Mrs. Jocelyn would be persuaded to hand them over. He discounted Somerset's suspicion that there might be some sinister party interested in the diaries for nothing of any moment had occurred since he had been on their trail. The letter ended, "Wish me happy, James. The lady and I are to be wed in December. I am the happiest man in the world. Ransome sends his regards."

Mrs. Jocelyn's letter, dated the day after the Earl's, was of a different temper. Somerset digested it for long moments. The name "Dalmar" occurred frequently, and in anything but flattering terms. It was very clear that something sinister was afoot, and that Mrs. Jocelyn held Dalmar to be responsible.

Somerset rose from his desk and went to the door to call his secretary.

"Ah, Fraser," he said as a sober young man in black frock coat entered moments later. "If you would be so kind, there are a couple of letters I wish to dictate."

Mr. Fraser immediately seated himself at a table to the right of Somerset's desk. He selected a pencil from a small rosewood box and adjusted the spectacles on the bridge of his nose. Only then did he look to his superior.

"To the Earl of Dalmar, etc. etc., etc.," began Somerset. "Dear David, I couldn't be happier with your news. Naturally I expect an invitation to the wedding."

"That's all, sir?"

"I trust you to amplify it appropriately. Fraser, how are you at forgery, by the by?"

"I beg your pardon?"

"Forgery. You know, copying another person's handwriting?"

Fraser eyed his superior askance.

"You did go to Eton, did you not?" asked Somerset, his brows lifting.

"I did, sir, but . . ."

"Good. In my experience, Etonians are always the best forgers. I'm glad to see that some things don't change. At my age, you know—oh, well, never mind that now. Where was I? Oh yes. 'To Mrs. Annabelle Jocelyn'—you'll find the address here. And make this flowery, and in French, if you please. The author of this letter is a female."

Somerset appeared to draw inspiration from the ceiling. Finally he said, "Oh, you know the background. Something to the effect that there are no other copies of the diaries and that Mrs. Jocelyn should proceed to reproduce them from memory. Oh, add, 'Thank you for the warning,' or words to that effect."

The pencil continued to scratch on the paper for some time after Somerset had finished speaking. "What address shall I write?" asked Fraser.

"The same."

"The Palais Royal?"

"Yes, that's the one."

"Do you wish me to include a copy of this forged letter to Lord Dalmar?"

Somerset fell into a brown study.

"Sir?" prodded Fraser after a prolonged silence.

The attaché seemed to come to a decision. "Let's play it by ear, shall we? Who's to say who, if anyone, is the villain of this piece? Trust to my experience, Fraser. In our business, it's better not to let the left hand know what the right hand is doing. That being the case . . ."

"Yes sir?"

"What? Oh . . . just send the letters, just send the letters."

Chapter Fourteen

Rosedale, the country seat of the Jocelyn family for four generations, was ideally situated between the inland county town of Lewes and the fashionable coastal spa of Brighton, and only a six-hour drive from London in fine weather. Though the manor itself was Elizabethan, the first Baron Jocelyn had brought it into the eighteenth century by giving the exterior a Palladian facing. Succeeding Jocelyns, finding themselves in more straitened circumstances through the second baron's predilection for gambling, thought themselves lucky just to hang onto the place. It was Sir Charles, the present baron, who had brought money into the family. At the age of thirty, he had formed a judicious alliance with Henrietta Routledge, heiress to Samuel Routledge the shipping magnate.

Sir Charles never questioned why he, an impecunious baron, should have captured the hand of such a well-dowered lady. To him, the reasons for the match were self-evident. He was, by birth and breeding, a member of the upper ten thousand. Through the first Baron Jocelyn came the hereditary and honorary post of Master of the King's Wardrobe. Besides a small pension, this gave him an entrée into Court circles. The Routledges were nouveau riche and of the merchant class. Their money in itself could not buy an introduction into the upper reaches of polite society. Only through marriage could Samuel Routledge's ambitions for his daughter be realized.

In point of fact, at nineteen, Henrietta Routledge could have taken her pick of half a dozen impoverished titles, and far more exalted than a mere baronetcy. Before her marriage, Henrietta, or "Harry," as she was then known, was a vivacious slip of a girl, with impish dark eyes and finely chiseled features. An only child and inclined to be spoiled by her father, she was of a headstrong bent, but this failing was tempered by a wealth of good sense and a loyal, affectionate nature. Though she was highly sought after, she was not flattered, sensible of the fact that it was her substantial dowry more than her person which lured her admirers. She enjoyed their attentions, but she was in no hurry to marry.

From the moment she set eyes on the handsome Sir Charles, however, she fell head over heels in love. Her father was scandalized, not merely because his only child was turning her nose up at the heir to a dukedom, but because he could not see how a high-spirited lass like his bonny Harry could ever be content with a dull stick-in-the-mud like Sir Charles Jocelyn, for all his good looks and fine breeding. In the end, her father had relented. Henrietta was the apple of his eye. He had never been able to gainsay her once her heart was set on anything.

Henrietta knew, when she married Sir Charles, that he was not in love with her. But she was young and believed that she could change the world. One gentleman's heart did not seem too onerous a task. Blithely she set out to make herself over into the kind of woman she thought would make her husband happy. Within three years, her father scarcely recognized her. Gone were the high spirits and hoydenish manners. Henrietta was as decorous and lively as a wax dummy, and so he told her.

In twelve years of marriage, Henrietta had presented her husband with five sons. Sir Charles was a devoted father. Motherhood became Henrietta. But she was miserable. And at the age of one and thirty, she had come to see that only pain and disillusion could attend a match where the two parties loved unequally.

Not that Sir Charles was anything but a considerate husband. Before the birth of their fifth child, he had visited his wife's bed dutifully once a week, and always on a Saturday night, mindful that on the following morning, the Sabbath, Henrietta could lie abed for an extra hour or two. His visits never lasted more than ten minutes, and after the birth of their third son, he had offered to cut them out altogether. Only Henrietta's desire for a daughter had constrained him to continue with the weekly visits. But after the birth of little Jonathon two years before, Henrietta herself had put an end to their married intimacy.

Sir Charles accepted his wife's preference like the gentleman he was. Henrietta was a gently bred girl who had matured into a woman of some refinement. She had done her wifely duty. More could not be expected of her. He did not consider himself a lusty man. Neither was he a monk. With due consideration, he installed a mistress at Brighton, not far distant from Rosedale. He did not love his mistress. In his whole life only one woman had ever captured his heart. She held it still—Annabelle, his brother's widow.

Since he was the soul of discretion, it never occurred to him that anyone, least of all his wife, would be wise to his transgressions. He was mistaken. As is the way of wives, within a month of his setting up his mistress, Henrietta knew every particular about the lady and her husband's visits to her. Mrs. Snow, the lady in question, was not so discreet as her protector. On the contrary, it amused her to flaunt her dubious position. As for Sir Charles's infatuation for Annabelle, Henrietta had recognized it before Sir Charles was aware of it himself.

Annabelle saw and understood little of what was going on. Though she prided herself on being a shrewd judge of character, she readily accepted people as they represented themselves. Hints, innuendo, speaking looks and suchlike were generally beyond her. She herself rarely said one thing while meaning another. She expected the same transparency in others. For some time she had been aware of a change in her sister-in-law. Since the birth of her last baby, Henrietta had become shrewish and ready to quarrel at the drop of a hat. Postpartum fidgets, Henrietta called it. And Annabelle believed her. Nevertheless, in spite of a ready sympathy for her sister-in-law's ailments, Annabelle had lost the taste for her company and would have rather been anywhere else but Rosedale.

241

The drive down was pleasant, but only because Dalmar was not a passenger in the coach. He and his brother acted as outriders. Annabelle had said not one word about the theft of the diaries which had taken place two nights before. Nor had the Earl, which had rather surprised her. She had expected him to gloat. But he'd taken one look at the fire in her eyes and the set jaw and had laughingly made himself scarce. She wondered what tack she should take and mulled the problem over in her mind as the miles sped by.

Apart from the perpetrators of the crime, only she, Bertie, and Lord Temple knew of the theft, and she'd sworn them to secrecy without knowing why. As far as the night watchman knew, the burglars had been disturbed before anything was taken. She didn't doubt for a minute that Lord Dalmar was crowing over his triumph, deeming her beaten. He'd learn soon enough that Annabelle Jocelyn was not some negligible gadfly he could brush away with impunity. On the other hand, she had learned to her cost that she'd underestimated the Earl at every turn. It behooved her to proceed with caution. She had a vision of Lord Dalmar passing the window of some bookshop, halting in his tracks, and turning with a stunned expression to stare at a display of purple-bound volumes. "The Memoirs of Monique Dupres," he would croak, and then faint dead away on the spot, knowing that she, Annabelle Jocelyn, had rolled him up, hook, line, and sinker.

Without thinking, she gave a crow of triumph.

"What's so funny?" asked her companion, looking at Annabelle with frank curiosity.

Fortunately, at that moment the coach lurched, and the ladies had their hands full grabbing hold of the two excited children.

Young Richard was in his element. Amy had never before been present during a Guy Fawkes celebration. Her dark eyes burned with excitement as he described the torchlight procession, the elaborate fireworks, the costumes, the mummers, and finally the huge bonfire, with its effigies of Guy Fawkes and Pope Pius IV, who was thought to have instigated the Gunpowder Plot.

"And we get to stay up past midnight," Richard informed

her, his eyes glowing at the thought of the late hour.

"How is it that Lewes has such an elaborate celebration to mark the anniversary of the Gunpowder Plot?" asked Bertie. "No other town goes to such extremes as far as I know."

"Oh, there have been bonfire nights at Lewes for hundreds of years," answered Annabelle, "and long before Guy Fawkes tried to blow up the House of Lords. I think it's a pagan festival which over time borrowed from this and that. No one knows for sure."

Having exhausted the topic of Guy Fawkes' Night, Richard soon introduced his second most favorite subject of conversation, and for the rest of the drive Annabelle suffered the dubious pleasure of hearing Lord Dalmar's virtues, his preferences, his bons mots and his profound grasp of things (to a child's way of thinking) extolled until she was sure such a paragon should be beatified and dispatched to heaven on the instant.

She'd been right about one thing: her sister-in-law went into high alt at her first glimpse of Amy. And no wonder, thought Annabelle. With her soulful dark eyes, so like her mother's, her flashing dimples, and that cap of unruly blond curls, the child was a living temptation to be spoiled by any female who harbored a mite of mothering instinct. And Henrietta had been saddled with five boys.

It soon became evident that this was to be a more elaborate house party than was typical for Rosedale and at that time of the year. As her maid unpacked her bags in one of the upstairs front bedrooms, Annabelle heard the grind of carriage wheels on the driveway below and the slamming of carriage doors followed by the indistinct buzz of people talking and laughing.

Dressed in a becomingly simple slip of gold silk, her bare arms prudently covered by a paisley shawl, she descended the stairs and came face to face with Colonel Ransome. Though she had known that Dalmar had been given carte blanche to invite whomsoever he chose, he had never once mentioned that the colonel was to be one of his party. Annabelle smelled collusion. Her first instinct was to turn on her heel and race up the stairs to Bertie's room and warn her friend of what was afoot. It was the trill of feminine laughter which arrested her in midstep.

Lady Diana, swathed from head to foot in black Russian sable, made a grand entrance, the center of a swarm of admirers, as was her wont. The footmen could not get near her. Ransome and John Falconer were at each elbow, removing the fur wraps from her shoulders. With a gurgle of laughter she threw her enormous muff in the air. Lord Dalmar made a dive for it and came nose to nose with Annabelle, the prize clutched to his chest like the spoils of war. He laughed self-consciously, a look of mingled alarm and sheer boyish devilry crossing his face in quick succession before he turned away.

"What's *she* doing here?" Annabelle asked Henrietta out of the side of her mouth as her sister-in-law came forward to greet the coachload of new arrivals.

"Didn't you invite her?" asked Henrietta, surprised at the question.

Annabelle's lips pursed in a most unbecoming pout. She met Henrietta's eyes with a blank stare.

Henrietta gave a low chuckle. "No, you're not that crazy," she said, and then added with a touch of malice that Annabelle was at a loss to explain. "You're about to have a taste of your own medicine, Annabelle. I wonder how you will like it?"

Before she could ask her sister-in-law to explain the mystifying remark, her eyes were drawn to the vision in blue velvet. Lady Diana, like a child at her first party, pirouetted before them, demanding recognition and acclaim. No one was tempted to laugh at the spectacle. It was as if everyone present recognized that what they were viewing was no mere mortal woman, but a work of art.

Vexed, Annabelle turned on her heel and made for the drawing-room, pulling her shawl more closely about her. She was sorry now that she'd chosen to wear the simple gold. Even dressed in a sack, Lady Diana could make every female present pale before her incomparable celestial beauty. *She looks as fragile as a snowflake, but I bet she's as hard as nails,* thought Annabelle. She grew impatient with her uncharitable thoughts and put them firmly from her.

Two gentlemen were in the drawing room, Sir Charles and his father-in-law, Sam Routledge. She planted a kiss on her brother-in-law's cheek and murmured, "How are you, Charles?"

"Annie-bud. Good to have you home again."

The pet name, an endearment of long standing, cheered her insensibly. No one but Charles had ever called her Annie-bud. It made her feel cherished and warm all over.

She gave her hand to the older gentleman and smiled when he kissed her fingers in the grand manner. "What are you up to, Sam?" she asked. "You've never kissed my hand before. Besides, hand-kissing is old hat."

"Tell Harry that," he said, and led her to a settee close to the blazing grate.

"She's been laying down the law again, has she?" asked Annabelle, accepting a glass of sherry from her brother-in-law's hand.

There was no necessity for Sam Routledge to elaborate. In the years since she'd been part of the Jocelyn family, Annabelle had observed Henrietta's impatience with her father's ignorance of and indifference to the prevailing modes of etiquette. He was a self-made man and proud of it. And though he was a little rough around the edges, his heart was in the right place. Annabelle had a soft spot for the old boy, as he had for her.

"Do you doubt it? If she had her way, I wouldn't be here for her party. She's scared I'll put my foot in my mouth in front of these swells." He gestured vaguely with one hand. "But I couldn't resist hanging on for one more day just to see you, Annabelle."

"You're too hard on her, Sam. Henrietta is no snob."

"Worst thing I ever did was marry her above her station," he said candidly. Seeing that his son-in-law was fiddling with a decanter on the far side of the room, out of earshot, he went on, "You should have seen her in her heyday, Annabelle. You wouldn't recognize her. She was an out-and-outer, a dasher, something like yourself! But now . . ." he threw his son-in-law a contemptuous look, "she's as dull as that old dog over there."

Annabelle choked on her sherry. "Really, Sam, Charles is very kind," she remonstrated.

"Yes, and so's the coup de grâce at a botched execution," he answered darkly. "But my gel ain't happy, I tell you, Annabelle. She just ain't happy!"

"She's still not over Jonathan's birth," commiserated Annabelle.

"Piffle! That ain't it. There's something else. I wish you would find out what's at the bottom of it."

"Oh, I don't think Henrietta would confide in me, Sam. We're really not that close."

He looked as if he might say more, but the doors opened, and the guests began to idle in for the pre-dinner sherry.

Twenty people sat down to dinner.

"Who are all these people?" asked Annabelle of Lord Dalmar before the company moved en masse into the dining room. Her head was reeling from so many introductions to new faces.

"I've never seen half of them before in my life." Lady Diana turned a brilliant smile on him. "Excuse me," he said to Annabelle with a trace of apology. "Your sister-in-law has evidently made this a formal do. I'm to take in Lady Diana. Be kind to Ransome. He's really not a bad fellow." And with a cheeky grin he left her and went to partner Lady Diana.

Annabelle was seated between Colonel Ransome and John Falconer. She lost no time in quizzing both gentlemen on topics which were of keen interest to her. But by the time dinner was over, all she had gleaned from Colonel Ransome was that he had been acquainted with Bertie some years before. Dalmar's brother proved only slightly less taciturn on the subject of Lady Diana.

"Oh no, there were no hard feelings when Diana broke the engagement. How should there be? It was not her doing. It was her father, the Earl, who was the instigator."

"But how is it that they come to be on such friendly terms? As far as I understand, Dalmar has been out of the country for five years or more."

"Correspondence, I suppose," was the careless answer.

Shocked, Annabelle blurted, "You mean that when her husband was alive, Lady Diana corresponded with Dalmar?"

Falconer, perceiving that he had inadvertently placed his

brother in an awkward position, hastened to exculpate him and only succeeded in damning him more.

"David has always looked out for Diana's interests. What I mean to say is, she looks up to him. That is, she has this effect on all of us poor gentlemen," and he laughed, rather hollowly, trying to lighten Annabelle's grim expression. Failing to elicit even the tiniest flicker of a smile, he prudently turned to the lady on his left and began an animated conversation on the spectacle that awaited them at Lewes on Guy Fawkes' Night.

When the ladies retired to the drawing room, Annabelle adroitly managed to place herself in the chair next to Lady Diana's. Mere whimsy, she told herself. By his nefarious scheme to rob her of the diaries, Dalmar had forfeited his place in her affections, or he soon would. She had made up her mind to cut him out of her heart, and when Annabelle set her mind on anything, even the fates could not subvert her from her course. Still, she was curious about the lady who she was certain would step into her shoes the moment the break with Dalmar became official.

"It was very kind in you to tear yourself away from town for our little house party," was Annabelle's opening conversational gambit.

Enormous, artless blue eyes were turned upon her. "David said I might come," lisped the Incomparable, as if that settled the matter.

Annabelle's brows lifted. "Your friends must miss you," was her only comment.

"Oh, I've brought them with me. David hinted that I might," and Lady Diana gestured with one delicate hand to the group of young ladies, strangers to Annabelle, who were gathered round the piano, selecting music for when the gentlemen should join them.

Smiling a shade too brightly, Annabelle murmured, "Do you generally travel with your own court?"

"Not generally, no, but David didn't want me to be bored."

Grossly affronted, Annabelle inquired, "Bored? In the country? Who ever heard of such a thing?"

Bertie, tête-à-tête with Henrietta, overheard the remark and flashed Annabelle a wildly disbelieving look. Annabelle's antipathy to country life was well known.

"I'm never bored in the country," confided Lady Diana, looking slightly pained at Annabelle's recriminating tone. "But David said that I wouldn't know a soul here, and he did not think I should be comfortable in such circumstances. David likes me to be comfortable," she concluded in all seriousness.

Bemused, Annabelle absently replied, "Oh yes, I've been assured that my fiancé always looks out for your interests."

A frown marred the beauty of that perfectly guileless face. "I wish you would not call him that," reproved Lady Diana softly.

"What?" asked Annabelle.

"Your fiancé. He was my fiancé before he was yours. And you don't hear me calling him 'my fiancé,' do you? Besides, David doesn't like the term. He told me so himself."

"But he is no longer *your* fiancé," explained Annabelle patiently. "You married Lord Merril, if you remember. And now you are a widow."

"Yes, and you married Mr. Jocelyn. And now you are a widow, too!" crowed Lady Diana triumphantly.

Annabelle regarded her companion in perplexed silence. Finally she offered, "Your esteem for Lord Dalmar is quite out of the ordinary. I wonder why?"

If possible, those celestial blue eyes widened even further. "David is very clever," she said.

"I'll give you that," returned Annabelle dryly.

"And he knows how to take care of a lady."

"How so?"

The beauty seemed to flounder for a moment or two before framing her reply. "He knows how to speak to servants and so on." She gave the matter more thought. "And he understands everything there is to know about a lady's apparel. And if the roof leaks or the carriage breaks down or the chimney goes on fire, oh yes, and if a horse goes lame, he knows how to get things fixed."

Annabelle blinked rapidly. "Doesn't everyone?" she asked cautiously.

Lady Diana gave one elegant shrug of her beautiful white shoulders. "I never trouble myself about such things. Why should I? There's always some gentleman at hand to take care of these bothersome details."

Annabelle looked at her companion with new respect. "How clever you are, to be sure!" she exclaimed, her admiration genuine.

A quick frown momentarily puckered Lady Diana's smooth brow. "Oh, don't say so!" she implored. "Gentlemen don't care for clever women." Her brow cleared. "Besides, it isn't so, or David would have told me."

"Oh?" was all that Annabelle could think to say.

"David says, it's on account of my mind never having been spoiled by an education." Observing Annabelle's blank look, she patiently explained, "He says that I'm an original and that learning would only be wasted on me."

Staring at that flawlessly vacant face, Annabelle could only murmur some polite commonplace. She'd never expected to feel sorry for her rival. But so it was. The girl was as thick as a door and proud of it.

Frowning, she asked, "Does Lord Dalmar pay you many such compliments?" She thought it shameless that he would so abuse an ingenuous creature.

"Oh, David admires me to distraction," was the artless rejoinder.

"How, precisely?"

"Oh, you know, the usual," replied Lady Diana vaguely.

"No. What, for instance?"

"I know he finds me more amusing than any other lady of his acquaintance. He told me so."

"Cad!" said Annabelle under her breath.

"I beg your pardon?"

Quickly rallying, Annabelle interposed, "A girl like you needs a husband. Some women just aren't cut out to look after themselves." Her mind busily began to review a list of suitable candidates for the position. Lord Dalmar's name was the first to be eliminated.

Lady Diana's smile was dazzling. "Haven't I just told you so? David would be wasted on a lady like you."

"I beg your pardon?"

"When did *your* roof last leak?"

"It never leaks," answered Annabelle in some confusion. Nor was it ever like to. With her usual foresight, Annabelle engaged the slater twice a year to give her roof a thorough going-over.

"Well, there you are, then," crowed the lady. "What use have you for a man?"

"Very little," answered Annabelle, smiling as comprehension dawned. "Perhaps I should offer for you myself."

"That's what David said."

"*What?*"

"But I told him you and I should not suit."

"Why shouldn't we?" asked Annabelle, beginning to wonder if she too had become as mad as a hatter.

"Because you're not tall, dark, and handsome, and you don't have broad shoulders, that's why," reposited Lady Diana and laughing, quickly decamped for greener pastures.

"Sly puss," said Annabelle to herself, and could not make up her mind whether to admire the lady for her animal cunning or be offended by it.

The gentlemen arrived soon after. Annabelle pretended an interest in a journal she had picked up, but she was aware of Dalmar's every move. He chose to sit by her, but she gave him no credit for this singular attention. On entering, every other gentleman had made a beeline for Lady Diana, and the barrier around her was almost impregnable.

She thought that the smile he angled her was particularly cozening. "You were too tardy," she said pertly, glancing meaningfully at the group surrounding Lady Diana. "It's the early bird that catches the worm, Dalmar."

"I didn't invite her," he said, ignoring the bait. "She's just too hen-witted to know when she's not wanted."

"Well someone must have given her directions or she would not be here," replied Annabelle reasonably.

"What I mean to say is, she would not take no for an answer. It would have been heartless in me to refuse her. Diana has so few friends."

Looking significantly at the group by the piano, Annabelle

murmured, "There were eight, last time I counted."

"Is she stealing your thunder? Is that why you've worn a face that could sour milk since she arrived?"

"No, that's not why," said Annabelle, stiffening up in spite of her resolve to appear casual. "And she's not stealing my thunder."

"Oh?" He let his eyes wander to the laughing group by the piano. "Better look to your laurels, Annabelle. Even 'The Milksop' has deserted you for Lady Diana."

"I am not so petty as to begrudge that pea goose the admiration of a gaggle of featherbrained cloth-heads," disclaimed Annabelle pettishly.

"But a *beautiful* pea goose, you will allow," responded Dalmar, leering. "And with the male of the species, when beauty and intelligence in a woman are put on the scales, beauty tips the balance every time. I'm speaking generally, of course. A connoisseur such as myself has a more discriminating palate."

In Annabelle's eyes, Dalmar's stock stood at an all-time low. Using every trick in the book, he'd tried to take Monique Dupres's diaries away from her. Behind her back he'd bought into her company and had dared to tell her how to run her business. He'd tried to bribe her. When all else had failed, he'd employed common criminals to steal what rightfully belonged to her. His nefarious methods might easily have cost her her life. Even his lovemaking was suspect. Every instinct urged her to throw his transgressions in his face. But Annabelle was too experienced a player to give her hand away. Her revenge would come later, with the publication of the French girl's memoirs. Let him gloat for the present. His victory would be short-lived. But oh how she longed to wipe that confident smirk from his face.

"A connoisseur of women? Is that how you see yourself?" asked Annabelle, trying for a coquettish air.

"Can you doubt it when I've chosen you for my consort?"

"But then, I'm not in your usual style, am I, Dalmar?"

"Beg pardon?"

Annabelle glanced around to see if they were being overheard by anyone. She lowered her voice and said confidingly, "Your

251

preference in ladies—you'll observe I'm too well bred to call a spade a spade."

Cautiously, he asked, "Annabelle, what are we talking about?"

"Carlotta, Mimi, Rosa, Yvette, not to mention a string of lesser Paphians," she answered, her smile cloying. "Beautiful red-headed widgens, every last one of 'em. You should have run true to form, Dalmar. With a lady who can put two and two together, you're out of your depth."

Inwardly, Dalmar winced, but he essayed brazenly, "I see you've blown my cover. Lucky for me you're a woman of the world, or so you boast. It's not every bride who would view her intended's past indiscretions with equanimity."

"No, nor be subjected to every intimate detail of his debauchery. How did you come by the nickname, by the by? 'Sir Spider' seems an odd name for a lecher."

Aggrieved at this show of malice, he said, "I thought you had a soft spot for 'Sir Spider.' As I remember, you said that he was an attractive rogue with no malice in him."

"No, nor scruples either," said Annabelle. "But at least I've solved the mystery of your interest in the diaries. It was your own good name that you wished to protect all along."

"You do me an injustice," he told her stiffly.

"That's not all I'd like to do you," he thought he heard her say, but at that moment Lady Diana called him to the piano, and he left his betrothed with noticeable alacrity.

This unpromising beginning between Annabelle and Dalmar set the tone for the days which followed. They bickered constantly, so much so that Dalmar began to give Annabelle a wide berth. No one who did not know them would have taken them for an engaged couple. Lady Diana was Dalmar's most devoted companion and where Annabelle was, Lord Temple was never far distant.

"What's going on?" asked Bertie of Annabelle as the ladies made an outing to Brighton to do a little shopping. Sir Charles and the gentlemen of the party were out shooting for the morning.

"I might ask you the same question," said Annabelle pointedly. It had not escaped her notice that Colonel Ransome and her friend became as stiff as pokers in each other's vicinity. "Who is this Ransome, anyway, and what is he to you?"

In normal circumstances, Annabelle would never have lowered herself to ask such a personal question. On this occasion, she wanted only to evade Bertie's searching glances and keen intelligence. She had taken no one into her confidence regarding her suspicions about who had stolen the diaries. It wasn't that she wished to protect Dalmar, she told herself. It was her own gullability that she wished to conceal. He'd made a laughingstock of her once too often.

As evasive as Annabelle, Bertie replied, "I don't know what you mean."

The rest of the journey was made in silence. At the Old Ship Inn on Ship Street, three coaches from Rosedale disgorged their passengers. The ladies divided into small groups and agreed to meet at the inn for luncheon. By unspoken, common consent, the older ladies, that is Annabelle, Bertie, and Henrietta, detached themselves from the more boisterous younger group, of which Lady Diana was the undisputed ringleader.

"I don't think they've got a grain of sense among the lot of them," said Henrietta absently as she stood watching the bevy of beauties cavort the length of Ship Street.

"I have it on good authority," said Annabelle wisely, "that such things weigh little with the male of the species."

"Little is the word for it," added Bertie. "A more empty-headed gaggle of widgeons I've never met up with, no, nor ever wish to."

"Were the young always so young, or are we just getting older?" mused Henrietta rhetorically.

The three ladies exchanged glances.

"Old tabby cats, that's what we are," said Henrietta, smiling.

"Green with envy," agreed Bertie.

"Speak for yourselves," reproved Annabelle. "How old are we— thirty, give or take a year or two?"

"I'll never see thirty again," said Henrietta.

"All right, all right! So I exaggerated a little. But we're a long

253

way yet till we reach our dotage. Good grief, those babies can't hold a candle to us!"

"Prove it," said Bertie, pulling a long face.

For a long moment, Annabelle stared at her companions. Finally, a slow smile curved her lips. "Follow my lead," she said, and linked arms with her friends.

With a newfound camaraderie they turned toward the warren of narrow lanes which ran off Ship Street, an unaccustomed recklessness lighting their steps. They trudged from shop to shop making a game of the outing. They exclaimed over bonnets they would normally never be caught dead in. They swathed themselves in transparent satins and cooed over black silk drawers imported from France. They tried out walking sticks and looked over bath chairs. They giggled and simpered and flirted brazenly with shopkeepers, scandalizing Brighton's more sober residents. On King's Road they came across a dress shop displaying gowns of a decidedly flagrant color and cut.

"We shouldn't," said Henrietta, halting Annabelle's move toward the doors. "I've heard of this place. The clientele are not the sort that a lady would care to meet in her drawing room."

"So much the better," said Annabelle with relish, and shepherded her reluctant companions over the threshold.

Annabelle boldly advanced into the center of the shop. Henrietta hung back, her eyes moving uneasily over the several flamboyant though indisputably modishly clad customers who were waited on by a bevy of young clerks. Her eyes came to rest on the tall, voluptuous form of a lady who was in the process of purchasing a beige pelisse trimmed lavishly with leopard skin. The eyes of the two women met and held. Henrietta stiffened. Annabelle noted the silent exchange and looked curiously at Henrietta.

"Who is she?" she asked under her breath.

"Mrs. Snow," whispered Henrietta, and turned away to examine a counter displaying leather gloves and slippers.

Mrs. Snow turned her back on the Rosedale party. In a clear carrying voice, she addressed the sales clerk. "As usual, Mary, charge these to the account of Sir Charles Jocelyn of Rosedale by Lewes."

At Annabelle's back, Henrietta gasped. Bertie, wise in an instant to what was going on, went to her side and had her soon ushered from the shop. Annabelle stood rooted to the spot studying the brazen hussy who dared broadcast to all and sundry that she was her brother-in-law's fancy piece. The lady turned full-face toward her, and Annabelle could scarcely believe what she saw. They might easily have been taken for sisters, though to be sure, Mrs. Snow's garments were more showy, and she used a heavier hand with her rouge and blacking. Only the hair, or what could be seen of it from beneath the brim of a high poke bonnet garishly decorated with yards of ribbon, was of a different hue. Annabelle's was the color of dark treacle. Mrs. Snow's was bright henna.

Unabashed, Mrs. Snow returned stare for stare.

Finally coming to herself, Annabelle said, "I shouldn't take the pelisse, if I were you. You'll only have to return it."

"What makes you say so?" asked the lady, adopting Annabelle's haughty air.

Annabelle was too angry to attend the interested stares of the several other "ladies" in the shop. In normal circumstances, she would have given the likes of Mrs. Snow a wide berth. But she took to herself not only the deliberate affront which had just been offered to Henrietta, but also the fact that Mrs. Snow's resemblance to herself was uncanny. In that moment, Annabelle's antipathy to red hair was converted into immutable loathing.

She advanced a step upon her look-alike and said heedlessly, and far from truthfully, "Sir Charles doesn't have two pennies to rub together. It's his wife's father who controls the purse strings. And frankly, I can't see him laying out his blunt for his son-in-law's doxy. My advice to you is to start looking for another protector."

Hot color suffused Mrs. Snow's cheeks. Her hands clenched in fury. Ignoring the titters, Annabelle spun on her heel and stormed out.

Nuncheon at the Old Ship scarcely improved the ladies' spirits after this unpleasant confrontation. The return trip to Rosedale was made in almost complete silence.

As Annabelle took her place at dinner that evening, her eyes searched Henrietta's face. As if aware of Annabelle's unspoken question, her sister-in-law returned a reassuring, albeit shaky smile. Annabelle thereupon turned her attention to Colonel Ransome and Bertie, on the opposite side of the table. They were engaged in their usual one-sided conversation. Surely the man must have deduced by now from his companion's stilted responses that Bertie did not wish to pursue the acquaintance. Some gentlemen were too obtuse for their own good, decided Annabelle.

Some moments later, a feminine trill of laughter, an uninhibited sound, startled Annabelle from her reverie. It couldn't be, she thought . . . but it was. Henrietta was laughing, and Dalmar was laughing with her. Annabelle could not remember when she had last heard her sister-in-law laugh so freely. Arrested, she stared at the two dark heads bent close together in an intimacy which excluded the rest of the company.

Her eyes flew to Sir Charles, and another shock awaited her. She observed that his sensibilities were ruffled by the spectacle of his wife flirting with another gentleman.

In other circumstances, Annabelle would have been happy to see her brother-in-law shaken out of his insufferable complacency. But all she could think was that in this long disastrous holiday in the country, Dalmar seemed eager to flirt with every other lady but herself. Was she so unattractive?

Unconsciously, Annabelle stretched her long neck as if to erase an invisible double chin. She turned to Lord Temple on her left and made some innocuous comment on the weather, always a safe subject, in her experience.

Before he could reply, the uncommonly strident tones of Sir Charles cut into every conversation.

"Henrietta, my dear, do share the joke." His face was slashed in a false smile. "Lord Dalmar must be in fine form indeed to wrest such unbridled laughter from a lady's lips."

Had Sir Charles always been such a stuffed shirt? wondered Annabelle. Wasn't a lady considered a lady if she gave way to genuine mirth? Evidently not, for the rebuke in Sir Charles's voice was unmistakable.

It was the Earl who took it upon himself to respond. Totally relaxed, smiling, he said, "Beg pardon, Sir Charles. You would only be bored by our conversation."

"I insist."

Like watching a tennis match at Hampton Court, thought Annabelle, suppressing a nervous giggle, all heads swiveled to view first one end of the table, then the other. The ball was in Dalmar's court.

"Very well," he said easily. "Your dear lady was under the impression, false, I assure you, that we veterans who served with Wellington in the peninsular campaign amused ourselves very much as we do at present." To the curious looks which were directed toward him, he said by way of explanation, "Lady Jocelyn puts too much stock in the tales she has heard of the balls and other amusements we enjoyed in Spain."

Stiffening up, Sir Charles pinned his wife with a piercing glare. "I lost a brother on the peninsula," he said, "and Annabelle lost a husband."

Henrietta colored. Annabelle stared. She could not believe that a husband whose infidelity was common knowledge could address his wife in such callous terms.

"A fine officer," interposed Colonel Ransome, "and a bruising rider to hounds, as I remember."

"You had hounds in Spain when you were fighting the French?" asked Annabelle incredulously.

"The hounds belonged to the Duke," replied Ransome. "He had them sent out from England. It was a welcome diversion when time hung heavily on our hands."

"I'm sure," murmured Annabelle ironically. She was remembering the other diversion which had occupied her husband in Spain when time hung heavily on his hands.

The soup was served, and Annabelle tooled her silver spoon through the thick, creamy liquid, hearing little of the banter which went on around her. She was thinking that more than half the gentlemen at the table had served with the British Army abroad. They were the lucky ones. For the most part they'd come back in one piece. She had been widowed. Poor Edgar, she thought, and was suddenly very glad that he'd had a son to leave behind after he was gone.

257

When she came to herself, she found that the tone of the conversation had changed. The military men had taken over, much to the delight of the ladies, and were outdoing themselves in relating outrageous tales of their exploits, none of them believable.

"He was a regular tear-away!" she heard Ransome explain to the company in general.

"Who was?" asked Annabelle in an aside to Lord Temple. There was no answer. She glanced at him curiously, noting the stiff back and the rigid way he held his soup spoon. "Can I get you something?" she asked softly. She'd often seen him like this before, and surmised that he was in pain.

He sent her a quelling frown, and Annabelle was instantly contrite. Lord Temple hated fuss of any description, and would not thank her for drawing attention to his war wound.

Lady Diana's girlish voice broke into her thoughts. "The man ought to have been court-martialed," she exclaimed. "Either that or locked up in Bedlam."

"Who are we talking about?" This time, Annabelle directed her question to the gentleman on her right, John Falconer.

"Major Hamish Crawford," he answered.

The name had a familiar ring to it, though Annabelle could not immediately place the gentleman.

"Oh, he was too successful to be court-martialed," answered Dalmar. "The Duke might deplore the risks he ran, but Crawford knew his job. He led the best reconnaissance unit in the army. The French put a price on his head, so that says something for the man's ability. It's true that his outfit was decimated every other time they moved out, but Crawford never asked his men to do anything he wasn't prepared to do himself."

"I think the Duke should have recommended him for a medal," interjected Miss Adam, one of Lady Diana's younger friends.

"What ever happened to him?"

The question was met with deadening silence. Several of the gentlemen were seen to exchange uneasy glances. It was Lord Temple who brought speculation to an end.

"An assassin's knife found him. In Brussels, wasn't it?" He

looked a question across the table at Colonel Ransome. "On the eve of Waterloo? His throat was slit."

Several ladies gasped. Then a babble of questions were hurled at Lord Temple and Colonel Ransome. But the gentlemen, becoming aware of the unseemliness of this turn in the conversation, refused to be drawn further.

It was only later, as she undressed for bed, that Annabelle remembered where she had come across the name before. Major Hamish Crawford was a minor character in Monique Dupres's diaries. More than that, Annabelle could not recall. It gave her the spur to continue with the task she had already embarked upon. Her last thought before sleep claimed her was that she would continue with the diaries early the next morning.

Chapter Fifteen

In the year of our Lord, 1815, Guy Fawkes' Day happened to fall on the Sabbath. The failure in 1605 of what was known as "The Gunpowder Plot" to blow up the Houses of Parliament in the reign of James I was observed throughout Great Britain with varying degrees of enthusiasm. In Lewes, the population marked the anniversary of this celebrated non-event with almost frenetic revelry.

The day started, predictably, with morning services in the old parish church of St. Michael's. The rector delivered the sermon, ostensibly an attack on those revolutionary agents of the devil who were the perpetrators of every malaise, imaginary or otherwise, which had affected the country since the failure of their plot to blow up the crème de la crème of the English aristocracy.

With the exception of a few blue-blooded zealots, no one put any stock in the rector's words. As everyone knew, he was following a time-honored tradition, and similar sermons were being preached at that very moment from every pulpit in the land. After a lapse of over two hundred years, however, the religious quarrel between Catholics and Protestants seemed very far distant. The old guard knew it. But the Jacobite Rebellions of the last century and the revolutions which had overthrown their counterparts first in America and then in France were too recent to be viewed with anything resembling equanimity. Times were hard, at least among the general population. It seemed politic to use every means at their disposal to persuade the hoi polloi that revolution in Britain would not only increase their misery but would also contravene divine law. Hence this annual diatribe against Catholicism on a national holiday which had been prescribed by king and parliament in 1605, had degenerated into nothing more than political rhetoric supporting the status quo.

Of everyone in the congregation that morning, some few were conscious of the unintentional irony in the rector's message. Dalmar was one of them. As the vituperation continued unabated, he was seen to exchange a meaningful glance with his friend Colonel Ransome. Both were military men and avid students of history.

As they well knew, Lewes's main claim to distinction lay in the celebrated battle which bore the town's name. In the thirteenth century, rebels under the leadership of Simon de Montfort had roundly defeated the armies of their king. Of more recent vintage, skirmishes between loyal royalists and rebellious roundheads had been fought in the very streets of Lewes. And irony of ironies, Thomas Paine, whose writings had fanned the flames of the American Revolution, had himself resided for a number of years in Bell House on the High Street. Dalmar's glance traveled the crush of worshipers and he wondered idly what thoughts they entertained behind their stoic demeanors.

Behind those sober faces, truth to tell, their thoughts were lively and for the most part dwelled on the pleasures which awaited with the advent of darkness. Guy Fawkes' Night in Lewes had become an excuse for general merriment, if not for a license verging on debauchery. That it had become the practice to turn the occasion into something more resembling a masquerade was held by some to be responsible for this shameful turn of events. For who would be able to point the finger when his neighbor donned a disguise and hid his identity behind a mask?

The rector's voice droned on. Young maids dreamed of stolen kisses from well-breeched lordlings. Untutored farm lads contemplated the delights of a tumble in the hay with some obliging tavern wench. Sober husbands entertained thoughts of carousing all night long with boon companions. Respectable wives plotted to clip the wings of their straying menfolk. And Annabelle wondered where she would find a pistol to complete the costume she had devised for herself.

She had decided to dress up as a highwayman. Inspiration played little part in her decision. Annabelle was a practical lady. Once before, she had made the mistake of costuming herself as the Empress Josephine. She had discovered that muslin and bare shoulders were not suitable for alfresco parties in November, even supposing the whole was covered by a warm woolen pellisse which was removed only when a torch was set to the great bonfire. As she remembered, though her front had been toasty warm from the fierce blaze, her backside had damn near petrified.

She was to congratulate herself on her foresight later that evening. With the setting of the sun, the breeze which buffeted the small country town of Lewes, wafting in from the Downs, had developed a distinct bite. She pulled her voluminous green mantle more securely about her. Only the children and young people seemed immune to the vagaries of the English climate. And Lady Diana, thought Annabelle with a stab of annoyance . . . well, she had done her duty. She had warned Lady Diana and her coterie of what they could expect. Her reward had been an incredulously murmured dismissal.

"Beauty has its price," one of the ladies had responded.

Hah! So did comfort! And she, Annabelle Jocelyn, was very glad that under her highwayman's disguise she was wearing two pairs of everything. Not for her the diaphanous costumes of the Greek deities the younger women had selected for themselves. She wondered how they were faring, and with only *silk* dominoes, too, to protect them from the elements!

Her eyes shifted to take in the figure of her companion. Bertie, very sensibly in Annabelle's opinion, was dressed from head to toe in velvet. It seemed reasonable to suppose that the Empress Catherine of Russia, which lady Bertie professed to be for the masquerade, would know a thing or two about circumventing the harsh Russian winters. *Vanity be damned,* thought Annabelle, and stamped her booted feet to stave off the cold.

It seemed that she and Bertie had been standing about for

hours in the crowded courtyard of the Bull, keeping an eye on the children. Earlier they had followed the torchlit procession of mummers and Morris dancers through the town's narrow streets. The place was packed with visitors who had arrived by the coachload to help the natives celebrate Lewes's gala event.

But the children had become overexcited and quarrelsome, and they had returned to the inn, where rooms had been reserved for the evening for just such an eventuality. They had been in the inn's courtyard ever since, attracted by the mummers' play, which was in progress under the glow of a score of lanterns and pitch torches.

Annabelle debated whether her presence would be missed if she slipped away to the private parlor Sir Charles had earlier bespoken. Every inn and tavern was bursting at the seams. It was fortunate that Sir Charles was known to the landlord. In addition to the parlor, the party from Rosedale had managed to secure four rooms for their use. She thought of the coal fire in the parlor grate and sighed audibly. Lady Diana and her court would put her down as a veritable Methuselah if she gave in to the temptation. Besides, she adjured herself, she had promised Henrietta that she would personally supervise the eldest two of her brood of five who had been permitted to make the trip for the occasion.

A burst of laughter and applause signaled the end of the mummers' performance. Before the audience had properly come to themselves, the actors whipped off their hats and were making the rounds. Patrons laughingly delved into their pockets for change.

"Mama, wasn't that splendid?" Richard, his face aglow, came racing over the cobblestones. At his heels, pursuing him as fast as her short legs could carry her, was young Amy.

"Yes dear," replied Annabelle, smiling to see her son's patent delight. "Quite splendid."

Spectators and patrons shouldered their way to different exits. Annabelle's eyes traveled over the crush. She thought that Lewes on Guy Fawkes' Night fell somewhere between Vauxhall Gardens on a national holiday and the Palais Royal under Allied occupation. Pickpockets abounded, as did ladies of ill-repute plying their wares. Her eyes lighted on a party of young bucks who were swaggering about, sending respectable matrons scurrying for cover with their low language and lewd suggestions. The undesirable element was only too evident this evening, thought Annabelle, frowning quellingly at two of the fops who had been ogling her intermittently.

"Shall we retire to the parlor for some refreshments?" suggested Annabelle. In another hour the bonfire would be lit, and soon after they could all go home to Rosedale. Then the children would be put to bed and the grown-ups would have their last party before leaving in the morning to return to London. The return to town could not come too soon for Annabelle.

Her suggestion was met with outraged protests from two young, shrill voices.

"You promised I could see the tumblers and fire-eaters, Aunt Bertie," cried Amy plaintively.

Bertie smiled an apology at Annabelle. "It's all she's been able to speak about for weeks."

Resigning herself to the inevitable, Annabelle said, "I'm game if you are. Though no doubt the gentlemen will ring a peal over us if we disobey their instructions."

They'd been warned earlier to stick close to the inn. Annabelle was more than happy to oblige. But the tumblers and fire-eaters were to be found on the hill on the outskirts of town where the bonfire was set. In the circumstances in which they found themselves, ladies did not go abroad without an escort, preferably a well-armed one.

"It was too bad of the gentlemen to abandon us to our own devices," said Bertie, voicing the selfsame thought that had occurred to Annabelle. "They should have returned by now. I wonder what is keeping them?"

"Mmm," answered Annabelle noncommittally.

She and Bertie had been left to their own devices because they had elected to look after the children while the rest of the Rosedale party took a turn around the town. Even Henrietta had deserted them. Annabelle could not remember a time when her sister-in-law had put her own pleasure before the needs of her family. She'd looked rather shamefaced as she'd asked Annabelle if she would mind looking after the two

Jocelyn boys.

"Where are your cousins?" asked Annabelle belatedly. "And where's Mary?" Mary was a young domestic attached to the Jocelyn household. When Annabelle had last seen her, she had been sitting with her charges, as engrossed in the play as they were.

"Don't know," answered Richard. "Can we go and see the fire-eaters, Mama? Oh, do say we may! Do! Do! Do!"

Amy took up Richard's chant.

"Silence," shrilled Annabelle, now genuinely alarmed.

She breathed a sigh of relief as Mary suddenly appeared at her elbow. It took a moment before it registered that Mary looked as alarmed as she herself felt.

"Where are the boys?" demanded Annabelle.

Between gasps, the frightened maid finally got out, "Oh m'um, I couldn't stop 'em. They took off down the 'igh Street."

"Show me," said Annabelle. Over her shoulder she yelled, "Stay here, Bertie, and look after those two."

She did not wait for an answer as she elbowed a clear path through the throng to the entrance to the courtyard.

"This way, m'um," said Mary, and turned right onto High Street.

Annabelle could not control a shudder of dread. The River Ouse was at the bottom of the hill. And James and Peter were two fearless hellions, for all their paucity of years. "If they haven't drowned, I'll kill them," she told Mary. "That's if Henrietta doesn't kill me first."

The poor girl burst into tears.

It was impossible to move rapidly. At every turn there were obstacles in their path; street-corner puppet shows, acrobats, jugglers, and everywhere bands of local urchins with hollowed out turnip lanterns begging for "a penny for the guy."

At the corner of Castle Gate, they halted.

"They could be anywhere," said Annabelle. "And in this crush, we would never find them. Pray that they haven't gone to the riverbank. But that's where we'll look for them, just in case."

They pressed on. As they approached the lights of the

Maiden's Head at the edge of the town, they could hear the strains of fiddles and the boisterous clapping and stamping of the patrons. Annabelle paused to catch her breath, trying to ignore the painful stitch in her side. Without warning, she was caught from behind by strong hands and dragged over the inn's threshold.

More incensed than alarmed, she turned on her captors. There were two of them, and though they were masked, like herself, she recognized them as the bucks who had been making sheep's eyes at her in The Bull's courtyard. She could tell at a glance that they were no gentlemen, but of a lower order, aping the modes of the upper class. Though their garments were fashionable, they were ill fitting, and of too garish a hue for Annabelle's taste. She judged them to be in their mid-twenties. She did not like the lascivious smirks they bestowed on her.

"Let me pass, gentlemen," she said, coldly polite. "You have no business to detain me." She looked down the length of her imperious little nose and gave them one of her "touch-me-and-you're-dead" looks.

"Take care of the other one," said the one Annabelle had guessed was the leader of the pair. "Chase her off. Anything. But make it quick."

Though his accents were not uncultured, Annabelle was far from reassured. Surreptitiously, she began to edge her way toward the door to the taproom. Her captor laughed and grabbed her by the shoulders.

"Cold bitch," he said. "I've got just the thing to heat you up," and he thrust his hips at her. "You've been panting for it all night."

Annabelle's scream was smothered by his hot lips. Through the folds of her cloak, his hands molded her breasts. She struggled wildly to free herself.

She heard the other man return.

"Quick, gag her."

A scarf was thrust into her mouth, but not before she had managed a piercing scream. It availed her nothing. The clientele of the Maiden's Head was very different from that of the more salubrious Bull. A coarse jest and a roar of laughter

267

were the only response her cry elicited.

"Any more of that and we'll have to share you with the whole damn lot of rutting bastards in there," said one.

Their intent was unmistakable: they meant to ravish her. With mindless, superhuman strength, Annabelle lashed out at them.

A fist caught her a glancing blow on the jaw, momentarily stunning her. Dazed, she allowed herself to be dragged out of the inn. She did not know where they had taken her until she heard the gentle lap of the water as it rippled over rocks and fallen trees. They were on the banks of the Ouse.

She was thrown roughly down and was dimly conscious that she had fallen against a haystack. Some farmer's field evidently stopped right at the river's edge.

In a moment she had freed herself of the gag. "Are you mad?" she shrieked. "You'll be hanged if you so much as lay a finger on me. There are dozens of willing females in town especially imported for what you have on your mind." She stared up at them, trying to gauge what effect her words had, but she could discern little in the dim light of the lantern that one of the men held high. A movement caught her eye, and she froze. The men were removing their masks. A paralyzing fear overwhelmed her. Wordlessly, she watched as the leader of the two unfastened the waistband of his pantaloons.

"Be quick about it," his companion told him. "If ever *he* finds out . . ."

"Shut your mouth!"

"Why? She won't tell anybody."

It was the cruel laugh which galvanized Annabelle into action. Without conscious thought, she fumbled in her cloak pocket and withdrew the antiquated pistol her brother-in-law had loaned her to complete her costume. It was a museum piece, and, of course, unprimed, but they weren't to know that.

"Hands up! Higher! Higher!" she croaked out, and dragged herself to her feet. Her voice quavered almost as much as the pistol she held with both hands.

They stood, hands held high, staring dumbly at her.

"She hasn't cocked it," said one.

What does that mean? thought Annabelle.

They lunged for her. Annabelle felt a pair of hands on her arms. Panic-stricken, she deftly wriggled out of her pelisse and made a dash for the other side of the haystack.

"I'm warning you! I'm warning you!" she yelled, and waved the pistol threateningly under their noses as they advanced upon her. Her back was to the river. But swimming was one of the things she had tried once and had never tried again. In that moment, she swore to God that horses and dogs would be her constant companions, and she would persevere with every blessed accomplishment she had ever forsworn. If only, oh, if only . . .

"Put the damn light down and hold her for me," said the leader. "I don't want any scratches showing on my face. He might get the right idea."

"No," said Annabelle hoarsely. She could not believe that this was happening to her.

The younger man took a step toward her, and Annabelle threw her pistol at him. He let out a howl of pain.

"Bitch! When we're done with you, we'll dump your body in the river."

Sobbing with terror, she fought their hands off. Only when they had wrestled her to the ground did she use up precious energy in screaming for help.

"Annabelle!"

For a moment, she thought she had heard the roar of a wounded lion.

"Annabelle!" And then she recognized the voice.

"David! Oh God, David! Over here!"

The two men released her and rose quickly to their feet.

"He's alone," she heard one of them say.

Then all hell broke loose. Dalmar charged into the circle of light and one of the men, the leader, grunted and went down. His companion was on the Earl in an instant.

Unsteadily, Annabelle rose to her feet.

"Get out of here! Now!" commanded Dalmar.

But Annabelle could not be so heartless as to leave him to his fate. Though he had winded the man who was beneath him, the man on his back had a stranglehold which he ruthlessly tightened. In fear and trembling, Annabelle approached the struggling men.

"Annabelle!"

She disregarded Dalmar's choked imperative. Meaning only to drag the man from his back, she caught hold of his coattails and pulled with all her strength. He released one arm from Dalmar's neck and tried to swipe her. Dalmar made good use of the opportunity he had been given. Straining, he broke the other's stranglehold, and in the next moment Annabelle found herself hanging for dear life to the coattails of a ferocious, spitting madman.

"Bitch! I'll kill you for this."

She dared not let go. It was, she thought rather hysterically, like having a tiger by the tail. Avoiding his vicious blows, she threw the full press of her weight on her heels and began to swing him in a circle. Instinct took over. She increased her pace and spun wildly. Round and round they went at a furious rate. She judged the exact moment when to let go. Like one of Congreve's rockets, the man went spinning and landed in the river. His yell of surprise and pain was very satisfying to Annabelle's ears. She saw him strike out for the opposite bank.

"You have a horrid laugh," she said, and wiped the feel of him from her hands.

When she turned back, the sight that met her eyes made her suck in her breath. Both men, their coats discarded, were on their feet and circling each other. But while her abductor clutched a wicked-looking knife in one hand, Dalmar was unarmed. Seeing at once that she could do nothing for fear of distracting the Earl, she sank to her haunches to watch and wait the outcome.

"I'm going to kill you for what you did to her," Annabelle heard Dalmar say in a voice that brought goosebumps to her flesh. She did not doubt that he meant it.

The other man laughed, but the sound was hollow, mere bravado. "When I kill you," he said, "I'll take her on your corpse. Then I'll kill her too." And he lunged for Dalmar.

The Earl leaped back, but the blow glanced along his arm, and a dark stain appeared on his shirtsleeve. Annabelle did not dare leave to go for help. If there was any chance that she might be of some use to Dalmar, she wanted to be there.

She could hear the strident breathing of the two men as they circled, and her own breathing increased to match their tempo.

The younger man lunged again. Dalmar fell back. His assailant charged, too late to stop himself when he realized that it was a feint. Dalmar's powerful hands grasped the other's outstretched arm. He brought his knee up, and at the same time drove down the hand that held the knife. Bone ground against bone with a sickening thud. The young man gasped, and the knife dropped from his nerveless fingers. He fell to his knees, his arm hanging loosely at his side.

"It was only a bit of fun," he whined. "I didn't do a thing to her."

Dalmar picked up the knife and stood, feet braced, towering over the beaten man. "Is he telling the truth?" he asked Annabelle.

"Yes," she whispered. She had never seen Dalmar so dispassionate. It frightened her.

"Annabelle, leave us." Dalmar's voice was soft, but she detected an edge of implacability.

She straightened. "We should take him to the constable," she said.

"Don't argue. Just do as I say."

Slowly she shook her head. She was trembling and could not seem to stop herself.

In three strides Dalmar was at her side. Her arm was taken in a bruising grasp, and she was shaken roughly. "Go and wait for me," he said. "There's a path beyond the trees. I'll meet you at the gate."

Tears welled in her eyes, and she threw herself into his arms. "Don't do it," she begged. "Oh please, David, don't do it. Just because he's an animal . . ."

Over Dalmar's shoulder she saw the man rise to his feet. He took a faltering step toward the river, his broken arm clutched tightly to his chest. In the same instant Dalmar turned.

"No!" cried Annabelle, and clung to him.

He cursed and tried to shake free of her.

"Run!" screamed Annabelle. "He means to kill you!"

But her abductor had already figured that out for himself. He needed no persuasion to propel himself into the icy waters of the Ouse. Dalmar threw Annabelle from him and ran to the edge of the bank in time to see the young man strike out for the other side. He did not even make the halfway mark before he sank from sight.

With eyes blazing, Dalmar turned upon Annabelle. She stood with her hands covering her face, weeping uncontrollably.

"I hope you're satisfied," he said cruelly.

"Did he . . . did he get away?"

Dalmar's hesitation went unremarked by Annabelle. "Yes, more's the pity."

"You would have killed him."

"He deserved to die." He found her pelisse and draped it over her shoulders. "Put your arms around my neck," he said, and swept her into his arms.

There was nowhere else she would have rather been. His protective power, in some sort, was the catharsis for the violation she had suffered at those other hands. She nestled against him, absorbing his warmth and strength, her head resting against his broad shoulder. She tried to put the scene she had just witnessed from her mind.

"How did you find me?" she asked at length.

"The maid, what's-her-name, said that you went to look for your nephews along the riverbank."

"Oh God, I forgot about the boys!"

"Rest easy. They're safe and sound, apart from the swats their father administered for throwing us all into high dudgeon."

He added the last to lighten her mood. She responded with a watery smile, then began to weep softly, and finally with deep, shuddering sobs. Without breaking stride he cradled her fiercely to him, crooning low, barely intelligible endearments against her temple.

When they came onto the High Street, there were few people about. The bonfire was to be lit at any moment, the climax of the day's festivities, and almost every soul was on the Cliffe, waiting for the master of ceremonies to set things in motion.

Inside the Bull, things were very much the same. The

taproom was practically empty of loiterers, with the exception of the odd crone who had imbibed a dram too much and had sunk into oblivion.

Calling for brandy and a pitcher of hot water, Dalmar carried Annabelle up the stairs to the chamber she was to share with some of the other ladies. Mary was there and hurried ahead of them into the room, lighting candles with a taper from the coal fire which blazed in the grate. Dalmar dismissed her with instructions to find their party on the Cliffe and convey the intelligence that Annabelle had been found but was in no shape to participate in the rest of the events planned for later that evening. When Mary had removed herself from the chamber, he set Annabelle gently on the counterpane atop the bed.

For a moment Henrietta could not believe what she was seeing. Annabelle was in her husband's arms! And he was kissing her passionately! And then it came to her. Of course! The woman in her husband's arms was Mrs. Snow. It could be no other, since her maid had given her the intelligence that Annabelle was feeling under the weather and had decided to forgo the rest of the night's revelries.

Rage and despair followed in quick succession. She tore her eyes away and forced herself to take an interest in the scores of masqueraders who paraded around the blazing bonfire. From their staggers she deduced that many of them were unequivocally in their cups. And whether from the license afforded from their nightlong carousing or because of the anonymity they were under the misapprehension their masks and costumes provided, few comported themselves with anything resembling dignity. Did her husband really suppose, she wondered bitterly, that she would not recognize the man behind the pirate's garb? Even in those flickering shadows and in that secluded nook under the cover of a spreading laburnum where he had stationed himself, she could identify him easily.

She felt the wet stab of tears in her eyes and swallowed spasmodically. The scene disgusted her! Sour grapes, a little voice whispered in her ear. It was true. If only *she* were the woman in her husband's arms, she would view the spectacle of other couples stealing kisses with far different eyes.

"Take a leaf out of Annabelle's book," Dalmar had told her. She still could not believe that she had confided so much to a total stranger. After the confrontation in the mantua maker's with Mrs. Snow, she had not been herself. She had locked herself in her room, and before she could talk herself out of her insane jealousy by reminding herself that every husband indulged in these little peccadilloes, Dalmar had been there, requesting her advice on a matter respecting a suitable bridal gift for Annabelle, or so he had said.

They'd never even touched on that subject. He'd taken one look at her red-rimmed eyes and had gently but remorselessly pried the whole course of her unhappy circumstances out of her, beginning with the vain hope she had entertained at the beginning of her marriage that she could make her husband love her.

She had expected the Earl to take the predictable masculine view and chide her for indulging such romantic fancies. Dalmar had done no such thing. On the contrary, he had listened with almost fatherly sympathy and had left her with that enigmatic piece of advice, "Why don't you take a leaf out of Annabelle's book?"

Only, it was not so enigmatic. Hadn't her own father been saying as much to her for years past? "Be yourself, girl," her father was used to say, "not this spineless wax impression of respectability. Who do you think you are pleasing?" And then, more darkly, whenever she corrected his speech or manners, "You're a dead bore, Harry, a dead bore!"

It was true. She was a bore, a dead bore, and she did not know if she could be the girl she once was. *It's too late*, she thought with something like despair. Charles seemed to be immune to her overtures, and there had been many since her conversation with Dalmar. She might as well not have existed for all the notice her husband paid her, if tonight was anything to go by.

Though she'd decked herself out as Nell Gwynn, one of Charles II's notorious mistresses, in an attempt to break the patterncard of rectitude she habitually presented herself as, her husband had not so much as glanced in her direction. As

274

the ladies had descended the Bull's narrow staircase, his eyes had been riveted on Annabelle, as had the eyes of every gentleman present. And no wonder! In that formfitting highwayman's get up, Annabelle's figure was revealed for what it was: perfection. And not even Lady Diana in all her feminine frippery could come close to the dash Annabelle projected, albeit unconsciously.

Mrs. Snow, also, for all their close resemblance, could not hold a candle to Annabelle's *panache*. *And my husband prefers the company of that vulgar, over-painted doxy to mine,* thought Henrietta, self-pity giving way to a simmering indignation. Her eyes involuntarily sought the object of her ruminations. Mrs. Snow's head was resting comfortably against Sir Charles's broad shoulder, unconscious or uncaring of who might witness their loverlike embrace. The eyes of the two women met and held, Mrs. Snow's lips curved in a slow smile of triumph.

So be it, thought Henrietta, finally tearing her eyes away. *I'm done with play-acting. My husband has found himself a conformable mistress. I'll be damned if I'll play the conformable wife for him. I have a life to live. It's time I got on with it.*

In that moment she turned her back on Sir Charles, both figuratively and literally, and glanced about her, seeking the other members of the Rosedale party. Her eyes alighted on Colonel Ransome and Mrs. Pendleton. If appearances were anything to go by, those two were involved in another of their tiresome spats. Though they pretended a hearty and mutual dislike, she was not fooled for one minute.

A movement caught her eye. David Falconer was beckoning to her, inviting her to join him and Lady Diana. She went with alacrity.

"They're just about to throw the effigy of Guy Fawkes on the fire," he said as she reached him.

"Hold onto your hat, then," she replied, her smile answering the look of concern she'd surprised in his eyes. "His head is stuffed with gunpowder."

The constable and some of his cohorts went around, warning the bystanders to step back from the flames. Henrietta ascertained that the children were safely under the supervision of Mary and Bertie and gave herself up to the sheer enjoyment of the occasion.

Silence descended as two stalwart men approached the blaze. With practiced movements they swung the "guy" back and forth in their arms as the crowd chanted in unison, "Burn him! Burn him! Burn him!"

The effigy of Guy Fawkes, complete with tall hat, went hurtling into the fire. A moment later the roar of the crowd was blotted out by a small explosion which rocked the center of the bonfire. Sparks went flying in every direction.

Again the chant was taken up by the crowd. "Burn him! Burn him! Burn him!" Henrietta added her voice to the others, but in her mind's eye it was not an effigy of the unfortunate Guy Fawkes who was cast into the fiery inferno.

Chapter Sixteen

Annabelle lay on the bed motionless, eyes closed, comfortingly lulled by the sounds of Dalmar as he moved around the room. In normal circumstances she would never have permitted his ministrations. Her parsonage upbringing had predisposed her to be the one who took care of others. But she was badly shaken, and almost childishly grateful for the reassurance that was offered merely by his presence. He bathed her sore jaw, then raised her head and forced her to drink from a small glass of brandy. No words were exchanged. But Annabelle submitted with uncharacteristic docility. With his strong arms around her she felt as warm and as safe as a chrysalis in its cocoon.

She did not know how long her thoughts drifted. She stirred. The room seemed too silent. Alarmed, she pulled herself to her elbows.

"David?"

He was sitting right by her, at the edge of the bed. Her initial rush of relief gradually evaporated when she became conscious of the hard, compelling scrutiny of those brilliant eyes.

"They meant to kill you," he said. "You do realize that?"

Her reply was unequivocal. "Yes." From the moment her abductors had removed their masks, she had known that her life was forfeit. They would never have taken the chance that she could later identify them.

A nerve twitched spasmodically in his cheek. "Drowning was too easy a death for those bastards!"

"Don't say so! Oh, can't you see? You're putting yourself on their level!"

His mouth twisted in an angry sneer. "You would say so, naturally, when I saved your life, not to mention your virtue. Or were you the instigator of that attack?"

"What?"

He was furious, and she could not believe it.

"Spare me the outraged innocence! Didn't I warn you not to leave the Bull? A woman on her own is fair game! You invited what happened to you tonight!"

Annabelle looked at him with eyes widened in shock. Her lips trembled. Reproachfully, she said, "The same way I invited what transpired in your rooms in the Palais Royal? The same way I invited . . ."

"Precisely!" God, he didn't know what was the matter with him! He didn't know what he was saying, nor did he care. She had put her life in jeopardy. If he hadn't gone looking for her—his mind refused to complete the thought. Residual rage fanned to life within him. Somebody had to pay for what he had been through in the last hour.

"Just look at you!" he raged. "How could anybody take you for a lady in that rig? You look as though you've been melted down and poured into those trousers! And what have you done to your hair? It's indecent the way you are flaunting every female curve and contour of your body!"

Indecent, provocative and so unjust. Couldn't she tell what she was doing to him? His eyes slid over every female curve and contour he had accused her of flaunting; the delicate arch of her long white throat, the pout of those full, ripe breasts, the tiny waist he could span with his hands if he had a mind to, the lush flare of her hips, and those long legs which would wrap around him, holding him so securely at the moment of climax in their lovemaking. God, she didn't have to flaunt anything. It was just . . . there! The tightening in his groin grew painful.

He had almost lost her, and he needed reassurance badly. Couldn't she see that? Apparently not.

"How do you feel?" he asked.

She eyed him warily. "Fine, fine. Just a little bit shaken. No, really, I'm fully recovered."

His eyes swept over her. "You're sure?"

278

"Quite."

He didn't have to think about what he was doing. He went to the door and locked it.

Annabelle watched mesmerized as he sat on the edge of the bed and removed first his boots and then his shirt and trousers. She didn't know where to look and fastened her eyes on the pulse that throbbed in his throat.

"It'll be hours before they're back," he told her. "They haven't even lit the bonfire yet."

Swallowing, she said, "I don't think I understand the male psyche. Honestly, David, I don't mean to invite anything. I didn't think . . ."

"You never do!"

She let that pass. "I am not inviting anything," she told him, not angry, not frightened, just forthright. There would be no misunderstandings this time, she promised herself. He had to admit that he wanted her too.

His voice was like molten steel. "I'm going to make love to you and there's not a damn thing you can do about it."

"No, but . . ."

"For God's sake, Annabelle! We are going to be married in a matter of weeks. If it's your father you're thinking of, put him out of your mind. I'll put things right with him if the occasion arises."

She stared at him blankly, trying to make sense of what he was saying.

Misunderstanding her silence, he said in a persuasive tone, "Pregnancy isn't the end of the world! So what if our first child arrives a month or so early? It happens to lots of couples. We'll just brazen it out. But don't turn me away now. Can't you see I'm going to pieces. Dammit, Annabelle, I need you now more than ever."

Pregnancy! Her heart turned over. The thought of having a baby, no of having *his* baby, made everything inside her ache with an indescribable yearning. Fantasies about babies had always had the power to tug at her heart-strings. But this was different. Awesome! Dalmar's child! Her blood sang. His seed would take root and fill her belly. Together, they would create a new life. It was a miracle! It was mystical! It was . . . and then she knew!

"You used the right word to get what you wanted," she told him. "You should use it more often. Oh come here, you big bully! Don't you know by now that I love you? Well, what's the matter? Cat got your tongue?" She smiled, an age-old feminine smile. "That's an invitation Dalmar. You won't get a better one."

She looked at him with wide, trusting eyes, luminous with love. Dalmar was too choked to speak. "I love you," she had said. No one, in his whole life, had ever said those words to him. He was shattered, but at the same time, he felt like ten feet tall.

He came down on her like a ton of coal. In five seconds flat, he had stripped every stitch of clothing from her back. He wasn't taking the chance that she would retract her offer. Not on that night of all nights. His need went beyond his lust for her woman's body. Pleasure was the furthest thing from his mind. He had damn near lost her! His drive to possess was like a raging bloodlust, a torment that ripped his self-control to shreds. She was alive. She was his. And only by joining his body to hers could the mindless fear inside him be laid to rest.

"Don't ever, *ever,* put me through that hell again," he told her, his hands almost fierce as they claimed her intimately. The violence of his touch took her by surprise. Beneath the press of his weight, he felt her stiffen. He groaned. "No! Don't hold back! Annabelle, give in to me!"

He raised himself slightly, his body trembling from the rigid control he was trying to impose. "I don't want to hurt you, but I can't stop now . . . Annabelle . . . please!"

Gradually, Annabelle relaxed beneath him. Her fingers splayed out across his back, gentling the tension which corded the hard, masculine muscles.

"It's all right," she whispered. "It's all right."

His fingers probed and invaded the intimate woman's flesh between her thighs. When she became slick and wet for him, his breathing stopped, then became harsh. Like an inferno burning out of control, desire exploded through him.

He couldn't wait; couldn't give her the time to catch up to him. "Forgive me," he expelled on a hoarse breath. He thrust her legs open and surged into her, losing himself in her soft woman's flesh. Involuntarily, feminine muscles contracted around him, and Dalmar went soaring over the edge.

When he finally pulled away, he could not look her in the eye. Such a thing had never happened to him before. He was supposed to be an accomplished lover, for God's sake, not some callow youth with his first woman. He was appalled at what he had done.

"I'm sorry," he said, breaking the silence. "I lost control."

He rolled to his side, pulling her with him, his arms cradling her tightly. "It won't be like that again, and that's a promise."

She cupped his face with both hands. "I love you," she said softly.

Their eyes held and locked. "I'll be honest with you," he said, swallowing a lump in his throat. He didn't know where it had come from. "I don't know what that means. But if it's any consolation, I've never felt for any woman what I feel for you."

She lowered her lashes, but not before he had seen some of the light go out of her eyes.

"Annabelle!" Her name was torn from him. He wished, then, that he had lied to her. Tightening his hold on her nape, he forced her to look up at him. "Can't you accept what I'm offering? I'll be a faithful husband. I'll never look at another woman, I swear. I'll never give our children cause to be afraid of their father. I'll take care of you, protect you, yet you'll still have a free hand to run your business empire. I'll . . ."

She silenced him by placing the index finger of one hand over his lips. "It's all right," she repeated, trying to gentle him of these new emotions which had raised a storm in his eyes. "I understand. Words are only tools to express ideas, after all. At the best of times, they are grossly inadequate." Her lips turned up in a siren's smile.

Fascinated, his eyes focused on the mole to the left of her tantalizingly curved mouth. He couldn't believe the effect this woman had on his body. "You're right," he told her, a new huskiness darkening his voice. "I've never been good with words. I'll show you what I mean."

He cupped her hand and brought it to his aroused, throbbing

281

manhood. She gave a start, and tried to pull back, but he prevented it.

"There are going to be no silent partners in this marriage," he told her, torn between amusement and ecstasy. "Just pretend you're starting on a new business venture and be your usual, thorough self."

His eyes held hers. Relentlessly, he stroked her fingers over every pleasure point in his body, compelling her to an intimacy he had never demanded from or allowed to any other woman. Under his careful tutoring, she gained confidence.

"Yes, like that," he groaned. "You're going to know every inch of me the way I know you."

This time he had himself well in hand when he pushed her into the depths of the mattress. He allowed her no modesty, but unveiled each cherished treasure first to his gaze, then to the caress of his hands and finally to the touch of his mouth. With infinite patience, he overcame each involuntary protest, every reluctance to permit him the freedom of her body. He savored her soft cries of pleasure as she writhed beneath the slow seduction of her senses. Only when she was mindless with need, calling out to him for release, did he yield to her pleading. But when he brought himself fully into her body, he taught her a new form of torment. His slow, measured strokes, denying her the fulfillment she craved, brought a torrent of anguished protest. He silenced her with a kiss.

He had never felt more of a man, never experienced so keenly the full depth of his masculine drive to possess. He wanted to enslave her, dominate her, control her, and at the same time, protect her from all harm. He would kill anyone who threatened a hair of her head. He did not think that so tepid a word as "love" could possibly express the ferocity of the emotions this woman aroused in him. Nor would he dare reveal such thoughts to Annabelle. She would be scandalized by his masculine arrogance. But what he could not reveal in words, he demonstrated by bringing her to the point where she could deny him nothing.

And yet, strangely, when he finally allowed the crisis to overtake them, as he thrust into her, hoarsely repeating her name, over and over, like a lover's litany, he felt the pull of *her* possession in every cell of his body. He could not give her enough of himself; could not deny the power she wielded over him, nor even want to. Possessor and possessed, one flesh, indistinguishable.

At the very moment that their passion spent itself, the sky outside their window blazed with light as thousands of fireworks were ignited over Lewes.

"What was that?" asked Annabelle, startled. She was still panting softly as her body recovered from the surge of sensations which had just swept through her.

Dalmar laughed and showered her with moist, tender kisses. "I think we started something," he said. "When we go on our honeymoon, remind me to give Vesuvius a wide berth. Though the volcano has not erupted in years, there's no sense taking chances."

With an answering smile, she responded, "Armageddon!"

"What?" He pulled back slightly to look at her.

She lowered her lashes. "The first time this . . . you know what I mean . . . happened to me in your bed, I thought the end of the world was upon us." A delicate pink suffused her cheeks.

Dalmar stared at her for a long moment then threw back his head and laughed.

"I don't see the joke," she said, pouting.

"Armageddon? The end of the world?"

"You don't know your Bible very well, Dalmar."

"That's where you're wrong. I know exactly what you are getting at. I'd just never thought of it that way before."

"I thought I was dying."

"And now?" His eyes were very soft, his voice low and caressing.

She flashed him a mischievous smile. "Oh, now I know I've died and gone to heaven."

He smothered her in a bear hug.

As the effigy of Guy Fawkes went up in a roar of flames, Amy looked about her with terrified eyes. She saw where refuge was to be found and made a beeline for the man who was standing beside her beloved Aunt Bertie.

Throwing her arms around Ransome's legs, she sobbed, "I want to go home."

"She's overtired and overcome with excitement," he told Bertie, and he lifted Amy high against his chest. Her arms stole around his neck and she buried her head against his shoulder.

"They threw a man on the fire," she whispered brokenly in his ear.

Soothingly, he comforted her, explaining that the "guy" was not a real man, but only a suit of old clothes stuffed with straw. He had finally quieted the sobbing child when scores of fireworks were let off simultaneously. Her frightened sobs began anew.

"Amy, you're missing the fireworks display," said Bertie, trying to distract the weeping child. "Oh, look at the rockets. And the Catherine wheels. You've never seen anything quite like this before." She touched her hand to Amy's shoulder.

"I want to go home," wailed Amy, shaking off the comforting hand.

"Richard doesn't want to go home," said Bertie hopefully.

"Well *we* are going home." Ransome spoke in a voice that would brook no argument.

Hoisting Amy more securely in his arms, he turned on his heel and made his way to the edge of the spectators.

"Where do you think you're going," demanded Bertie, running to keep up with him. "I have not given you permission to take Amy away. She is my responsibility, not yours. Put her down this instant, d'you hear?"

Ransome stopped dead in his tracks, and Bertie stumbled against him. His expression was livid as he turned to face her. In a furious undertone, he said, "If she's not my responsibility, I know whom I have to thank for that! And say one more word to me in that vein, madam, and you'll rue the day that you were born."

Scandalized at being addressed in such terms, and even more shaken as the full significance of his words registered, Bertie could only stand and stare.

Ransome did not so much as spare her a backward glance. He pushed his way through the throng with Amy sheltered against his powerful chest. Bertie picked up her skirts and went racing after him.

"I know what you're thinking and you're wrong," she said, gasping more from fear than exertion. "Amy is my niece, d'you hear, my *niece!*"

He did not slow in his stride as he began the descent which led to the bridge into Lewes. "I might ask," he said, a sneer coating his voice, "why Amy should be the spitting image of my mother. There's a miniature of her in my possession. Remind me some time to show it to you."

"It's not possible," said Bertie, her voice low and lacking conviction even to her own ears.

"Oh, I'll allow that her eyes are yours," he said. "But in everything else, she is a Montague through and through. I should have suspected as much when you were so diligent in keeping her away from me for the duration of this houseparty. I'm surprised you allowed her to come to Rosedale in the first place. Why did you?"

With more honesty than caution, she blurted out, "I didn't know you were invited."

"Ah," he said, a wealth of meaning conveyed in the short reply.

Her uneasiness growing with each passing second, quickly, sharply, Bertie cried out, "This changes nothing. Surely you see that?"

"I beg to differ." His voice was as soft as silk. "My dear, this changes everything. D'you suppose I'll allow my own flesh and blood to be raised by strangers? Think again, Mrs. Pendleton."

She lambasted him with a furious oath.

"Keep your voice down," he bit out.

"Aunt Bertie, you're angry." Amy lifted her sleepy head, and glanced from one white face to the other.

Ransome's hand closed around the small head and pushed it back to the comfort of his shoulder. "There, there, pet. We'll soon have you home," he soothed.

The rest of the way to the Bull was made without one word being exchanged between the two of them, though, from time to time, each addressed a few words to Amy.

Ransome lost no time in hiring a chaise for the return trip

to Rosedale.

"We should wait here for the others," Bertie pointed out.

He shrugged indifferently. "Suit yourself. I promised Amy I would take her home and that's what I intend to do."

Rosedale was not "home" to Amy, but Bertie wisely refrained from telling him so. She could see that in his present mood, Ransome wasn't prepared to wait for time nor tide. He barely allowed her enough time to scribble a message for the others, giving them their direction, before he climbed into the chaise. Fearing that he would leave without her, she thrust the note at the landlord with some garbled instructions and went hastening after him.

In the carriage, though he might have laid Amy on one of the banquettes, Ransome chose instead to cradle her in his arms. The child was asleep but that did not stop him crooning soft words of comfort against her hair.

Torn between apprehension for the future, and a terrible regret for what might have been, Bertie finally said, "Paul, please, Amy is my sister's child. She's happy there. It doesn't matter who her natural parents are. Can't you understand that?"

In voice she scarcely recognized, he said, "I presume your sister has a husband?"

"Yes, but . . ."

"I'll talk to him. I have no doubt this thing can be settled amicably between gentlemen."

"No," she whispered.

"What do you care?" he baited. "It will make little difference to you. No demands will be made upon your time. You can see Amy as little as you do at present, if that's what you wish."

Each word pierced her like a poisonous barb. Her first instinct was to retaliate with all the fury of her wounded pride. She swallowed the senseless, accusatory words, and stared out the window.

His voice reached out to her in the darkness. "You must hate me very much."

She thought of the terrible heartache she had suffered at this man's hands.

"Bertie?"

"I had good reason," she answered at length.

"You never gave me a chance to explain."

She laughed softly, derisively. "Tell me, Colonel Ransome, how does a man explain away a wife?"

"I never lied to you!"

"No, but you let me think you were unattached. She came to see me. Did you know that?"

"She told me. And afterwards, I could not find you." A pleading note crept into his voice. "Bertie, I would have taken good care of you if only I had known; if only you had given me a chance."

"Yes, the way you took good care of your wife, I suppose?"

Frustration and anger surged through him. "You know nothing about the circumstances of my marriage."

Her voice held a chilling finality. "No. And I don't wish to know. Can't you get it through your head? It's over and done with! How many times do I have to tell you?"

"It will never be over! Because of Amy, there will always be a tie between us."

There was much that she might have said in rebuttal. She was too spent to summon the energy.

When they reached Rosedale, Ransome ordered the coachman to wait. Bertie followed him up the stairs. On the landing, they changed places and she led the way to her own chamber.

"Amy sleeps with me," she told him by way of explanation. Curiosity got the better of her. "Why did you tell the coachman to wait?"

With undiminished tenderness, he laid the sleeping child on the trundle bed next to the tester bed. He straightened without haste.

"I'm going back to Lewes," he answered.

Instinct warned her not to question him further, but she could not stop herself. "Why?"

Without blinking an eyelash, he responded, "There's a brothel there that I've become acquainted with. Of late, I find that I've had surfeit of the company of well-bred ladies."

She felt as if she had been slapped. Turning her back on

287

him, she fumbled for the fastenings of her pelisse. Slowly, with trembling fingers, she began to undo them.

"Bertie, one word from you and . . ."

"Don't let me stop you, Colonel."

Silence filled the room. She heard the click of the latch as he closed the door. Moments later, a carriage door slammed and the sounds of horses and carriage wheels came to her through the open window.

Mrs. Rosie Snow was in a towering temper, which was evident to anyone who knew her by the square set of her shoulders, the jut of her chin and the brisk, impatient strides which carried her away from the scene of revelry on the Cliffe. There was further evidence to be seen if one had a mind to examine her more closely. No one did. For on that dark stretch of road which led from the bonfire to the outskirts of Lewes, few were about with the exception of the odd man and his maid, who melted into the shadow at anyone's approach. Mrs. Snow scarcely saw them, so lost was she in her bitter ruminations.

To her cost, she had mistaken the character of Lady Jocelyn. It seemed that the prune-faced, curds-and-whey drab could become a veritable she-cat when she had a mind to. She had underestimated that lady. Which was why her protector, Sir Charles, was at that very moment in the bosom of his family and she, Rosie Snow, was left to find her own way home. Intolerable! And it had been contrived so effortlessly. Devious bitch!

And everything had started off so well! She'd been delighted when Sir Charles had made no objection to her presence at a public masquerade where it was quite possible that in the course of the evening she might very easily rub shoulders with his wife. The poor man was under the misapprehension that their costumes would conceal their identities, for there was always a plethora of pirates and shepherdesses at such events. She had known better. But she'd had no wish to rob him of his illusions. Why should she? It gave her a perverse pleasure to look these well-bred, top-lofty ladies in the eye and watch them squirm when it registered that she, Rosie Snow, could lure their men from them by merely crooking her little finger.

Her first inkling of trouble had caused nothing more than a small ripple of annoyance. She'd been locked in an embrace with Sir Charles when he had suddenly pulled back.

"My God, she's staring at us!"

"What?" She'd been dazed from the ardor of his kiss. There had never been any doubt that Sir Charles was a skillful, demanding lover.

"Henrietta, she's looking this way."

The eyes of the two women had clashed.

"Of course she doesn't recognize us," she'd crooned. She couldn't help smiling her triumph at the other woman. "Besides, she's a well-bred wife. Even if she does, she'll look the other way."

There had been no resumption of the kiss. Sir Charles had been ill-at-ease from that moment on. But it was after the fireworks display that he'd lost interest in her completely.

"What the devil does she think she's doing?"

His eyes were fastened on the group of merrymakers who were dancing to "The Grand Old Duke of York." Henrietta was at their center. As the fiddlers increased the tempo of the music, she picked up her skirts, baring herself to the knees.

Sir Charles could not drag his eyes away from the picture his wife presented. With head thrown back, eyes flashing, she linked arms with the man who was partnering her, and was spun around with great gusto till she was swung off her feet. Breathless and laughing, she'd turned her face up to her partner. It was an invitation the young man could not resist.

"He's kissing her!" Sir Charles ejaculated, and started forward.

She checked him with a hand on his sleeve. "What's the harm? You were kissing me. And if she did recognize us, she'll only throw it in your teeth. Leave well enough alone, why don't you?" Her voice turned low and husky. "There's a room waiting for us at the Maiden's Head." She pouted prettily. "Don't you want to be private with me?"

The gesture was lost on him. His eyes were still locked on the dancers. Manufacturing an ingratiating smile, she turned into his arms and rubbed herself suggestively against his length. His

289

interest in Lady Jocelyn wavered. Brazenly, she took his hand and cupped it around one breast. He groaned and crushed her to him.

A terrible wailing, a child's cry, rent the air, and the music suddenly stopped. Sir Charles pushed her away.

Testily, showing a temper she was normally at some pains to conceal, she broke out, "Oh do let us get away from here. It's only some rash child who has scorched his fingers. It happens every year."

"It's Peter! My God! What next?"

She'd turned to follow the direction of his anxious gaze. Lady Jocelyn was fussing over some tow-headed boy. She straightened and looked straight at them.

Sir Charles's voice was hoarse when he exclaimed, "She can't mean to bring him here?"

But it was very evident that that was exactly what Lady Jocelyn *did* mean to do.

As if petrified with horror, like some marble statue, Sir Charles stood and gaped as his wife approached. She was only a step away when he came to himself. His face crimson from chagrin or guilt or a combination of both, he quickly placed himself between the two women.

"Henrietta!" There was a desperate appeal in his voice. "Please! Remove yourself at once, and take Peter with you!"

With great good humor, and as if she did not give a brass button that she was breaking every rule of deportment in the book, Lady Jocelyn said, "It *is* you, Charles. I thought as much. This wretched child has got himself burned and must be attended to at once. Every one of our party seems to have disappeared. Would you be so kind . . . oh!" She peeked over her husband's shoulder. "Good evening, Mrs. Snow. Peter, this is Papa's friend, Mrs. Snow. Say how-do-you-do."

The sniveling child mumbled, "How do you do, Mrs. Snow."

"Henrietta!" Sir Charles looked fit to be tied.

"Harry!" The cry came from the young man who had partnered Henrietta in the dance. "We're ready to begin whenever you are!"

290

"Harry!" The name evidently did not sit well with Sir Charles.

"It's what all my friends call me," returned Henrietta gaily. "Now be a good boy, Peter. Papa will look after you. Oh, by the by, Charles, I haven't seen James and Richard in an age. I wonder what has become of those boys?"

"Richard knows lots of bad words," interjected Peter. "And now I know them too." His tears subsided into dry, rasping sobs as he contemplated his good fortune in having such a knowledgeable pedant for a relation.

Trying to give the appearance of a man who has the situation well in hand, Sir Charles blustered, "Really, Henrietta, I fail to see . . ."

"Ta, ta," she said, turning away. "I really must go. Don't worry about the boys. I don't think any harm will come to them. They've just wandered away again. And Mary has gone after them. But the burn on Peter's hand is a nasty one. It really ought to be attended to. Good bye, Mrs. Snow. Lovely to see you again!"

Of course, after that little display of wifely spite, the night had been ruined. There was no question that Sir Charles would leave his young sons to fend for themselves, or even permit his mistress to come within hailing distance of them. She'd been rudely and summarily dismissed and told to remove to Brighton forthwith!

The very thought of the way he had looked at her, the way he had spoken to her, as if he were turning away second day's mutton, made her seethe with resentment. Well, she would show him! There were gentlemen in the Maiden's Head, if she was not mistaken, who would be glad to keep her bed warm. She smiled at the irony of Sir Charles paying the shot for the room where she meant to cuckold him.

Lost in the sweet delights of her vengeful thoughts, she became careless. She paid no heed to the carriage which bore so relentlessly down upon her. Mercifully, she did not suffer long, and knew nothing when her lifeless body was thrown into the river.

Chapter Seventeen

"Annabelle! What the deuce?" The stunned expletive came from Lord Temple as he pushed through the door to the breakfast room.

It was the third time in as many minutes that Annabelle had heard those words, or words very like them. Self-consciously, she touched her fingers to the bruise on her jaw. "I had an accident," she said. "It was clumsy of me. I tripped over my feet and fell against the bed-post."

It was a lame excuse, and one that had been concocted by Dalmar to spare her embarrassment. It was his design to put the whole matter of the attack on her before the magistrates in Lewes just as soon as she had quit Rosedale. Not for the world would he permit her to be badgered by over-zealous bureaucrats. For who was to say whose version of the truth the Law would accept? Annabelle saw the sense in his logic. Moreover, she had no wish to become the object of speculation or worse—pity to her friends.

At the prolonged silence, she glanced up from her bowl of porridge, the only sustenance she could force past her stiff lips, and her eyes swept over the Viscount. He hadn't moved a muscle, and looked to be rather white about the gills. But then, so did Charles this morning and the two other occupants of the room, Colonel Ransome and Bertie. She knew that it was going to hurt like blazes, but she couldn't help herself. She grinned, then groaned almost simultaneously.

By way of explanation, she said, "From the looks of us, we

should be under a doctor's care. Speaking for myself, I think I'll give Lewes a miss next Guy Fawkes Day. The boredom and predictability of Bath has become suddenly appealing."

No one answered her attempt at levity. She stifled a sigh and wished that Dalmar or some of Lady Diana's crowd would put in an appearance. The tension between Ransome and Bertie was almost tangible. She couldn't wait to shake the dust of Rosedale from her feet. *Only an hour to go,* she consoled herself, *and we'll be on our way to town.* Perhaps then Colonel Ransome would take the hint and leave off his opportuning of her friend. Couldn't he see that Bertie wanted none of him?

On the other side of the breakfast-room door, there was stir. Doors opened and slammed. Girlish laughter and giggles rose to an alarming crescendo. Sir Charles gazed fixedly at the door. It opened to admit Henrietta followed by Lady Diana and two of her young friends, the Hon Miss Loukes and Miss Cranbrook. Their glances flicked over the sober faces of the room's occupants. Lady Diana whispered something in Henrietta's ear and the two of them dissolved in giggles.

Annabelle had to look twice at her sister-in-law, else she would have scarcely recognized her. It wasn't that Henrietta had changed her appearance, or had adopted a new mode of dressing, Annabelle decided, but she *did* look different. And then it came to her. It was in the eyes and in the facial expression. Henrietta looked positively animated. And becoming! And years younger! Annabelle could not tear her eyes from her sister-in-law. Neither could Sir Charles.

In the ladies' wake came the other houseguests. Annabelle's eyes brushed Dalmar's. No one observed the betraying pink which stole across her cheekbones. It was Henrietta who was at the center of all conversation.

In answer to a question put by Lady Diana, Henrietta said, "They're country dances. That's why the steps are unfamiliar to you. You're not like to come across them at Almack's or in a London ballroom."

"But how do you know them?" lisped Lady Diana. "I'm sure I never had so much fun in my life."

A chorus of voices gave their assent to Lady Diana's observation.

"I learned the steps as a young girl," replied Henrietta. "Those were the only dances that I knew until I married and made my bow to society." She smiled, the oddest mixture of whimsy and regret. "In those days, I wasn't aware of how uncouth and wild the movements were."

"What dances?" asked Dalmar in an aside to Sir Charles.

"Vulgar country dances," responded that gentleman irascibly, but careful not to let his voice carry. "You missed the spectacle. My wife taught the whole damn town of Lewes a series of dervishes that made our Morris dancers look like a procession of paid mourners following a hearse."

Dalmar's lips twitched, but he managed gravely, "Did she, by Jove?"

There was a clamor of raised voices from the ladies. "Oh, do say you will, Harry! Do say you will!"

Sir Charles became aware that his wife was looking a question at him. "Beg pardon. I wasn't listening," he said, none too graciously.

Lady Diana pounced on him. "Harry must come up to town and teach us the steps for my ball. Oh, they'll be all the rage. And I'll be the envy of Lady Jersey and those horrid lionesses of Almack's."

"More like you'll lose your vouchers to the place, the whole lot of you!" expostulated Sir Charles.

"What a fuddy-duddy thing to say!" observed Miss Loukes in a carrying undertone.

"Well, Charles?" asked Henrietta boldly. "Do we or do we not go up to town?"

He could not hold her stare. "The house has been shut up," he mumbled into his napkin.

Annabelle, who was blissfully unaware of the eddies which flowed beneath the surface, immediately offered to accommodate them both for as long as they wished, and then wondered at the glower Sir Charles shot her.

"Well, Charles?" persisted Henrietta.

Bristling under a sea of curious stares, but sticking to his guns, Sir Charles drawled, "I'm afraid it's impossible." He calmly cut into a prime piece of sirloin. "I can't spare the time at present!"

"You can't spare the time," repeated Henrietta, coming very close to mimicking him.

"No," replied Sir Charles without elaboration.

Henrietta's laughing accents cut across a chorus of groans and protests. "I don't give up so easily." Turning to Annabelle, she said, "We'll make this a hen party. Just you, Bertie and I."

"What about the children?" demanded Sir Charles, more astonished than angry. "You know how they abhor town life."

Henrietta threw him a disarming smile. "You're right, of course." He beamed at her. "I wouldn't dream of taking the boys with me. You'll manage them, won't you, dear, with Mary's help?"

No one could mistake the look which crossed Sir Charles's face. *Churlish*, thought Annabelle. And since Henrietta had never in *her* memory left her children to the care of servants overnight, even Annabelle was conscious of the strained atmosphere.

"Then that settles it," said Dalmar, slapping Sir Charles on the back. "Don't worry, old chap. I'll keep an eye out for the ladies, and you can rusticate with a clear conscience."

As it happened, young Richard elected to stay with his cousins at Rosedale for a week or two.

"Perhaps Amy would like to stay, too," offered Annabelle, addressing Bertie.

It was Colonel Ransome who answered. As he handed first Annabelle, then Bertie into the closed carriage, he said, "That will not be convenient."

He climbed in behind them and reached for Amy. With a crow of delight, she practically flung herself on his lap. Round-eyed, Annabelle darted a quick glance at Bertie's revealing profile. She would have to be very obtuse, indeed, thought Annabelle sagely, not to put two and two together under these circumstances.

As soon as the carriage pulled to a stop in front of the entrance to her house on Greek Street, she was out the door like a shot, reaching for a fractious, sleepy-eyed Amy. Bertie was only a step behind her, foiling Annabelle's discreet attempt to provide the two Friday-faced lovers with privacy to bring their differences to a satisfactory conclusion.

An implacable masculine hand on Bertie's arm yanked her backward. She landed with a thump against the banquette, and the door was unceremoniously slammed shut in her face.

"Driver, a turn around the park, if you please," Annabelle heard Ransome command stridently. She half turned on the front step, and watched as her coachman urged his team forward.

"Well!" she exclaimed, somewhere between outrage and thwarted curiosity. "That man is just too full of his own importance!"

She spent the next hour showing young Amy over her new domain. In the nursery, where Richard's knights were set up, Amy was in her element. Annabelle watched in some amusement as Nancy and nurse tried to divert the girl to unexceptional toys more suitable for a young female. But Amy was very vociferous in her rejection of anything that smacked of "prissy."

"Oh dear," said Annabelle to the two bemused maids, "if I'm not mistaken, Amy is suffering from a surfeit of male influence, Richard and his cousins. Oh dear!" she said again as the object of her conversation gleefully rerranged Richard's knights and infantry to suit her own taste. Annabelle was not quite sure that Richard would view this desecration with anything resembling equanimity. She had visions of the normal household tranquillity which prevailed in Greek Street being shattered by the spats of noisy, quarrelsome children. The prospect made her shudder.

She was in the morning room, which also served as her study, when she heard a footman open the front door to Bertie. Though she trusted her companion implicitly, events had made Annabelle cautious. Without thinking, she gathered the pages of Monique Dupres's memoirs, which she had newly committed to paper, and thrust them into the bottom drawer of her Sheraton escritoire.

She'd made remarkable progress, she thought, and no wonder. She'd been driven by an unwholesome curiosity to uncover the shady goings-on of one "Sir Spider." The first time she'd come across the knave, he'd been only one of many such characters who marched through the pages of the French girl's manuscript. She hadn't paid much attention. But that was before she knew his identity. Dalmar!

And though the diaries opened in Vienna, she had concentrated all her powers of recall on what had transpired in Brussels, where "Sir Spider" had first put in an appearance. Vienna was only of academic interest. Brussels drew her like a magnet.

But oh, she could not shake herself of the unpalatable conviction that she had become something of a peeping-Tom— a ridiculous notion for a publisher to entertain.

On reflection, however, she was forced to admit that she had lost that professional sense of objectivity which had served her so well in the past. It could not be otherwise. Through an unusual set of circumstances, she had become privy to the most intimate, sordid details of Dalmar's past. And none was more sordid than the episode she had spent the last hour regurgitating.

Scandalous! And so mortifying to read another woman's description of the virile attributes of the man she, Annabelle Jocelyn, was soon to marry. Apparently Monique Dupres had taken a more thorough and leisurely inventory than she had permitted herself.

Behind the building anger, she sensed another, more elusive emotion. With elbows on the desk, she palmed her closed eyes and strove to identify it. And then it came to her. Self-doubt, inadequacy, a sinking feeling that she wasn't enough woman to satisfy a lusty man like the Earl. It wouldn't be the first time that such a thing had happened. She hadn't been enough woman for Edgar either.

It was illogical but she felt like a betrayed wife all over again. Which was ludicrous, she chided herself, since Dalmar's indiscretions could in no wise be deemed as infidelity. They had not even known each other when he had been stationed in Brussels. She sighed; she shook her head and tried to shake herself of her blue-deviled temper.

In such a frame of mind, Annabelle finally caught up with Bertie in the nursery. She saw at once that the poor girl was almost beside herself.

"You've been gone for hours," she observed quietly.

Bertie turned up a tear-streaked face and opened her mouth to answer. A watery sob escaped her lips.

"Come away," said Annabelle softly, careful not to attract Amy's interest to the drama which was unfolding.

Bertie allowed herself to be directed to Annabelle's small private sitting-room on the floor below. Tea and biscuits were sent for. Annabelle kept up a flow of inconsequential small talk until the servants withdrew.

The door closed. After a long and thoughtful pause, Annabelle introduced what she hoped was a neutral topic of conversation. "Amy seems to be settling in well," she remarked. "I've given her the room next to yours. I hope I did right?"

The response which met this innocuous observation floored Annabelle. Bertie burst into a torrent of tears and, between gulps, became involved in a long and convoluted explanation of which Annabelle could make neither head nor tail. Feeling somewhat alarmed, she fetched a small silver flask of "medicinal" brandy, which she kept secreted in her sewing basket. Having liberally dosed Bertie's tea (and her own, as an afterthought), she commanded her to swallow the whole. Few argued with Annabelle when she adopted an autocratic air. Obediently Bertie drained every last drop of liquid in the small china teacup.

"Now, then, shall we start over?" said Annabelle, her voice carefully devoid of any overt sympathy.

The calm, assured tone seemed to strike just the right balance. Bertie fumbled for her handkerchief, blew her nose, and generally dallied till her composure was somewhat restored. Finally she looked into Annabelle's troubled blue eyes and said tremulously, "Paul, that is, Colonel Ransome has asked me to marry him."

"Oh." It was the last thing that Annabelle had expected to hear. "All things considered," she continued doubtfully, "I suppose it's the best course." She was thinking that Ransome and her friend could not be in the same room together for five minutes but they became as stiff as starch. Still, if the man was Amy's father . . .

"That's a matter of opinion!"

"I beg your pardon?"

"Don't you see?" cried Bertie passionately. "I don't wish to marry him! How should I, after what passed between us? But I don't have a choice in the matter."

Bertie had never taken anyone fully into her confidence on the matter of Ransome and Amy's parentage. It was a wretched episode she thought she was long over—the old, hackneyed story of a green girl who had loved unwisely and too well. She'd never suspected that the man she'd given her heart to had a wife in town while she was hidden away in the country, until that wife had burst into her little house in Chelsea and blown her world apart. She'd told Annabelle very little about her history except to imply that her marriage had not been a happy one. Having said as much, she knew that Annabelle would not press her to reveal the details of her background. In point of fact, she had invented the late Mr. Pendleton as an act of sheer desperation when she was alone, single, and pregnant with Amy. Afterward she had kept up the pretense out of habit and a very real fear that Ransome might one day discover her whereabouts if she kept her own name.

At that moment she wished she had taken Annabelle into her confidence. She longed for a little disinterested advice from someone whose judgment she valued. Absently, nervously, she twisted the handkerchief in her hands into knots. Though she could not bring herself to reveal the full magnitude of her deception, and omitting any reference to the imaginary Mr. Pendleton, she began to unburden herself, relating only the essentials of her unhappy circumstances.

Annabelle listened without interruption. Her expression betrayed neither the shock nor condemnation which Bertie half feared she would surprise on her friend's face. Her story at an end, Bertie searched Annabelle's eyes anxiously.

"Annabelle, perhaps you can advise me. What should I do?"

Annabelle hesitated. Cautiously, she asked, "You're quite sure you don't wish to marry the man?"

"Hardly!" responded Bertie with a semblance of defiance. "And the feeling is mutual, I'm sure."

"Then why has he offered?"

"He wants Amy, naturally. He never thought of offering for me until he was sure that she . . . oh well . . . no sense going into that now." A fresh wave of tears welled in her beautiful pansy brown eyes.

"My dear, you don't have to marry any man if you don't wish to," pointed out Annabelle reasonably.

Between sniffs Bertie got out, "Oh Annabelle, you're such a simpleton sometimes. Haven't you learned yet that it's a man's world? Where do you think we went this afternoon? To my brother-in-law's, that's where! And Paul and James have decided between them that everyone's interests are best served by my marriage to . . . to the father of my child."

It's a man's world. The truth of that unpalatable statement was incontrovertible, thought Annabelle. For the most part, men ordered things to suit themselves. Women, the weaker vessels, were forced to accept the confines of that submissive role which was fashioned by society, buttressed by law, and sanctified by church—all bastions of male power. It took an exceptional woman to break out of that rigid mold. But it could be done. If a woman used the wits she was born with, she could thumb her nose at the male species and still stay on the right side of public opinion.

Very gently Annabelle stated, "Nevertheless, no one can force you to marry Ransome unless you wish it."

It never occured to Annabelle that her friend was concealing more than she had revealed. Bertie said that she did not wish to marry Ransome, and Annabelle believed her. She could not guess that what stuck in Bertie's craw was the fact that the gentleman had offered marriage only after he had deduced that he had fathered her child. In point of fact, as is the case with most people, though it was advice Bertie had specifically asked for, it was reassurance she'd hoped to receive. She was disappointed and did not know why.

The conversation lost focus and drifted into other channels. By and by their thoughts turned to Henrietta and her projected sojourn in Greek Street. With a gaiety they were far from feeling, they set their minds to devise some outings to entertain Henrietta when she should arrive. They were determined that everything should be done to ensure that she did not mope for her absent children. "For a more maternal lady I've yet to meet," said Annabelle knowledgeably.

As it happened, Henrietta took them by surprise and landed on their doorstep late of that very afternoon. In her best hostess manner, Annabelle invited her sister-in-law to look upon her home as if it were her own. Before the evening was out, it was very evident that Henrietta, or "Harry" as she now insisted on, had taken Annabelle at her word.

When Dalmar and Colonel Ransome dropped in after dinner, the main floor public rooms were fairly choked with people, most of them intimates of Lady Diana. Annabelle was still dazed from the speed with which everything had been arranged. She'd thought to spend a quiet evening nursing her sore jaw, now artfully covered with paint and powder. But events had simply overtaken her with the force of a hurricane.

"What the deuce is going on?" asked Dalmar of a slightly abstracted Annabelle as she greeted him at the door.

"An impromptu party to welcome Henrietta, I mean Harry, to town." She couldn't help being a little stiff with him. The episode in Monique Dupres's memoirs was still very fresh in her mind. Her greeting to Colonel Ransome was only a trifle warmer.

The gentlemen appeared not to notice, or perhaps they could not hear her for the uproar. In one room, which the guests themselves had cleared of furniture, a rollicking reel was in progress. It was Bertie's nimble fingers which hammered out the music on the piano.

The gentlemen's eyes slowly traveled the crush of people.

"It's rather a young crowd for Greek Street, wouldn't you say, Ransome?" observed the Earl. "And not a literary type in sight." He turned a laughing face upon Annabelle. "You won't be able to combine business and pleasure at this sort of do."

"I'm scarcely in my dotage," retorted Annabelle. "And I'm not averse to pleasure. Why ever would you think so?"

"I don't think so, and with good reason."

She chose to ignore the sardonic smile and intimate tone. They idled their way to the room where the dancing was taking place. When the reel came to an end, the dancers stamped and hooted their displeasure. Ransome excused himself and went with alacrity to sit beside Bertie on the piano bench. Catching sight of Dalmar, Henrietta detached herself gently from her partner who was apparently reluctant to let her go.

"You're in looks tonight, Lady Jocelyn," murmured Dalmar, bowing over the hand she offered him.

"If I am, I have you to thank for it." Rather shyly, she added, "I'm following your advice, you see."

"And Sir Charles?"

Her smiled faded momentarily, then flashed more brilliantly than before. "There's always much to occupy him in and around Rosedale." A mischievous glint crept into her eyes. "I should feel guilty, I suppose, for dumping five boys in his lap. But frankly, I don't give a straw."

"I'm sure it couldn't happen to a worthier person," said Dalmar. "Console yourself with the thought that time won't hang heavily on his hands."

They laughed companionably.

Annabelle shot a keen look at first one and then the other. She was on the point of asking them to explain themselves when Lady Diana gave a trill of pleasure and threw herself at the Earl.

"Darling," cooed Lady Diana in the voice that always reminded Annabelle of her father's dovecote at the bottom of their garden in Yorkshire, "I swear you take the shine out of every other gentleman in the room. Isn't he the handsome one, Annie?"

Dalmar smiled a lazy smile, and Annabelle snorted indelicately. From the corner of her eye, she watched as the Earl made a slow assessment of the girl through the veil of his lashes. That he fancied himself something of a connoisseur of females had never been in doubt. With a studied indifference she could scarcely sustain, Annabelle greeted The Beauty.

Dalmar's greeting was more effusive. "Diana! Goddess of the moon," he fairly purred, and he brushed the tips of her fingers with his lips. "Tonight you outshine the moon itself. What do you say, Annie?"

"There isn't any moon tonight," she blurted. Three pairs of eyes trained upon her. Lamely she explained, "It's been overcast all day."

A stab of annoyance flashed through Annabelle at the amused, almost complacent twinkle which lurked in Dalmar's eyes. She was jealous and he knew it. Worse, she'd been churlish to Lady Diana for no good reason. It wasn't the lady's fault that she had the good fortune to be young, titled, rich, charming, and beautiful beyond compare. Everyone liked the girl. Even *she* liked the girl.

Trying to make amends, Annabelle voiced the next idle thought which flitted into her mind. "It wouldn't be fair to the rest of us ladies if you had brains, too."

Dalmar choked on his laughter, and Annabelle wished the floor would open beneath her feet. Thankfully, Lady Diana could pluck a compliment out of thin air.

"You're too kind," she murmured and dropped those enormous eyes becomingly.

Annabelle was saved from further embarrassment by a young blade who solicited her hand for the next dance—a waltz, she was relieved to discover. And since this was a very informal private party, no young lady was denied the pleasure of treading her toes to the beat of the wicked, voluptuous dance which had taken the ballrooms of Europe by storm.

Over her partner's shoulder, she surveyed the dozen or so couples who crowded the small space which had been turned into an impromptu dance floor. She still found it hard to believe that she had consented to this spur-of-the-moment affair. She was not by nature an impulsive person. Quite the reverse. Her calendar was carefully plotted weeks in advance; her attention to detail, meticulous to a fault. She never expected to enjoy her own parties. She was too conscientious a hostess to forget herself for a moment. Yet here she was, tripping the light fantastic, as Milton would say, as if she hadn't a care in the world.

Her eyes traveled the throng of people. Of the scores who filled her small house, she did not think she was acquainted with more than a handful. It was Lady Diana who had brought most of them with her. In effect, it was Henrietta and Lady Diana who were hosting the party. Everything had been thrown together at the last minute and, wonder of wonders, no one seemed to be suffering one jot. Truth to tell, Annabelle could not remember when her guests had enjoyed themselves more. There was a lesson for her here, somewhere, mused Annabelle.

"May I say how very becoming you look in that frock, Mrs. Jocelyn?" she heard her partner say.

The compliment quite took the sting out of Dalmar's perceived neglect of the niceties. She knew she had never looked better in her daffodil silk with its overdress of gold-shot gauze. It did wonderful things for her nondescript hair which wasn't quite brown, nor yet black, now that the dye was wearing thin. He had not spared his compliments for the other ladies. Why was he so niggardly with her?

"You dance the waltz divinely," said young Mr. Loukes.

Cliché, thought Annabelle, but quite acceptable for all that. She smiled into Mr. Loukes's bland brown eyes. He was no more than a boy, really. But if he wished to practice the finer points of the art of flirting, she was quite prepared to indulge him.

Batting her great sooty eyelashes, Annabelle murmured, "Why Mr. Loukes! I bet you say that to all the girls!"

"No, ma'am," he answered seriously. "I always make it a point to pass up the eligibles in favor of the older ladies when the waltz is announced." At Annabelle's blank look, he added by way of explanation, "Debs my own age don't know the steps. They don't get enough practice, you see, on account of Lady Jersey. They're like to lose their vouchers to Almack's."

It was after that inadvertent set-down that Annabelle became the life of the party. Unsparing of her advanced years, and ignoring pinched toes, aching muscles, and especially Dalmar's mocking, knowing glances, she applied herself to learning the steps of every blessed country dance Henrietta introduced for the delectation of their guests. Not even the moon goddess herself could outshine her in gaiety.

By the time the last guest had taken his leave and Bertie and Henrietta had trudged up the stairs to bed, Annabelle felt sure that the smile on her face had petrified. Wearily she traipsed through the ground-floor public rooms, taking inventory. She was pleasantly surprised. Though she was sure that Greek Street had never witnessed such a wild, unholy party, the damage appeared to be minimal.

In the drawing room she plunked herself into the plump cushions of a white satin sofa. With shoes discarded and hair askew, she closed her eyes and reflected on the folly of trying to keep up with the young.

It was how Dalmar found her some few minutes later.

"I thought you'd gone," said Annabelle, quickly rearranging her hair. She blessed the caprice which had made her resist the impulse to loosen her stays. "But I'm glad you're here. You never did tell me what the magistrates at Lewes had to say."

"It was as I thought," he said carelessly, and took the chair beside her.

"Yes?" She gave him an expectant look.

"They didn't know where to begin searching for those two blighters. I'm afraid they got clean away. But that's not what I wish to speak to you about. There's something of greater importance that needs to be said."

His expression was hooded, his voice grave. Annabelle became instantly alert.

"What could be more important than finding the men who attacked me?" she asked incredulously.

Impatiently, he answered, "They are of no moment! Will you listen to me, Annabelle?"

She could only stare at him, and after a pause, he went on more deliberately, "About the diaries . . ."

"Oh no! Not that again," she blurted out. "Look, Dalmar, as far as I'm concerned, we've exhausted that as a topic of conversation."

"It's not a topic of conversation. It's a bone of contention," he said fiercely. After a moment he went on more levelly. "Annabelle, this is your last chance to surrender them gracefully. After this, I'll wrest them from you, by fair means or foul."

Annabelle had never got round to confronting Dalmar about the theft of the diaries. In point of fact, when her temper had cooled sufficiently, she was more than half convinced that she had misjudged him. Not that she doubted for a minute that he was capable of such outrageous conduct. But from what she knew of his character, it seemed more in keeping that he would boast of his success if he had bested her—as she would do if their positions were reversed. There was a rivalry there between them which neither was slow to exploit. In her opinion, it was part of the attraction which held them together.

But in two weeks, Dalmar had not once, even obliquely, baited her with his victory. And now his own words absolved him. Like a ferret on the scent of a rabbit, he was still hot on the trail of the diaries, thinking that she had them in her possession.

In a manner of speaking, she supposed that she had. In the fortnight since the manuscript had been stolen, she had religiously reconstructed almost a half of it. But she was wiser now. She kept the work under lock and key in a drawer in her bedchamber. She did not think that any thief would go undetected if he tried to burglarize her house in Greek Street. She had taken the precaution of alerting a few chosen members of her staff to be on the watch for suspicious strangers.

Not for a moment did Annabelle distrust anyone of her immediate acquaintance. She was convinced that the malefactor was one of the many titled gentlemen who were portrayed in Monique Dupres's memoirs. And the field of suspects was so wide that it seemed to her the task of discovering who had done the deed was hopeless.

All this she might easily have confessed to Dalmar if she had not believed that his immediate response would be to say *I told you so* in that superior way she so much detested. If he only knew it, she thought irritably, she was far more likely to give up the idea of publishing the diaries if he stopped hounding her. He just could not see that it was his high-handed methods that made her dig in her heels. She could be just as intractable as he.

She said nothing of what she was thinking. In some perverse way, though inside she trembled at the thought, she was curious to see how far Dalmar would go to get the diaries. Moreover, his supreme confidence and his arrogant assumption that she was no match for him rankled. It brought to mind Bertie's passionate avowal, "It's a man's world."

Her eyes narrowed on the figure of the Earl. Unhappily for

Dalmar, in that moment Annabelle saw beyond the particular gentleman who was sitting at his ease in her drawing room. He was the archetype, a representative of that predatory species which she labeled, rather derogatorily, "men in general." In their ranks, she numbered Edgar, Sir Charles, and Colonel Ransome. She knew the breed well. And recent events had only confirmed her conviction.

"I give you fair warning, Annabelle. I won't be swayed from my course by my affections."

"Dear, dear! That *does* sound serious," she answered flippantly.

"You'll be laughing on the other side of your face when next we meet if you don't surrender those diaries this instant."

"Did anyone ever tell you that you are a poor loser?" she drawled.

"Hand over those diaries!" he shouted.

"Certainly not! Those diaries are private property—mine, to be exact. Bailey's has nothing to do with them." Deliberately, falsely, she baited him. "They'll be ready in a day or two to go to the printers, and in very short order, Monique Dupres's memoirs will be selling like hotcakes from Land's End to John o' Groats."

Thunderstruck, he stared at her.

Adding insult to injury, she said in a kindly tone. "Now don't get your hackles up, Dalmar. No one will hold you responsible. I'm not having them printed here. They'll be done by another firm, so you see, if there's any trouble, you and Bailey's will be completely exonerated.

His face contorted into a mask of fury. "And that's your last word?"

Mutely, Annabelle nodded.

He had risen to his feet and was towering over her like some huge bird of prey. She had to forcefully remind herself that it was Dalmar, and in spite of the menacing posture, he would do her no harm.

He uttered an explosive oath and strode to the door. At the threshold he pivoted to face her.

"May I remind you of our pact?"

She knew at once that he was referring to their agreement to keep their business and personal lives separate.

Rising to her feet, she nodded her assent.

"I'll hold you to it."

As angry as he, she answered, "You do that, Dalmar. But I promise you, you'll never get those diaries away from me as long as I have breath in my body."

With one last, furious look, he flung over his shoulder, "God, you make the temptation almost irresistible, do you know?"

Chapter Eighteen

When Dalmar walked into Annabelle's office at Bailey's the following morning, she greeted him with a smile. Though she had not forgotten their blistering argument of the night before, other things had robbed the recollection of its sting.

On her desk lay a report from Albert, her second-in-command, and orders for books which had just come off the presses. He'd done a remarkable job, she thought, in ferreting out new avenues of distribution for the cheap cloth-covered editions she planned on producing. Her ambition had been realized, and in future, Bailey's books would be found not only in the more prestigious bookshops, but also behind the counters of drapers, grocers, and general mercantiles in some of the great centers outside London. It was a first in the publishing world, and Annabelle was elated at the coup Bailey's had pulled off.

She was eager to share her success with someone. Of everyone she knew, the Earl was more qualified than most to enter into her excitement. He'd shown a remarkable grasp of how her business was run. He was her partner. She'd acted on some of his suggestions and found that he had a sound head for business. But her most cogent reason for wishing to share the glad tidings with Dalmar was personal. She wanted to bask in his admiration. Rising quickly to her feet, she went forward to greet him.

It was the chill of his silver gaze which stopped her in her tracks. She fell back a step as two other gentlemen entered behind the Earl. Their expressions were somber. One of the men was wearing a black coat.

"Is this the lady in question?" asked the man in black.

"It is," said Dalmar.

"Am I addressing Mrs. Annabelle Jocelyn?" asked the gentleman, his eyes pinning Annabelle with a calculating stare.

"Yes," she answered, and flashed the Earl a questioning look. But Dalmar's gaze was trained steadfastly on the scene outside the small office window.

The man in black turned to his subordinate. "Let the record show that Lord Dalmar identified the suspect." His eyes flicked to the Earl. "It's in her favor, Your Lordship, that she did not dispute your identification."

"I'm aware of that. Just get on with it, man! I haven't got all day."

Annabelle watched in numbed silence as the clerk made notes. "David, what's going on?" she asked, her throat strangely dry. She became aware that all the normal, comforting sounds of a busy publishing and printing house were absent. The whole building had gone as quiet as a tomb. It frightened her. She tried to catch Dalmar's eye to no avail. Nor did he answer her question. That frightened her even more.

The man in black addressed her in slow, sonorous tones. "Mrs. Annabelle Jocelyn. I am a constable of the law, and I must ask you to accompany me to Bow Street for questioning."

"Am I under arrest?" she asked. Her fingers curled around the edge of her desk, and she sagged against it for support.

"Not at the moment. But serious charges have been laid against you."

"And . . . and if I refuse to go with you?"

It was Dalmar who answered. "Don't be a fool, Annabelle! These gentlemen are officers of the law. They mean business! You'd better listen to what they say."

For the first time since entering her office, he looked at her directly. Those glittering, steely eyes showed no mercy.

"What charges?" she asked, turning her attention to the constable.

"Suspicion of murder."

The answer stole her breath away. She made a strangled,

choking sound as she sucked air into her lungs. "What are you talking about?" Though her voice was hoarse, it had risen a notch.

"Monique Dupres," said Dalmar, his face a mask of implacable coldness.

Stunned, uncomprehending, she looked from one to the other. A flicker of pity momentarily softened the constable's eyes. There was no such softening in the Earl.

"But I left her alive and well in Paris."

"It's true, miss," said the constable. "We have it from the foreign office." He extended a scrap of paper. Annabelle took it and looked at it blindly. The constable's voice gentled. "If you can prove your innocence, you have nothing to fear. The girl was a British spy, as you can see." His eyes met the Earl's. "It seems more like that one of those Frenchies did her in," he offered.

The chill in Dalmar's voice matched his expression. "You're forgetting, constable, that Mrs. Jocelyn had the opportunity. Whether or not she had the motive remains to be seen. Now get on with it."

Annabelle was so shaken that she could not follow the conversation. She turned to Dalmar and said pleadingly, "Tell me the truth. Is she dead?"

He answered her with brutal honesty. "Yes. Her throat was slit during the riot in the Palais Royal."

A shudder passed over Annabelle. By degrees, she came to herself and tried to focus on what the constable was saying. "What did you say?" she asked blankly.

The constable coughed and shuffled his feet uneasily. He cleared his throat. "If you hand over the documents, miss, you're to be released into Lord Dalmar's custody. Otherwise I must ask you to accompany me to Bow Street for questioning."

"Documents?" said Annabelle. "What documents?"

"Diaries," answered Dalmar succinctly.

Sudden comprehension jolted Annabelle. Her eyes locked with the Earl's. "The diaries!" she said. "So that's why you're here."

"Yes," replied Dalmar, and folded his arms across his chest. An unmistakable flash of triumph came and went in his eyes.

313

"Why don't you make things easy for yourself, Annabelle? Just hand them over, and we can all go home."

Annabelle's lip curled. She rounded furiously on the constable. "I don't have the diaries," she told him. "They were stolen from this very office a fortnight ago."

"A likely story," snorted the Earl. "Constable, I adjure you to do your duty."

"It's the truth, damn you! Lord Temple can verify my statement."

In a not unkindly tone, the constable said, "I'd advise you to hand over those documents, miss, or I shall have to take you into custody."

"But I don't *have* the diaries," yelled Annabelle.

"I did warn you, miss. Now come along."

He made a move to take Annabelle by the arm. She shook him off and backed herself into a corner of the room.

"I'm not going anywhere with anybody," she cried out. "I don't believe you are officers of the law! You're impostors, that's what you are!"

Out of the corner of her eye, she saw the clerk scribbling furiously, no doubt recording that she was resisting arrest or some such thing. Her temper soared.

"I'll give you something for the record," she railed, and snatched the notes from his hands. She ripped them to shreds and scattered the pieces like a handful of confetti.

"Where are they, Annabelle?" Dalmar's voice was dangerously quiet.

"Inside my head!" she spat out.

His eyes held hers, and he said with bone-chilling finality, "Take her away. I'll start the search here. If we don't find anything here, we'll try her house on Greek Street."

"I hope you've got a warrant or whatever it is you need before you open one drawer on my premises," she warned him, "or I'll be the one filing charges."

"You forget, these are my premises, too."

"I don't want you in my house!"

"I've got a warrant. Everything's above board."

But everything wasn't above board, and they both knew it. Annabelle stood panting, glaring up at the Earl. It seemed she

314

could do nothing, say nothing to shake him from his purpose. In that moment, he was a stranger to her, a very disciple of the devil. Though clear, rational thought was beyond her, all through her body she felt an overwhelming sense of betrayal.

Her tone was as venomous as she could make it when she said, "Have a good look round when you're in Greek Street, Dalmar. I promise you, it will be the last time you ever cross my threshold."

He seemed totally relaxed and slightly bored. "Now who's the poor loser?" he drawled.

Thus Annabelle, generally esteemed for her cool logic and calm, imperturbable nature, completely lost her head. Incensed beyond endurance, without weighing the consequences, she lashed out at the object of her distress. Her open palm struck Dalmar full across the face.

A lesser woman would have cowered before the blaze of fury which distorted the Earl's normally saturnine features. Annabelle struck him again.

He grabbed her by the shoulders. Kicking, biting, scratching, spitting like a wildcat, she went for him. Her strength was unequal to his. She was shaken like a rag doll. Pins fell from her tresses to scatter on the floor. Her hair cascaded wildly about her shoulders. Still she fought him.

Her arms were seized from behind.

"Put the manacles on her!"

"But your lordship . . ."

"Do as I say."

Bands of adamite confined her wrists. Far from subduing Annabelle, the action incited her to further violence. She kicked out at her captors, screaming abuse at them. They bound her ankles together. Dalmar's glittering eyes betrayed his murderous frame of mind. Annabelle did not care.

"Take her away!" he bit out. "No doubt a cold cell and a dish of want will bring her to her senses."

Bound hand and foot, Annabelle resorted to the only weapon left to her. She lashed the Earl with the rapier blade of her tongue.

"You spawn of Satan! You degenerate! I should have known what to expect from a man who murdered his own father!

You'll never get those diaries! I swear I'll publish them! I'll make you the laughingstock of all England! The foul stench of your name will disgust all decent people!" Screaming like a fishwife, uncaring of who heard her, Annabelle cursed him up hill and down dale.

"Gag her," said Dalmar curtly.

Kicking, bucking, screaming, she resisted the smothering gag. It took two pairs of hands to hold her down and Dalmar to finish the job. He turned her over. Hatred, pure and unadulterated, glittered in her eyes. He stepped back.

The sound of his soft, sardonic laughter shocked even the constable and his clerk. Annabelle heard it, and closed her eyes. After a moment, she went as limp as a rag doll.

"I warned you that I would teach you a lesson," said Dalmar.

Complete silence reigned in that small room.

He turned his back on her. "Take her away," he said.

Like a rolled up carpet, Annabelle was hoisted under the arms of the two officers of the law. Ever afterward, she would shudder when she remembered that scene as they carted her down the stairs and out the front entrance. She opened her eyes briefly then shut them again as she met the shocked stares of her employees. She wished then that she were dead.

The short carriage ride to Bow Street was made in a matter of minutes. She offered no resistance when she was dragged to her feet. On entering the premises, she kept her head down and her eyes averted. But no one in that noisy crush of people paid her any attention. She was deposited in an airless room with a small barred window, its only articles a dirty cot, a broken-down chair, and a chamberpot.

"Think yourself lucky, miss! The public cells are down-stairs," said the constable. "You're getting special treatment, you are."

She was scarcely aware when the gag was removed and her wrists freed of the iron manacles. Nor did it register when the constable turned the key in the lock of the door.

Disoriented, in shock, she stood motionless in the center of the room. It was the cold which finally got a response from her. She had no cloak and the room was unheated. Removing a filthy blanket from the bed without even looking at it, she draped it over her shoulders and sank down onto the chair. For the next three hours, she scarcely moved a muscle. But behind her vacant expression, her thoughts were frantic.

"How did it go, then?" John Falconer regarded his older brother with raised eyebrows.

Dalmar shrugged out of his greatcoat and flung himself down on a wing chair. "Not as I expected," he said grimly. "I don't think I'll go near her for a few hours yet. By that time, perhaps her temper will have cooled. I take it Ransome is still out?"

"I haven't heard him come in."

"He wasn't too pleased with the outing, I take it?"

Falconer grinned. "He had no objection to taking Mrs. Pendleton and her niece for a spin. But I think he was wishing Harry, Lady Jocelyn, at Jericho."

"Yes, well, I didn't wish to alarm the ladies when the house was being searched. They were better out of it. God, I need a drink!"

"It's only eleven o'clock in the morning," objected Falconer. "What's brought this on?"

The Earl strode to a massive Jacobean sideboard. He opened the door at one end and withdrew a bottle of brandy and two glasses. "Join me?"

"Thank you, no."

"I bungled it."

"What? Didn't you find what you were looking for?"

"Oh yes. But it's Annabelle I'm thinking of. She'll never forgive me. God, I'll never forgive myself! It finally happened, you see."

Alarmed more by his brother's haggard expression than the terse words, Falconer threw down the letter he had been perusing.

"Good God, David! Don't keep me in suspense. What finally happened?"

"I lost my temper. I manhandled her."

"You beat her?" asked Falconer incredulously.

A shudder passed over the Earl's tall frame. "Thank God, no! It didn't come to that!"

He bolted the drink in his hand and poured himself another. For a long moment he stared down at the amber liquid in the glass he was holding. "I'm my father's son, after all, it seems," he said. "Blood will out, so they say. If I ever doubted it, what happened this morning has brought me to my senses."

"What rot! David, how can you *think* such a thing? You're nothing like the man we called Father. He was a bully, a wife beater, a cruel, unfeeling monster."

Impatiently, Dalmar cut in, "Words which Annabelle would not hesitate to apply to me."

He slumped into a chair beside the hearth and stretched out his long legs to rest his booted feet against the brass fender.

Falconer studied the dejected droop of Dalmar's shoulders, the compressed lips, the shuttered expression. Very softly, he asked, "What happened, David?"

"Leave it!"

"But . . ."

"It's over! For God's sake, just leave it alone, can't you?"

The rough, almost despairing words effectively silenced the younger man. Falconer knew his brother too well to try to force his confidence. The disparity in their ages as much as the circumstances of their wretched childhood had shaped their relationship. A younger sibling did not encroach upon the privacy the elder wished to maintain, particularly if that elder was Dalmar.

Lost in thought, Falconer gazed absently at the intricate leaf design on the white marble mantel. *It's over*. The words held the ring of finality.

"Do you mean the marriage won't take place?" he asked, voicing the thought which had crossed his mind.

"That's precisely what I mean. What's this?" Dalmar stretched over the arm of his chair and picked up a packet which lay on a low walnut side table.

Recovering slowly from the shock of Dalmar's words, Falconer stared blankly at the envelope as his brother tore it open.

"It's from the British Embassy, from Somerset, in Paris.

318

When did it arrive?" Dalmar quickly scanned the contents.

"What? Oh, this morning, when you were out. Is it important?"

Dalmar crumpled the single sheet in his fist and tossed it into the grate. "No. It's not important—only congratulations on my forthcoming marriage. Not even a word about those wretched diaries."

Silence descended, and the eyes of both men were drawn to the grate as flames licked round the crumpled letter till it turned to white ash.

"At least I got the diaries," said Dalmar finally. "I'll send them to Somerset through diplomatic channels."

"I never did understand why they were such an issue with you. Would it have mattered so very much if Annabelle had published them?"

Dalmar did not answer immediately. He clasped both hands behind his neck and stretched to ease the tension across his shoulder blades. "Who's to say?" he observed at length. "I thought so. You forget, Monique Dupres was murdered. At the time there was a suspicion that her death and the diaries were linked. It was possible that Annabelle stood in some danger."

"But correct me if I'm wrong—you never did tell Annabelle about the French girl's murder?"

"No. Not until today." He became lost in thought. A look of revulsion crossed his face. "O God, I wish . . ." His voice faded. "No," he went on, coming to himself. "I never did get around to telling her about the French girl's death. At the beginning, as I said, Annabelle was under suspicion, and Somerset—well, you know how devious he is—he constrained me to silence. There was a chance that the murderer might give himself away."

"D'you mean, laying a trap?"

"Something of the sort. In retrospect it seems ludicrous. Annabelle isn't a murderess, and no one has made a move to take the diaries away from her, in spite of what she said." Observing the question in the younger man's eyes, Dalmar explained, "This afternoon, she swore they had been stolen. But I found them in Greek Street."

Falconer's fingers played idly with the folds of his white

linen cravat. The speculative look he leveled at his brother was carefully shielded by the sweep of his lashes. "Then my question still stands," he said. "Why have you taken such extreme measures to stop publication of the diaries?"

Dalmar shrugged eloquently. "For the usual reasons, I suppose. There is the matter of public opinion. Then again, I don't doubt that Annabelle will be served with a rash of lawsuits. And yes, I admit, I don't fancy the embarrassment of having myself portrayed in the lurid pages of such a travesty of literature."

"I thought you didn't give a brass button for public opinion?"

"Yes, well *that* was before I thought I was to be married."

There was a brief silence before Dalmar went on, as if speaking to himself, "But you didn't ask the important question."

"Which is?"

"Mmm? Oh, *Will Annabelle ever forgive me?* I think I frightened her out of her wits."

"Why *did* you lose your temper, David?"

Stirred from his lethargy, Dalmar exclaimed. "Dash it all, John! Do you never give up?"

"No," answered Falconer, with more confidence than he was feeling. "It's a Falconer failing. Runs in the family, you know."

By degrees Dalmar's grim expression relaxed. He chuckled. "*Touché*, halfling! When did you get to be so perceptive?"

A cushion hit him square in the chest. "Halfling, is it?" demanded Falconer. He pulled awkwardly to his feet and launched himself at the Earl.

Without a second thought for impeccable Weston tailoring, or for the delicate Sèvres porcelain ornaments balanced precariously on the Sheraton tables nearby, they wrestled each other to the floor, hooting and howling like two schoolboys who had been let out of the schoolroom.

On the other side of the library door, lackeys eagerly stood in line for a turn to peek through the keyhole, till the Earl's majordomo spoiled their sport. Old Raggett scattered them with the mere raising of one bushy gray eyebrow. When the coast was clear he put his ear to the door. He recognized the sounds. It was either a slaughterhouse or boys at play, but certainly nothing to be alarmed about. Fleetingly, he thought of the old lord, the present Earl's uncle. A new era had begun in the house in Cavendish Square. Somehow he knew the old boy would be smiling.

Dalmar was far from certain that the new era he had hoped for was due to be ushered in. In point of fact, he was certain that his conduct had put him beyond the pale. Misgivings and self-doubt plagued him. It was not so much his high-handed ordering of events to suit his purpose which troubled him. He could not be sorry that he had wrested the diaries from Annabelle. But the vicious, uncontrollable rage which her open defiance and barbed tongue had unleashed in him was unforgivable. The same rage had once incited him to turn on his own father—with lethal results. That very morning he had turned on Annabelle. Now, his rage spent, he felt only despair. With bitter self-reproach, he railed at himself for bringing all his hopes to nothing. And yet it seemed he was powerless to change. *Like father, like son.* The thought drummed in his brain, tormenting him beyond endurance.

He had always feared that he carried the seeds of his father in his own body—that bad blood coursed in his veins. A sensible man would have forsworn idle dreams of domestic bliss. Then what ailed him? Annabelle, of course. She had slipped under his guard and, like a fool, he was off and crying for the impossible. And with what disastrous results! He did not think he would ever forget that look of mingled hatred and contempt which had blazed at him from her shocked eyes.

He wondered what she was thinking, and then decided it was better not to know. He had no wish to face her, but he refused to take the coward's way out. Though his brother or Ransome could just as easily effect her release, he thought he owed her the chance to thoroughly abuse his character for his sins. And this time, he was resolved to take his punishment without a murmur. Like a condemned felon mounting the scaffold, he set his face toward Bow Street and his fate.

When he reached his destination, he saw by his watch that three hours had passed. He could not seem to stop the trembling which wracked his limbs. On the steps of the Bow Street office, he inhaled deeply, then pushed through the doors.

"Annabelle?" For a moment he was not sure that the girl sitting so forlornly on the solitary chair was she. He saw her shoulders lift, and recognized the gesture.

She made no answer, but her eyes followed him as he took a few paces around the small cell. "I beg your pardon," he said. "They told me you would be given a small room. I had not known to expect this!" He was appalled at the conditions of the place.

When she answered, her voice, low, steady, and quite without passion, was the death knell of all his hopes. "It's of no moment. Was this all a hoax, Dalmar?" She gestured vaguely with her hand.

"Not entirely. I wanted to put the fear of death in you. I happen to know one of the magistrates. He owed me a favor. The rest you can surmise."

"And there is no magistrate waiting to question me?"

"No. Only if the diaries were not found."

A small, fleeting smile touched her lips. "And you found them?"

"Yes."

"The French girl, Monique Dupres, was she truly murdered?"

"Yes."

"And was she a spy?"

"Not to my knowledge."

"I see."

He came to within a pace of her and for the first time noted the filthy blanket that covered her shoulders. Without thinking, he snatched it from her. "My God, Annabelle. This rag isn't fit for a beggar!"

He could not be certain, but he thought she flinched from his touch before she rose to her feet. "I was cold," she answered again in that low, dispassionate voice which cut him to the quick.

A tray lay on the floor beside the bed. On it, evidently untouched, was a hunk of coarse bread and a bowl of stew.

Frowning, he asked, "Have you eaten?"

"Yes, thank you," she answered, as polite as he.

They were like two strangers who had nothing to say to each other. She was free to go, but he could not bring himself to say the words that would take her out of his life forever.

"Annabelle, I want you to know that I bitterly regret what happened this morning."

He was aware of her hands fisting at her sides. "Thank you," she said, and moved restlessly away from him. "I accept your apology."

Her words slew him. He knew her so well. She would not, could not, sever a relationship with bad feeling. She too carried the seed of her parent. Absurdly, he regretted that he would never have the chance now to meet her father.

Her back was to him. For one unguarded moment, he allowed his eyes to blaze with all the pent-up longing, all the passion, all the love (he was past denying it) that only she had ever brought to life within him. When she turned to face him, his expression was hooded.

"We had a good race," he said with a smile that didn't quite reach his eyes.

"Yes, didn't we?" She gazed steadfastly at her clasped hands.

"And I take back what I said. You're a good loser."

The break in his voice betrayed him. Her eyes flew to his, but his smile never wavered.

"Thank you," she murmured. "But I don't believe that there can be a winner in the course that was set for us."

He inclined his head gravely in acnowledgment of the hit. Everything had been said. And it was sheer torture to keep her with him a moment longer.

"You're free to go, Annabelle. My carriage is waiting. There are a few loose ends I have to tie up here, so I hope you'll excuse me if I don't escort you to your front door?"

"I didn't expect it," she said, and pushed past him as he held the door for her.

"Wait!" He removed his greatcoat. "You'll freeze without this." He saw the indecision reflected in her eyes, and knew that she wished to avoid any excuse that might lead to another meeting between them. Very gently, he said, "You may leave it in the coach once you reach home, if you wish."

"Thank you," she said, and remained motionless as he draped the greatcoat over her shoulders.

For one brief moment he allowed his hands to skim over her arms and back in a pretense of adjusting the voluminous folds of the garment. "That should do it," he said, and dropped his hands to his sides.

She turned her head up. As if she were asking the time of day, she said, "Lord Dalmar, will you send the retraction to the papers, or shall I?"

A muscle tensed in his cheek, but he answered easily, "I'll take care of it. Don't give it another thought."

He watched as she slowly wended her way to the exit. She did not look back, nor did he expect her to. It wasn't Annabelle's style to weep over spilt milk. He fully expected that in the next few weeks she would throw all her energies behind some new and interesting project. As for himself, he shrugged, he'd get by, one way or another. Without warning, the Earl of Dalmar lashed out at the great wooden door with his tightly clenched fist, and for the space of a few seconds an unnatural silence descended on Bow Street.

When she arrived home, Annabelle had very little to say for herself. As was to be expected, Henrietta and Bertie were frantic with worry and fairly hurled questions at her. In as few words as possible she told them that she had come under suspicion for the murder of a French girl in Paris, that she'd been cleared of the charges and that, as of that moment, she was no longer engaged to the Earl. Her cool, polite smile and transparently brittle composure surprised the ladies into silence.

In the morning room, Annabelle found the day's post. She absently leafed through it. Only one letter excited any interest. She saw that it had come from Paris. Opening it carefully, she smoothed out the single sheet it comprised. As was her habit, she glanced first at the date and then at the signature at the bottom of the page. Monique Dupres's name leaped out at her.

She thought she screamed, but no one burst in to investigate what had provoked the shocked cry. After a few moments, she had herself sufficiently in hand to read the letter calmly, though her hands were shaking. Again and again her eyes scanned the page, beginning with the date and ending with the girl's signature.

When she finally laid it aside, she stared blindly into space. According to Dalmar, the girl was dead. Yet in her hand was evidence which refuted his claim. If there was some reasonable explanation for the discrepancy, Annabelle was resolved that the Earl was the last person she would approach for enlightenment. She mused on the problem for some few minutes and reached a decision.

There was only one course open to her if she wished to pursue the matter. She would have to make the journey to Paris. All things considered, the plan had merit. She had to do something to distract her thoughts from Dalmar. Yes, she thought, a trip to Paris might just be the ticket, given her circumstances.

And she did not know why, in a day of unparalleled, unremitting misery, she should choose that moment to start bawling her head off just when she had decided, unequivocally, that she was going to have a grand time.

Chapter Nineteen

Dalmar made no secret of the fact that he had come into possession of Monique Dupres's diaries. He also gave out that he had taken it upon himself to destroy them. In fact, without divulging any of the background, and careful not to mention Annabelle by name, he made a joke of it. His object was merely precautionary. Though he did not think that Annabelle stood in any danger, he wished it to be generally known that the diaries were no longer a threat to anyone.

At White's, at Brooks, and at most of the gentlemen's clubs, it became almost the only topic of conversation for a full sennight. And blueblooded gentlemen who had been in blissful ignorance of their jeopardy suddenly became aware of the catastrophe that had damn near overtaken them. Not unnaturally, the Earl became something of a celebrity.

It was Lord Temple who brought the report to Annabelle's ears. He tracked her down at Bailey's.

Her mild, almost indifferent comment, "It was to be expected," baffled the Viscount.

"I had thought Dalmar was a cut above that sort of thing," he observed.

"Did you? No. To such a man winning is everything. It was not to be supposed that he would keep quiet about his success." And as though she'd lost interest in the conversation, she gave her attention to the columns of figures on the page she held in one hand.

Temple eyed her consideringly for some few minutes. At

length he observed, "I know the diaries were stolen some few weeks ago. So what exactly did Dalmar get hold of?"

"Very little," she answered. "I had not the time to recopy as much as half the manuscript."

"Recopy?"

"From memory."

"Ah, I thought perhaps you were hoaxing me."

Her eyes, so unrevealing of late, lifted to meet his. "Why should you think so?"

"So! You plan on giving Dalmar his just desserts?" He smiled as if appreciating the joke. "I take it he knows nothing of this gift you've been hiding under a bushel?"

"I did not take him into my confidence, no. But you are mistaken, Gerry, to think I care one way or the other about revenging myself on the Earl."

"What? You have no plans to publish the girl's memoirs?"

"Not in the immediate future, no. But if and when I do, you may be sure it will be a matter of principle. Personal feeings no longer enter into it."

"Tell that to Dalmar!"

This last brought a ghost of a smile to Annabelle's lips, but it was evident that there was little to amuse her in the subject of the Earl.

When Lord Temple finally excused himself and left her to her labors, she found her powers of concentration quite dissipated. Sighing in annoyance, she tossed to her desk the column of figures she had been perusing when Lord Temple had walked in.

Albert could not return to Bailey's too soon for her comfort, she thought. Perhaps then they could begin to make a start on the press of business which had accumulated in his absence and through her neglect. Then again, she asked herself, was it fair to leave Albert with so much in the way of responsibility, not to mention chores, while she went gallivanting on the continent?

Patently unfair, she admitted, but very necessary for all that. Until her curiosity about Monique Dupres was satisfied, there could be no peace of mind for her. In spite of what Dalmar said about the girl's death, she remained unconvinced.

Not only did she have the girl's letter to disprove his assertion, but she had also belatedly remembered that the bank draft in the sum of two thousand pounds, which she had paid for the diaries, had long since cleared her bank. She did not know what game Dalmar was playing. She only knew that she did not trust him, at least with respect to anything which touched on the diaries.

No. It went deeper than that. She could never forget the Earl as he had been in that very room when he had ordered her bound hand and foot and gagged. That man was a stranger to her. To say that she did not trust him was an absurd understatement. He terrified her! That murderous expression! Those remorseless eyes! That brutal touch! She did not doubt that, given enough provocation, the man could do murder.

Hard on that thought came the awful spectacle of herself as she had been when she had dared him to do his worst. Her hand tightened involuntarily on the pencil she was holding. It snapped. A sob tore from her throat, and she hurled the pieces to the floor. That girl, too, was a stranger to her, and one she did not care to know.

Let it go, she told herself. *The engagement is over. The retraction has appeared in the papers. You are well out of it. Just let it go!*

For the next two hours she forced herself to take up the reins of her business. She answered correspondence, scheduled book releases, and consulted with the managers of the several departments that made up Bailey's. No one watching her would have guessed how much willpower she expended to appear with her usual air of competence. Inside Annabelle was shaking. A week had passed since that dreadful, never-to-be-forgotten scene in her office with Dalmar and the constables. Though she had returned to her desk the very day after, and had brazened through a morning at Bailey's of which she could recollect not one jot, she still half expected snide remarks and furtive, speculative glances from her employees. Annabelle worried herself unduly. Her place in her subordinates' esteem was secure. It was the Earl who earned their dislike.

Her intimates held to a more moderate position. Having no real notion of what had occasioned the rift between Dalmar and Annabelle, they remained on friendly terms with them both. There had been some hope at the beginning that two people who were obviously made for each other would soon come to their senses and effect a reconciliation. That hope was dashed by the subsequent conduct of the two unhappy lovers, for Annabelle proposed a jaunt to Paris under the escort of her most devoted and constant companion, Lord Temple, and Dalmar embarked on a life of unmitigated dissipation.

"What the hell's got into him?" asked Ransome of John Falconer as they stripped the groggy Earl of his garments. "This is the seventh consecutive night."

Dalmar, spread-eagled on his tester bed in Cavendish Square, grinned lopsidedly up at the ceiling and immediately launched into the refrain of a ribald drinking song.

Falconer averted his nose. "It's not what's got into him that worries me, but who and what the hell he's been getting into. He smells like a brothel!"

"What would you know about brothels?" asked Ransome, grinning broadly. He had to fight the Earl to get his boots off.

"I'm not married," said Falconer. "And if Annabelle ever gets wind of what's going on, my brother, drunken sot, can wave good-bye to his chances in that quarter."

"I think he already has," said Ransome, suddenly grave.

"Yes," said Falconer. When he reached for Dalmar's shirt, his hands were none too gentle.

It could not be expected, in that small, exclusive society of which she was a member, that Annabelle would long remain in ignorance of Dalmar's mode of living. Nor did she.

Her first inkling came when she stepped out of a milliner's shop in Bond Street and literally bumped into him. The hatbox went rolling. At her back, Bertie sucked in her breath.

Dalmar's strong hands cupped Annabelle's shoulders, steadying her. Their eyes locked. She had to fight the impulse to sway into him, and pulled back slightly.

"Dal?"

The contact was broken. Dalmar went to retrieve the hatbox, and Annabelle's eyes strayed to the auburn-haired lady who had so familiarly addressed the Earl. She looked to be no more than a girl of twenty or so, and the daring cut and color of her garments betrayed her profession. In that moment Annabelle felt as if she had swallowed a jagged shard of glass. Speech was beyond her.

She took the hatbox from his hand without a word of thanks. He tipped his hat, gave her one speaking look which she could not interpret, and moved off to offer his arm to the lady, who was impatiently tapping her foot.

When Annabelle next saw the Earl, they were at the opera, and it gave her no more pleasure to note that he had fixed his interest on a different lady. He was in the most notorious box of the theater. It belonged to Harriette Wilson, the queen of London's demireps and, if female tattle was to be believed, the most fastidious in her choice of consort.

Annabelle regretted then that she had allowed her friends to persuade her to accompany them to the King's Theater. But it seemed that they had come to an understanding among themselves, namely, as far as she could judge, that under no circumstances was she to be left to her own devices. Thus Henrietta, Bertie, Lady Diana, and it went without saying, her coterie of young friends, scarcely let her out of their sight, unless it was when she entered Bailey's forbidding portals. They seemed determined not to give her time to think. She thought it sweet of them, but quite misguided.

She was sure that with one thing and another there were a hundred things more pressing which begged her attention than a night at the opera. In her mind's eye, oblivious of the musical drama which unfolded on the stage, she began to tick them off, one by one.

At the interval, a delicate white hand settled on her wrist. She looked up to meet the anxious eyes of Lady Diana. "Don't refine too much upon it," said the girl. "Gentlemen will be gentlemen, you know. I'm sure he's only trying to make you jealous." Under her breath, she added, "Poor boy!" Annabelle heard her and smiled.

She was more than a little ashamed of the uncharitable thoughts she had formerly entertained with respect to the girl. She had discovered that there was in her nature such a sweetness of disposition, such a depth of unaffected solicitude, that one could forgive not only the small understanding, but the youthfulness and beauty besides. An impulsive creature, not prone to swings of temperament, Lady Diana was the perfect antidote for anyone who wanted to wallow in self-pity. She saw the best in everyone. It was no wonder, thought Annabelle, that the girl was uncommonly popular.

She followed the path of Lady Diana's eyes. Harriette Wilson's box fairly teemed with gentlemen who had come to pay their respects. Annabelle was not sorry that Lord Dalmar was having plenty of competition for the fair Cyrene's favors.

For Annabelle's ears only, Lord Temple intoned, "Now if only *that* little filly could be persuaded to set down her memoirs! I'll wager *she* could tell some tales out of school."

Annabelle's eyes widened a fraction. "Now *there's* a thought," she mused, and directed her gaze, now turned speculative, upon the dazzling beauty. Even from that distance, the hue of the lady's locks was unmistakable. Auburn, thought Annabelle, and turned up her nose.

Her next encounter with the Earl left her thoroughly shaken. He turned up, as drunk as a lord, during one of her literary soirées in Greek Street. Her bête noir, the poet, was honoring her guests with a reading from his latest opus, dull-as-dishwater stuff, in Annabelle's opinion. She was just wishing that she could inject a little more excitement into what was a not very memorable evening, when some unholy, mischievous demon took it upon himself to grant her heart's desire. In staggered the Earl, each arm fastened securely (for support more than anything else, thought Annabelle uncharitably), around the bonny, buxom figure of what could only be described, loosely and politely, as a Drury Lane vestal. Both girls had red hair.

Annabelle was instantly on her feet. The Earl took one look at her, and an expression of utter confusion swept his face.

"What are *you* doing here?" he asked, swaying alarmingly.

"I *live* here," she retorted.

Several of the gentlemen went to remonstrate with the Earl. Lord Temple's voice carried above the others.

"*Really,* Dalmar, this is the outside of enough!" he said. "You should be ashamed to expose the ladies to behavior unbecoming in a gentleman."

Dalmar frowned. "What ladies? Oh, *these* ladies." His glazed eyes tried to focus on the squirming, giggling girls in his arms. "What are you doing here?" he asked them in some perplexity. "I thought I left you at Mother Finch's."

"Oh là, sir," said one, "aren't you the funny one? You paid us a golden guinea to come to your house where we could show you . . ."

"Wrong house!" roared Dalmar, a sudden sense of the awful reality piercing his drunken stupor.

He bowed with as much dignity as he could manage. "M'apologies, Mrs. Jocelyn," he mumbled. "Ladies, gentlemen," and he retreated with more celerity than one would have expected to see in a man in his sodden condition.

Annabelle directed a look of utter appeal at Murray, her friend and fellow publisher. He came to her at once.

"Someone should see that he gets home safely," she said in an anguished undertone.

"Leave it to me," he said, and went after the Earl.

From the raised voices and ensuing mayhem which erupted in the foyer, it was evident that Dalmar had taken the notion that Murray mean to deprive him of his spoils. Annabelle did not wait to hear the outcome.

Gesturing to a maid to close the doors to her literary salon, she said, "Do go on, Cameron. You were coming to the interesting part, I believe, where our hero contemplates the efficacy of suicide."

Annabelle was known to possess a certain sangfroid which some said was the equal of Wellington's. But this display, as one wag was heard to say in an aside, should have the Duke looking to his laurels.

Staring into the middle distance, the poet began, "Forsooth . . ."

A loud bang followed by a shrill scream issued from the other side of the closed doors.

"What fair or foul . . ." supplied Annabelle helpfully. Not even the ghost of a frown wrinkled her smooth brow.

"Eh? Oh, of course," said the poet, looking at Annabelle doubtfully. She nodded her encouragement. Poetlike, he gazed steadfastly at the ceiling, as if willing it to inspire him. In slow, measured tones, he droned out the canto which was, so he humbly confessed, the quintessence of his philosophy.

"Forsooth, what fair or foul wind finds . . ."

The sudden crack of a pistol shot split the air. Everyone froze. Annabelle rose gracefully to her feet.

"Supper is just about to be served," she said. "Will you excuse me? I think I heard the signal which tells me I'm wanted in the dining room. Do go on, Cameron."

"Forsooth, what fair or foul wind finds
The deities themselves shall ne'er forfend.

"Quite candidly, it's your best yet."

"And that's honesty with a vengeance, if ever I heard it," said Thomas Longman, the younger, to his neighbor from behind his hand.

Thus encouraged by his mentor, the poet, preening a little, began over. But as soon as their hostess had quitted the room, her guests were on their feet like a shot, and the excited hum of their conversation quite drowned out the drone of the unfortunate poet's voice.

In the foyer, Annabelle found Dalmar rolling on the floor with Murray and three footmen kneeling over him. The front door stood open. Of the two buxom red-haired wenches there was nary a sign.

"Oh my God, is he dead?" she cried out, and rushed to the Earl's side.

He grabbed her hand and held it to his cheek. "Annabelle," he repeated over and over, "Annabelle."

"He damn near killed me," said Murray. "How could he even *think* I would wish to take one of those doxies off his hands? I am more discriminating than he, begging your pardon, Annabelle."

"Where is the wound?" asked Annabelle.

"In the ceiling," replied Murray testily. "His lordship is merely suffering the effects of an overindulgence of every vice known to mankind."

"Known to *gentlemen!*" corrected Annabelle, not bothering to hide her rancor. "I'll send for a hackney."

"Don't trouble. There's one at the door."

With the help of two footmen, Murray assisted Dalmar from

the house. On the front steps the Earl seemed to catch his second wind. At the top of his lungs, he bawled out the lusty words of some half forgotten refrain, improvising handily when memory failed. Appalled, Annabelle shut the front door firmly behind him.

When Henrietta and Bertie arrived home from a very gay card party at Lady Diana's (literary soirées were not their cup of tea), they found Annabelle at the top of a stepladder examining a large hole in the plaster ceiling.

"Was it a memorable party?" asked Henrietta, eyeing the ceiling with some misgiving.

Her careless words opened the sluice gates. At first, there was a trickle. And then came the deluge.

More anxious than they cared to admit, the ladies helped the weeping girl from her perch and hurried her to the small upstairs sitting room where they were sure of finding the secret supply of "medicinal' brandy. After much hunting for glasses, they made do with three demitasse cups.

When Annabelle had finally choked out the course of events of "one of the worst nights of my life," the ladies sipped their demitasse brandies in companionable silence.

"Men!" observed Henrietta finally.

That one word expressed exactly the sum total of all the exasperation they were feeling on a subject which was by and large an enigma to them.

"When do you go to Paris?" asked Bertie.

"Not for another week or so, when Albert returns."

"Look, why not pop off sooner, say tomorrow or the next day?"

"No," responded Annabelle. "It's impossible. I have a mountain of correspondence to catch up. There must be twenty manuscripts on my desk, some from regular contributors, which I simply must read. If Albert were here, it could be done. But we're at a critical stage right now. Albert must remain at his post until the goods are delivered and distributed."

Henrietta and Bertie exchanged glances over Annabelle's bowed head.

"She's got to get away from here," mouthed Henrietta silently.

Bertie nodded. "Look," she said, "haven't I lent you a hand before? Couldn't I take over for a week or so till Albert arrives? It wouldn't be the first time I'd read manuscripts for you. Or perhaps you found my work unsatisfactory, and don't like to say?"

"'T'isn't that," protested Annabelle. "You know I trust your judgment implicitly. But I had thought . . . dash it all, Bertie . . . you are my companion. I had hoped that we could go to Paris together."

"Paris," murmured Henrietta. "I wanted to spend my honeymoon there, you know, but it was impossible, because of the war. Charles always said that we should go there one day. I don't suppose he even remembers his promise. Well, men never do. Do they?"

One desultory comment led to another, and by the time the ladies had tucked a very grateful Annabelle into her bed for the night, the decision had been taken. Bertie would hold the fort on the home front, and Henrietta would accompany Annabelle to Paris.

Outside her door, and before returning to their own chambers, Bertie laid a detaining hand on Henrietta's sleeve. "D'you think we did the right thing in keeping that story about Lewes from her? I don't think she knows."

Bertie was referring to that morning's paper, where there had been a small column on Lewes. Two bodies, as yet unidentified, had been pulled from the River Ouse. One was of a young man with a broken arm. The other was that of a woman. In both cases, foul play was suspected. At Lady Diana's party, the talk had been of little else, since many of her guests had been members of the house party at Rosedale.

"I don't think she's fit to take any more shocks for the present," replied Henrietta, her voice barely above a whisper. "I remember how she was before, you see, when Edgar sent Richard home to her. She's at breaking point now. Surely you've noticed? First she becomes all stiff and proper, then she withdraws completely. Though I didn't think so at the time, I'll say it now: Bailey's was just the right thing for her."

"A distraction, you mean?"

"Yes. Though it was more than just a break from the usual

336

run of things. A trip to Paris may not fit the same bill, but it can't do any harm that I can see. At the very least, it will shield her from Dalmar's goings-on."

"Men have a lot to answer for," said Bertie.

"My dear, don't we all?" chided Henrietta gently, and moved off down the hall.

Bertie stood staring after her for some few minutes. When she turned in, she was lost in thought.

"Women have a lot to answer for," observed Colonel Ransome. "D'you realize that this is the tenth consecutive night we've stripped him and tucked him into bed?"

"I should! I've got the bruises to show for it," answered Falconer with feeling. "If only he would stop fighting us."

The object of their conversation came to himself with a start. He reached for his brother and grabbed him by the shoulders. "Tell me it was a dream," he implored.

"It was a dream," soothed Falconer.

Dalmar shook him violently. "Liar! Liar!"

Ransome pried the Earl's powerful grip from the younger man's shoulders. Dalmar covered his eyes with the back of one outflung arm.

"It was the wrong house. It was the wrong house," he said brokenly.

"What's he talking about?"

"A nightmare, I imagine."

Dalmar laughed, a sound that alarmed his two companions. "She'll never forgive me," he told them.

"If memory serves, you said that last week," said Falconer with barely concealed hostility.

Dalmar turned his face into the pillows. And Falconer felt the first warming of pity as it began to melt the edges of the hard vise of anger which had gripped him all week.

Softly, he said, "I'll give you odds, a hundred to one, Davie, that she does forgive you."

Ransome's eyebrows lifted. "What do you know about it?" he asked.

The younger man shrugged. "They always do. I remember

337

my mother. Women in love. They're . . . vulnerable."

"Aren't we all?" observed Ransome, his eyes resting thoughtfully on the Earl's inert form.

It took forty-eight hours for the Earl to "sober up," as they said below stairs, or "recover his equilibrium," as they gave it out above stairs. Either way, he was miserable.

But it was his mental anguish which was the more acute. He knew that he must offer an apology to Annabelle for all the distress and unpleasantness he had occasioned, but he scarcely knew where to start. In his opinion, there was no excuse for his abominable behavior that would stand up to the light of day.

He had thought to erase her from his mind by losing himself in the bodies—oh God, and so many—of other women. The old adage "The best way of forgetting a woman is another woman," which had served him so well in the past, now appeared ludicrous. Not only had the ploy not worked, but it had left him in his sober moments feeling as guilty as all hell.

But his case was hopeless. There was no question of reconciliation. Even if Annabelle would have him back, which he very much doubted after brazening to her face that he was a thoroughgoing libertine, he would not permit it. He had frightened her half to death. In all conscience, he did not think he could give a firm undertaking that such a thing would never happen again. And he'd be damned before he would see her recoil from his touch! He was not forgetting how she had shrunk from him when she had bumped into him on Bond Street. Before he saw her turned into a replica of his mother, he would see her shackled to Lord Temple, he virtuously perjured himself.

Heartsore, headsore, and bitterly ashamed of the depths to which he had sunk, he debated whether or not he should face Annabelle in person or affect his apology through the medium of a letter. As it happened, the decision was taken out of his hands.

He came down to breakfast on the second morning following what he ever afterward referred to euphemistically in his mind as "the debacle" at Annabelle's literary salon to find trunks and valises strewn around the front vestibule.

"Is someone going somewhere?" he asked on entering the breakfast room.

Ransome and his brother were at the table. Rather shamefaced, Dalmar tried to return stare for stare.

It was Colonel Ransome who answered. "Actually, we're both going somewhere. Paris, to be exact. My furlough is about over, or had you forgotten?"

The Earl had forgotten, but he did not wish to say so.

"Paris, John?" he said, addressing his brother, and took the chair opposite. The odor of grilled kidneys and kippers fairly turned his stomach. "This is rather sudden, is it not?"

"In a manner of speaking," replied that gentleman, grinning unashamedly at his older sibling's evident discomfort. "Do try the braised liver," he baited. "It's melt-in-your-mouth tender."

The Earl's lips compressed tightly. After a moment, he was able to say, "Thank you, no. I'll stick to the coffee, if you would be so kind."

Falconer obligingly filled the Earl's cup. "It was decided on impulse," he said, answering Dalmar's original question. "Harry and Annabelle are off to Paris. The rest of us decided to go along for a lark."

"The rest of us?" asked Dalmar.

"Diana and her cohorts. Oh, and Lord Temple."

There was a silence.

"Oh," said Dalmar, and studiously downed the scalding hot coffee. "Is there any particular reasoning why it should be Paris?"

"Not to my knowledge. The girls simply want an outing. It will be all properly chaperoned with abigails, et cetera, if that's what's worrying you."

Dalmar carefully replaced his empty coffee cup. "You're not sweet on Henrietta Jocelyn, by any chance, are you?" he demanded.

"Certainly not!" Winking broadly at Ransome, Falconer continued, "It's the other lady I fancy. And now that you've given me a clear field . . ." Observing the thunderous look which crossed Dalmar's face, he hastiliy concluded, "I was only funning, dear chap! Don't get your hackles up!"

Visibly relaxing, the Earl asked at length, "When do you leave?"

"Within the hour."

"And you, Ransome?"

"Not for a day or two. I still have some unfinished business to attend to."

Ransome's "unfinished business" went by the name of Mrs. Bertie Pendleton. He paid a call on Greek Street the following afternoon and found her, in spite of the cold weather, in the garden with Amy. They were playing a game of catch.

Amy saw him first and raced to his outstretched arms. He flung her high in the air and caught her safely as she hurtled to earth. Her squeals of delight scattered the robins and starlings which were feeding on the fruit of a nearby rowan tree.

"I think she likes me," he said as Bertie came up to them.

"Do it again!" squealed Amy.

He did, with the same gratifying results.

"Let's go inside," was all the comment Bertie had for this happy reunion.

Ransome squared his shoulders. She'd promised to give him his answer before he left for Paris. He had already made up his mind that he would not accept a refusal.

Bertie sent a reluctant Amy upstairs to the nursery and led Ransome to the morning room, or Annabelle's study, as it was generally known. Restlessly, she touched first one object and then another on the open escritoire and finally picked up some papers just to give her hands something to do.

"I'm helping Annabelle out," she said nervously. "Things have fallen behind at Bailey's. Those wretched diaries, you know. Or perhaps you didn't know?" She was babbling and could not seem to stop herself. "After they were stolen, Annabelle devoted all her time and energies to putting them together again."

"Dalmar did not steal the diaries," he said, as gently as he could make the reproof. "He made no secret of the fact that he had taken them."

"What? Oh, no, you mistake me. I mean, when thieves broke into her office, the first time, and attacked her."

340

If Ransome had been any other gentleman, perhaps he would have passed over Bertie's surprising remarks. But he was a colonel in the British Army, and one, moreover, whose special field of operations was espionage. It was only natural for him to question Bertie further until he had all the facts before him.

The more he probed, however, the more taciturn his quarry became, and she evidently regretted the impulse which had led her to say so much. Ransome changed his tactics.

"It's a pity she didn't report the theft," he essayed, "or the thieves might have been apprehended."

He struck lucky.

"That's what I told her at the time," said Bertie. "She might even have had the diaries returned to her possession and saved herself all her subsequent trouble."

"That would certainly have saved her '*putting them together again,*'" he said with emphasis, trying to look knowledgeable.

"Oh. You know about that?"

He gave her his "don't-try-to-pry-my-secrets-from-me" smile, and said very vaguely, "Remarkable."

"'Tis, isn't it?"

"Quite!"

"Though you know, Annabelle's memory is no better than the next person's when it comes to remembering dates and so on."

"That surprises me!"

"Well, of course, it's shocking. How she can regurgitate books whole and forget a friend's birthday is beyond anything."

Ransome had ferreted out exactly what he wished to know. He was not unfamiliar with the phenomenon. In his employ, he had once had a spy who possessed the exact same gift. A very useful man to know, as he remembered.

He relaxed somewhat, and said more naturally, "But I didn't come here this afternoon to talk about Mrs. Jocelyn. I'm here for my answer."

"Yes," said Bertie, peeping up at him through her lashes.

Without asking her permission, he led her to a Sheraton side chair and pushed her into it. Straightening, he took several paces around the room before turning to face her. He permitted himself a few moments to compose himself.

"I'm not going to accept a refusal from you, and that's flat," he said.

"Yes," said Bertie.

"You will cast my former conduct in my teeth. I give you leave to do so. I was a married man. That my life was not worth living, and my wife a slut of the first rank, those subjects I won't even go into."

Taking her silence for encouragement, he pressed on. "Bertie, having met you, I just could not give you up. Try to understand, dear girl, I could not take the chance on telling you of my circumstances. Honor meant nothing to me. I see now that my conduct was unforgivable. But, my darling girl, have you any idea what I went through when you left me without a word?"

"Yes," said Bertie.

"You put me through hell! But . . ." he lowered his voice, striving to gain command of himself. "Our circumstances are different." He inhaled deeply. "Bertie, doesn't a father deserve the chance to know his own child?" he pleaded.

"Yes," said Bertie.

"Haven't I paid the price for my sins?"

"Yes," said Bertie.

"My dear girl, do you want to bring me to my knees? Do you want me to beg? Do you want me to humble myself and tell you that I love you still and that I have never stopped loving you?" He went on one knee and clasped both her hands in his. "I'll do all of these things and more," he said passionately. "Please, just tell me what I have to do to change your refusal to a 'yes.'"

"Nothing," said Bertie.

"Bertie!" The cry was wrung from him. "I swear I'll do anything you ask of me."

"Then you had better marry me," said Bertie.

"What?"

He looked deeply into her eyes. The love he saw reflected there stunned him. "You don't hate me?" he murmured.

"I've never stopped loving you, Paul," she said, and buried her head against his shoulder. "I only wanted to hate you. Can

342

you forgive me? I've had time to think about it. You see, I wasn't blameless either, though I tried to pretend I was."

"But you were!" he protested.

"Sh! I won't let you say so. What we did was wrong. But I've learned that life is too short to waste on regrets for the past."

He would never accept her verdict on their brief love affair, but he did not voice that thought. "Then kiss me, Bertie," he said. "We've wasted too much time as it is."

She went into his arms without a protest.

Chapter Twenty

Colonel Ransome lost no time in seeking out Dalmar to apprise him of the interesting information concerning Annabelle which Bertie had let slip. Though he did not think there was any urgency, he spent the remainder of the afternoon and early evening combing all the respectable gentlemen's clubs, and not-so-respectable gentlemen's dives, where there was some likelihood of finding the Earl. But no one could give him Dalmar's direction.

He returned to Cavendish Square feeling not a little irritated with his friend. The Earl had been wallowing in self-pity, not to mention debauchery, for more than a week. It was time, thought Ransome, that Dalmar pulled himself up by his bootstraps and went back to the business of living. No sooner did that thought occur to him than he was smitten with self-reproach. When he had found himself in similar circumstances many years before, his conduct could not stand up to scrutiny either. In that moment, it seemed to him that a terrible lie had been perpetrated. In truth, it was men who were the softer sex. The women of his acquaintance suffered their misfortunes with an enviable fortitude.

He was ascending the stairs to his chamber when the Earl's voice hailed him from the library door.

"Do we celebrate or drown our sorrows?"

Ransome pivoted. His eyes swept the tall figure of the Earl. Dalmar appeared to be perfectly respectable, and as sober as a judge.

Smiling broadly, the colonel retraced his steps. "You may congratulate me," he told Dalmar. "She has accepted me."

With much backslapping and good natured cajolery, they entered the library together. No time was lost in toasting the lady's health.

"When does the marriage take place?" asked Dalmar, settling himself more comfortably into the depths of his wingback chair.

Ransome noted that Dalmar was nursing the glass of champagne in his hand as if it were hemlock. Swallowing a smile, he reached for the open bottle and replenished his own empty glass.

"As soon as may be, but not soon enough for my taste."

The Earl arched one brow.

"Bertie wants Annabelle to stand up with her when she says her vows," explained Ransome. "If I had my way, we would wed tomorrow, before I leave for Paris."

"What are your plans?"

"I'm selling out. You need not look so astonished. The war is over. I was never one of those career soldiers. I've done my duty. Henceforth I have every hope of adopting the quiet mode of a country gentleman. In short," Ransome sipped his wine thoughtfully, "in short, the appeal of family life, with my wife at my side and a quiverful of children at my knee, is about as much excitement as I shall ever wish for."

Some of the light went out of the Earl's eyes, but he had a smile in place when Ransome looked up. "A laudable ambition," he murmured and inwardly winced at the trace of bitterness he could not erase from his voice.

Ransome tactfully changed the subject. "But, my dear chap, what am I thinking of? I have something of a particular nature I wish to say to you." And he recounted his conversation with Bertie as it touched on Annabelle.

The Earl heard him out in silence. Finally, he said, "Am I to understand that Annabelle has it in her power to write down, word for word, a complete version of Monique Dupres's diaries?"

"You are."

"I've never heard of such a thing!"

"Haven't you? It's a strange phenomenon, but not unheard of. I think there is a name for it, but I've forgotten what it is."

"She never said anything to me about this—this trick memory!"

"No! Nor did she tell you about the break-in at Bailey's."

The Earl jumped to his feet and paced furiously about the room. "This is nonsensical! I have my own man at Bailey's. He said nothing to me about a burglary or an attack on Annabelle."

"It happened at night. Perhaps that's why."

"What the hell was she doing there at night? And why didn't she report it to the authorities, or tell *me?*"

Mildly, soothingly, Ransome replied, "Who can say how a woman's mind works? But there is no cause for this alarm, surely?"

Dalmar impatiently combed his fingers through his hair. "How can I say? This puts a different complexion on things. The diaries were stolen—you're sure of that?"

"Quite. So you see, if someone was after them, he's got what he wanted. And as I told you, she's rather shy, or so Bertie said, of boasting about this particular gift of hers. Few people know of it. It's not likely that she'll be troubled again."

"I can't see that that follows. Knowing Annabelle, she'll start over and publish those damned diaries if only to spite *me.*" Dalmar threw himself into his chair. "I don't like it, Ransome," he said. "I just don't like it." A thought sprang to his mind, and he sat forward in his chair. "She was attacked at Lewes!"

"You never mentioned that before!"

"I had my reasons." He was on his feet again and striding to his desk. He returned a moment later with a folded newspaper. "Here, read that!" He pointed to the bottom of the page. "It arrived this morning."

Ransome took the paper from him. When he had finished reading it, his face was very grave. "So," he said, "the woman they pulled from the river Ouse has been identified."

"Mrs. Rosa Snow."

"Annabelle's double, according to Bertie."

Both men looked at each other for a long interval.

"What now?" asked Ransome softly.

Dalmar as already striding for the door. "We leave for Paris as soon as may be."

Annabelle was having the time of her life. Every one of her friends should have known it. She told them so a dozen times a day. And she was very careful to keep a smile pinned on her face from the moment she stepped out of her chamber in the Hotel Breuteuil till the moment her maid, Nancy, blew out the candles at night. The strain of it all was beginning to tell on her.

"What's on for tonight?" asked Henrietta, her comprehensive glance taking in the group of elegantly dressed young people who made up their table in the hotel's public dining room.

"The Palais Royal?" suggested Annabelle hopefully.

In the three days since they had arrived in Paris, she had fallen in with her companions' wishes. Like any group of tourists, they'd done the sights. She had hoped for a little time for personal business. But her friends were too solicitous by half for her own good. She had not had a moment to call her own. And since they stuck to her like glue, she had determined to achieve her real object in coming to Paris right under their very noses.

"The Palais Royal," she repeated with more conviction when she observed the uncertain frown which puckered John Falconer's brow. "I've been there before," she said, and added persuasively for the ladies' benefit, "The shops in the galleries will bowl you over. You've never seen their like before. London milliners and such like are very provincial in comparison."

"Shops? Why didn't you say so before?" asked Lady Diana. "I thought it was just some ancient relic of a building like all the others we've traipsed through in the last three days."

"Hardly," interposed Falconer. "And not to put too fine a point on it, it's not the sort of place where a lady of quality would wish to be seen."

"Do tell us more," purred the Honorable Miss Loukes, batting her eyelashes at the young man. She had taken a fancy to him, and didn't try to conceal it.

"It's a warren of gaming houses and . . . and suchlike," he ended lamely.

If he had lavished the place with extravagant encomiums, he could not have whetted the ladies' appetites more.

"You mean, it's wicked?" asked Henrietta, her eyes as round as saucers. "A den of iniquity?"

"Precisely!" he exclaimed. He cast a wild look at the other gentlemen at the table.

It was Mr. Loukes who answered that look of urgent appeal. "Put one foot in that building," he told the ladies flatly, "and you'll be accosted by every loose screw who thinks you are no better than you should be."

Mr. Loukes had sadly mistaken his audience. These damsels were no set of shrinking debs but, or so they accounted themselves, a bevy of dashers quite up to the mark on all suits.

"But if Annabelle went there . . ." began Miss Loukes persuasively, only to be silenced by a ferocious frown from her brother.

"We haven't been to the cathedral yet," pointed out Falconer.

The ladies groaned their disappointment.

"Quite frankly," said Lady Diana, "I think you gentlemen are too nice in your notions for my taste."

A chorus of female voices seconded her opinion.

The gentlemen became more entrenched in their position.

It was Lord Temple who poured oil on troubled waters. "When were you last there?" he asked John Falconer.

"Some months ago. September, to be exact."

"Not long after the occupation? Well, that explains it. I assure you, things are very different now. It's quite the thing for English ladies to do a tour of the Palais Royal. As long as they are well escorted, I don't see the harm in it. No, really, Wellington's discipline is very much in evidence. The guards patrol there regularly."

The other gentlemen gradually gave way before Lord Temple's considered opinion. He was their senior by several years and an acknowledged man of the world. In comparison, they felt like very small fry indeed. Only one gentleman held to the strength of his convictions.

"All the same . . ." began John Falconer.

Annabelle rushed into speech before he could turn the tide of opinion. "If you don't wish to come, John, suit yourself. Frankly, I don't wish for anyone's escort. I'm quite prepared to go with only my maid."

After that unequivocal declaration, the gentlemen gave way. Not unnaturally, the ladies were delighted.

In the attaché's office at the British Embassy in the Rue St. Honoré, three gentlemen sat conversing around the warm blaze of an open fire. Two of those gentlemen bore the marks of a long and wearying journey. Their spurred boots were mired to the knee; their cloaks, which were thrown over the back of a chair, were filthy and soaked through. Lines of exhaustion lent each man's countenance a forbidding aspect. One of those gentleman's voices was raised in anger.

"What the hell do you mean, Somerset, by keeping that information from me? When Annabelle wrote you that the diaries were stolen, you should have informed me at once!"

"Get a grip on yourself, David," said the attaché soothingly. "Perhaps I should, but try to see things from my perspective. I could not know why Mrs. Jocelyn distrusted you so. But it was very evident that she did. You, on the other hand, were supremely confident of your power over her. I could not see what harm it would do for things to run their natural course."

"What you mean is you did not trust me! My God, man, I told Annabelle that Monique Dupres was murdered! What was she to think when your forged letter reached her, calling me a liar?"

"But David, how was I to know what was going on?" The attaché spoke quietly, with exaggerated patience, as if to soothe the outburst of a fractious child. "It was very evident from Mrs. Jocelyn's letter that she believed the French girl was still alive. And as I understood, that is the story we agreed on."

The Earl was not placated by this facile explanation, but thinking it better to curb his anger for the moment, he went on levelly, "And now you tell me that she might very well be in danger? Well, get on with it, man! Get to the point, for God's sake!"

Exchanging a telling glance with Colonel Ransome, who was hunched forward in his chair, his hands extended to the blaze in the grate, Somerset began, "I was about to write you a letter explaining . . ."

"Yes, yes, I understand all that. The point, Somerset, what is the point?"

Stifling a sigh, Somerset rose and went to his desk. He unlocked a drawer and withdrew a sheaf of papers, which he tossed in the Earl's lap.

"You sent me these," he said. "They are incomplete, but certainly attributable to Monique Dupres. The handwriting, as one would expect, is Mrs. Jocelyn's."

"If you are asking me if I knew that it was Annabelle's handwriting, why don't you just come right out and say so?"

Ransome stirred himself and turned to slice the Earl a warning look. Dalmar put his hand over his eyes.

"I'm sorry. No, I did not recognize the handwriting. Perhaps I should have. To be blunt, I had no wish to read such pap. I only glanced at it before sending it off to make sure that I had the right stuff."

"Oh, you had the right stuff all right. Let me show you." Somerset retrieved the loose pages from Dalmar's clasp and leafed through them till he found what he was looking for. "Here, read this."

Dalmar sat up straighter in his chair and held the page up to the light.

"Two days before the Battle of Waterloo," Somerset explained to Colonel Ransome, "Monique Dupres was in her bedroom in the house her protector had rented in Brussels on the Rue Ste. Catharine."

"The Rue Ste. Catharine?" asked Ransome, lifting his head.

"Like many British visitors, she was packing her valises in anticipation of leaving the battle zone. After all, who knew what the outcome of that confrontation between Wellington and Bonaparte might be? A carriage had been ordered to begin the first leg of her journey to Antwerp and safety. At least, that is what she wants us to believe."

"Are we talking about the night of the Duchess of Richmond's ball?" asked Ransome.

"Ah, that interests you, does it Colonel Ransome? I thought it might."

Dalmar tossed the page he had been reading onto a table by his elbow.

"Perhaps I'm suffering from exhaustion. But there's nothing there of any interest that I can see," he said. "So she saw two men going into number 25 Rue Ste. Catharine and five minutes later only one of them came out. So what?"

"May I see?" said Ransome, and picked up the page the Earl had discarded.

"You will note," said Somerset, like a man who had been vindicated of some nefarious crime, "that the girl very often, though not always, chooses to conceal the identity of her characters behind a descriptive soubriquet."

"I recognize one of them," said Ransome. "It's Major Crawford."

For a moment the name did not register with Dalmar. "Major Crawford? Oh, of course, she calls him *'Le Roux'* because of his red hair. Wasn't he the fiend who was responsible for the butchering of the flower of England's chivalry in those do-or-die raids in Spain?"

"He was," said Somerset.

"And was butchered in Brussels for his sins," added Ransome.

"From all accounts, he merited his fate," the Earl remarked indifferently.

"And if I am not very much mistaken," said Ransome, his voice beginning to vibrate with excitement, "whether unwittingly or by design, Monique has just revealed the identity of Crawford's murderer."

"The devil she has!" exclaimed Dalmar.

Ransome rose to his feet. "I'm sure of it," he said. "Didn't you read to the end of this? Crawford and a companion entered the house at eight o'clock. Five minutes later his companion leaves, alone. At half past eight, two other officers enter the house. Dalmar, I investigated the murder of Major Crawford. He died before the Duchess of Richmond's ball. The two fellow officers—they were to go with him. They found him with his throat cut."

"It was quite deliberate, I think," mused Somerset.

"What was?" Dalmar's mind was still trying to assimilate what Ransome had just told him.

"Ransome just wondered whether Monique Dupres had revealed the identity of Crawford's murderer unwittingly or by design. It was quite deliberate, in my humble opinion."

His two silent companions barely managed to restrain their impatience.

Smiling, Somerset went on, "Well, you haven't read the rest of the diaries, you see. And I have. There's no reason for the girl to include such an ordinary, insignificant event. Who cares if two men go into a house? I saw at once that there was something different about this passage. There's no bedroom scandal in it. And suddenly, for no apparent reason, she begins to call Major Crawford "Le Roux," when she mentions him by name elsewhere in the diaries. D'you know what I think?"

Resisting the urge to betray a temper which was near to exploding, Dalmar managed, "No. Tell us what you think."

"I think the girl was blackmailing the murderer. And perhaps, as a gesture of intimidation, she let this passage stand."

To Dalmar's blank look, the attaché elaborated, "She was thumbing her nose at the man."

"Your powers of deduction overwhelm me," said Dalmar. "Have you deduced who the murderer is yet?"

"Unfortunately, no," said Somerset. "I've approached everyone I can think of. But no one is acquainted with the particular epithet the girl applied to Crawford's companion."

"*Poultron?*" said Ransome. "No, I've never heard of it."

"What did you say?" asked Dalmar.

"*Poultron,*" repeated Ransome.

"*Poultron,*" murmured Dalmar. "Now why does that word have a familiar ring to it?" He closed his eyes and allowed his head to fall back. His two companions studied him in silence for a long interval. His lips moved, repeating the soubriquet, but he uttered no sound.

Slowly, he opened his eyes. "Everything fits," he said.

353

"Everything makes sense now. The theft of the diaries. The attacks on Annabelle. Those murders—Crawford, Monique, Mrs. Snow—they're all of a piece."

"What are you saying?" asked Ransome.

"I'm saying that I think I know who the murderer is. Come on! Let's make haste!"

"But where are we going?"

"To the Palais Royal, or the Maison D'Or, to be more precise." The Earl was already on his feet and draping his sodden cloak over his shoulders. "If she hasn't already done so, Annabelle will be eager to verify whether or not the French girl is still alive. I see now that *that* was her purpose in coming to Paris."

Ransome shrugged into his cloak. "But who is the murderer?"

"I'll tell you what I think on the way. There's not a moment to lose. Pray God, we're not too late."

The Palais Royal was not so very different from Annabelle's recollections of it, though she was glad that Lord Temple's words had not been an exaggeration. There were many British visitors to be seen, most of them respectable, and some of them of the first stare. He'd been right about the Horse Guards too, Annabelle noted. They fairly swarmed all over the place. The sight of them gave her confidence and strengthened her resolve to follow the outline of a plan which had half formed in her mind.

To give her friends the slip was easier than she expected. Once she'd led them up the stairs to the first floor makeshift galleries, the ladies soon became absorbed in the serious business of bargain hunting, and, to their chagrin, the same gentlemen who had scolded them for their spurious curiosity became absorbed in the other "ladies" who sauntered by, unattached, and who eyed them boldly.

Annabelle lingered in a milliner's shop trying on hats, but all the time, her eyes scanned the faces of the shop's patrons. Her moment came. No one's eyes were on her. She opened the door to the back stairs and slipped through.

Her heart immediately began to race at an alarming pace. Her nerves were stretched taut and it was not to be wondered at, she thought. Her mind went back to the night of the riot, when she had first met up with the Earl. In that poorly lit, less populated part of the palace, as she carefully descended the stairs with her velvet pelisse hugged tightly to her, she had the strangest feeling of déjà vu. It would not have surprised her to see the Earl come looming out of the shadows, but whether to stalk or protect her, who was to say?

In the gardens, the lanterns were all lit. It seemed that all Paris had come out to view the sideshows. Annabelle passed tumblers, organ grinders, jugglers, acrobats, and even a man with a performing bear on a leash. It reminded her so forcefully of Lewes that she could not stop an involuntary shudder. She traversed the edge of the central fountain and came to the huge arched porticoes with the covered promenade beneath. It was here that Annabelle's phenomenal memory deserted her.

There were so many massive Tuscan columns, so many bays, all of them identical, that she could not with anything resembling certainty say which of them led to the Maison d'Or and Monique Dupres.

Her steps slowed, and she scanned the stalls and shop facades for numbers, but in that dim light she could see very little. And then she saw it. A jeweler's shop window, and the entrance beside it. She took one step toward it, but at that moment her attention was caught by a press of people who pushed out of one of the courtyard cafés on her right. Snatches of conversation in German, French, and English carried to her ears, but one voice riveted her to the spot. Like a stag at bay, she lifted her head and turned to confront the danger which threatened. *It's only a figment of your imagination, my girl,* she scolded. But even as that thought occurred to her, he stepped beneath the halo of an overhead lantern. It was Dalmar.

His face was set and forbidding; his cheekbones seemed to be gouged out of granite. Perhaps it was a trick of the light, but she saw a remorseless twist to his mouth, a merciless glitter in those eyes of stone. She had once likened him to a pirate or a brigand. She thought, then, that he might easily be taken for an executioner.

Thoughts chased themselves in her head in dizzying confusion. She did not know why he had come to Paris, or why, of all places, he should be in the Palais Royal. She sensed a terrible danger stalking her. It might be irrational, but it was as real to her as the reticule she clutched in her hand. She panicked, and like any trapped animal, she looked for a way of escape.

With a small cry, she whirled about and elbowed her way frantically through the crush of people. Her one thought was to return to her friends and the safety of the galleries.

"Annabelle!"

He had seen her. His hoarse cry of command at her back intensified her efforts to evade him. At one point she went sprawling, and her reticule rolled out of her hand. That this was the work of pickpockets was never in question, but Annabelle could not let that deflect her from her purpose. She saw a hand snatch the reticule from the ground. She let it go without a protest, and pulling herself to her feet, pushed on.

She burst through the entrance to the backstairs and screamed when strong masculine arms enfolded her.

"Annabelle, what's wrong?"

With fists flying, she pounded against her captor's broad chest. She was shaken roughly.

"Annabelle! Stop it! D'you hear? Stop it!"

"Oh God, Gerry, is it you?"

Lord Temple's eyes anxiously scanned her white face. "Annabelle, what is it?"

"Dalmar!" she choked out. "Oh, please, Gerry, just get me away from here before he finds me."

He didn't argue with her. He simply grasped her by the elbow and half dragged her along. "In here," he said, and pushed her into a cupboard under the stairs. He stepped in behind her and pulled the door shut.

"Annabelle!"

She pressed closer to Temple. Dalmar's cry was very close at hand. Behind that one word, she sensed the terrifying force of his rage and frustration.

"David, is that you? What the hell are you doing in Paris?"

Annabelle recognized John Falconer's voice.

"Never mind that now!" Dalmar shouted up the well of the staircase. "Is Annabelle up there with you? Did she come this way?"

"No," shouted Falconer. "She seems to have given us the slip. But don't worry. Temple is looking for her."

"Damn!" muttered the Earl under his breath. "Hang on, I'm coming up."

Annabelle heard his footsteps as he took the stairs two at a time.

"He's gone," said Temple. "Now let's get you away from here."

"You're quite safe here."

"I . . . I didn't know you had rooms in the Palais Royal, Gerry."

"Didn't you? Here, let me take your wraps. Now sit down and I'll get you something to steady your nerves."

Déjà vu, thought Annabelle and crossed her arms to control her trembling. She accepted the glass of brandy Temple proffered and sipped slowly. For some reason, she wanted to delay the interrogation she knew must come. For something to say, she said, "It must be very expensive keeping up two sets of rooms. And you can't be in Paris that often, surely?"

He studied her over the rim of his glass. "Curiosity killed the cat," he said, and smiled the oddest smile.

Annabelle felt a shiver of something she could not name and withdrew her gaze.

His voice laced with amusement, he said, "If you must know, Annabelle, like many gentlemen, when I'm in Paris, I always arrange to have rooms at my disposal in the Palais Royal. I'm a single man. And it's convenient. Does that answer your question?"

"Oh," was all that she could think to say. She began to cast around in her mind for a safe topic of conversation when she heard the key turn in the vestibule. The color washed out of her face.

"It's only my man," said Temple reassuringly. He pulled himself awkwardly to his feet. "I'll send him to fetch a hackney, and when the coast is clear, I'll get you out of here. Now drink up your brandy like a good girl."

He was out of the room for only a moment or two. Annabelle set down her glass and took stock of her surroundings. Temple's rooms were very similar to the ones Dalmar had taken her to on the night of the riot. But this time it was not the Earl who was her champion. She felt the loss more keenly than she would have wished. Suddenly she felt bone weary and passed a hand over her eyes.

When Temple returned, she saw that he was limping. "I shouldn't have involved you," she said. "You're not fit for this kind of excitement."

She could see at once that her words had angered him. He lowered himself carefully onto a straight-backed chair.

"My dear Annabelle," he drawled, "don't let this collection of old bones gammon you. I assure you, I'm well able to take care of myself."

"I'm sorry. I didn't mean anything by it. It's only that Dalmar . . ." When he sliced the air impatiently with one hand, Annabelle's words died altogether.

"D'you think that I'm not a match for Dalmar?" He snorted derisively. "It doesn't take brawn to fell an adversary. Only brains." His voice moderated. "But time grows short. Let's leave that for the moment, shall we? I want to know why Dalmar is here, and why you are afraid of him."

She didn't like the way his eyes narrowed on her. She didn't like the hard edge in his voice. For a moment she thought of telling him to mind his own business. But instinct warned her that he was not in the mood to suffer a show of feminine rebellion. Moreover, she was conscious that she owed him some sort of explanation for her near-hysterical behavior.

"I don't know why Dalmar is here," she said.

"I had it from Falconer that the Earl was fixed in London."

"So I understood."

"Well *something* must have made him change his mind."

"Apparently." She saw his lips compress and quickly elaborated. "No, really, Gerry, I haven't a clue why he is here. And I'm certainly no longer in Dalmar's confidence."

"Then tell me why you are afraid of him."

"It would take eons to explain my antipathy to the man," she parried. "Can't we just leave it at that? Please, take me back to the hotel. Truly, I'm not feeling well." And that last was no evasion, she thought. Her head was swimming unpleasantly.

"All in good time," he answered. "But until our hackney arrives, indulge me a little by answering a few questions."

"Oh, very well," she said, not very graciously.

"You told me that you had committed only half the girl's diaries to paper?"

For a moment she could not think what he was getting at.

"Annabelle, how far did you get with the girl's diaries?" he said in a voice which shocked her out of her lethargy.

"Not very far," she admitted at once. "As I told you, there was not the time to put down as much as half."

"So, he knows nothing of Brussels as yet?"

To Annabelle's ears the conversation had taken a nightmarish turn. Just out of reach, in some dim recess of her mind, was the key to a puzzle which had begun to to tease her.

Frowning in concentration, she said, "Why do you say that he knows nothing of Brussels?"

In tones of strained patience, he replied, "It stands to reason. The diaries begin in Vienna. You mentioned it in passing some time since."

"Did I?" she murmured. She knew that she had not. At all events, she did not wish to embark on a long and involved explanation of her reasons for passing over Vienna in favor of Brussels. Even to herself, she could not defend the vulgar curiosity which had tempted her to that course.

"Brussels has nothing to do with anything," she said, and frowned at her slurred speech. "If you ask me . . ." She did not know what was wrong with her tongue.

"Yes?" he prompted.

"What? Oh! I'll warrant he's here to get to Monique Dupres before I do." The more she thought of it, the more merit the notion gained.

"That's impossible," he said.

"I don't see why! He doesn't know that I have the diaries committed to memory. It wouldn't surprise me one whit if he thinks I'm here to renegotiate their purchase. He's going to try and buy her off, that's what!" Her bosom heaved with indignation at the very thought.

"He's not here to see Monique Dupres."

Like a quarrelsome child, she turned on him. "Why do you persist in saying so?"

Deadly quiet, he answered, "Because the girl was murdered."

Silence, dark and turbulent, filled the room.

"Do you know what I think?" asked Temple softly.

Her mouth strangely dry, Annabelle could only shake her head.

"What I think," said the Viscount, "is that Dalmar believes that you are in some sort of danger."

"Danger?" she whispered. "Why should I be in danger?"

She choked back a sob when he stretched like some graceful jungle feline.

"Did it never occur to you, Annabelle, that whoever stole the diaries might have something to hide? I mean something criminal, of course."

"No," she said.

"For the sake of argument, let us suppose that such a person exists. Wouldn't you say that your uncanny knack of recall might prove something of an inconvenience? That it might conceivably lead some poor devil to the hangman's noose?"

The sinister meaning of his words struck her with blinding clarity. "But there's nothing in the diaries to incriminate anyone," she burst out. "At least, not of the sort to incite any rational person to do me bodily harm."

"Isn't there?"

"No!" She shook her head vehemently.

"No evasion this time," he said, his manner as charming as Annabelle had ever seen it. "Does Dalmar know about Brussels? It's the only explanation, you see, that makes sense."

She felt as if someone had just walked over her grave. "Yes," she answered. "I didn't even make an attempt to put down Monique Dupres's recollections of Vienna. Well . . . Brussels was more interesting, you see. But truly, Gerry, there was nothing there to incriminate anyone."

"It's of no moment," he said, but she knew from his expression that it was.

"I don't see why it makes a difference," she said reasonably.

He passed a hand over his eyes. "If only I had known that you had begun to reconstruct the diaries with Brussels! But how should I? Damn! I should have acted sooner." He looked up and caught her wary expression. "Don't take on so!" he said, smiling. "No real harm is done. And I'll keep Dalmar away from you, I promise."

She did not know what prompted her to say, "I've quite given up the idea of publishing the diaries. It was an idiot notion to begin with."

"If only you had listened to me when I first voiced that thought," he said, "none of this might have happened." He looked at his watch.

He was waiting for someone or something, she thought, and remembered that he had sent his man for a hackney. Though she had no real facts to go on, only her instincts, she made up her mind then that nothing on God's earth would constrain her to enter a closed carriage with Lord Temple. Dalmar was on her trail. Completely reversing her former opinion, and without any rational explanation to account for it, she clung to that thought.

Temple rose, and she rose with him. "That must be my man now. Will you excuse me? Drink the rest of your brandy, Annabelle," he admonished, and drained his own glass. "It will soon be over."

He waited until she had lifted the glass to her lips. As soon as he turned his back on her, she took a step toward the window, uncaring and only half aware of the brandy which slopped on her gown. But her legs would not seem to hold her up. She staggered.

It will soon be over. Was his choice of words deliberate or merely unfortunate? *Who cared?* Every nerve in her body, every hair on the back of her neck screamed at her to make a bolt for it.

Think, she chided herself. She felt sure that for the moment at least she was safe. It did not seem as if he meant to harm her

361

in his own rooms. He thought her compliant, unsuspecting. But as soon as she was within hailing distance of any passersby, she meant to scream bloody murder. And it was all so unnecessary! She was sure she did not know anything!

She leaned on the back of a chair for support. There was something very far wrong with her, something more than just a reaction to the awful chain of events which had overtaken her.

He's poisoned me, she thought. *Dear Lord, he's already murdered me. And I'll never know the reason why!* That galling thought put new starch into her drooping backbone.

Swaying on her feet, she forced herself to pick up a brace of candles. Her time was up. There was very little to be done now. Her one thought was to give Dalmar some clue to what had happened to her. With an unsteady hand, she torched the drapes at the window, and turned aside as the flames licked slowly up their length. "Oh God," she said. "Oh God, please . . ."

Several things happened simultaneously. Doors slammed, people called out, and a pistol shot exploded outside the door. Annabelle dropped the candelabra in her fright.

The door burst open and Temple stumbled in. *This is it,* she thought, and raised her brandy glass threateningly, meaning to strike him. He evaded it easily, grabbed her from behind with one arm across her chest, and held a wicked-looking knife to her throat.

"Douse that fire!" The voice was so achingly and comfortingly familiar.

"Dalmar!" she breathed.

The Earl stood on the threshold, disheveled, his boots mired to the knee, his dear face showing unmistakable signs of fatigue. He was the most beautiful sight she had ever seen in her life.

"I knew you'd save me," she told him. "Like St. George and the dragon."

She was dimly aware of the two men who entered behind him. They tore the smoldering drapes from their poles and flung them on the floor.

"If you've harmed a hair of her head . . ." said Dalmar, edging closer to his quarry.

"Stand back!" warned Temple, and he pressed his blade into Annabelle's exposed throat, drawing a drop of blood. "She's merely drugged. But if you want her to remain in one piece, you'd best do as I say."

"I'm not drugged," said Annabelle crossly. "*You* are, Gerry. I switched glasses, you see, the first time you left the room. Any moment now and you'll keel over."

With an explosive imprecation, Temple flung Annabelle from him. He sprang past Dalmar, cutting a wide swath with his knife in a bid for the open door and freedom.

The Earl's arm shot out, and in a movement which was entirely familiar to Annabelle, he brought the Viscount's arm down on his knee. The knife went flying. The Earl caught Temple a crashing blow to the jaw. Annabelle heard the crack of bone on bone and winced. Temple sprawled against a delicate side table, overturning it, and fell heavily to the floor.

Dalmar took a step toward the fallen man, fists clenched, murder in his eyes. "Get up," he ground out. "Get up!"

Annabelle put one hand to her aching head. "I lied," she said. "I *am* drugged, and he's as sober as a judge."

Comforting arms closed about her shoulders. "Are you all right?" asked John Falconer.

"John, get her out of here," she heard Dalmar say in a voice that allowed no argument.

Shaking off Falconer's hands as he tried to draw her away, she cried out, "There's another one. He's gone for a hackney."

"No, he hasn't," said Dalmar. "We've got him, thank God. Who do you think led us to you? Now get her out of here, John. I have some unfinished business with Lord Temple."

Nothing could have cleared Annabelle's head more effectively than those uncompromisingly sinister words, and spoken in such a cold tone.

Her head came up, and she looked directly at the Earl, willing him to look her in the eyes. "No," she said. "You can't do it. Leave it to the law, David. You're not God."

Dalmar did not spare her a glance. "For the last time, John, will you get her out of here?" he said.

If he had cursed or raised his voice, or railed at her, Annabelle could not have been more frightened.

Strong arms swung her off her feet. "No!" she protested, striking out wildly. "For the love of God, David, don't do it!"

"Ransome, go with them," said Dalmar.

The other man seemed to hesitate. "Why not do as Annabelle says, and leave the law to take its course?" he suggested quietly.

Dalmar made no answer, and after a moment, Ransome followed after Falconer and Annabelle. He closed the door softly behind him. Lords Dalmar and Temple faced each other across the width of the room.

Neither man said anything until the sounds of Annabelle's screams had faded.

Temple dragged himself onto a sofa. "I don't think you have a case that would stand up in a court of law," he said, rubbing first his jaw and then his arm.

Dalmar smiled faintly. "Temple, you have murdered four people. That's four separate trials. You might spend years in the Fleet just waiting for each case to come up."

"And neither of us would want that to happen, would we, Dalmar?" Temple looked almost boyish when he grinned.

"It would be too distressing for Annabelle," agreed the Earl.

"If it's worth anything, I wouldn't have let her suffer, you know."

There was an imperceptible tightening in Dalmar's jaw. "You're too kind," he murmured.

Temple's eyes dropped. A short pause ensued, each man lost in private reflection.

Finally, Temple asked, "What are you going to do with my man?"

"Very little, I'm afraid. In exchange for his miserable life, you see, he led us to you. He'll be on the first ship that leaves port for the West Indies."

"You recognized him, I take it?"

"The man from Lewes? Oh yes, I recognized him, all right. I'm not like to forget the man whom I pulled off Annabelle as he was about to ravish her."

The Viscount started. "That was never part of the plan! Good God, he deserves to die! If I'd known, I would have killed him myself."

Dalmar made no reply. From his coat pocket he pulled a dueling pistol and began to check the chamber and then the muzzle.

Not a flicker of emotion registered in the Viscount's face as he watched the Earl's careful, deliberate movements.

At length, he offered, "I see you're not asking me any questions. There might have been extenuating circumstances, you know."

Dalmar flicked him a contemptuous glance. "I'm not interested in excuses," he said.

"I wasn't about to offer any," said Temple, his control showing the first sign of a crack.

There was slight softening in the Earl. "I allow that you had some justification for ridding the world of Major Crawford. By your lights . . ."

"By anyone's lights! Would you have tamely accepted what I've had to endure all these years? My body is never free of pain. It's been one damn operation after another, and more to come. And for what? For one man's bid for glory. He never cared anything for the men under his command. We were just pawns in a game to him!"

The Earl answered steadily and without heat. "Monique Dupres is beyond pain, poor girl. And that Prussian officer, I forget his name."

"She was a mercenary bitch! She was blackmailing me—she and that Prussian whoremonger of hers! Can you imagine, they thought I'd let them ride roughshod over me without a whimper! Well, I taught them that they had very much mistaken their man!"

"Incredible!"

"They never had any intention of sticking to their part of the bargain! They sold the diaries from under my nose. Yes, and laughed in my face when they told me!"

"And Mrs. Snow?"

"That was a mistake! I thought she was . . ." He stopped dead in mid-sentence.

"Annabelle," supplied the Earl. "Are you ready? Would you care for a glass of brandy first or . . . ?"

"Now who's being kind!" A bitter smile twisted Temple's lips. "Thank you, no! Just satisfy my curiosity, if you will. How did you come to put two and two together?"

"It was in the diaries," said the Earl. "I recognized the soubriquet, you see."

"*Poultron?* But no one knew me by that name. It was an obscenity invented by Monique Dupres."

"She must have mentioned it to me, sometime or other." Dalmar shrugged carelessly. "Forgive me, but from the moment I first saw you, I put you down as a milksop. I could never rid myself of that word in connection with you, even when I came to see that it was a misnomer. Once the significance of the girl's description of the events in the Rue Ste. Catharine was pointed out to me, everything fell into place."

It seemed that everything had been said. Lord Temple dragged himself to his feet and faced the taller man. "Are you to be my executioner?" he asked.

"It won't come to that, I hope. You were once a very brave soldier, so I've been given to understand. You served your country well. I think you know how best to protect your family and friends."

"Annabelle, you mean. You wouldn't do as much for anyone else."

"Very true," said the Earl.

The two men exchanged a long, level look.

"Thank you," said Temple. "I think I know my duty."

Dalmar inclined his head gravely. "If you wish to leave a note or some such thing . . ."

"I think not. You may spread the word, if you like, that Lord Temple lost rather heavily at the gaming tables. That, at least, is no lie."

As Dalmar turned aside, Temple said, "I was just wondering what they will make of the scorched drapes when they find my body?"

"I expect they shall think you went a little mad," was the quiet rejoinder.

"Yes. Perhaps you're right. I did go a little mad, didn't I?"

Without answering, the Earl placed the pistol on a table just beyond Temple's reach. "Don't botch it," he said. "I can't give you the coup de grâce. I'll be just outside the door." He exited the room.

Annabelle heard the report of the pistol shot as they took the last turn in the stairs.

Chapter Twenty-One

It was a very subdued group which made the return trip from the Palais Royal along the Rue de Rivoli to the Hotel Breteuil. Annabelle had finally succumbed to the effects of the laudanum with which Temple had liberally laced her drink, and she slept the sleep of the just. Now and again, as the coach lurched, she moaned her distress, but otherwise she seemed quite content and lay passively curled up in John Falconer's arms.

"What do you think Temple would have done with her?" asked Falconer. He still could not credit that a man with whom he was on the friendliest terms could sink to such depths.

"A knife in the throat in the Bois de Boulogne, I shouldn't wonder," answered Ransome. "It's close at hand, and decent folks stay away from it at night. I make no doubt that the only thing that saved her from her fate at the Palais was the awkwardness for Temple of avoiding so many of our chaps who were on patrol duty."

"I can scarcely believe that he would have gone through with it, though."

"You may be sure that he would."

"You sound very sure of yourself."

"My dear Falconer, a man who has murdered once doesn't cavil at another."

"I suppose so . . . only . . . I wish . . ." The rest of what he had to say was swallowed up in a sigh.

"I don't blame your brother," said Ransome.

"And you think I do? I assure you, I do not."

"Well then?"

"I'm thinking of Annabelle. She will never understand what drives a man like David."

"No. And he knows it."

Once the hotel was reached, the sleeping girl was given into the charge of Nancy, her maid. Annabelle was scarcely under the covers when Dalmar arrived upon the scene. Without looking to left nor right, nor asking anyone's permission, he barged into her chamber.

Nancy, who had been setting the room to rights, straightened and turned to face the Earl. Though she recognized him at once, she did not let his exalted position or title weigh with her. It would have surprised Annabelle to know the magnitude of her sharp-tongued, stiff-as-starch maid's devotion to what she conceived was her mistress's best interests.

Dalmar advanced into the room, and Nancy went to meet him.

"Your Lordship," she began. But the scathing words which trembled on the tip of her tongue died unspoken. There was something in his expression, something in his eyes, or perhaps in the way he carried himself, as she later explained it to cook, which made her forget herself. She turned aside and hovered covertly in the background.

Not a word was spoken. The Earl merely stationed himself at the side of the bed and gazed steadfastly at the softly breathing girl. As if aware of that intense scrutiny, Annabelle stirred, and one inert hand drooped over the side of the bed. Dalmar covered it with one of his own and brought it to his lips. But before Nancy could begin to think of remonstrating with him, he had tucked Annabelle's hand beneath the covers and he quit the room.

Downstairs, in the hotel lobby, Dalmar consulted with Ransome and Falconer. The story they concocted was simple and to the point. Annabelle, wandering away and becoming lost in the vast corridors of the Palais Royal, had been set upon by pickpockets. Falconer had found her and taken her straight on to the hotel, where he had met up with the two other men by chance. Respecting Lord Temple, they were to plead ignorance, though the Earl briefly related how the affair had ended.

"It's for the best," said Ransome, and Falconer readily concurred.

"I leave her in your hands then," said Dalmar, addressing his brother.

"What? Aren't you going to hang on for a bit?"

"Somerset is still in the dark. Someone has to put him in the picture. I'll cadge a bed at the Embassy for the night and see you when you get back to town. See that you give Annabelle an accounting of how Temple met his end. At least he died with honor."

They had idled their way to the front steps.

"You're not leaving so soon? You've only just got here," protested Falconer.

"You forget, Ransome and I have other business to attend to. The matter of Temple's manservant. He should be off our hands in a few hours."

"I wish you would stay on for a bit," said Falconer desperately.

"There's nothing to keep me here," was the clipped rejoinder.

Falconer could think of a score of reasons why his brother should linger in Paris. But before he could articulate a single one of them, his hand was firmly shaken and he found himself saying his *adieux* to the two older men.

He turned back into the hotel and found a quiet nook where he could keep an eye on the front entrance and be on hand to greet the rest of his party when they should return from the Palais Royal. He settled himself to read one of the British papers the hotel stocked for its English patrons, but his mind was restless and refused to absorb the printed word.

It was not the events of that night which occupied his thoughts but another, more distant occasion and one of far more personal significance for himself. He remembered another woman who had been rescued from the clutches of a tyrant and who had turned on her rescuer, damning him for his sins. It seemed his brother was fated to be repudiated by the significant women in his life. And after tonight, he knew that no woman would ever get close to him again. The injustice of it all made him want to shake his fists at an indifferent deity who seemed to have turned his back on his creation.

November slipped into December. Temperatures dropped. The days grew short, darkness descending well before the dinner hour. Many of the grand houses around Mayfair were practically shut up for the Christmas festival as lords and ladies repaired to their country estates for the innumerable house parties which had been arranged.

For the lower orders it was business as usual. The most they could hope for was an early end to their labors on the eve of the holy day itself. For what man earning his bread by the sweat of his brow could afford the luxury of more than the few statutory holy days which were scattered throughout the year?

Bailey's had never been busier, a circumstance for which its proprietor and managing editor was heartily thankful. Leisure was something Annabelle assiduously avoided, for when time hung heavily on her hands, her thoughts invariably turned to Dalmar, and the Earl was one subject she refused to think about.

Since that night in the Palais Royal when he'd ordered his brother to carry her from Lord Temple's rooms, she'd only once set eyes on him, and that was at Bertie's and Ransome's wedding. They hadn't exchanged more than the barest civilities. She had not even thanked him in person for his rescue, since the Earl had quit Paris long before Annabelle had recovered from her drugged stupor.

It was John Falconer who had seen her through those few nightmarish days in Paris, and some kind elderly gentleman at the Embassy, whose name she had forgotten, who had explained the awful chain of events leading up to that harrowing night. And then she'd been told, quite severely, to forget the whole thing as if it had never happened.

She'd managed to obey the attaché's advice tolerably well, for her friends knew nothing of what had transpired and did not subject her to the rash of questions she might have otherwise expected. They were sorry to hear of her brush with pickpockets and scolded her severely for wandering away, but their conversation was mainly of Lord Temple's surprisingly sudden demise, though some few had known of his fatal predilection to gaming.

In London, Dalmar was conspicuous by his absence. Annabelle learned that he had taken over the management of his vast estates in Hampshire. She deemed it for the best, and set herself to emulate his example. She fell into her former pattern of spending the mornings at Bailey's, the afternoons in company of her young son, and the rest of the interminable hours in her calendar she filled up with as many parties and outings as were offered, even supposing there was a dearth of company in town.

Henrietta stayed on in Greek Street, since nothing could persuade Annabelle to remove to Rosedale. And though Sir Charles wrote to his wife, in no uncertain terms, reminding her of her duty to her sons, she prevaricated. Now that Bertie was married, she wrote to him, Annabelle was quite alone in the house, servants notwithstanding. And the dear girl could pretend as much as she liked that she had not a care in the world, yes, and do a creditable job of pulling the wool over the eyes of the ton, but she, Henrietta Jocelyn, was not deceived. Beneath that false smile and exquisitely made-up face, Annabelle was miserable. And until such time as a suitable companion was found, Henrietta advised Sir Charles that she could not see her way clear to returning to the bosom of her family.

For three weeks or more, a lively correspondence between Sir Charles and Lady Jocelyn was kept up. But nothing that Sir Charles committed to paper, and his logic could not be faulted, made the least impression on his wife. No one was more sensible than she of what she owed her family. But such arguments, in her present frame of mind, counted for nothing. If Sir Charles had written one affectionate word things might have been different. He did not, and Henrietta dug in her heels.

It came as no surprise to her, on returning to Greek Street from one of their evening jaunts, to find Sir Charles pacing Annabelle's small drawing room as if he were a caged tiger.

"What brings you to town, Charles?" asked Annabelle,

dutifully pecking his cheek.

The question obviously startled him. Under cover of greeting her husband, Henrietta murmured, "It's as I told you. Half the time, she's not all there. Well, you'll soon see how things stand."

They did not spend more than ten minutes conversing together, and to every subject that was introduced, Annabelle contributed only monosyllables. Her mind was miles away.

"What's wrong with her?" asked Sir Charles when they had retired for the night.

"She's been like this since I first came up to town. I had hoped that the trip to Paris might pull her out of the dismals. But since then, it's only got worse. It's Dalmar, of course. She's pining away for him."

"What—Annabelle wearing the willow? That doesn't sound like her!"

"It won't last forever. One doesn't die of a broken heart. That is, after all, only a figure of speech. And Annabelle is a sensible girl. Given time, she'll get over it."

Though her cool, rational words had a visible effect on Sir Charles, Henrietta did not notice it. At that moment, becoming aware that her bedchamber gave every evidence of masculine occupation, she exclaimed, "What can that girl be thinking of! She's moved your things into my room. Oh well, that is easily remedied."

Meaning to ring for Nancy, she moved toward the bell-pull. Sir Charles stayed her hand.

"For God's sake, Henrietta, have you taken such a disgust of me that we cannot spend one night together under the same roof as man and wife?"

Her eyes widened in surprise at the heat in his words. Obediently she allowed him to lead her to a small bedside chair.

"There is only one bed," she pointed out.

"We've shared a bed before."

"But never for more than five minutes together. You'll find that I'm a restless sleeper."

"How do you know?" he asked, towering menacingly above her. Not a trace of levity could she detect in his expression.

"How? I . . . I just do know, that's all."

"Have a care, Henrietta! If I thought for one minute that you'd shared someone else's bed when you'd refused mine, I'd take a whip to you, and then I'd damn well kill your lover."

For five whole weeks, Henrietta Jocelyn, née Routledge, had had a taste of independence. Perhaps it was not all that it was cracked up to be, but it had been an experience for all that. Men years younger than she had pampered, flattered, and courted her with soft words and long, languishing looks. But never once had she been tempted to betray her marriage vows, in spite of an errant husband who ignored her very existence, unless it was in her role as mother to his heirs. And her reward for her unswerving fidelity was this—to be reviled for a sin that belonged more properly to her accuser.

She sprang to her feet, and Sir Charles fell back a pace before those flashing eyes. She went at his chest with her index finger as if to hammer home her words.

"In the first place, my name is Harry. I was never really that insipid creature whom you chose to call 'Henrietta.'

"In the second place, I did not refuse your bed. You turned me away, quite deliberately, by making the experience as tedious as a bowl of curds and whey. Five minutes of your time was all that I was worth to you. Don't you think I know that you spent the whole night through in the bed of your mistress, Mrs. Snow?

"In the third place, I am not the malefactor here, you are. And if I was unfaithful to you, which I deny, it would be no more or less than you deserve.

"In the fourth place . . ." But Henrietta's anger was suddenly spent, or she had forgotten what she meant to say. At all events, she turned aside and moved to the hearth where she stood, arms crossed, staring into the dying embers of the fire.

Sir Charles came up behind her. Very gently he turned her to face him. "Is it too late to make amends?" he said, angling her a lopsided grin.

She refused to look at him, and the desperation of his situation lent urgency to his words. "There's no one warming my bed now, Harry," he said.

"No," snorted Henrietta. "But not by your design. If someone hadn't murdered the poor woman, she'd still be there—I was going to say in the background, but that's a joke! The whole world saw how you brazenly carried on with her at Lewes."

"I didn't know you cared!" he yelled.

"I'm human. I have my pride!" she shot back.

"Pride? Who the hell cares about pride? I'm talking about love."

"Love?" she said the word scathingly. "I've long since given up trying to make you fall in love with me."

"But I *do* love you! Don't you believe me? Oh God, can't you forgive me? How was I to know that I meant anything more to you than an entrée into polite society? That's all your father wanted for you, wasn't it?"

She looked at him doubtfully. That look gave him hope, and he pressed his advantage. "Ours was a marriage of convenience. You were so very young. And I was so damn blind."

She angled her head back and studied his intent expression. "Why now, Charles? Why come to me now?"

He could not explain it even to himself. He shook his head. "You've never been away from home before. Your life has always been your family. I think I took your presence for granted. When you weren't there, I realized that our home had lost its heart."

For a moment he held her at arm's length, his eyes searching hers anxiously. Then, finding what he wanted to see, he smiled and swept her into his arms.

In the end, Annabelle allowed herself to be persuaded to spend the Christmas holidays at Rosedale. For one thing, not to do so would have caused a serious rift between Sir Charles and Henrietta, for the latter refused to leave Annabelle in the lurch. For another, Richard added his persuasions. Christmas with his cousins was infinitely preferable to what his mama proposed—a quiet twosome in Greek Street with only church services and a walk in the park to leaven the boredom. And finally, Albert had long since returned from the north. Bailey's could very easily be left in his capable hands.

But Rosedale was anything but an enjoyable experience for

376

Annabelle. Though she was happy to see a new cordiality between Sir Charles and Henrietta, she could not shake herself of the conviction that her presence was superfluous.

Thinking to relieve the loving couple of the responsibility for entertaining her, she began to spend a good deal of her time with the children. But even there, she was soon given to understand that her presence put a decided damper on things.

The boys had been at one of their favorite games—knights and dragon slaying. It went without saying which part Annabelle was assigned. She could not like the ferocity of her young nephews and son when they came at her with their drawn wooden swords. Nor were they any more gratified by the way she played her role. It was Richard who explained it to her.

"Dragons, Mama, are not nice creatures. They are wicked. They don't give knights second chances."

"But I don't like hurting people," protested Annabelle.

"No," said Richard prosaically, "but dragons do."

It was with relief on both sides when Annabelle took herself off, belatedly remembering that she had letters to write. But her young son's words revolved in her mind, though why this should be so, she could not fathom.

With so many hours in a day to get through, Annabelle became a little restless. If there were scores of things to occupy one in the country, she was sure that she could not think of a single one that she could not do better in town, with the exception of riding and hunting, and these overrated sports held no interest for her.

It was here that a ripple disturbed her conscience. She had a vague recollection of making some wild promises to the Deity when those awful men had set upon her in Lewes. And then it came to her! Of course! She had pledged that she would persevere with every blessed accomplishment she had ever forsworn if only the Lord would send his angels to watch over her. And the Lord, in his wisdom, had sent Dalmar. It was an arresting thought.

It was only natural that from there, her thoughts should wander to other occasions when the Earl had intervened to save her. Her memories jolted her. For each time that she had called upon the Lord's help, it seemed that her prayer had conjured up Dalmar. As a coincidence, it was positively uncanny, thought Annabelle. She dismissed the queer notion that began to take root in her mind. Dalmar an angel? Blasphemy! He was no more an angel than he was a knight in shining armor!

Annabelle, however, was not one to trifle with the Deity. Nevertheless, she was far from eager to follow through on her part of the bargain she had made at Lewes. She searched her mind for every possible avenue of escape. None presented itself.

In fear and trepidation, and in a borrowed riding habit, she approached her brother-in-law's head groom and advised him that she was willing to submit herself to the rigors of riding lessons. The poor man balked. In his considered opinion, some few people and horses were best kept on opposite sides of a fence. Among the former he numbered Annabelle.

It was unfortunate that the only docile beast in his master's stable should be something of a freak.

"In spite of 'is size, 'e's as gentle as a lamb," he told Annabelle reassuringly. "And 'e's too old to do more than a fancy shuffle even when 'e's spooked."

"What's his name?" asked Annabelle.

The groom hesitated, then shrugged philosophically. "Goliath," he said, and waited for the lady to take to her heels.

But the lady had more gumption that he had given her credit for.

"Well, lead him out and let's get on with it," was all that she said.

Annabelle's equestrian ambitions were fortunately very modest, and exactly matched her God-given talent in that field. By the end of her stay at Rosedale, she was able to mount and dismount (with the aid of a mounting block and groom, naturally), and she enjoyed many a leisurely ramble through Rosedale's barren pastures and commodious park. She could not have been more delighted with her meager progress if Bailey's had prised Lord Byron from John Murray's tenacious grasp.

It was on just such a ramble that John Falconer came upon her. He reined in his mount and waited patiently as groom and rider slowly descended the rise of a hill. When Annabelle drew level with him, he edged his horse forward.

"Do you always ride with your eyes closed?" he asked, startling her.

Her eyes flew open.

"John! How do you do?" she cried out.

He found the warmth of her welcoming smile more than a little gratifying. "Good to see you again, Annabelle."

"I suffer from vertigo," she explained, and quickly closed her eyes when the ground seemed to heave up to meet her. "Or perhaps it's *mal de mer.* Or both. No matter, I'm not about to let such trifles get the better of me. What brings you to Rosedale?"

Swallowing a laugh at the picture of Annabelle, eyes tightly closed, hanging for dear life to the pommel of her saddle, and mounted on a veritable colossus of a horse, he said easily, "Just passing through on my way to meet some friends in Brighton. I thought we'd take this opportunity to catch up on all the news."

She turned very quiet at that, but brightened a little when they entered the house. "Harry will be delighted to see you again," she said, making for the morning room.

He followed behind her and shut the door quietly. Surprise etched her face when she turned to look at him.

"I've already made my bows to Harry and Sir Charles. It's you I came to see, Annabelle, as if you didn't know."

"How is he?" she asked without preamble, and gestured for him to take a chair close to the one she had selected for herself.

"Sober, celibate, and as miserable as sin, you'll be happy to hear."

"*That* does not make me happy," she protested faintly.

"Doesn't it?"

He did not know why a note of recrimination had crept into his voice. It had not been his purpose in coming out of his way to see her to lay everything at *her* door. And he was sure that the thought of effecting a reconciliation between the two ill-starred lovers had never once crossed his mind. Good grief! He was only a younger brother and highly sensible of all the disadvantages attaching to that role.

What then? He'd expected better of her. Though she'd said very little in the aftermath of Temple's death, it had seemed to him that she'd been excessively severe in her judgment on Dalmar. That rankled, for it placed her firmly in the camp of "public opinion," and public opinion had never been kind to David Falconer.

Perhaps he judged her too harshly. He was in no position to know all the circumstances surrounding the rift between Annabelle and his brother. He didn't wish to know. He only wished . . . he didn't know what he wished.

He expelled a sigh on a long breath. "Forgive me. I don't know why I should give you the sharp edge of my tongue. That's not why I came out of my way to see you."

"Why did you come?" she asked.

He stretched out his long legs and absently flexed the stiff muscles of one knee. It was a moot question, and he took his time before responding.

He tilted his head and smiled up at her. "I don't believe I've ever told you how I got this gammy leg, have I?"

"No," she said, more than a little relieved at this innocuous turn in the conversation. "I've often wondered. But you know, John, most of the time I'm scarcely aware that you have a slight limp. It doesn't seem to incommode you excessively, does it?"

"No. Only at balls or when I'm fatigued. My leg was broken when I was a boy, you see, and the bones did not knit properly."

"Oh, I'm sorry."

"I was lucky not to lose my life."

"It must have been a terrible accident," she said consolingly.

"Actually, it wasn't exactly an accident. It was my father's doing. If David hadn't been there, I think he would have killed me."

Haltingly at first, and then with growing confidence, he began to relate the events which led ultimately to his father's demise and to his brother's ostracism by polite society. As his voice quietly droned on, it seemed to Annabelle as if Rosedale's safe and sunny morning room gradually receded and she was transported to a different place and time. Though Falconer's words were dispassionate, almost conversational, the scene which unfolded in her mind was vibrant with color, quickening a sensitivity to every emotion, every nuance of thought of the characters she saw like moving pictures inside her head.

She had never doubted that Dalmar's father was a bestial sort of a man, controlling his dependents with the unfailing strength of his right arm. It was not such an uncommon story. But never in a hundred years could she have imagined the frightful reality which Falconer's words evoked.

No one had ever thought that Robert Falconer would turn on his younger son. For some inexplicable reason, it was the elder boy, David, who incited him to his worst fits of passion. The mother, a delicate creature, cowed by years of verbal abuse and beating, very rarely interfered. And the family was too ashamed to take anyone into its confidence, though servants' gossip had long since spread tales.

Dalmar had some respite when his uncle, the Earl, took a hand in things. He sent the boy away to school and in the holidays had him stay at Gilcomston, his estate in Hampshire. It was only when the father was known to be away from home that Dalmar ever chanced a visit to see his mother and a younger brother who now bore some of the brunt of his father's ungovernable temper.

It was inevitable that Dalmar should be surprised by his father on one of these clandestine visits. There was a ferocious quarrel. But Dalmar, at seventeen a tall and manly youth, was in no mood to be cowed by a father he despised and no longer feared. As a boy he had known helpless fury as a victim terrorized by a bully of a father. That experience had given him the spur to equip himself so that in any field of combat he could acquit himself well.

Only his mother's anguished pleas had persuaded him to back down and remove himself before Robert Falconer's rage turned against the other members of the family. Within minutes of Dalmar's leaving the house, however, Robert Falconer had vented his spleen on his wife. John, distraught, and meaning only to protect his mother, had gone at his father with fists flying. A backhanded blow to the side of the head had sent the boy staggering to the top of the long staircase. Another blow had sent him toppling over. He'd grabbed for the balustrade and missed it by inches.

It was his mother's screams which had brought Dalmar racing back to the house. Far from being brought to his senses by this wanton act of violence, Robert Falconer seemed to be in the throes of a terrible dementia. In spite of the appeals of servants who came running on the scene, he went for the boy as he writhed and moaned at the foot of the great oak staircase. But Dalmar had entered the house. He saw at once what was afoot, and went for his father.

It was the first time Dalmar had pitted his strength against his father, and the very first time that Robert Falconer had ever backed away from a fight. Though raging like a madman, he'd left the hall abruptly, to the great relief of every one present. Dalmar had been on his knees, tending to his brother's injuries, when Falconer had returned with a rapier in his hand. There was never a doubt in anyone's mind that Falconer meant to exact a terrible revenge for his son's rash interference.

With only a chair to protect him, Dalmar fended off the wild blows and thrusts which were aimed at him. From somewhere a servant found a foil and threw it to the young man. When he discarded the chair and faced his father, a terrible silence descended on the great hall. It was as if everyone knew that in this fight there would be no quarter asked or given. A final reckoning was to be made, one way or another.

"And . . . and Dalmar ran his father through?" asked Annabelle when Falconer came to the end of his recitation.

"Thankfully, yes," said Falconer with an indifference which shocked Annabelle's ears. "Else David would be in his grave and I might not be here to tell the tale. The real story, of course, was suppressed. It was easy to bribe the servants. My father was the most ill-natured of masters. However, gossip was rife. And there was no way to suppress the stories that got about. My uncle, the Earl, deemed it expedient for David to go abroad. And so he went to India."

"And your mother?"

"Oh, she turned on David. There was a breach there that was never patched up. It was to be expected, I suppose. In spite of everything, you see, she still loved my father."

"Oh."

"Yes, 'oh!' There's no accounting for it, except perhaps to say that after one of those terrible bouts, my father was always consumed with bitter self-recrimination and reproach. Until the next time, of course."

"Why . . . why are you telling me all this?"

He passed a hand wearily over his eyes. "God, I don't know! I've never before revealed the circumstances of that night to anyone. I suppose I had it in mind to exonerate David's character. Damn it all, Annabelle," he burst out, "he has some justification for his aversion to men who terrorize women— yes, and for a mistrust of their promises to reform!"

"You don't have to justify Dalmar's character to me!" she softly remonstrated.

"I don't?"

"I'm sure I don't know why you should think so."

"But—it's what David thinks!"

She cocked her head and gave him the strangest look.

"Well, what else should he think when you have acquitted yourself very much in the manner of our mother?" Rather bitterly, he added, "I'm sure there's no understanding the logic of women!"

"Your mother?" she said incredulously.

"I'm not saying that you are like her in character. If anything, you are her antithesis. Well, why do you think David and I are drawn to women like you? I'll tell you why. It's because you would never allow us to indulge our vicious Falconer tempers with impunity."

"You will never convince me that you have a temper, John!" said Annabelle, smiling.

"Don't say that! That would mean I take after my mother— perish the thought!" His face became the picture of consternation. "I beg your pardon. I didn't mean that the way it came out. I don't wish you to think I fault my mother for what she was. All I meant—"

"I know," said Annabelle, in a not unkindly tone. "You don't wish to be thought a poor, gormless creature who is henpecked by managing females such as myself."

"Something like that. Good God, no!" He laughed.

"Annabelle, you're putting words in my mouth!"

He could never decide afterward whether or not Annabelle had taken charge of the conversation by interjecting that piece of frivolity. At all events, their conversation drifted into less personal channels, and Dalmar's name was not mentioned again until Falconer ruthlessly brought it up moments before he took his leave of her.

She had walked him to the front door and out to the stables and had kept up an incessant flow of chitchat which he found almost impossible to dam.

Finally, at the end of his tether, annoyingly aware that he had been humbugging himself and that he did, indeed, wish to effect a reconciliation between Annabelle and his brother, he threw caution to the winds and rudely cut in, "If you decide that you want him, you're going to have a fight on your hands."

She didn't pretend to misunderstand him. "A fight? With whom?" She was thinking of Lady Diana, or perhaps some other lady who had come lately upon the scene.

Falconer accepted the reins of his steed from a stableboy and mounted into the saddle. Correctly interpreting the train of her thought, he said, "It's not another lady, if that's what you're thinking." Disregarding a natural reluctance to broach an indelicate and insensitive subject in hopes of drawing off any resentment she might still be harboring against the Earl, he said doggedly, "And as for his dallying in the petticoat line, that does not signify."

"Oh, doesn't it?" she answered dryly.

"You have my word on it that since he's gone down to Gilcomston, he has adopted the mode of a monk."

"How very . . . salutary," she commiserated.

His brows knit together as he tried to decipher what the ironic tone might or might not signify.

"Annabelle, there is a greater obstacle by far," he persisted.

She had evidently lost the thread of what he was saying. "What obstacle?" she asked.

"Dalmar himself. I think he's lost confidence. He's not the same person. Do you know what I think?"

"No, what?"

"I think—and this is only conjecture, mind you—I think that he suffers from a terrible foreboding that he might turn out to be just like my father."

"But that's preposterous. Why would you even think so?"

A ghost of a smile, faintly self-mocking, touched Falconer's lips. "I harbor the same secret dread with respect to myself."

Chapter Twenty-Two

In Gilcomston, his country seat in Hampshire, the Earl of Dalmar had shut himself away in his study, and was ostensibly hard at work on estate accounts. At that moment he was sprawled inelegantly in a well-worn leather armchair, his feet propped on a great oak desk, and staring disinterestedly at the long windows on the far wall. With the pencil in his hand, he drummed an idle tattoo against one booted foot.

The door handle rattled. Dalmar's feet dropped to the floor, and he adopted an air of concentration as he bent over his ledgers.

"Still at it, I see," said John Falconer pleasantly as he sailed into the room. In his hand he held two letters. "These just arrived by post. One for you," he tossed one letter on the desk, "and one for me. From Annabelle, if I'm not mistaken. I wonder what that tear-away is up to now?"

He draped himself over a commodious armchair which hugged the hearth and became involved in opening and reading the one-page epistle. From time to time he chuckled softly. For the Earl he spared not a glance.

Dalmar picked up the letter his brother had tossed to him. He weighed it carefully in one hand. He turned it over. He examined it from all angles. He sliced a look at his younger brother's carefully averted profile. At length he emitted a soft sigh and deftly pried it apart with a jewel-encrusted silver letter opener which lay at his hand.

He wasn't sure what to expect. It was a full month since he

had last seen her at Ransome's wedding. She'd been very cold with him then, not that he blamed her. He did not wish for any converse with the lady—not even a letter. Just yesterday, he had actually been surprised into laughter. Genuine laughter, not the mechanical grimace of bared teeth and a forced bark, but the real thing. He was making progress. He was sure that he could tear her from his heart and mind, given time—say, a hundred years or so. He carefully smoothed out the single sheet and began to read.

It was a bread-and-butter letter thanking him for his timely rescue from Lord Temple. In passing, she mentioned his good offices during the riot at the Palais Royal and also at Lewes on Guy Fawkes' Night. He didn't like the tone of the letter. It was too serious, too polite, too formal, and just the sort of thing he would expect Annabelle to write to a perfect stranger. Only at the end was there a flash of something which captured Annabelle's flair for irony—or was it sarcasm?

"I always thought," he read, "that angels were robed in white and possessed a magnificent set of wings. So now I know."

Now what was he to gather from that? Did she imply that he was an angel? He reread the letter several times. No, that could not be right. Perhaps she referred to herself. To his surprise he discovered that he was grinning. He considered the phenomenon and concluded that he felt decidedly lighter of heart. It was too much to say that Annabelle had forgiven him for his vicious conduct on the day she had been dragged to Bow Street, nor had she mentioned that episode in her letter. But there was just a hint that she no longer regarded him so completely beyond reproach.

He looked up and caught his brother's curious eye upon him. The smile faded from his face.

"A thank-you note for my part in her rescue from Temple," he said. If his brother had any thought of a reconciliation between himself and Annabelle, he wanted to nip that hope in the bud. He was grateful for this lessening of hostility on Annabelle's part, but it would never do to let himself be persuaded that he could trust himself in any volatile situation with Annabelle. And with her, it went without saying, there were bound to be many of those.

He looked pointedly at the letter in Falconer's hand. "And yours?" he asked, studiously casual.

"Oh." Falconer waved the page negligently in the air. "She spent a week in York with her father. It seems that she's brought the old boy back to town with her. I say, David, d'you think you could spare me for a week or so?"

"You've only just got here!" exclaimed the Earl in a slightly aggrieved tone.

"Yes, I know. But Annabelle's giving a welcoming party for her father. Well, you know what Annabelle's parties are like. Anything can happen. I wouldn't want to miss it for the world."

A dark tide of color rose in Dalmar's neck. He turned away and observed mildly, "I thought you detested town life."

"Did I say that?" Falconer seemed to give the notion some thought. "By Jove, you're right," he said. "I believe I did, once upon a time. Well, I've had a change of heart, 'tis all."

Dalmar pinned his brother with a penetrating stare. "Is Lady Jocelyn to be in town?"

Falconer's brows shot up. "Not to my knowledge. Last time I heard, she and Sir Charles were holidaying in Paris. Why do you ask?"

"No reason. Then there's nothing more to be said except 'Don't do anything I wouldn't do!'"

"Good God!" exclaimed Falconer, laughing. "What a boring fate! I hope to do a hell of a lot more than you've been up to of late, dear brother."

He quickly ducked as a missile came flying toward him, missing his head by inches. The candle bounced off the wall and rolled under a chair.

"You can always come with me," suggested Falconer hopefully.

"I wasn't invited."

"But Annabelle never invites people to her parties. Like bad pennies, they just turn up. You should know that better than anyone. Oh, I beg your pardon. I didn't mean . . ."

"Forget it. No, really . . . there's quite enough here to occupy me for months to come."

"And all of it pressing," said Falconer sardonically. "Have it your own way. I'll keep you posted on my direction." To his brother's arched brow, he responded, "Well, with Annabelle, who knows where we might end up? Last time Paris, next time, Berlin, for all I know."

Dalmar's look was thoughtful as his younger sibling sauntered from the room.

"It was a lovely party," said the vicar to his daughter, his eyes thoughtful as they rested on the top of her head.

"Yes, wasn't it?" she replied.

Annabelle sat on the hearth, arms clasped around her knees, her spine resting against the front of her father's chair. His hand was on her shoulder. It was a comforting position, she thought, and one which reminded her forcefully of childhood days. They would often sit thus, talking over the day's events or merely absorbed in private reflection.

"Who was that woman?" asked the vicar at length.

"The one who disrobed in front of everyone?"

"Yes, that's the one."

"She said she was an artist's model and had mistaken the house. And when no one stopped her entering the premises, she was sure she had the right address. D'you think she was telling the truth, Papa?"

"Oh, I think so," answered the vicar with a small, private smile.

"It had occurred to me," said Annabelle, "that it were more prudent to send out cards for my parties. Then the porter could turn away interlopers at the door."

"Is that the custom in London—to send out cards?"

"Papa, that's the custom everywhere."

"Strange," said the vicar, "I've never followed it."

"No, and neither have I. Still . . ."

"My dear, you refine too much upon it. To have the porter turn away strangers at the door! It seems so . . . un-Christian! And really, no one was offended by the lady."

"True," agreed Annabelle.

"And she seemed to enjoy herself, once she was persuaded

to put her clothes back on."

"You don't think she ruined my party?"

"Good heavens, no! Quite the reverse, I should say. Your young man, Dalmar—he was not present, I think someone told me."

There was a long pause as Annabelle slowly assimilated the unwelcome turn in the conversation. She became involved in tracing a path with her fingers through the thick pile of the rug. "I did not expect him," she said in a small voice.

The vicar regarded her bowed head with a sapient eye. "Am I to take it, then, that the marriage is put off altogether?"

"I shall never marry," said Annabelle with ringing finality, then ruined the effect she wished to achieve by emitting a pathetic little sniff and several hiccups in quick succession.

Wordlessly the vicar dangled a pristine white handkerchief in front of her face. Annabelle accepted it with an incoherent expression of gratitude and blew her nose.

"There's a good girl," said the vicar consolingly. "Now why don't you begin at the beginning and tell Papa all about it?"

The words were so achingly familiar, thought Annabelle, though it was years since she had last heard them. She half turned her head and regarded her father through the wet spikes of her lashes. He was still a fine figure of a man, she thought, in spite of a bald pate and a slight stoop to his shoulders. He was a man who laughed a lot, to which the fine lines around his eyes and the deep slashes in his cheeks amply attested. She'd once told him, half in earnest, that she thought that on Judgment Day he would plead on behalf of the devil himself. There was not much that shocked the reverend Jonathan Summers. Still, she was his daughter. . . .

"Can't you tell me?" he softly encouraged.

And then the whole damning story, suitably expurgated, came pouring out of her.

"Oh Papa," she cried, "if you had only seen me that day when he came to Bailey's with the constables to take the diaries away from me, you would not have recognized your own daughter! Such language! Such wild, uncontrollable behavior! Do you know, I slapped him twice? And I knew the consequences would be severe. But I was past caring. I was beside myself, like some deranged bedlamite. And after everything he had done for me! And he—he was only trying to protect me, as future events were to prove. I knew it even then. But a wicked humor had taken possession of me. I did not even recognize myself," and she buried her nose in her sire's damp handkerchief, and proceeded to dampen it some more.

"You don't think," pointed out the vicar reasonably, "that the provocation was great? That perhaps the young man has much to answer for, that his methods are, forgive me, my dear, a trifle ruthless?"

"Very ruthless," agreed Annabelle readily, "as was to be expected." To her father's look of surprise, she responded, "It's almost frightening, this obsession he has about protecting me at all costs, yes, even from myself."

"A caprice?" murmured the vicar.

"A sacred trust, more like. He's like a guardian angel, and oh, Papa, guardian angels aren't all that they're cracked up to be, as I've discovered."

"Then if the man's character is unpredictable, it's best to sever your ties to him," said the vicar thoughtfully. "You did the right thing."

With a small, impatient shrug of her shoulders, Annabelle responded softly, "Oh no, Papa, if it were only that, I should not care. I can predict Dalmar like, well, like the hands on that clock over there. Can't you understand—it's myself I don't know."

The vicar was not very sure that Dalmar was the man he would have chosen for Annabelle. He did not like the sound of manacles and gag. But whatever the circumstances of that incredible encounter, he could not, in all conscience, permit his dear daughter to be crushed under the weight of her guilt.

"So you stepped out of character for a moment or two," he said, "and the experience has left you shaken."

"Mortified," responded Annabelle in a muffled undertone.

"It was the same with Jacob," mused the vicar.

"Was it?" asked Annabelle, swiveling her head round to gaze at her sire. As she remembered, they had once had a gardener of that name.

"You recall that he robbed his brother of his birthright.

Shocking!" said the vicar.

"Did he?" asked Annabelle doubtfully. "I didn't know Jacob *had* a brother."

"Esau was his name."

"Oh, *that* Jacob. You're telling me stories from the Bible, Papa." She smiled up at him. It was just like old times again.

"And yet he got over that unhappy episode and made his peace with Esau. And the Lord used him to effect mighty things."

Annabelle sighed inaudibly. She should have known that her father would start to moralize sooner or later. "Yes, Papa," she intoned politely.

"And think of King David," said the vicar, warming to his subject.

"I have you there, Papa! King David was a veritable hero!" crowed Annabelle, interested in spite of herself.

"You're forgetting Bathsheba," he corrected, "and her poor husband, Uriah."

"I had forgot," said Annabelle contritely.

"Yes, David connived at the poor man's death."

"Scandalous!" hissed Annabelle. "Sometimes, Papa—and I hope you don't think this is blasphemy—but I think the Lord needs his head examined! King David should have been punished for what he did!"

"Were you always such a Biblical illiterate?" asked the vicar, the smile in his voice robbing his words of any real censure. "We'll let that pass. But my point is that everyone, unless he's a blessed saint, steps out of character a time or two in his lifetime. Look at Edgar!"

"Edgar," said Annabelle musingly. "I don't recall . . . you will have to refresh my memory, Papa. Does he appear in the Old or the New Testament?"

"Edgar, your late husband," said the vicar dryly.

"Oh, *that* Edgar."

"He wasn't a bad man, you know. Well, look how he made provision for his son, Richard. He must have suspected that he stood to forfeit your good opinion once Richard's existence became known. But he didn't compound one error by adding another. He did his duty, and I've always admired him for it."

"Poor Edgar," said Annabelle, and lapsed into a meditative silence. "Perhaps I've misjudged him," she said, striving to be generous.

"And then there's Annabelle Jocelyn," said the vicar, regarding Annabelle's bent head with a soft, knowing eye. "So you've seen yourself in a new light, and you're shocked by what's been revealed."

Annabelle cocked her head to one side. "Did you ever step out of character, Papa?" she quizzed. "I just can't imagine it."

"Oh yes," said the vicar. "I do it all the time. Well, we all do, to a greater or less degree. But one lives in hope, you know. That is, after all, our creed."

They sat in companionable silence for a long interval. At length, Annabelle stretched and slowly rose to her feet. She pressed a kiss on top of the vicar's bald head.

"Thank you, Papa," she said. "I think I've learned a salutary lesson."

"And the young man, Dalmar?"

The smile she bestowed on him was appallingly familiar to the vicar. An involuntary shiver danced along his spine.

"Oh, he's in need of a salutary lesson," said Annabelle. "And I'm just the one to give it to him."

The Earl of Dalmar received the first intimation of what was in store for him on a Friday morning. It arrived in the form of a one-page epistle from Annabelle. It seemed that the lady wished to buy him out of her publishing business. She was prepared to offer him very generous terms, so she wrote.

Dalmar mulled the matter over in his mind. There was no real reason, he thought, why he should not accede to her wishes. But something in him resisted, something that refused to accept the severing of this last link between them.

He wondered where the capital to buy him out was to come from. As he well knew, Bailey's was in the throes of expansion, and every spare penny that Annabelle had was tied up in the business. She was up to something. He could smell it— something that she knew he would put a stop to if he had any say in the matter. He decided, then, rather indignantly, that nothing on God's earth could make him tamely relinquish his half share in Bailey's.

On Saturday morning, another epistle arrived at Gilcomston, this time from John Falconer. It appeared that the young man was having such a good time in town that he proposed to stay on for another sennight, if his brother could spare him. Dalmar snorted. As they both knew very well, in February, things were very quiet in the country. Most of his time was spent at books and ledgers, and a very dull time of it he was having. As if anyone cared.

As he read further, a laugh was startled out of him. He could picture Annabelle's party as if he were there. Was there to be no end to the scrapes she got into? The girl needed a keeper. He'd thought so from the moment he'd first clapped eyes on her. How damnably unfortunate that he had to disqualify himself from taking on that role for circumstances beyond his control.

The next paragraph in Falconer's letter brought storm clouds to the Earl's brow. This, he thought, even for Annabelle, was skating too close to thin ice—Harriette Wilson, London's most notorious courtesan, to be observed entering Bailey's by its front doors! And to leave standing outside in the street for a good half hour or more, her equipage—for who could mistake its distinctive blue satin trappings?—that was tantamount to courting social disaster for Annabelle. What could the girl be thinking of?

It was here that the Earl came very close to suffering a mild apoplexy. *She wouldn't dare!* he thought, and on the next breath, *Who says she wouldn't?*

He'd spiked her guns once before, in the matter of Monique Dupres's memoirs. And though every word was imprinted in her memory, she had given her word to Somerset that she would never commit them to paper. But Annabelle hated to be bested in anything. He should have expected, thought Dalmar, that she would find some way of demonstrating her utter contempt for all his schemes to order her life to suit himself.

"Damn her to hell!" The roar reverberated through the great house, from cellars to attics, sending innocent little mice scurrying for their holes, and turning startled servants into statues of stone. It was only when his lordship's curricle was observed to be safely disappearing in a cloud of dust down Gilcomston's stately drive that whispering servants dared come together in clusters to decry their unhappy lot. The proverbial Falconer temper was flying at full mast.

"''ere," said cook, a certain Mrs. Flood by name, as she waved her spurtle under old Raggett's long nose, "A' thought the new earl were a downey 'un. 'E ain't never show'd us that 'orrid side o' 'is character a-fore."

"No," agreed that august gentleman, carefully removing a speck of lint from the sleeve of his new scarlet livery. He appeared to fall into a brown study. Emerging a moment or two later from his reverie, he smiled rather oddly and observed, "The old lord was a bit of Turk, if ever there was one."

"Ain't that the truth," concurred Cook readily.

"D'you know what I think?"

"No, wot?"

"I don't think we'll see the likes of the old lord again." His tone was faintly regretful.

Mrs. Flood blinked owlishly. She looked askance at the butler's straight-backed figure. "An d'y know wot I says, Mr. Raggett?" she asked, deceptively mild.

"No, what?" asked Raggett absently.

"Amen to that!" she roared. "That's wot! Amen to that!"

The Earl arrived in town too late to present himself at Greek Street. And since he was not expected in Cavendish Square, and young Falconer did little more than rack up there for the night, the caretakers had made no provision for visitors. He had to content himself with a cold house and indifferent victuals.

A fire was soon kindled in the study, however, and Dalmar set himself to while away the hours with a good book and fine brandy till his brother should return from some vaguely specified party. He had a long wait.

Falconer arrived when it was almost three of the clock in the morning, and though he greeted his brother effusively, he wanted nothing more than to crawl into a comfortable bed.

396

Another hour was to pass before he had his wish, for Dalmar cross-examined him most particularly on the very minutiae of Annabelle's comings and goings. As far as Falconer knew, there was nothing worth the telling. He could not know how his carelessly thrown out words set the Earl back on his heels.

Falconer went off whistling, and Dalmar poured himself another drink. He digested his brother's words in growing resentment. Annabelle, commissioning Robert Loukes to bid for her on a hack at Tattersall's? And Annabelle, quite the thing, and as if she was not terrified of horses, mounted on that same hack and joining a party of riders in an outing to Richmond? There was more. Annabelle was in the market for a dog, and though she had yet to settle on anything definite, Lady Diana had undertaken to present her with a puppy from her own dam's litter when she next went home to the country. Dalmar was sure he did not know what the world was coming to. And then, a blinding shaft of comprehension pierced him.

He slammed his glass down, shattering it into a thousand pieces. He did not care. Swearing savagely, he lurched to his feet and began to pace furiously about the room.

Annabelle Jocelyn was involved with another man! Everything pointed to that conclusion. There was no other explanation for this recently acquired resolve to overcome her aversion to dogs and horses. And damn it all—he had promised himself once that *he* would be the one to help her subdue these absurd phobias. It was not to be borne!

He closed his eyes and breathed deeply for several minutes. This would not do. Annabelle was beyond his reach. He had not the right to meddle in her private life. With a wrenching pain, he dragged his thoughts from the possible suitors to her hand who sprang to mind. *Let it go,* he told himself resolutely. *What she does in her private life is no longer your concern.*

No, but he was still her partner. And he would be damned if he would see her risk Bailey's for the dubious privilege of publishing Harriette Wilson's memoirs. By degrees, and all unconsciously, his outrage at the thought that another man had already replaced him in her affections subtly transferred itself to this more legitimate grievance. Bailey's would buy Harriette Wilson's memoirs when hell froze over, or his name wasn't David Falconer!

The following day was Sunday, and Dalmar was obliged to contain his patience until church services were over before presenting himself at Greek Street. He was kept kicking his heels in a downstairs anteroom for a full ten minutes only to be finally informed that Annabelle was not there. The intelligence was given to him by a gentleman who introduced himself as Annabelle's father. The two men sized each other up in the space of one quick, comprehensive look.

"Where is she?" asked Dalmar, returning stare for stare with the stiff-backed, dragon-faced gentleman.

Jonathan Summers involuntarily flexed his muscles. Though he could give the younger man more than twenty years, he thought that he might still acquit himself with honor in a bout of fisticuffs, though to be sure, he had not attempted such a feat since his Oxford days.

Every muscle in Dalmar's body tensed. Man of cloth or no as Annabelle's father might be, to a man of action like himself there could be no mistaking that stiff challenging posture. He sensed the exact moment Jonathan Sommers began to relent, and relief swamped him. It was inconceivable that he should be forced to defend himself from an attack by Annabelle's father. He might inadvertently hurt the old boy, and that would be one more thing for which Annabelle would never forgive him.

"Where is she?" he repeated.

"At Bailey's. She's gone to fetch . . ."

But Dalmar was already striding from the room.

The vicar quietly followed him out and stood pensively at the bottom of the stairs long after the front door had closed. Annabelle had called the man her guardian angel. To his way of thinking, the Earl had the look of an avenging fury. *Ah well,* he thought, *the Lord works in mysterious ways. And Annabelle, provoking chit, takes after her Maker.* He did not think the Lord would take offense at the small joke.

It took Dalmar only five minutes to reach his destination. The front doors to Bailey's stood open. Outside, on the pavement, waited a burly footman whom Dalmar recognized as one of the men whom he had employed to protect Annabelle. He dismissed him from his post with a curt word, entered the building, and barred the doors behind him. Annabelle Jocelyn, he determined, could scream bloody murder, but nothing would save her from his righteous wrath. He took the stairs two at a time and stormed into her office as if he were in the first wave of invaders scaling the battlements.

With a little cry, she spun to face him, and the stack of papers she had been clutching to her bosom went scattering in all directions.

For the longest time, she could do nothing but stare at him, mouthing choked, inarticulate gibberish. He was a fearsome sight, she thought. His dark hair was wild and windblown, his brows slashed in a fierce frown, and those gray eyes, oh God— the storm in them could easily blow away a mountain. She drew herself up to her full height and tried not to be intimidated by the fourteen stone of powerful masculine sinew and muscle which dwarfed her. It was hard to remember that he was her guardian angel. In that moment, if he had yelled some bloodcurdling battle cry and come at her with mace and drawn broadsword, it would not have surprised her one jot.

She had to fight that first almost overpowering instinct to drop to her knees and scurry under the desk like some frightened little rabbit. Everything was working out just as she had engineered it, more or less, she consoled herself. Only, she had thought that the scene of this battle would be her drawing room in Greek Street with reinforcements, at hers to command, standing by. This vast, empty building did nothing to bolster her shaky confidence.

"I . . . I came by to pick up some policy papers," she said for something to say, and gestured weakly to the mess of papers scattered around the floor. "I like to read them once in a while just to refresh my memory." Her tone was not nearly as confident as she had hoped it would be. If only he would stop staring at her as if he were a starving lion and she a plump chicken who had wandered into his line of vision. "You'll be happy to know I'm taking your advice. I mean to abridge them, you see, so that . . ."

She jumped when his fist slammed against the closed door.

"You never learn, do you?" he said, baring his teeth. "Have you forgot what happened in this very office the last time you tried to thwart me?" His voice rose to a roar. "I'm not letting you publish Harriette Wilson's memoirs, and that's final."

She didn't feel very angry. In fact, she was quite shaken. But she knew exactly what she had to do. She loved him too much not to take the gamble. And when it was all over, they would either live happily ever after, or one or both of them would hang for murder. What had she to lose? she asked herself philosophically.

Baring her own teeth in a reasonable counterfeit of his snarl, she yelled back, "If I want to publish Harriette Wilson's memoirs, there's not a damn thing you can do to stop me. Go on Dalmar, go on! Run and fetch your Bow Street constables. Where's the gag? Where are the manacles?" And she held out her arms in a derisory, taunting gesture. "Put me in prison and throw away the key! See if I care!" And for good measure, she added, not quite truthfully, "You don't frighten me, David Falconer."

There was nothing counterfeit about the Earl's next move. He grabbed her by the shoulders and shook her till she was sure her teeth had loosened. "I won't allow you to put yourself at risk!" he yelled at her.

"Liar!" she stormed back. "You don't give a fig about me! It's yourself you're thinking of. You don't want the world to know what a libertine you are."

At last Annabelle had hit upon the one thing which had the power to fan the tiny flame of her resentment until it burst into a genuine conflagration—Dalmar and his redheads!

She pushed out of his arms and glared doggedly into his set face. "You've hurt me far more than Temple ever did! My God! I didn't deserve that! In front of all my friends and in my own drawing-room, of all places!"

"Annabelle," he groaned, stretching out a hand to conciliate her. She slapped it away, and he let his arm drop to his side.

"So your pride was hurt. I'm sorry for it, Annabelle," he said, very stiff and proper. "But our engagement was broken. You can't fault me for turning to other women."

Like a furious spitting kitten, she paced before him. "Sir Spider!" she hissed, and sliced him a look of pure venom. "I never saw the birthmark which gave Monique Dupres the idea for that epithet! Where exactly is this intimate spot on your body which she mentions in her diaries?"

Dalmar said nothing, but his ears burned scarlet.

Annabelle emitted a derisory snort and continued her pacing. "You are mistaken, Lord Dalmar, if you think I fault you for turning to other women. It was the public display which earned my disgust." She halted and slowly brought her head up. Her eyes dared him to touch her. "I had expected some consideration, some semblance of dignity. I'm sure no one could name a single one of *my* lovers. No, because I conduct my *affaires* with a modicum of discretion."

"This has nothing to say to anything," said Dalmar stonily. "And we have wandered far from—*what* did you say?"

With a nonchalance she was far from feeling, Annabelle brazenly repeated her observation.

She didn't like the way his eyes closed. She didn't like the way his hands fisted at his sides. She didn't like the way his muscles bunched along the powerful arms and shoulders. And she most particularly did not like the way the smooth line of his jaw had hardened into granite.

"His name?" said Dalmar through set teeth.

Attempting to inject a little levity into a very tense moment, Annabelle archly exaggerated, "Would I stick at one, Dalmar? None of them was very memorable. I'm sure I've forgotten half their names already." He must know that she was joking.

The silence vibrated with leashed violence. Not even when she had been in that room in the Palais Royal with Lord Temple had Annabelle experienced such a frightening sense of her peril. She quickly ranged herself on the other side of the desk. How could she have been such a fool, she chided herself belatedly, as to deliberately provoke the full force of his anger against herself?

Placatingly, she offered, "What odds? I didn't do anything you yourself weren't doing."

He opened his eyes and pinned her with such a look that Annabelle was sure she must be nailed to the floor.

Hastening to make amends, she rashly interjected, "Don't forget, you said so yourself, the engagement was broken. That means we were both free agents. I promise not to cast your women in your teeth if you promise . . . *aahh!*" She screamed as he lunged for her.

He stalked her like a hound on the scent of the fox. With commendable presence of mind, Annabelle kept the width of the desk between them. She cast one anguished look at the closed door and wondered if she should bolt for it.

"First," said Dalmar, gnashing his teeth furiously, "I'm going to tear you limb from limb and grind your bones into dust. And then you're going to tell me the names of your lovers. And then . . ."

"You've got the sequence wrong," she scrupulously pointed out. Not even the flicker of a smile touched his lips. *Oh God, she thought despairingly, has the man no sense of humor?*

Slapping her hands palm down on the flat of the desk, in a voice calculated to intimidate—the one which never failed to win an argument in the world of commerce—she stated unequivocally, "Enough is enough! You may not have noticed, but you've just broken one of your own cardinal rules. Don't forget, Lord Dalmar, our personal and business lives are to be kept entirely separate. Now, if you wish to discuss the matter of selling out your share of the business in a reasonable and civilized manner, I am open to suggestion."

She evaded his long reach with only inches to spare. And by the time he had vaulted the desk, she was halfway to the door. She dragged it open. His hand lashed out and slammed it shut. As the door handle was wrenched from her grasp, she felt the pain of it right down to her toes. Her temper flared.

She spun to face him. With both hands she beat a tattoo upon her heaving bosom. Though he was only inches from her, she baited, "Come on, Dalmar, come and get me, if you dare. I'm not afraid of you, you overgrown tadpole! Touch me—I'm warning you—touch me and I'll knock your block off!"

He did more than touch her. Like a ton of coal, he came crashing down on her, flattening her against the door till she thought her ribs would break. Strong fingers closed around her throat.

Torn between anguish and fury, he let his fingers tighten alarmingly. "If you *ever* again let another man touch you," he railed in her ear, "I'll wring your bloody neck before I murder you."

"It's one of my policies," she hurled back.

"What is?" he bellowed.

"What's sauce for the goose is sauce for the gander! And don't you ever forget it, David Falconer!"

They were both panting hard from a combination of exertion and spent anger.

"Did you say those words to another man?" he asked, his voice harsh with emotion.

She couldn't think what he was getting at. He administered a rough shake to loosen her tongue.

"Well?" he demanded. "Did you tell some other man that you loved him too?"

"Of course not!" she replied at once. "How could I, when I still love you? Besides, you don't really believe that there were other men, do you? But I mean it, David Falconer, I'm warning you, next time, next time . . ."

His whole body went rigid, then gradually relaxed as the meaning of her words slowly penetrated. "Oh Annabelle," he said, "oh Annabelle, can you ever forgive me?" For a long, agonizing interval she was silent, and he groaned in despair. "When I thought I had ruined my chances with you, I went crazy. Can't you understand? Nothing mattered anymore. Those women, I don't even know who they were."

It was several moments before he realized Annabelle could not find her voice for tears. Cradling her face with both hands, he implored, "Don't cry, love. Please don't cry. I'm not worth it."

She let out an anguished cry and threw herself into his arms. "*Never, never* say such a thing again, or I shall *hit* you, David Falconer! You don't know, *can't* know what you are worth to me."

She went on in a similar vein for several minutes, her words muffled against the lapel of his coat. When she began to talk incoherently of guardian angels and knights in shining armor, he thought it time to intervene. He kissed her swiftly

"Is it true? Can you still love me, knowing what I am?" he

403

asked softly.

"What are you?" Her eyes were brimming with tears and unabashedly luminous with a love she did not try to conceal from him.

"I'm my father's son," he said, his voice choked with emotion. "A man with bad blood in his veins."

"Haven't you been listening to a word I've been saying?" she asked passionately. "You're not the man your father was, nor anything like him. Even if you are a hard man, I know you to be a man of honor. You live by your convictions. You've proved that many times over."

She drew in a deep, calming breath, knowing that her next words might be the most important she had ever said in her life. "Forgive me, my dear, for not trusting you more. I should have known from our first encounter at the Palais Royal what manner of man you are."

"Admit it! You were terrified of me even then!" he said roughly.

Smiling through her tears, she said, "You *tried* to terrify me, you odious man! But you didn't succeed. How should you, when you almost lost your life defending me? I can never forget that duel you fought with the Frenchman, even if you can."

"As I remember," he said softly, "it was you who saved me. You came dashing down those stairs and diverted his attention."

"I saw the whole of it, did you know, just shadows against the wall? I couldn't tell who was who until I saw one man go down and the other come in for the kill. And then I knew." At the recollection she shivered.

"What did you know?"

"I knew that you had too much honor to kill a man who was wounded. It just isn't in you."

He let out a long, shuddering breath. "Annabelle, about Lord Temple . . ."

She covered his lips with the tips of her fingers. "Don't," she whispered. "There's no necessity to explain yourself to me. Once I began to think things through, I knew that I could trust you to do what you thought was right. It's been like that

404

from the beginning, only events and circumstances have sometimes blinded me to the truth. Can you forgive me?"

His voice shaking with emotion, he said, "It's I who should be begging your forgiveness. Oh God, when I think of how I took those damn diaries away from you! I'm no better than my father!"

"How can you think that?" she cried out. "Would John admire you, or Ransome, or Bertie, or Henrietta, if you were anything like your father? Would Richard love you? Would I?"

Grinning whimsically, he said, "You left out Lady Diana."

"Diana doesn't count," said Annabelle, brushing away her tears. "She's such a dear that she loves everybody indiscriminately."

He laughed and shook his head. Framing her face with both hands, he asked in a more serious vein, "Are you going to deny that sometimes I frighten you half to death?"

Sniffing, Annabelle retorted, "I didn't say you were perfect. So you needn't get a swelled head. But," her lips curved in a self-satisfied grin, "I just proved that no matter how much I provoke you, you'll never do me any harm. It's just not in you."

"What? I don't think I understand."

"You don't really believe that I was going to publish Harriette Wilson's memoirs, do you? It was all a sham to rile you, so that I could prove to you that there's nothing to fear when you are in one of your rages."

"Good God!" He slammed his fist into the door, and Annabelle jumped. "You were taking one hell of a chance," he roared. "Have you no sense, woman?"

"No!" she yelled back with equal force. "Loving someone means that you are willing to take a chance on them. Haven't you learned that yet?"

She really believed everything she was saying. He could see it in her eyes. He had never felt more humbled in his life, or more . . . cleansed. It was as if this one adorable, willful, fearless girl had put the specters of his past to flight.

It took him a moment to find his voice. "Oh Annabelle, Annabelle," he said, "there's not another woman like you."

She pulled back and looked up at him through her sooty lashes. He was fascinated by the pout to her lips.

Between sniffs, she said, "Those women—they all had red hair."

For a moment he was baffled and did not know how he should answer her. The last thing he wished for was a discussion on the nameless, faceless women he had shamelessly used in the weeks following the final break with Annabelle. Feeling his way carefully, he said, "Don't you like red hair?"

"What kind of question is that?" she said petulantly. "You know I dye my hair."

He had to ask. "Annabelle, why do you dye your hair?"

"Because it's red, of course, and I absolutely detest red hair."

It was impossible to say anything in reply. He fought the temptation to give in to his laughter. Her next words sobered him.

"At least we can part as friends," she taunted.

He turned instantly truculent. "I may murder you one of these days, but give you up? Never!"

She smiled a very watery, feminine, knowing smile. "You don't frighten me, Dalmar. And *that* for your famous Falconer temper," and she snapped her fingers under his nose.

He threw back his head and laughed. "Oh, Annabelle," he said, "God help me, I love you."

She grinned like a Cheshire cat. "I love you too," she breathed, and nestled her head on his broad chest.

Moments later she felt his fingers tangle in her hair. He brought her face up, and his eyes, assessing, devoid of any trace of humor, gauged her bemused expression. She recognized the look on his face.

"You're mad!" she choked out, and made a helpless motion of one hand to take in the small room.

"I can manage," he countered, "if you help me."

"There isn't room to swing a cat in this little boxroom," she desperately shrilled. "Not a spare inch of floor space or a couch or . . . or whatever!"

His fingers were already at the back of her gown, slipping the

406

small buttons from their buttonholes. "There's a chair and a tabletop," he said huskily. "I'll let you choose."

"That's very good of you, I'm sure. But if you think I'm going to let you . . ."

"I love you," he said. "I love you," and his lips swooped down, cutting off any protest, kissing her again and again, melting her resistance, persuading her to yield to the intimacy he had been too long denied.

And it felt so good, so right, so absolutely what the doctor ordered, thought Annabelle dizzily, that she would not have cared if they had been a pair of equestrian performers in Astley's Royal Amphitheater. Where there was a will, there was a way, and where there was love, everything was possible.

Epilogue

The gray light of dawn cast its first feeble rays over the Georgian city of Bath. In the Christopher Hotel, in High Street, in an upstairs chamber with a view over the River Avon and to the hills beyond, Annabelle slept in the arms of her husband.

As the new day progressively filtered into their chamber, Dalmar gazed tenderly down at the softly breathing girl fitted so closely to his length, and he reflected on his good fortune. Annabelle was his. The thought humbled him. Again and again he had to remind himself that they were man and wife. Again and again the vows he had so solemnly sworn to her drummed in his mind like a lover's litany: *to have and to hold from this day forward, to love and to cherish, till death us do part.*

His lips brushed her ear. "I love you," he whispered.

Annabelle sighed and nestled closer.

Gently, so as not to wake her, he lifted the bed covers and feasted his eyes on the softly rounded figure of his naked wife. He pulled back slightly to make a space of a few inches. Annabelle grew restless, emitted something cross and unintelligible, and closed the distance between them. Dalmar smiled.

He loved the way she crowded him in bed; loved the way she possessively curled herself around whichever part of his anatomy lay to hand; loved the way she trustingly allowed him to arrange her inert limbs to suit his own purposes.

His eyes roamed familiarly from the curtain of glorious,

flame-red hair spread across his pillow to the lush curve of the feminine leg which he had drawn over his hips. Inevitably his breathing quickened. His body grew hard. Oh God, he thought, he loved a hell of a lot more than what they did in bed. But words could never adequately express the ferocity of emotions this one girl could so effortlessly arouse.

"Annie-love," he crooned. He didn't give her time to come to herself. He wouldn't dare. Even on their honeymoon, he did not doubt that Annabelle planned to manage every blessed minute of their time. They would get to that later. But for the present . . .

Her eyelashes fluttered. She stirred and turned up her head. Her lips were only inches from his. "David," she breathed, "what time is it?"

His tongue sank into the silky, moist recesses of her mouth the moment before he claimed her with his body. He felt her surprise, then savored her instinctive, voluptuous movements as she responded to his hungry possession. He fed her passion with deep, powerful strokes and dark sensual words.

It was a quick coupling. He scarcely gave her time to recover.

"Again," he said.

And this time he claimed her slowly, bringing her again and again to the verge, delaying the final moment of rapture till he thought he would go mad with wanting her. Her response to him never ceased to awe him. She needed him almost as much as he needed her. She was so giving, so loving. She made him feel things he had never believed in . . . until now.

She was still panting hard in the aftermath of their lovemaking when he pulled away. He rolled to his side, stretched one hand to the bedside table, and retrieved a rolled-up scroll tied with a red ribbon. He thrust it into her hands, then turned back to the bedside table and lit a candle.

"What's this?" she asked.

"A policy paper," he answered shortly.

Her eyes lit up. "I love policy papers," she said, and dragged herself into a sitting position, tucking the ends of the bed sheet under her armpits.

Dalmar smiled at the gesture and negligently clasped his

hands behind his head. At ease and yet on his guard, he propped his broad shoulders against the bedrest and studied her with covert interest.

She presented a curious dilemma for him, he thought. For while he admired her mettle and knew without a doubt that a lesser woman would not do for him at all, he was determined to be master in his own house. And perversely, without Annabelle's consent, his very reasonable and very masculine ambition was doomed to come to nothing.

Her look was frankly curious. "Have you come round to my way of thinking?" she asked. "Honestly, David, when there's a policy in place, things run so much more smoothly. But I've told you this before."

"I could not agree with you more," he said, surprising her. "Now read it and tell me what you think."

She removed the ribbon and unrolled the heavy vellum document. From time to time, as she read, she chewed on her bottom lip. Dalmar found that he was holding his breath.

She was silent for so long that he felt compelled to jog her memory. "As policies go, I think it's fairly lucid in its design." He was careful to sound faintly bored and affected an interest in the intricate folds of the bed canopy overhead.

"As clear as crystal. In fact, patently transparent, if you don't mind my saying so," came the clipped rejoinder.

He chanced a quick sidelong glance at her. The expression on her face was unmistakable. Definitely mulish.

"There are only two major clauses in the whole document," he replied defensively. Her peeved look decided him against mentioning a third and very minor clause which was hidden away on the back page. It was only a piece of frivolity, after all, he reasoned, and he did not think that Annabelle was in a frame of mind to accept his feeble attempt at levity. No, better by far to persuade her to the reasonableness of his two major clauses.

"True," agreed Annabelle. "But they are very comprehensive. You are to be congratulated. I admire well-written policies."

"Thank you." To his ears it did not sound as if she meant the words as a compliment.

411

"But if I agree to these terms, you have virtually the last word in how I run my business, and how I conduct myself in private, isn't that so?"

"Annabelle," he protested, "I'm not an ogre. You won't find me unreasonable." With a blend of tenderness and blatant cajolery, he went on, "Surely it's not too much for a husband to ask of his wife—that he be permitted some say in how she goes on?"

She cocked her head to one side and gave him the strangest look. After a moment's consideration, she said, "I'm not most wives, David. You must remember, I'm used to ruling the roost. I don't think I could take direction very easily."

"Who's talking about direction? That's not what I meant. Think of Bailey's. We're partners, aren't we? And after a few false starts, we're getting along amazingly well, wouldn't you say?"

"Amazingly," replied Annabelle. "But that's because, by and large, you've left me to run things the way I see fit."

"Don't you see? That proves my point. I'm an agreeable fellow. As husbands go, you'll find me very accommodating."

"Mmm!" said Annabelle. "I don't think that's much of a recommendation, David."

"You don't think I was right to try to stop publication of Monique Dupres's diaries?"

"Well," said Annabelle, squirming under his direct look, "I'm not infallible." When Dalmar's eyebrows rose fractionally, she said, "All right. I admit that sometimes I'm a bit headstrong for my own good. But if you hadn't taken that high-handed attitude, I wouldn't have dug in my heels."

"I've learned my lesson," he said. "Haven't I proved it?"

Annabelle could not in all honesty deny that he spoke nothing less than the truth. And she'd discovered to her great surprise that she rather enjoyed having him for a partner.

Shyly she offered, "We do work well together, don't we?"

Surprise and pleasure etched his voice. "Do you think so?"

"Oh yes," said Annabelle. "I'm coming to rely on your advice. Do you know, you have the makings of a first-class entrepreneur?"

Dalmar's jaw sagged. When he had recovered from the

412

shock of her words, he said, "I love working with you. In fact, I love doing everything with you."

He moved closer. Annabelle inched away.

"About the policy," she said.

"What about it?" He had almost given up hope that Annabelle would agree to his terms.

"What I was thinking," she mused, and her eyelashes fanned down, veiling her expression, "what I was thinking was this: if we were to make the terms of this document reciprocal, I would not be averse to accepting it. In other words, would you be prepared to allow me a similar latitude in *your* affairs?"

She was thinking that Dalmar had just bought a major share in some tin mines in Cornwall. The company was simply begging for some astute man or woman of sound business sense to reorganize it from top to bottom. And as for Bailey's, Albert was more than competent and pressing for more responsibility. And she was restless and ready for a new challenge.

"Reciprocal?" asked Dalmar cautiously. "Do you mean we should both have an equal say in the ordering of our private lives and that our business ventures should be joint?"

"Don't you think that's fair?" asked Annabelle, slanting him a carefully artless look.

"Oh, I think so," he quickly agreed. He was thinking that he had just bought a major share in some tin mines in Cornwall. The company badly needed reorganizing from top to bottom. Only, he was not sure where to begin. And managers were sometimes known to rob their employers blind. But if he could inveigle Annabelle into taking hold of the reins for a time, it would greatly relieve his mind. And her services would cost him next to nothing, he reasoned, or very little. To cover his eagerness, he frowned.

"I have no objections to what you suggest," he said, striving for a casual tone. "Does this mean you would be willing to help me set things up with that company I've just bought over? Not that I would expect you to devote all of your time to it, you understand."

"Well," said Annabelle, feigning reluctance, "I suppose I could spare myself from Bailey's for a short while. It's the least I could do, under the circumstances."

413

She lowered her lashes to conceal the flame of victory which she suspected had kindled in her eyes.

He pretended an interest in the carving on one of the bedposts to conceal his gloating smile.

After a moment he said, "Do we shake hands on it or what?" He was hoping it would be the "what."

"We'll get to that later," said Annabelle. She had that look about her which told Dalmar that she was in her "business" frame of mind. "Have you got a pencil handy?" she asked.

Resigned, Dalmar dutifully fetched a pencil for Annabelle.

"Thank you. Just a few changes of the wording here and there," she said, "and we shall have ourselves a document that will serve us very well."

Dalmar propped himself against the backrest of the bed and cupped his neck with his laced fingers. From time to time, he offered suggestions. He fetched more paper. Within an hour, the simple one-page policy he had given to Annabelle filled four complete sides.

"There," said Annabelle. "I think we've covered every eventuality. What do you think?"

He took the papers from her fingers and began to read. Annabelle raised herself on one elbow and watched him anxiously.

From time to time, as he read, Dalmar smiled. Annabelle had added any number of variations to his original proposal, but the substance of his intention remained pretty much as it had been. She had accepted that, as her husband and protector, he had some say in decisions which affected her well-being. As a last resort, he could forbid her involvement in any undertaking which might provoke insult or injury to her person. She was giving in to him. It was a heady thought. And if he had to surrender a few trifling liberties to secure her acquiescence, he counted the cost to himself as almost negligible.

"Will it do?" asked Annabelle at length.

"It's perfect," he purred.

Annabelle smiled. He was giving in to her. It was a heady thought. Did he realize, she wondered, that he had just agreed to be a paragon of a husband which few gentlemen could hope to emulate? Whether he knew it or not, Dalmar and his

414

redheads (with the exception of herself, naturally) would be forever parted. And if she had to surrender a few trifling liberties to secure his acquiescence, she counted the cost to herself as almost negligible.

Dalmar turned on his side to face Annabelle more fully. "I never expected this to be so easy," he said frankly.

"Neither did I." There was wonder and surprise in her voice.

"We're both strong-willed characters, and used to getting our own way," he pointed out.

She absently combed her fingers through the dark cloud of hair on his chest. "That's the beauty of policies," said Annabelle, with something like a smirk. "It's all spelled out in black and white. And if we get into an argument . . ."

"The policy will settle it for us."

"That's the general idea."

"There's something to be said for policies after all," he said, and bounded from the bed.

Annabelle had been so gracious, so accommodating, that he was seized with a sudden urge to reward her. He strode to the clothes press and began to search for something suitable to wear for the day ahead. At his back, Annabelle became involved in reading the policies.

"I'm sure you have the day all planned," he said, "so just tell me your pleasure and we'll be on our way. What's it to be? Shopping in Milsom Street? A stroll to the Pump Room for a glass of Bath's invigorating brew? The new Assembly Rooms? Or how about a walk around Sidney Gardens?"

The voice which reached his ears was low and husky. It didn't sound like Annabelle's.

"David, come here."

When he did not heed her summons at once, she repeated the command. Obediently he padded back to the bed. Her eyes were sparkling with some emotion he could not define. Was it anger, he wondered, or amusement, or . . .

"Did you think you could get away with this?" she asked, and pointed with her index finger to the original policy paper, the one done up with the red ribbon.

He knew at once to what she referred. In very small print, on the back of the document, was the third clause which he'd hoped to slip by her.

He angled her a sheepish, cozening grin. "You can't blame a man for trying," he said.

"Shocking," said Annabelle, frowning. "You meant to take advantage of me."

Dalmar shifted uncomfortably. He wasn't wearing a stitch of clothing and was beginning to feel the ignominy of his position. "It was just a bit of fun," he said placatingly. "Where's your sense of humor?"

Annabelle snorted. She tapped the rolled vellum document against the palm of one hand. Her eyes brazenly swept over him. "You're not forgetting," she reminded him huskily, "that this policy works two ways. That what is sauce for the goose is sauce for the gander?"

"Oh, quite!" he answered.

Slowly, deliberately, she drew back the covers, unveiling her naked beauty to his eyes. Fire licked through his veins. She crooked her little finger.

"Well? What are you waiting for?" she asked. "Need I remind you that, according to your very own policy, when one gives the signal, the other must be prepared to do his or her conjugal duty? David," she positively purred, "I think I'm going to love having you at my beck and call."

Some things a man just didn't argue with, thought Dalmar. They had a whole lifetime ahead of them to work out who would call the shots in their marriage. He was sure he looked forward to every minute of it.

Laughing, he said, "Annabelle, I promise you, this is one policy I'm going to hold you to," and before she could change her mind he covered her with his body.